I0745608

Where Shadows Grow

Copyright © 2020 Alanna Peterson

All rights reserved. No part of this publication may be reproduced in any form or by any electronic or mechanical means, including information storage and retrieval systems, without permission in writing from the publisher, except by reviewers, who may quote brief passages in a review.

This is a work of fiction. Names, characters, organizations, places, and events portrayed in this novel are either products of the author's imagination or are used fictitiously. Any resemblance to actual persons, living or dead, companies, events, or locales is entirely coincidental.

Publisher's Cataloging-in-Publication Data
Names: Peterson, Alanna, author.
Title: Where shadows grow / Alanna Peterson.
Series: Call of the Crow Quartet
Description: Seattle, WA: Rootcity Press, 2020.
Identifiers: LCCN: 2020911242
ISBN: 978-1-952149-03-0 (pbk.) | 978-1-952149-04-7 (epub)
Subjects: LCSH Agricultural laborers—Fiction.
| Post-traumatic stress disorder—Fiction.
| Family—Fiction. | Friendship—Fiction.
| Iranian Americans—Fiction. | Asian Americans—Fiction.
| Northwest, Pacific—Fiction. | Science fiction. | Adventure fiction. |
BISAC YOUNG ADULT FICTION / Thrillers & Suspense
| YOUNG ADULT FICTION / Cooking & Food
| YOUNG ADULT FICTION / Diversity & Multicultural
| YOUNG ADULT FICTION / Social Themes / Mental Illness
Classification: LCC PS3616.E84268 W44 2020 | DDC 813.6—dc23

Book design by Unflown | Jacob Covey

Printed and bound in the United States of America
First printing 2020

Published by Rootcity Press
Seattle, WA
rootcitypress.com

Where Shadows Grow

ALANNA PETERSON

CALL OF THE CROW QUARTET

BOOK TWO

ROOTCITY PRESS

SEATTLE

*To food chain workers
everywhere,
without whom our tables
would be empty*

I.

The Tangled Skeleton

Andi

TUESDAY, AUGUST 11

THE DISTANT CHEERS OF THE AUDIENCE ROSE AND FELL, RHYTHMIC as ocean waves. But there was nothing peaceful about these swells: they were unpredictable and strong, the kind that could pull you under and never let you go.

Andi Lin moved her hands to her lap, leaving a damp fog outline on the vinyl chair. She fidgeted with the bracelets they'd given her in Wardrobe. "To give you more sparkle," they had said.

"Your face looks sweaty," the makeup artist muttered. "Close your eyes."

Andi obeyed, feeling the brush sweep across her forehead. Fragrant flakes of powder perfumed the air. The cloying scent tickled her nose.

When she opened her eyes, her face in the mirror looked much paler than usual. Maybe they thought she would look "prettier" that way, or maybe they didn't have quite the right match for her skin tone. Then again, her nerves weren't helping matters either.

"All set." The artist took off the smock protecting Andi's dress, gesturing towards the backstage room where Cyrus was waiting. "You're on in five minutes."

Andi felt like wiping off her pink lip gloss and tearing away through the halls. Why had she ever thought this would be a good idea?

Cyrus looked up from his phone, catching her eye as she entered the room. "Wow. Alexandria. You look…magnificent."

"You dress up nice yourself," she said. Cyrus looked pale, too, though he was light-skinned to begin with. They had styled his hair in an artfully messy way and dressed him in a suit, complete with bow tie. The two of them looked almost like they were going to prom or something, instead of appearing on Lillian Page's afternoon talk show.

She slid onto the couch beside him, running her fingers through her long black hair. "I don't think I can do this."

He took her hand, not saying a thing about its clamminess. "Of course you can. It'll go just like we practiced, then it'll be over. We didn't come all this way just to turn back now. Besides, we have to do this. For the greater good."

"Don't say that," she said. He responded by shooting her a bewitchingly adorable grin.

Cyrus's phone buzzed as someone peeked in the door to give a one-minute warning. Andi stood up, her knees shaky. What if she fainted as they walked out on the stage? That would be so embarrassing.

She smoothed her hair and reached her hand out to Cyrus, but he was staring at his phone with obvious dread. It continued buzzing insistently in his palm.

"Who is it?" she asked.

"What? Oh. My dad."

"Aren't you going to answer? He probably just wants to wish you luck."

"Luck!" Cyrus said, like this hadn't even crossed his mind. As if to make up for his odd reaction, he laughed. "Of course. No, better not to talk now, I'd rather wait till after the show."

"Is everything okay?" The worry that had been stalking her all day, only recently overshadowed by stage fright, crept in again. Just after her phone alarm had gone off at 4 a.m., Andi had received an unexpected text from Cyrus: Change of plans, don't pick me up, I'll meet u at the airport. That had been strange, considering he lived less than a block away and it was no trouble to swing by and get him.

He'd arrived for their early morning flight to LA minutes before it took off, huffing into the cabin with his backpack askew. Once he'd settled into the seat next to hers, he apologized. "Long night. I'll explain later. Better get some sleep before the show."

She had asked the same question then. "What's going on? Is everything okay?"

He'd gazed at her with heavy-lidded eyes, stifling a yawn, and said, "Everything's wonderful. I'm going to California with a beautiful girl and we're going to see… amazing stuff like… stars… celebrities, I mean, and… stucco and… palm trees…."

He'd slept in the car, too, but as soon as they arrived at the studios they had been sucked into the chaotic whirlwind of wardrobe and rehearsal and makeup and everything else, so she hadn't had a chance to ask him anything more.

Now, his mouth twitched upward, but she knew his fake smile when she saw it. He didn't get a chance to respond before someone wearing a headset appeared and ushered them out of the room. "You're on."

They walked into the bright lights and deafening applause. Andi tried not to think of tidal waves sweeping her off her feet. She looked for her parents in the front row and saw them beaming, adding to the intensity of the light.

Lillian shook her hand. Andi forced herself to keep smiling, to not think about how sweaty her palms were, to not get tripped up and tongue-tied. Just keep it like they'd practiced.

Once they sat down, Lillian jumped right in. "We're thrilled that you could join us today. It's been almost two months since Tara Snyder, the woman who allegedly abducted you, was arrested, and your terrifying ordeal ended. How are you doing now?"

Andi glanced at Cyrus, but he sat there silent, looking shell-shocked. She wasn't prepared for that. During rehearsal, he'd been his usual wisecracking self, and she'd assumed he would take the lead. But when he didn't, she took a deep breath, and her voice came out soft, but not shaky. The audience listened intently, like they had been waiting a long time to hear from her.

"We're pretty good," she answered. "We're so grateful for all the support we've been given from our families, our doctors, our community... everyone's been so generous."

Cyrus was nodding. "We feel really lucky," he added.

"And how are your brother and sister doing?" Lillian asked Cyrus.

Cyrus flinched subtly. "They're fine. Not interested in doing interviews, though."

"So your brother made a full recovery from the respiratory infection that had him hospitalized for weeks?"

"Like I said, he's fine." Earlier, too, Lillian had pried for details, and Cyrus had remained just as firmly tight-lipped as he was now. They would never talk about Naveed's lingering health problems on the air. That wasn't their story to tell.

Lillian added, "I've heard that new cases of the infection have started turning up throughout Washington state. They're calling it Multidrug-Resistant *Klebsiella*, or MRK." She pronounced it "murk," the same way Andi's doctors had. "Sure sounds like a nasty bug. Be careful out there, y'all. Keep that hand sanitizer at the ready, like Dr. Ben always says!"

Andi was sure that her face must be flaming red. She hadn't heard anything about new cases of MRK; Lillian hadn't mentioned this during rehearsal either. It struck her as terrible news, especially since Cyrus, Naveed, their younger sister Roya, and Andi had been the first patients infected with this new strain of *Klebsiella pneumoniae*. The bacteria had evolved into antibiotic-resistant superbugs because of the filthy conditions

Tara Snyder's research cows lived in, and Andi had only led Cyrus and Naveed into that barn because they were trying to escape. Andi had long been worried the disease was still out there, still spreading, but until now she'd tried not to dwell on it too much.

Andi took another deep breath, trying to calm down and pay attention. Lillian was smiling so sweetly, but her pancake makeup now seemed to conceal a cruel inner face.

"Coming to terms with what happened must have been hard," Lillian said with exaggerated sympathy. "How has the experience affected you?"

"Things won't ever be the same for any of us." Andi didn't really want to talk about that; she couldn't even put into words how deeply it had changed them all. If Lillian could go off-script, though, why couldn't she? "But I think what hurts the most is that the rest of the world has moved on. Whenever people talk about this, it's always about Tara Snyder and what she did. It's never about Nutrexo, the food company she worked for. It's definitely not about their CEO, Richard Caring, who okayed the EcoCows in the first place. The whole project only existed because Nutrexo owned Genbiotix, a pharmaceutical company! And what about the fact that all the problems we saw are widespread across the whole food industry? Livestock are still being kept in horrific living conditions, which could lead to more infections like MRK. We might have stopped EcoCow milk from being sold, and Nutrexo is gone now, but Genbiotix spun off into its own company, and they're still out there—"

"Making life-saving medicine, such as the only known effective treatment for MRK," Lillian interrupted.

Ouch. So she wanted to play hardball? Fine. Andi was about to respond when Lillian continued, "Cyrus, I've heard that you're doing particularly well now. Tell us about your summer job. It sounds like you've gotten quite the unique opportunity."

Andi felt like she'd lived this moment before: there was a humming in her ears, an outwardly attractive but inwardly callous person sitting opposite her. Lillian wasn't going to let Andi speak; her eyes flashed warningly. *A little too far, dear. Wouldn't want to offend the sponsors.*

Cyrus said, "Oh, yeah, I've been working at Parapluie Bistro, one of Chef Thierry Marchand's restaurants. It's been amazing. I've learned so much there."

Andi's heart sank. She'd hoped he would jump in to support her. She thought that was why they were here, to remind people that this fight was not over, that it was just beginning. But instead here he was, chattering on about some Persian-style dish he'd developed for the dessert menu. Lillian looked pleased. Andi tried to catch his eye, but he wouldn't look at her.

"Sounds delicious!" Lillian said when Cyrus finished talking.

"Yeah, it's been a busy summer, between that and the website my friend and I launched—devilandcyborg.com, not that I'm trying to plug it or anything," Cyrus said.

"Well, aren't you talented," Lillian fawned. "It's so inspiring to see how well you're doing despite everything you've been through. Thank you both for being here."

"Thank you for having us," Cyrus replied with a smile so fake that Andi was sure she wasn't the only one who noticed.

Lillian turned back to the camera. "Up next, a special report from Dr. Ben on the silent killer lurking under your sink."

Andi stood up, not even trying to act pleasant now that the cameras were off, and walked off the stage. As she exited, she saw Dr. Ben waiting in the wings with his smarmy smile, ready to be embraced by the crowds.

"*Silent killer?* Isn't that a little over-dramatic?" Andi said to Cyrus as they returned to the backstage room. She was still annoyed at him for not supporting her out there, but she really needed to vent. "They're probably talking about some disinfectant or whatever, but they make it sound like sink gremlins are going to pop out at you whenever you open a cupboard."

"Sink gremlins." Cyrus chuckled. "Hey, wasn't Dr. Ben the one selling that supplement you took?"

Andi rubbed her temples. She really didn't want to think about that right now—her head hurt at the mention of it. "Well, he had the Metafolia guy on his show and called it a 'miracle product.' If that's what you mean."

"Maybe I should rush out on the stage and throw down a white glove. Demand satisfaction for indirectly harming my girlfriend."

"It was no big deal. Anyway, it's in the past." And yet, something still nagged at her. Even though she'd ended up in the emergency room after taking the herbal supplements several weeks ago, the experience hadn't been entirely unpleasant. Throughout the whole fiasco, she'd felt strangely… peaceful.

Cyrus's grin faded. "Alexandria, you rocked it. I'm sorry I couldn't really talk about that stuff, I froze up and all I wanted to do was get out of there, but you… I like seeing that side of you. Your righteous indignation."

The apology helped, a little. "Lillian didn't. She totally cut me off. Had to get back to a safe topic of conversation."

"Well, I think everybody watching will be able to tell what's up. The truth is uncomfortable sometimes."

"I can't believe what she was saying about MRK. Why didn't she mention that at rehearsal? I hate it when people keep stuff from me."

Cyrus shrugged. "Who knows why anybody…." He trailed off, staring at his phone. Andi saw him swipe open the screen. Two new voicemails.

Andi checked her own phone. She'd gotten a sweet voicemail from her ah-ma in Berkeley, who had apparently organized a viewing party with a bunch of other Taiwanese retirees, as well as a few congratulatory texts. Andi's parents had messaged that they'd meet her after the show was over to celebrate. She responded with a thumbs-up.

Cyrus took her hand. "Let's go."

"Where?"

"Anywhere. Outside. Find a palm tree to sit under."

There were no palm trees outside. Just a big parking lot, the maze of studios, their gigantic hangar-like buildings, the trailers parked nearby.

They walked. Cyrus played back his voicemail, and Andi tried to listen, but the volume was too low for her to divine anything. All this stress was making her head hurt again.

Finally, he shoved his phone back into his pocket, exhaling loudly as he slowed to a stop. She waited for him to say something. He didn't.

Andi stepped in front of him. "Cy? What's going on?"

He looked around, as if to make sure no one was watching, and then he hugged her, leaning his head onto her shoulder, angling his mouth toward her ear. Speaking very softly. "I don't really want to talk about it, and please don't tell anybody, but Naveed had to go back to the hospital last night."

The news hit Andi brick-like, even though it was what she had suspected. "Oh, Cy—what happened?"

"It's just, his feet… his hands, too… apparently he's been having this pain, and it got really intense last night… like, bad enough he couldn't even walk… and… and he…."

Cyrus swallowed hard. It hurt Andi to hear this, and she could imagine how awful that confrontation must have been, so she didn't wait for him to finish. "That's horrible," she said, though the word seemed inadequate. "But I thought he couldn't feel anything in his hands and feet? Because of the nerve damage?"

"They think it's related to his neuropathy," Cyrus said slowly, recovering his voice. "It's a pretty common complication—that's what my dad's message said. But they're going to do a bunch of tests, so they can rule other things out."

"But he doesn't have to stay there, right? They let him go home?"

"No. They admitted him. Sounds like it'll be a few days at least."

"Oh no, but his birthday's coming up…."

"Not for another week. I'm sure he'll be home by then."

All this information was hitting Andi in waves. "Can I tell Brooke?"

"No," Cyrus said quickly. "Better not. I really don't think he wants to talk to her right now. If he does, he can contact her himself."

That seemed fair enough. Their breakup was so recent, and Brooke was off in the wilds of British Columbia with her mom and older sister anyway. "Why didn't you stay?" Andi asked. "Shouldn't you be with him?"

Cyrus sounded pained. "He doesn't want me there."

"Because… because you made him go?" Andi asked.

Cyrus let out a strangled sound that she took as a yes, and she rubbed his back, trying not to think about that terrible evening when they'd all gone out to celebrate her seventeenth birthday at Parapluie. But the memories came anyway, in small vivid bursts: Naveed crouched in the back alley after freaking out inside the restaurant, sweat-drenched and struggling for breath; Brooke suggesting they call an ambulance; Naveed suddenly springing up, grabbing her by the wrists and slamming her against the wall; Brooke gasping, eyes wide with shock, as he yelled, *No! Don't make me go back there—I'm never going back, never—*

It made Andi's heart hurt to think of Naveed turning that same anger onto Cyrus, who had been so patient with his brother. She squeezed him closer. "Don't worry. He'll forgive you once he feels better."

He sighed and pulled away. "Thanks, Alexandria. You're right. This is for the best. They'll take care of him, get things worked out. I guess we might as well enjoy our goddamn vacation." He held his arm out. "Now. Back to the studio, so that Dr. Ben can tell us the truth about those murderous sink gremlins."

Roya

TUESDAY, AUGUST 11

ROYA MIRZAPOUR WANDERED ALONG THE ROCKY BEACH, FARTHER and farther from Auntie Leila. If she just paid attention to the slippery stones beneath her feet, maybe she could guide her thoughts away from the bad places they wanted to go, away from the question she kept coming back to. *Should I have gone with Maman? Did I make the wrong choice?*

Up until this morning, her vacation had been going wonderfully. A few days before, Roya and Maman had journeyed up north by car and ferry to visit Auntie Leila, Baba's younger sister. She was a marine biology postdoc in Oregon, but was spending the summer doing research on the San Juan Islands off the Washington coast, and had invited them to join her for a few weeks in the cabin she'd rented on Lopez Island.

Auntie Leila liked to go down to the beach at low tide and comb for treasures, and taught Roya about all the hidden things that come out when the water is low. Roya learned about the different kinds of sea birds, about the orca pods who swam through the waters occasionally, about the habitats of sea lions. She learned how to identify different types of seaweed: the long hollow tubes of bull kelp, the bright green nori, the air-filled bladderwrack like small, puffy hands.

Even better, it was the first time in her whole life that Roya had Maman all to herself, and getting away from home had released the heaviness that had been weighing them down for the past several months. The day before, as they'd explored tidepools, Roya had crouched to get a closer look at a bright purple sea star, humming to herself as she raked her fingers through the sloshy wet stones since she wanted so badly to touch the creature but knew she shouldn't, and Maman had come up beside her and encircled her in a hug, kissing her on the cheek, even. "Oh, Roya-jaan, I love you so much," Maman said, and it was so strange and out of the blue but that only made it more amazing, because it had been so long since something like that had happened, so long since her mother had been anything but a distant half-ghost, but here they were on the beach and Maman was solid and real and spilling over with this sudden, astonishing affection, and Roya drank it in, letting it fill her completely.

At the end of each day Roya fell asleep in a loft bed in the cabin, ceiling slanting low overhead to remind her of home, but with a window above so she could see the stars. Still, every night she ended up crawling over to Maman's bed after the nightmares came.

Maman had woken her up early this morning, so early it wasn't even light yet. Roya knew something was wrong by the fierce way Maman hugged her, by the tremble in her voice. She told Roya that she needed to go back to Seattle because Naveed was in the hospital again, quickly adding that he'd be fine but they needed to keep him there for a few days. Maman said she wouldn't be gone for too long, and that Roya could stay here with her auntie. If she wanted to come back, though, that was fine too.

Roya got an itchy feeling in her belly, a sort of irritation, like something small was trapped in there and trying to get out. She knew her answer immediately: she wanted to stay. But she felt bad saying that out loud. It wasn't like she didn't want to see Naveed; she did, of course she did, but no way was she trading tidepools for hospital rooms, especially since

Cyrus was in California and wouldn't be there to lighten the mood. But it wasn't fair that Maman had to leave this place just when she was starting to come alive again, and it wasn't fair that Roya had to let her go.

"If it's really okay… I think I'll stay here," Roya whispered. "But give him a big hug for me."

Maman squeezed her close. "I'll come back as soon as he gets discharged. And I'll call you every day."

Roya made him a get-well card while her mother finished packing up. It was hard to get back to sleep after Maman kissed her goodbye, because she kept thinking of her brother, wondering what exactly was wrong with him, knowing how awful he must feel to be back in the hospital… and meanwhile Roya was on this beautiful faraway island, being selfish, wanting to keep Maman all to herself.

When Auntie Leila finally woke up, she'd suggested a morning low-tide walk on the beach. Now, as Roya stepped toward a piece of driftwood, thinking she'd dig through the rocks to look for shells and sea glass, something caught her eye on top of the bluff behind her.

She turned and saw a girl with pale skin and dark braids watching from the shadow of the tree line. A shapeless linen dress hung from her thin frame.

"Hey!" Roya called out, scrabbling up the bluff as quickly as she could, but by the time she got up top, the girl was retreating into the woods. Roya was about to start after her when she heard Auntie Leila yelling her name.

"Roya! Come back down to the beach. We can explore the woods later. I want to show you something."

Roya cast a wistful glance backward, but the girl was gone. If she'd ever really been there at all. The way she had moved, like a frightened animal, making so little noise as she darted through the trees. Her dress, her braids, the longing in her eyes. She looked like she'd stepped out of a story book.

"I saw a girl over there, by the woods," Roya confessed to Auntie Leila when she returned to the beach.

"A girl?"

"Yes. Maybe the same age as me, or a little older, but she looked strange. Old-fashioned."

Auntie Leila frowned. "I didn't see anyone. Here, look what I found."

It was a pretty amber-colored agate stone that seemed to glow in the weak sunlight. Auntie Leila said she could have it, so Roya slipped it into her pocket, but she almost forgot to say thank you. Her mind was still far away.

Then her auntie gasped, and Roya followed her gaze. There, way out at sea, was a whole pod of orcas! Roya counted five dorsal fins, but wasn't sure how many there really were, because they kept moving.

"My binocs!" Auntie Leila exclaimed, scrambling across the rocks to her backpack, but Roya didn't want to lose sight of the whales. They were swimming fast, so she ran down the beach to keep them in her view, around a narrow corner that she couldn't usually walk on because it only appeared during low tide.

Then she was on a new beach. This one was sandier, but small, and Roya stopped when she realized she'd nearly run into an enormous sea lion.

It barked at her before disappearing into the water. Roya was relieved he hadn't attacked or anything, but at the same time felt bad for disturbing him. She fixed her gaze back out at the sea. The orcas were gone.

Disappointed, Roya turned around—and saw that she had been standing in front of an outcropping of rock that jutted into the ocean. It was curved into an arch of stone, maybe three feet tall. A doorway into darkness.

After squinting into the shadows to make sure no sea lions were in there, she crawled into the small cave. Barnacles scraped at her knees. Inside it was dark, and only the quiet drippings of water broke the silence. Something was in there, though, something pale in the gleam of light shining through the opening. Roya scooted closer, and drew in her breath when she realized what it was.

A skull. A *human* skull. And not only the skull—it looked like an entire skeleton, huddled there on the ground in a heap of bones, bones not in their right places, bones washed around by tides.

Roya didn't want to look at them, but at the same time she did. When she worked up the nerve to inspect them more closely, she noticed a small dark shape planted firmly in the sand underneath. Roya reached toward it, thinking she knew what it was, shivering as she nudged the waterlogged skeleton aside and closed her hand around solid, rough metal.

A key. An old, rusted iron key.

She slipped it into her pocket with the agate just as Auntie Leila crouched in the cave's opening. "Roya! What are you—"

"I found something." Roya pointed at the tangled-up skeleton. She was about to mention the key, too, but stopped herself. Auntie Leila would probably take it away. But Roya didn't want to give it up. Somehow, it felt like the key belonged with her.

The police came, later. Roya watched them carry the bones out piece by piece. In the harsh daylight they looked small and fragile, and too wet. By then a crowd of onlookers had gathered, murmuring to each other, wondering.

One of the police officers took her aside to ask some questions. Roya was nervous to talk to them, but Auntie Leila stayed close, keeping an arm around her the whole time, and the officer was friendly. As they were wrapping things up, Roya asked, "Will you be able to figure out who it was?"

"It's not likely," the officer said. "Sometimes we can use the teeth, but they're all worn away. Whoever they were, they died a long time ago."

For some reason, this made Roya think of the old-fashioned-looking girl she'd seen on the bluff. She reached into her pocket, closing her hand around the key, feeling its rough edges, its weight in her palm.

Find her. The thought flew in from nowhere, almost as if it were a message transmitted by the key itself. Roya gripped it harder, knowing what it meant, knowing what she needed to do.

Find the girl.

Cyrus

CYRUS STARED OUT THE WINDOW, FINGERS TWITCHING, TRYING with all his might not to touch his phone. Andi leaned against him in the back seat, scribbling musical notes onto composition paper. Up in front, her mom, Joyce, was navigating their rental car along Highway 101 while her dad, Jake, noodled on the guitar.

They'd been sitting in stop-and-go traffic for over two hours, and Cyrus had long ago maxed out on the amount of time he could amuse himself by counting palm trees. But he'd made a promise to Andi. She thought he spent too much time on his phone, which he had to admit was kind of true. So for this portion of their vacation, he'd agreed to only check it a few times a day.

She'd promised to do the same, and seemed to be having no trouble, but it was killing him already. Especially since his best friend Dev had been left with the task of managing their website while he was gone. According to the frantic messages Cyrus had received the day before, the site had crashed thanks to the huge influx of traffic after his appearance on Lillian's show. Dev said that downloads of the game they'd developed remained steady, but views of the video series they'd recently started had gone way up.

Andi hadn't seemed impressed when Cyrus had first explained to her about their channel. He was aware that some people didn't find gameplay videos narrated by a couple of almost-sixteen-year-olds very interesting, but he'd hoped she wouldn't fall into that camp. Luckily, though, Andi had come around after he showed her the first episode, where he and Dev played an old-school Zelda game while talking about a bunch of random stuff, including Dev's obsession with katana swords and the derivation of the word "rupee." They were only three episodes in, and already the series had attracted a wide audience. The videos took a lot of time to put together, and Cyrus often spent long nights editing them after his restaurant shifts, but it was worth it. Their new game was coming along slowly, and they needed to do all they could to stay at the front of their supporters' minds.

Cyrus didn't want to think about all he was missing out on by being offline, all the comments and mentions and potential opportunities that were passing him by. But this was preferable to dwelling on the deeper things that haunted him.

His thoughts kept returning to the thin black notebook buried underneath the balled-up socks and T-shirts in his backpack. Taking it had been a mistake, he knew that. And yet, when Khaleh Yasmin had given him a ride to the airport at the crack of dawn so that his dad could stay at the hospital with Naveed, Cyrus made her wait outside as he spent an extra five minutes searching the bedroom he shared with his brother. He told himself he was protecting Naveed, because what if his parents found the notebook instead? Whatever was in there, it probably was for the best that they didn't see it. Right?

Cyrus had found it when he slid his hand under the mattress of Naveed's bottom bunk; he'd stuffed it into his backpack and thundered down to the car. All day, during the flight, the interviews, the after-show party, the dinner with Andi and her parents at a fantastic sushi restaurant, it had been at the back of his mind. Yet he was so exhausted when he got to their hotel room that he didn't open his bag at all, he just took off his shoes and climbed into the cot they'd wheeled in for him, so that Andi could have one of the beds and her parents the other. It had been a long time since he'd had a night of uninterrupted sleep, and he fell into a deep, dreamless slumber instantly.

They'd let him sleep late, and he woke up panicked that Andi had gone through his bag, but of course she hadn't. She wasn't the kind of person who would do that. Still, his stomach clenched just thinking about it. He should have told her the whole story the day before at the studio, but he'd found himself unable to get the words out. Which was probably for the best. If she knew what had really happened, if she knew what Cyrus had done, she probably wouldn't want to be with him anymore. He could still hardly believe that she liked him back, and couldn't stand the thought of losing her.

So he shoved down the guilt, vowing not to think about it, deciding to take the advice Baba had given when they hugged goodbye. "Your brother's going to be fine, Kourosh," he'd said, pronouncing Cyrus's name the Persian way. "You deserve a vacation. Try to enjoy it."

And their vacation was truly beginning now. They were leaving LA for Santa Barbara, where Jake had arranged for them to stay with an old friend.

Eventually they exited the freeway, driving nearer to the ocean, and soon found themselves in front of a black iron gate. Joyce rolled down her window and identified herself on the intercom. The gates swung open.

Cyrus looked at Andi quizzically, but she was gawking too. "This?" she said. "*This* is where we're staying? I thought we'd be, like, sleeping on the floor at some surfer's apartment."

Jake pretended to be hurt. "What, you think I don't have any rich friends? No floor-sleeping here. We'll be staying in the guest house."

"Guest house?" Andi repeated. "Who *is* this guy?"

Jake turned around to look at his daughter. "His name's Brennan Walsh—but please don't make up your mind about him until after you meet him."

Brennan Walsh. The name sounded vaguely familiar to Cyrus.

"What's that supposed to mean?" Andi was asking suspiciously.

"He's the founder of Bountiful Earth Market. And their CEO," Jake added, almost in a mumble.

Andi sat up straighter. "We're staying with a food industry CEO, and you didn't even *mention* this to me?"

"Like I said, don't judge him until you've gotten to know him. He's a good person. When we met back in the day, he was working in PR at the record label, but he gave that up so he could do something more meaningful. He really cares about sustainable food and wants to make it more available to everyone."

Andi flopped back into her seat. Cyrus took her hand to show that he was on her side, but Jake's explanation made him realize where he'd heard the name before. "Hey, you know what? They keep talking about Brennan Walsh at the restaurant. They're catering an event for him next month. A benefit for the Walsh Foundation."

"Huh! Small world," Jake remarked.

They lapsed into awed silence as they drove up the circular drive and parked in front of the main house. Bougainvillea vines arched on trellises around them, and there were palm trees everywhere.

"So this is why peaches at Bountiful Earth cost $10 apiece," Andi said under her breath. "Not because the people who grow and harvest them are being fairly compensated, or because they're organic or whatever. Because you're paying for this." She gestured at the fountain sending picturesque sprays of water through the air.

Jake turned around. "Hey, enough with the cynicism. Give him a chance, Peanut."

Andi looked like she was about to say something else, but just then one of the gardeners waved and approached the car. Jake rolled down his window.

"You Joyce and Jake?" the gardener asked, and they nodded. "Here, bring your car around this way. Mr. Walsh will be back in time for dinner, but until then you're welcome to explore the grounds. There's a path off the back patio that leads down to the beach."

They thanked him and he pointed them toward a narrow driveway curving off to the right. Through a thick arbor of trees was another mansion. Cyrus couldn't believe this was the so-called "guest house." It looked bigger than his entire home in Seattle.

They entered into a wide, airy living area decorated with sleek, modern furniture. There were three bedrooms, each with its own adjoining bathroom—the luxury of this was almost more than Cyrus could bear—and a gleaming kitchen, and an avocado tree off the back patio. Cyrus chose the ground floor bedroom, right next to the kitchen, and asked Andi if she wanted to head down to the beach. She excused herself to get ready.

Once in his room with the door shut, Cyrus checked his phone and responded to a couple texts from Dev. Then he dumped out his backpack, changing into his swim trunks as soon as he found them, but leaving his T-shirt on.

And there it was, haunting him again. The notebook. It had fallen open on his bed, the pages full of Naveed's neat Persian script. Cyrus wasn't sure whether to be relieved or disappointed. This must be the notebook his brother had used for copying passages from the texts he studied with Khaleh Yasmin. Though Cyrus had stopped learning the language years ago, after Maman finally gave up on forcing him to go to Persian school on Saturdays, he recognized the names of the poets whose books lined their shelves: Rumi, Hafez, Forough Farrokhzad.

But—all of this had been written Before. Cyrus could tell by the neatness of the handwriting. Naveed had lost quite a bit of his fine motor skills, and his penmanship now was spidery and hard to read.

Cyrus fluttered the pages. There, in a section toward the back, were pages with the new scrawl, written in English. He swallowed hard. He'd been right after all—this was the same notebook his brother had been scribbling in all the time lately. His eyes fell upon one of the pages, but he didn't read for long before he slammed the notebook shut.

He wrapped it in a dirty T-shirt and stuffed it into the bottom of the backpack, then shut it in the closet. Nope. He wasn't going to look again. One peek had been enough.

Cyrus wandered into the well-stocked kitchen. He cut a slice from the loaf of sourdough they'd gotten at a bakery earlier, then picked a ripe avocado outside. He mashed it onto the bread, drizzled it with olive oil and sprinkled it with sea salt, then ate it on the patio underneath the tree. It didn't taste nearly as good as it should have. Cyrus pushed his plate away, telling himself, *Naveed's going to be fine. Others are taking care of him now. I'm free. I'm free.*

Andi opened the screen door. "There you are!" She had changed into a cute sundress, aqua bikini straps peeking out from beneath, tying at the base of her neck. He found himself astounded by her, the way he so often was.

He stood up and extended his hand. "M'lady? Care to take a turn with me in the gardens?"

She gave him a huge smile that zinged straight through to his heart, causing him to forget everything else. "But of course, m'lord."

They linked elbows and walked along a gravel path, underneath a sprawling orange tree whose fragrant fruit glowed golden against the dark branches, the green leaves.

"This is going to be amazing," Cyrus said as they walked, his excitement returning. "We can go to the beach... check out the university... the farmer's market... I'll cook you dinner and we can eat on the patio...."

"Mmm. Hey Cy, you know... that whole thing with Lillian's show is still bugging me. How everyone just wants to forget about what happened with Nutrexo. Maybe that's why Lillian was the only one who got back to us, but all the actual news shows said we needed a 'fresh angle.' I was thinking—what about MRK? Isn't the spread of a new disease reason enough to get people to care about factory farming and all that other stuff? Maybe we could pitch that to the news people, and talk about our experiences?"

Cyrus searched for the right words. He appreciated what Andi was trying to do, but he didn't have any desire to appear on television ever again. "Maybe? I don't know, to be honest I don't really want to go around making myself out to be some sort of poster child for MRK. I didn't even get it that bad, so I doubt anyone would be moved by my stories of having a fever for a couple days and coughing up nasty-looking phlegm."

Andi was quiet. He knew she was thinking about Naveed, who had come ridiculously close to dying several times while battling his MRK infection. But Naveed wouldn't want to talk about that on some news show. Besides, Cyrus was willing to bet that his brother was more concerned with the weedkiller that Tara Snyder had tested on him, causing the nerve damage—and, apparently, the intense pain—that plagued him now. But she was locked up awaiting a trial that wouldn't happen for many months, and the herbicide was banned from sale, so those things, too, were old news.

They turned a corner, and Andi leaned closer. For a second he thought she wanted to kiss him—but, no luck. "Hey, so how's Naveed doing?" she asked. "Have you heard from him?"

Cyrus's heart beat faster. "No. I don't think he wants to make a big deal out of it, you know? My parents are being pretty vague about what's going on over there." This was mostly true. They had filled him in on the new diagnosis, but he wasn't about to bring that up with Andi now. "You don't have to worry, though," he went on. "It sounds like he's doing okay."

"Good. I was starting to wonder. I texted him a few times yesterday, but he never wrote back."

"Oh, yeah, I don't think he has his phone right now." *Just tell her,* Cyrus's brain insisted. *Just say it. She needs to know.* But it was like there was an impenetrable barrier between his mind and mouth, and the words just wouldn't come out. Instead, he added, "But I can have my parents pass on a message."

"Okay. I just want him to know that he can call me anytime. I'm sure he's pretty upset, being stuck there."

That didn't even begin to cover it. "I'll tell them," he lied. She smiled, lightened, like a weight had been lifted from her and dropped on his own head.

Cyrus slowed to a stop. His feet felt leaden. "Andi, um… would you mind… I mean, the whole situation is just so depressing, do you think we could, like, make a pact not to talk about it for now?"

"Of course. I understand."

"Thank you," he sighed, relieved.

She pressed closer, looking him straight in the eye. "And you," she said. "You, m'lord. How are *you* doing?"

Oh, it felt so good, her sweetness, her concern. The way she was patient with him, giving him the time to figure out how to talk about it, and when he was ready, she'd listen. She understood what he needed, and that was a beautiful thing. "Alexandria," he said, loving the way her name sounded on his tongue. "Whenever I'm with you, I am absolutely magnificent."

They continued their stroll down the steep path that led to the sea. Cyrus whooped and took her hand tight in his, pulling her along. She laughed behind him, and he kicked off his flip-flops when he made it to the beach, tearing for the water. The waves roared in and receded, sucking the sand away from his feet. The ocean water was warm. He threw off his shirt and stood before Andi in his swim trunks, which he might have felt self-conscious about ordinarily, but the ocean had infused him with some sort of fast-acting invincibility potion.

Andi was looking him over, so he flexed a (somewhat flabby) bicep and said, "Oh yeah, you know you want a piece of this."

She chuckled. "What's gotten into you?"

He couldn't explain the sudden manic excitement he felt, the *freedom,* so he ran into the waves, diving clumsily into the warm water. He looked back to see Andi startled on the beach, pulling her dress over her head to reveal her bikini underneath.

"Jesus, I thought you were about to drown or something." She pressed her hand to her heart, as if he'd worried her very much.

"I *am* drowning," Cyrus said dramatically, sitting up, the waves crashing against his back. "Quick, save me, save me!"

She shook her head, but walked closer to the water. God, she was hot in that bikini. Cyrus wanted to roll around with her in the sand.

He rolled onto his back instead, and swam out past the waves breaking on the beach, enjoying his buoyancy in the saltwater. Andi swam up beside him.

"This place is awesome," Cyrus said. "I never want to leave. Can't we just stay forever? Maybe I could be Walsh's personal chef or something, and you could go to UC Santa Barbara, bike there every day...."

He reached over to hold her hand in the water. She laced her fingers with his. He wondered if her lips would taste salty, if he were to kiss her now.

They bobbed in the water, the waves pulling them closer and closer together. He pushed aside a wet strand of her hair. She did the same with his, but let her hand linger on the side of his face. "You still have your glasses on," she observed. "They're getting wet."

She was touching his cheek now, the back of his neck. He liked it. Didn't want her to stop. He was nervous that this wouldn't go right, and hesitated, but she leaned in close, and then she did it: she pressed her lips firmly to his, and they kissed.

She tasted like salt and mint, and Cyrus lost himself in the glory of that moment, in the perfection of all that surrounded him: the beach, and the waves, and the sun, and the girl.

Suddenly, everything really was fine. Everything was magnificent.

<u>6 mordad</u>

the sparrows are hungry and i can't afford bread
seeds would be better but such things don't exist
in this dead place

when the birds grow desperate enough
they will begin to eat glass
i admit i find this appealing

i disappear between the pages   i am losing
my borders   i am the butcher
bone-handled knife slicing through marbled flesh
the heads of the sheep beyond the filmy glass
they watch me still   through their dusty dead eyes

now the sparrows are crunching at the window
leaving holes   shredding tiny bellies from within
i blame myself for letting it get this far

whenever my eyes close
i see red   does that mean i'm angry
or just human   i am alive but decomposing
i will soon be wearing the clothes
of children   skin and bone
skin and bone   you can't see
what you can't
name

Roya

ROYA COULDN'T SLEEP. THE NIGHTMARES HAD COME, AS USUAL, and she'd crawled drowsily over to Maman's bed, but it was empty: a reminder that she was gone. Roya didn't want to bother Auntie Leila, who got grumpy when woken in the night, so she stared out the skylight instead, trying to chase away the images from her bad dream by watching the stars fade into daylight.

It didn't work, though. She kept seeing Naveed superimposed over the dark night sky, clawing his way into the loft, plastic tubes dangling from his arms and his chest and his nose, his hands all wrapped in bandages and his eyes deep in shadow. He saw her, too; he crawled closer, tubes thwapping against the floorboards, he had come to tell her something, and even though he couldn't talk because there was a bigger tube coming out of his mouth, making hissing sounds with every breath, she knew what he was saying.

You made the wrong choice.

At dawn, Roya got up. She pulled a sweatshirt over her pajama top, left a note for her still-sleeping auntie, and walked to the beach alone.

The fog was thick, so she didn't go too close to the water, staying back by the big rocks instead and listening to the waves and the gulls and the seals. The sounds returned her to the normal world, and gradually the vision of her nightmare-brother started to fade.

Maybe things would have been different if Naveed could've just come with them in the first place. But Maman had worried that Lopez was too remote in case of an emergency, and besides he had an appointment that he couldn't miss this week, so Baba had decided to stay home with him.

At the time, Roya hadn't felt bad about leaving. He didn't really talk to her, or anyone, very much anymore. Lately, he stayed in his room except for at mealtimes, when he picked at his food and Maman tried to get him to eat more and he yelled at her and stormed back up to his room. Roya would sometimes knock on the door afterward to check on him, but he never let her in.

Those first few days on Lopez had been so wonderful that Roya had hardly thought about him at all. Now, though, this struck her as an unquestionable betrayal.

You made the wrong choice.

A flood of emotion overtook her, and she began to cry. *Stop being a baby,* she scolded herself, but she couldn't help it. She missed him *so much.* She missed the way he had been before, the person that he couldn't seem to find his way back to, the brother who had told comforting stories when she was sad, who had made her the wooden flute that she couldn't bring herself to play anymore, who had always listened to her, even when no one else would.

But there wasn't anything she could do to bring him back.

As she sobbed into her knees, she sensed movement and looked up. A gull, maybe? Or, she thought with sudden excitement, a crow? But it was no bird. Instead, a person materialized from the fog.

Instinctively, she shrank back, but the figure kept coming closer. Roya was about to get up and run away—until she saw who it was.

The girl stopped a few feet from Roya. She was sucking on the end of one of her braids, and was wearing the same linen shift as the day before. This time, though, she also wore a knotted cord around her waist, from which hung a leather sheath with an elaborately-carved dark-wood handle sticking out of it. A knife, Roya realized, but this didn't frighten her; a strange thrill bloomed inside her instead.

The two girls looked at each other for a moment, neither saying a word. Roya pulled her hand into the sleeve of her sweatshirt and attempted to wipe her tear-stained face.

Unnerved by the girl's silence, Roya finally asked, "Are you... are you real?" She realized how stupid this sounded, but at least she hadn't blurted out, *the key told me to find you.*

The girl took the braid out of her mouth and flicked it behind her shoulder. "Of course. Are *you* real?"

She was smiling now. Her yellowed teeth twisted in on themselves. She looked somehow young and old at the same time.

Roya knew she was taking too long to respond, but she was feeling decidedly unreal at the moment, so she didn't say anything.

"What's wrong?" the girl asked. "Did someone die?" She said it almost eagerly, as if hoping the answer was yes.

Roya shook her head slowly.

The girl pursed her lips. "Oh. It's only, when I saw you yesterday, I could feel it, your energy—it felt like you'd lost someone. I wanted to talk to you then, but I'm not allowed to leave Orcinia, so I couldn't let your mother see me."

Orcinia? Roya thought, but she said, "My mother? Oh, no, that was my Auntie Leila."

"Do you live with her?" The girl studied Roya intently, like she was the most important thing in the world.

A flush of warmth spread through Roya's body. "No. She's just watching me. Because my mom had to leave."

"So you miss your mother, and that's why you're sad?"

"Sort of." Roya was tempted to tell her everything. She hadn't been able to talk about what had happened with anyone, really. This girl, though, looked like she actually cared. Like if Roya was hurt, she was hurt, too. "Actually, I did kind of lose someone."

The girl perked up. "Then maybe I can help you! By the way, I'm Kasandra, but you can call me Kass. What's your name?"

"Roya."

"Okay, then, Roya. Tell me about this person you lost. They're not dead?"

"No." This was hard. How could Roya possibly explain what she meant?

"Hmm. Too bad. I mean, not too bad that they're alive, it's just that sometimes it's easier to find them if they're dead."

Roya was intrigued. "It is?"

"Yes, because sometimes pieces of people stay behind, when their bodies go. They can still communicate. You just have to become receptive to receiving their signals."

She spoke about it so matter-of-factly. Roya wanted to know more, but Kasandra kept talking. "This is a special place, this island. The boundaries between our world and the spirit world are very thin here. So, your person, is she missing?"

"Not she. He. And no, not exactly. I know where he is, but he almost did die a few months ago and I think that made him lose part of himself and turn into someone else. I want to help him go back to the way he was."

Kass looked thoughtful. "Makes sense. Sometimes, people who almost cross over leave pieces of their soul behind in the spirit world. Are we talking about your father?"

"No. My big brother."

"Ah. Okay. That's good, because you're bound by blood. But the problem's very complicated. Sounds like a job for my nan. She's really good at this."

Roya hugged her knees closer. "Has she ever helped you find someone you lost?"

Kass turned to her, for the first time looking almost angry. But her expression quickly softened. "You don't live here, do you." It was a statement, not a question. "How long are you here for?"

"I'm not sure." A horrible feeling started brewing inside. What if Maman left her here for a long time? What if she got so wrapped up in Naveed's problems that she forgot about Roya?

No, she wouldn't forget her only daughter. "Probably a week or so," Roya finished. "But you live here, in… what's that word you said? Orss… something."

"Orcinia. It's not far." Kasandra waved an arm vaguely. "I should go, before Nan realizes I'm gone. I have to serve breakfast to the acolytes. And don't tell anyone you saw me here. But will you… will you come back tomorrow? Same time? This is the only time of day I can get away."

Roya had so many questions. What was Orcinia? What were acolytes? But she nodded.

The girl broke out into a grin so huge that Roya could see all of her twisted teeth. "Promise?"

A wave crashed against the rocks. Roya breathed the salt-filled air. She hadn't made the wrong choice. This was exactly where she was meant to be. She smiled back. "Promise. Tomorrow, same time."

Kass spat on her hand, then extended it. "Saliva is one of the humors," she said, by way of explanation. "I know. It's definitely a lesser one. Not as good as blood. But it'll work for now. It can still bind things." She looked at Roya. "Your turn."

Roya spat on her own, then the two girls' hands met in a handshake. There was something strange about Kasandra's hand; it was like holding something ropy and old. And it may have only been Roya's imagination, but it was almost like she could feel invisible yarn sprouting around their two hands. Binding them.

Andi

ANDI HELD CYRUS'S HAND AS THEY WALKED OVER TO BRENNAN'S house for dinner that night. She still felt electric after that salty kiss, as if she were a lightning bolt bounding around in the clouds. She crunched along the gravel path, holding on to Cyrus, remembering how good it felt to touch his skin in the rocking waves.

Her mother looked back at them, and Andi pressed closer. She considered kissing him again, just for the sake of annoying her mom, who hated public displays of affection. Andi still couldn't believe her parents hadn't bothered to tell her where they'd be staying. Despite her dad's insistence that Brennan was different, she wasn't looking forward to dinner with a CEO at all.

They arrived at the main house just as Brennan opened the front door. Like nearly all of her dad's friends, he was white, which was also unsurprising considering his powerful position and obvious wealth. But with his long-ish brown hair and middle-aged paunch, he looked more like an aging surfer than a business executive.

Her father introduced them, and Brennan invited them inside. "Care for some fresh juice? I just made it: mango-apple-ginger-carrot."

"Sounds great," Cyrus said.

"No, thanks," said Andi. Even though she knew, rationally, that the chances of Brennan Walsh drugging her drink in full view of her parents were basically nonexistent, she wasn't going to trust him until he'd earned it.

Brennan poured juices for everyone else and led them past the expensive-but-not-very-comfortable-looking furniture in the living area to the back garden. Once they had settled into lawn chairs by the pool, he asked, "Guest house working out all right for you? Sorry that I won't be around much during your stay, but I'm off to New York for the rest of the week."

"Oh, yeah? Hey, remember the time Mile Seven played at CBGB?" Andi's dad asked. "And you... with the potted ficus... and the cowboy hat...." He practically collapsed in a fit of laughter.

Brennan chuckled. "Yeah, that was classic. Do you remember, Joyce?"

"Hardly. I was really... out of it that night."

Andi glanced at Cyrus with a subtle eyeroll. She wasn't really in the mood to hear about the drug-fueled rock-and-roll exploits of their youth.

"Unfortunately, it won't be fun this time," said Brennan. "Some Wall Street investors are angling to acquire my company. I don't even want to go, but these past few years have been rough. The rest of the board insisted I hear them out."

"You don't want to sell?"

"No! They want to take the company public, but I'm not interested. I want to be invested in the communities we serve. I don't want to spend my life obsessing over our stock price so that our shareholders get richer. That's how you end up with companies like Nutrexo."

Okay, maybe Brennan wasn't that bad. Not that Andi would admit this out loud, but still. She found herself relaxing a little.

Brennan waved a hand. "Just one of the many unpleasant things I'm dealing with these days. On top of all that, my mother passed away last month."

"Oh no, I'm sorry to hear that," Andi's mom said.

"I've been there. It really shakes you up. I'm sorry, man," her dad added.

"I still can't believe it. I mean, she was getting up there, but she was healthy. Then one night she had a stroke, and that was the end. But you know what's weird? When I went to clean out her stuff, her cupboards were full of boxes and boxes of this herbal supplement. I mean, I'm all for natural products, but this one has a ton of ingredients, some I've never even heard of… and I can't help but wonder…."

"What was it called?" Andi asked, guessing she might know the answer.

"Metafolia. That guy on TV, Dr. Ben or whatever his name is, was all over it a couple months back."

"Wow, how weird," her father said. "Andi tried that when she was recovering from her concussion—"

"And it didn't work out so well," Andi finished. She didn't want to talk about it with a veritable stranger, even though Metafolia had been on her mind ever since she'd seen Dr. Ben at Lillian's show.

Several weeks earlier, Andi's ah-ma had sent along a bottle of Metafolia. It was supposedly effective for "restoring the body to wellness," a claim that sounded so vague as to be almost meaningless. By that point, though, Andi was growing desperate, still occasionally sidelined by intense post-concussion headaches and attacks of vertigo. So she'd started taking the supplements, not expecting much. But one evening in late July, she'd been watching a movie with her mother, and the screen went all shimmery. It had felt like she'd be able to walk through it, and she'd leaned forward—but only succeeded in toppling into the coffee table and ending up on the floor. Her mother promptly freaked out. Andi stayed perfectly calm herself, if a bit disappointed. Even though it made no sense, she felt like she'd been on the verge of discovering something profound, and her mother was preventing her from grasping it.

Somehow she'd ended up in the car, and her mom was driving too fast, taking the curves so quickly that Andi threw up out the passenger side window, then started laughing because it was so absurd, it was like genuine rock star behavior, but her mom hadn't seen anything funny about it. When they arrived at the hospital and her mother explained that she'd fainted, everyone was very concerned, the vomiting was a bad sign apparently, and no one seemed to care that it was only because her mother was driving so recklessly, or that Andi wasn't even sure she'd lost consciousness in the first place. But because of her previous concussion and the headache that kept growing in intensity as the hours passed, this earned her a night in the hospital, multiple brain scans and hyper-anxious parents, followed by yet another week of so-called "cognitive rest" at home: limited television, computer use, texting, even listening to music.

After discovering that her blood pressure was extremely low, the doctors asked if she was taking any medications or supplements, and her mother mentioned Metafolia. Even though Andi didn't tell them about the shimmering screen—not wanting to appear crazy on top of everything else—they thought it was probably the reason for her "little fainting spell," as one nurse annoyingly called it.

Now, Brennan looked at Andi with interest. "You had some side effects?" She nodded, giving no details. "Interesting. It makes me mad, you know. There's hardly any regulation of these things, and people take them because they think they're harmless if they're 'natural.' I thought about suing, actually."

"Really? We considered that, too," her father said. "Didn't want to go to all the trouble, though."

"Oh, lawsuits are a headache for sure," Brennan said. "And what we really need is more oversight of these companies by the FDA. It's appalling how poorly supplements are regulated, thanks to DSHEA. I should probably put in a word with Senator Bittner... I know she's interested in these issues."

The mention of the FDA tickled Andi's brain, bringing her back to a place she generally tried not to go. She remembered sitting in Tara Snyder's lab, hearing her say, *The FDA already approved the EcoCow milk based on the evidence we provided.*

The conversation moved on, but Andi wasn't listening anymore. She was thinking about all the shows that had turned her down when she was finally ready to talk, because their story was no longer news. Thinking about the way that Lillian had silenced her.

They want a fresh angle? she thought. *Then I'll give them one.*

Cyrus

AFTER AN AMAZING DINNER OF GRILLED SALMON AND LEMON-drizzled asparagus, Brennan suggested they walk down to the beach while the cook was putting finishing touches on dessert. Cyrus, still feeling rather euphoric after his and Andi's earlier kiss, offered Andi his hand, and she took it. They lagged behind the others, strolling slowly through the dusk.

"He doesn't seem so bad," Andi mused.

"Brennan? No, he seems all right. I guess some CEOs aren't evil. What a world, right?"

"Right," she repeated distantly.

As soon as they stepped onto the sandy beach, Cyrus's phone buzzed. He looked up at Andi, not wanting to break the promise he'd made.

"Go ahead," she told him.

He slowed down to pull it out of his pocket, hoping the text wasn't from his parents. It didn't sound like things were going too well over there, at least not at the moment, so he was nervous what he might find.

Cyrus angled his phone away from Andi, but to his surprise it was just a photo from Auntie Leila. In it, Roya crouched on the beach, a half-smile on her face, gray stones beneath her, gray skies behind.

He laughed in relief. "That beach looks a little different from this one, huh?"

Andi peeked over his shoulder, then Jake and Joyce leaned in to look. So Cyrus held it out to Brennan, who stared at it curiously. "Where's that?"

"Oh. Lopez Island."

"Lopez?" Brennan asked. "Huh. Thought it looked familiar. Whereabouts are they staying?"

"I have no idea," Cyrus had to admit. "I've never been there."

While Brennan was studying the picture, another text from Auntie Leila buzzed in. Guess what your sister did yesterday? Discovered a human skeleton in a cave at the beach. Someone who died ~30 years ago, a woman, they think. Pretty wild right? Anyway she's watching a movie right now but you should call her tomorrow k?

"Whoa, that's weird." Cyrus showed Andi. "But I don't know. Finding a skeleton? Somehow, it's just so *Roya.*"

He texted Leila back. Interesting! ok I'll call in the morning, love the pic btw, but when he put his phone down, Brennan was still staring into space, apparently deep in thought.

A wave crashed against the rocks nearby, sending a spray of tiny droplets onto their faces. Brennan turned toward the house. "Best get back. Dessert's probably ready by now."

"What are we having?" Cyrus asked as he returned his phone to his back pocket.

"Cheesecake, I think."

Cyrus held back a squeal of delight. His mouth was already watering.

They trekked through the jungle-like garden, passing the pool and spa, following the path illuminated by solar-powered lanterns. At the main house, they climbed the stone steps up to the back deck overlooking the ocean.

Their desserts were already waiting for them at their seats. Everyone had their own small, round cheesecake with a gorgeous marbled-chocolate top served with a drizzle of raspberry coulis. Cyrus eagerly dug into his—oh, the texture, so perfect, so unbelievably light!—but before she even picked up her fork, Andi was saying to Brennan, "What kind of evidence would you need in order to file a lawsuit against Metafolia?"

Brennan looked surprised for a moment, but quickly recovered. "Well, I kept all the bottles I found at my mother's house. I could have them sent off for testing. They have this 'proprietary blend' in them—I have no idea what that contains, but it's not uncommon for certain supplements to be laced with prescription drugs. Still, I don't know that there's any way to link them to my mother's death at this point, unfortunately. No autopsy was done."

"But what if I were to testify about what it did to me?"

Cyrus almost dropped his fork. He couldn't believe Andi was volunteering to be grilled by some lawyer about her experience with Metafolia. She hadn't exactly seemed eager to talk about that stuff earlier.

Brennan also seemed curious. "It depends. What happened, if you don't mind me asking?"

"Why don't you tell him, Mom," Andi said. "You remember the details better than I do."

Joyce launched into the story of Andi's night in the ER. Cyrus was a little alarmed to hear it from her perspective; he'd only heard it from Jake and Andi, both of whom had downplayed the whole thing, but it sounded a lot more serious the way Joyce told it.

While her mom talked, Andi sliced her cheesecake into chunks, then cut each one into smaller pieces. She didn't take a single bite. Before long, her plate had turned into an unappetizing, pale pink mess.

Joyce was going on about dangerously low blood pressure and fluid resuscitation when Andi cut her off. "Thanks, Mom, I think he gets the point. Do you know if anyone else has been harmed after taking it?"

Brennan shook his head. "I don't know. But if there have been others…

we might even want to consider a class action suit. In any case, though, we're going to need strong medical evidence."

"I'm sure Andi's doctor would testify," said Joyce. "He seemed convinced that the supplement was the problem."

"Definitely," said Jake.

"Maybe you should sue Dr. Ben, too," Cyrus said. "I wonder if he got kickbacks or something for promoting it on his show."

Brennan laughed humorlessly. "Not a bad idea. Got to start with the actual product, though. Prove it's unsafe before taking any further action."

"Do you know anything about the company?" Jake was asking.

"Not much. It's run by this guy named Geoffrey Walker. It's strange, he looks kind of familiar to me… but I don't know anything more than what's on their website, which isn't much."

"So when can we get this going?" Andi asked. "I mean, if it's hurting people—if it's maybe even *killing* people—we need to get the word out as quickly as possible, right?"

"Yes, but we'd better have airtight evidence before making any accusations," Brennan said. "I'll talk to my lawyer next week. In the meantime, you could speak with your doctor, see if he'd be willing to testify, and if he's aware of any other cases like this. I'll be in the Seattle area in September for a benefit gala with my charity foundation—maybe we could catch up then."

"I might have to work, actually," Cyrus said. "Turns out my restaurant— the restaurant I'm working at, I mean—is catering that event."

"Oh, you work at Parapluie? Chef Thierry and I are old friends." Brennan paused. "You know what? You're all welcome to come to the gala as my guests. If you're available, of course. The food will be amazing, plus Senator Bittner will be attending, so we could talk about what it would take to put together a bill to fix some of these FDA loopholes. It's ridiculous that it's so easy to get supplements approved for sale, but so hard to prove they're unsafe."

The conversation turned to politics, and Andi excused herself to the bathroom. Cyrus sat back and zoned out. If only Andi hadn't mutilated her cheesecake, he would've gladly eaten it for her, but he settled for scraping every last bit of coulis off his plate and taking one more heavenly bite.

After they finished dessert, they thanked Brennan and made their way back to the guest house. Andi seemed lost in thought; the two of them walked slowly, far behind her parents.

"That cheesecake was so good," Cyrus mused, not knowing what else to say. "I wonder how they made it so fluffy? Mine always turn out too dense."

Andi turned to him. "Hey Cy, remember what I was saying earlier, about needing an angle? Well, forget MRK. I looked online, and couldn't find anything about new cases. I bet Lillian was just saying that to see how we would react."

This didn't really make sense to Cyrus—why would Lillian lie about something like that?—but Andi continued, "Metafolia. That's our angle. It isn't just supplements that are poorly regulated, it's food additives in general. For the FDA to approve something, all the company needs to do is provide data showing that it's safe—and I'm sure it's easy enough for them to design their studies so that it ends up looking harmless, even if it isn't. So we can relate it back to what Tara Snyder was doing with the EcoCow milk in Blazin Bitz Crave... and maybe that senator Brennan mentioned can help change the regulations if there's enough public support...."

Cyrus wasn't sure if she realized how hard that would be, but he liked seeing her excited about something. "I bet the CFJ would be all over that," he said. "Maybe you could talk to my mom about it when we get back."

"That's a good idea. Or I could ask Brooke—she's always trying to get me to come to their meetings. Maybe we could start planning a new campaign," Andi said.

Cyrus's gut tightened. Brooke's mom worked with Maman as co-director of the Coalition for Food Justice. Had Maman told her what had happened with Naveed? If so, it might have gotten back to Brooke....

"I could talk to Dev, too," said Cyrus, trying to distract her from that train of thought. "If you worked on the content, we could maybe make a new website? Since NutrexoTruth.com was so effective?"

She stopped suddenly, underneath a lemon tree that arched over the pathway.

"What do you think?" he asked, figuring she'd continue talking about Metafolia, or Brennan, or the CFJ, or anything other than what she actually said.

"I think… that sounds perfect." She smiled and stepped closer, adding, "And… I think that I'd like to kiss you good night."

His heart soared, and he thought he might replay those words in his head for all eternity. But then—just before their lips touched—he remembered something else she'd said, something that released a tiny flutter of dread deep inside him: *I hate it when people keep things from me.*

He would tell her. Eventually. Just not right now.

Then his thinking brain turned off, because her lips were kissing his so tenderly, so softly, and he held her close in the warm lemon-scented breeze, under the light of the waning moon.

<u>Excuses</u>

7/20: "Can't stay long, helping my mom w/CFJ stuff."

7/23: "I have an appointment this afternoon, see you tomorrow."

7/26: "My sister got in last night, we're going to Pike Place today. Want to come?" (no.)

7/27: "Dawn and I are going to the lake. Cy and Andi said they'd meet us there. You should come!" (not up for it.)

7/28: "Gotta get ready for my job interview at the juice bar. Wish me luck!"

7/29: "I got the job! They want me to start tomorrow! They need me full time, but I'll come over after work and bring you some juice."

7/30: "Work was great. Sorry I can't come over. Too tired."

stop charting it's too depressing the diagnosis is obvious to anyone reading the signs

doubt brooke will come around much anymore now that she's working.
been trying to reach farhad, i prefer conversations w/him anyway.
not like he ever talks about his time in evin
not like i ever talk about my shit with him
it's just that he doesn't watch me every second
looking
for another sign
that i'm broken

he understands what it's like
to have your entire life ripped away, stolen,
leaving you with
nothing

even though she pretends to, i don't think brooke
in her privileged life
could ever truly get that

she's impatient with the way i drift through time
the days come and go
they can't touch me i can't touch them
this is who i am now   a living ghost

sometimes i wish i was in tehran with farhad
we could go all over the city
  wait in line at the bakery for sangak
  spend all day wandering through the grand bazaar
  we could travel through iran together
  visit his grandparents' pistachio orchards
  the tombs of the poets
  eat mulberries straight off the tree
but then i think about trying to get on a plane
  (what if i'm on one of their lists?)
and i think about the smog
  (would i be able to breathe?)
plus where would i even get the $$ since i'm not working anymore
and that's all it takes to remember that i'm stuck here.

but finally some good news.
my feet are tingly tonight, my fingers too.

pins and needles, kind of.
don't want to jinx anything but maybe they're waking up?
maybe if i could touch her skin again, feel it under my fingertips,
maybe that would help us find what we lost.

i just want to feel something

anything at all

Roya

THURSDAY, AUGUST 13

ROYA WOKE UP AT DAWN AGAIN THE NEXT MORNING AND SNUCK through the quiet house, grateful that Auntie Leila was such a heavy sleeper. When she emerged on the foggy beach, Kass was already huddled on a log twirling a braid in her fingers, a woolen cloak wrapped around her shoulders.

As soon as she saw Roya, she stood up. "I'm glad you came. I know what to do about your brother—but we'll need to gather a few things first."

"Okay." Roya was glad that Kass had jumped right in. "What do we need?"

"It would help if you have something of his. Some hair, a piece of his clothing. I can wait if you need to run back and get it."

Roya thought about this. She tugged on the sleeve of her sweatshirt, an old hand-me-down that she was pretty sure Naveed had once worn. "This used to be his. Will that work?"

"It'll do." Kass met her eyes. "There are a few other things we need from Orcinia. But you have to be quiet and stay out of sight. And you have to give me your word that you won't tell anyone about any of this."

"Of course. I'm really good at keeping secrets."

Kasandra seemed satisfied, so they set off. As they walked through the forest, she explained, "I'm not allowed to leave because it's not healthy on the outside. Everything's made of chemicals these days, and everyone's obsessed with money instead of paying attention to what's important. The outside is toxic to bodies and minds. Besides, it might be dangerous. Nobody on the island likes my nan because she's a witch."

"A witch?" Roya felt another unexpected thrill.

As if figuring Roya was concerned with this news, Kasandra added, "Don't worry. She's not a *bad* witch. She helps people."

Roya wanted to find out more, but couldn't think of the right questions to ask as they made their way through the forest. The dim light of dawn barely pierced the canopy of trees. The darkness of it made her think of the sea cave, of the key she had found. She had been carrying it with her everywhere. Even now it bumped against her leg as she walked, heavy in her pocket.

Soon they came to a tall chain-link fence. Kasandra walked along it slowly, stopping when she reached a certain spot. At first glance, the fence seemed as strong and whole as ever, but when she looked closer, Roya could see that the joints had been cut vertically for several feet, so that the sides could be pushed open and crawled through.

"They don't come back here very often," Kass was saying. "No one knows about this. So no telling."

Roya wished she'd stop saying that. Of course she wasn't going to tell anyone. But she hoped that whatever Kasandra had planned wouldn't take too long, so that she'd be back to the cabin by the time her auntie woke up.

Once inside, the two girls crouched in the bushes. While Kass waited for the perfect moment to emerge, Roya surveyed Orcinia. The main building was a rustic wood cabin. Two large yurts straddled each side. Their canvas walls reminded Roya of circus tents, only less colorful. Near the yurts was a covered area filled with half a dozen picnic tables and an outdoor kitchen. In the distance, fields and greenhouses stretched as far as she could see. A small barn was filled with bleating goats, and the chickens in the coop next door clucked quietly, giving Roya a fleeting pang of homesickness.

Kass led Roya to a spot underneath the front steps of the main house: a shallow root cellar, where the shelves were lined with wooden crates and glass jars and burlap bags of potatoes, and bundles of drying herbs and garlic hung overhead. The smell of apples lingered in the musty air.

Once they were safely hidden, Kass took off her cloak hood. "This is where I was born," she whispered.

Roya thought she meant this generally, as in within the walls of this house, but Kass swept her hand in a circle across the dusty ground beneath their feet. "Right here. Mother wanted to get some blackberry jam, and I started coming so fast—Father barely came down in time to catch me."

Roya touched the ground, too, tracing the circle that Kass had drawn. "Do you have any brothers or sisters?" she asked.

"No. And my parents are both dead."

Roya was just beginning to digest the horribleness of this when Kass continued, "Mother was the first baby born here in Orcinia—she almost didn't survive the birth but my grandfather saved her. He named her Miracle. Father was an outsider, though. He came here as an acolyte and fell in love with my mother so he stayed, but they both died when I was five."

"How?" Roya asked before she could stop herself.

Thankfully, Kass didn't seem offended. "Nan says that my father injured himself when he was splitting firewood, and they had to chop off his hand to try to save him, but germs got into his blood anyway. She says that's what killed him."

Roya squirmed. She didn't like thinking about blood infections. Or amputation. Or death.

Kass looked around, as if to make sure no one else was listening. "But it's not true. I remember. There was no wood-chopping accident." She lowered her voice further. "He shouldn't have made Grandfather angry."

She said it neutrally, not like she was upset about it or anything, but it nevertheless sent an involuntary shiver through Roya. She turned toward the shelves, pretending to be interested in the jams.

"Mother died of a bad sickness a few months later. So now it's just me and Nan and Grandfather and the acolytes." Kasandra crouched in front of a cupboard and started rummaging through it.

"What's an acolyte?" Roya asked.

"A student." Kass pulled a small brown bottle from the cupboard, then took a few leaves from various hanging herb bunches and wrapped them in a cloth napkin. "They come here to learn things from Nan, and from Grandfather when he's here, but most of them don't stay long. Most don't even last the whole moon cycle—they're more like tourists, only here for the ceremony, because they want to talk to somebody who's gone, tell them things they never got to say. Some of them stay for a long time, though. They help with harvesting."

"So your grandfather… is he here now?" Roya hoped the answer was no.

"Not right now. He's gone a lot. He's a prophet—the gods can talk to him. They guide him, help him understand what to do. Mostly he's on the outside, spreading the word, looking for new acolytes." Kasandra tucked all the items she'd gathered into the canvas pouch slung over her shoulder, along with a narrow wooden box that she handled very carefully. "That's all we need from here. Follow me—we're going past the barn, I bet Nan's in there, so make sure she doesn't see you."

Roya focused on staying as quiet as possible as she walked behind Kasandra, who led her back into the thick forest beyond the fields. Her heart beat rapidly: she was excited, but nervous. What did Kass have in mind? What were they going to do?

Finally, they came to a clearing. They stood, Roya saw as she turned around, inside a circle of birch trees, their white papery trunks glowing in the pale sunrise.

"This is where we have our ceremonies. There are thirteen birches, one for each moon." Kass led Roya past the fire pit in the center of the clearing, ringed by stones splotched with hardened candle wax. "But we're not going to stay here—we're just gathering sticks for the poppet."

"The poppet?"

"You know—like a little doll. Here, I'll find some on the ground while you get the living ones from the trees. First, you have to ask for the tree's permission, then break a stick off of each one, and picture him while you do it. Think about your intentions, what you want for him. Concentrate hard. It's important."

Roya nodded. This made sense. She walked up to the first tree and placed her palm on its trunk, mentally requesting permission before breaking off a thin branch. She thought about Naveed and tried to picture him the way he used to be, happy and healthy, but for some reason she had a hard time doing it. The image of his monster-self from her dream kept intruding.

Once she had gathered all thirteen sticks, Kass said, "Time to go. Don't want to get caught."

They made their way back through the fence and forest, up to a high bluff overlooking the beach. The dawn spread its gray light over them.

Kasandra removed her knife from its sheath. "Stay right there. I'm going to cast the circle. For protection."

Roya stayed still as Kass traced a circle around and over them with her knife. Once that was finished, she started unpacking her bag. Out came the cloth napkin, the small bottle, the wooden box. Then she took out a different ivory-handled knife with a curved blade and cut a few lengths from a spool of twine. "Let me see your sleeve," she added, and from that she teased a small thread, which she cut off and wrapped around one of the sticks.

She began fastening them into the shape of a person, tying off two legs, wrapping twine around a small section for the neck, sticking a small bundle out of the chest perpendicularly to make arms. As she worked, she asked, "What's your brother's name?"

"Naveed."

"Naveed? What kind of name is that?"

"It's Persian." That was Roya's default response whenever people commented on how "unusual" her family's names were. But Kass only looked at her blankly.

"My parents were born in Iran," Roya added.

Still, Kass stared uncomprehending, like she'd never heard of it.

"It's a country? In the Middle East?"

"Oh," said Kass. "Is it close to Russia, then?"

"Yes. Pretty close."

"My father was from Russia." Kass set down the stick bundle, which now looked very much like a doll. She opened the wooden box, removing a goblet and two tall, wide candles. From somewhere, she produced a match and lit them.

Kass opened the cloth napkin and pressed something into Roya's palm. It was a seed of some sort, a hard, round one that looked kind of like a cherry pit. "While I get ready, hold this. Think about him. Remember your intentions."

Then Kass pulled on her hood again—Roya thought it made her look delightfully witchy—before crumbling the herbs into the goblet and pouring in the contents of the bottle. From it came a thick, red liquid. Roya wasn't watching too closely, because she was examining the engravings on the goblet: a woman with three heads, one looking left, one forward, and one right.

"That's Hekate," Kasandra told her. "Goddess of the underworld, of crossroads and borders and doorways. We use this chalice in our ceremonies, too—she's the one who helps us communicate with the dead."

Roya nodded: this, all of this, made so much sense to her. It all felt so right. She held the seed tightly, trying to pack it full of as much love as she could.

Kasandra picked up her knife, gripping it with both hands. When she spoke, her voice sounded different: lower, more serious.

To the poppet, she said, "You are Naveed. I name you Naveed. Anything that happens to you happens to him." Then she drew deliberate lines around him with the dark-handled knife from her sheath, carving symbols into the air. Roya watched, transfixed, because it really did feel like Kass was harnessing something. The world grew quieter. Even the wind stopped blowing. The candles burned brightly.

"Naveed, I see you happy and healthy, healed and whole. May you become well, from your body to your soul," Kassandra chanted. She glanced at Roya. "Say it with me."

Together, they repeated the spell twice more. Then Kass dipped her knife into the chalice. It came out red and dripping. The way it clung to the blade, Roya could tell it was not wine. "What's that?" she whispered, not wanting to interrupt.

Kass didn't seem to mind. "Blood. From a goat we slaughtered on the new moon. Here, hold up your hands."

Roya did as she was told, making sure the seed was still safely cradled in her palms. Kass dripped blood into her hands, and goosebumps exploded on Roya's arms as the seed grew slippery red.

Kass then held the still-dripping knife over the poppet. She moved it slowly from the head to the hands to the chest. Blood trickled through the sticks, pooling on the ground.

"Are you sure this is right?" Roya asked, because something strange had come into her just then. Something like a sickness, a worry.

"Yes. Now: you put the seed back in his chest. Right in the middle, to restore his heart."

Roya obeyed, again, though her hands shook and she almost dropped the seed. She couldn't say what was wrong, exactly. Just that she wasn't sure whether this magic was going to help or hurt.

Kass took her knife with both hands, and was carving more symbols above the poppet when suddenly she drew in her breath. The knife dropped to the ground.

"What happened?" Roya asked. "Is something wrong?"

Kass didn't answer. She stood up quickly, pinching the poppet's head inside the napkin she'd wrapped the herbs in, and threw the doll off the cliff into the churning sea below.

"What are you doing?" Roya almost screamed it, frantic, as she ran to the edge of the bluff to look down at the water. She expected to see the poppet floating there; it was only made of sticks, it should have bobbed right back up, but she could see nothing in the water but a faint red tint to the foam.

Roya turned around to see Kasandra kneeling next to her knife. She reached her hand out to pick it up, then drew away, as if afraid to touch it.

"How could you do that? You said… anything that happened to the doll would happen to him… and it's… it's going to drown…." Roya looked down at the water again, but nothing had resurfaced.

"No, no, it'll be all right," Kasandra said, but her voice was unsteady, like she was trying to convince herself. "The water will cleanse him, you'll see."

"What's wrong with your knife?" Roya asked. Kasandra still hadn't picked it up; she was crouched there with one hand hovering over it. Roya stepped closer, wondering if she would be able to feel the answer radiating in the air, but when she got close, Kass scooped the handle up with the cloth napkin and returned the knife to its sheath.

"Nothing's wrong," she said. "But this is going to be harder than I thought. We need to try something else. Here—tomorrow I'll bring our Book of Shadows. That will tell us what to do."

Roya had the distinct sensation that Kass was trying to distract her. But Roya couldn't forget that little poppet who was still underwater, sinking to the bottom of the ocean, as if that seed she'd planted in his heart had been an impossibly heavy stone.

Andi

THURSDAY, AUGUST 13

ANDI LAY ON HER BED TRYING TO FALL ASLEEP, THE MARINE breeze wafting through the open window. She could hear the waves out there whispering. Or, she thought drowsily, maybe it was the whales. When she was younger, maybe ten or so, she'd had a brief but intense obsession with humpback whales, and had fallen asleep every night to a recording of their mournful aquatic moans. Because of her perfect pitch, she easily picked up on the subtleties of their vocalizations, and had created a tonal language for them in her head.

Apparently, she'd been weird even back then.

She reached for her phone, knowing that she was only pondering whales because she was trying so hard not to think about something else. It couldn't be avoided anymore, though.

Why hadn't Naveed called?

They had been in Santa Barbara for a few days now. And it was wonderful. For the first time in months, she'd finally been able to relax. It also felt good to have a purpose again, and though she hadn't done anything about Metafolia yet, she looked forward to working on website content and getting in touch with Brooke as soon as she got home.

During the day she distracted herself with Cyrus, keeping the pact they had made that first day at the beach not to talk about Naveed. Just this morning, Cyrus had volunteered the only detail she'd heard so far: "Sounds like they're making progress—the new meds are helping. They just have to watch him one more night, so he should be headed home tomorrow."

Which was great and all, but Andi knew that every day in the hospital probably felt like ten to Naveed, and she kept expecting to hear something from him. Who else did he have to talk to, after all? He had stopped hanging out with all his old friends, had quit his job at the bookstore, had broken things off with Brooke, had some mysterious but obviously terrible argument with Cyrus. But he hadn't answered any of her calls or texts.

Andi didn't know what to make of this. She'd thought they had some sort of deeper understanding, ever since the conversation they'd had the day after her Metafolia-induced ER visit back in July.

She'd been slightly loopy from painkillers that morning, and frustrated at being sentenced to another week of cognitive rest. She hadn't really wanted to tell Cyrus about it; the whole thing was kind of embarrassing. They'd been planning to go to Parapluie for her belated birthday celebration that evening, so she wrote him a text to cancel. Not feeling good today, need to just stay home and sleep. Can we reschedule?

So she was surprised when someone knocked on her door later, waking her up. Through the crack in the door—she wasn't allowed to close it all the way—she saw Cyrus, looking adorably concerned, holding a foil-covered baking dish.

"Your dad told me what happened," he said. "I brought you some brownies. With caramel-pecan frosting."

"Wow. Thanks." She sat up, even though a stab of pain shot through her head when she moved.

"And, um, these two wanted to tag along too." He opened the door all the way, and Andi was surprised to see Naveed standing there, half-smiling, a bouquet of dahlias in one hand, Brooke's hand in the other.

Andi tried to hide her amazement. She knew what a big deal it was to get Naveed out of the house.

"Hey, I hope you don't mind us coming over?" Naveed was sweating, she noticed, and out of breath. Her house was less than a block from theirs, but it was probably the longest walk he'd taken in a while.

"Of course not," Andi stuttered.

Cyrus set the brownies down on her desk. "I'll go find a vase for the flowers."

"Are they from next door?" Andi wondered aloud.

"Yeah, they were hanging over the fence," Naveed said.

Andi thought about Mrs. Rochester, about her prized dahlias, how she fertilized and pruned them and actually entered them in contests. It all seemed like something straight out of a fairy tale, and the words were out of her mouth before she could stop them. "I hope Mrs. Rochester didn't see and put a curse on you or something."

For a second, Naveed looked shocked, a dark shadow darting across his face. Andi was about to add that she was only joking when he grinned. "Worth it," he said, and laughed, just a short chuckle, but it made the whole room brighter somehow.

Cyrus returned with a vase full of water and placed the flowers inside. Naveed was looking around her room, and Andi was suddenly self-conscious about the state of it, the sheets of composition paper scattered around, piles of dirty clothes, records from her dad's collection stacked in a corner.

"Why don't you sit down," Brooke was saying to Naveed. Andi scooted over in her bed, toward the wall, patting the space beside her.

Naveed didn't seem to be listening. He was still taking it all in, and had the strangest expression on his face. It was the same look she'd seen that first day they'd met at her dad's old record store. That look of curiosity, of wonder.

Brooke guided him to the bed, and he settled in against the headboard. She sat next to him for a minute, but as soon as she spotted the records, she got up and started thumbing through them. "Ooh, Sonic Youth! Can I put this one on?" she asked.

"Sure." Andi accepted a brownie from Cyrus and demolished it quickly, cupping one hand beneath it to catch the crumbs. Brooke played DJ at the record player, and Cyrus squeezed in behind Andi, letting her rest against him, and with his arms encircling her she felt supremely good. Naveed, as usual, was quiet and distant, but whenever Andi peeked over at him he had a faint smile on his face. *This is nice*, she thought as she nuzzled her head into Cyrus's shoulder. *Can't we all just stay like this forever?*

But soon Cyrus checked his phone and said they had to be going. "Your dad didn't want us to stay long, and Brooke has to get Naveed to the PT clinic." Naveed didn't say anything in response. He had turned his back to them, and now that Andi listened for it, she could hear his deep, rhythmic breathing.

Brooke sighed. "I really hate to wake him up," she said. "I wish we could just let him sleep."

"Well, how about we go get the car and come back? I'll drive, then you can leave straight from here," Cyrus suggested.

"Cy, you don't—"

"I know, I know, but I *do* have my learner's permit, and besides it's just right around the block. Please?"

"Fine. We'll be back in a few minutes."

Cyrus kissed Andi on the forehead, promising to come back soon, and blew her one more kiss from the doorway before he and Brooke left.

The music was still on, Bjork's *Homogenic* spinning in the record player. Andi turned away from Naveed, so they were back to back. She heard her dad in the doorway a moment later, checking on them, then leaving, and once he was gone she pressed the soles of her feet to Naveed's. She imagined transferring things into him, the love she felt, the acknowledgment of how much it meant that he had come to visit her.

"Bachelorette" began—dizzy, breathless violins spiraling into rhythmic drums—and it made Andi feel like the two of them were on a rocking boat, adrift on a perilous sea. She curled her toes into his, enjoying being close to him: he was usually so far away from her, from everyone. Then she pulled her feet away. What was she thinking? Her heart was with the boy who had baked her brownies, not the one who'd stolen flowers.

Naveed stirred. He coughed quietly for a moment before saying, "Oh, shit."

Andi turned over.

"I fell asleep? In your bed? Oh God, I'm so sorry." He wiped his mouth, which was a little drooly. He was obviously mortified.

"It's okay," she said. Then, before he could ask, "Cy and Brooke are coming right back. They went to get the car. So they can take you to your appointment."

He closed his eyes. "Okay. I wish… I wish I could stay here instead. Sorry, I can't believe I… it's just… some nights I can't get to sleep."

"It's fine. Really."

He didn't make a move to get up. Instead, he turned to her, studying her with his big dark eyes. Dark eyebrows, eyelashes, irises; dark undereye circles. All of him so dark. "You understand, don't you, Andi," he said. "You and I, we're the ones… we know what it's like to have… setbacks."

"Yeah. It sucks. And now I get to spend the whole week in bed doing nothing. Again."

"It's horrible." He met her eyes. "But I'm so glad you're all right."

The way he said it, with so much tenderness—she could hardly stand it.

He paused for a minute. She didn't say anything, because she could feel it, something in him building, something he needed to get out.

"I hate this," he finally said. "I *hate* it. I know I should be thankful it wasn't worse, but… it's hard to explain, how the neuropathy feels, like I'm drifting just above the ground. Like I lost my anchors to the normal world, and now I'm half here and half somewhere else. Like I can never fully be part of things anymore. Every time I stand up, or try to do some stupid thing like button a shirt, something that should be so easy, I'm faced with it over and over again, I'm forced to remember what she did, how she made me this way. I can never get away from it. From her."

His eyes, so pleading, were filling up. She didn't think she'd ever seen him cry, and wasn't sure if she could take it. A sudden, intense impulse seized her: to gather him up, to cup his jaw in her palm and feel the ridge of his cheekbone with her thumb, to hold him and hold him and hold.

She restrained herself, banishing those inappropriate thoughts from her head. She wished she knew what it felt like to love a brother. Did it feel something like this, such a deep longing for their happiness, such a great desire to make them better, no matter what it took? Andi tried to tell him all this with her eyes, not knowing what words to say. There was nothing she could offer that wouldn't sound hollow.

Naveed sniffed, rubbing his eyes with the heel of his hand. "Do you ever feel like that, Andi? Like you'll never escape? Like the days are just so endless, and there's nothing to look forward to?"

"Um… yeah, sometimes." She didn't like where this conversation was headed, so she said, "Maybe it would help to get out more. Go places, do stuff to distract you, replace the bad memories with good ones… not that that's how it works, I know that, but… anyway, it's been helpful for me. And starting something new. Having a project."

"I hate going out," Naveed said. "Everybody watching me, knowing who I am, knowing what happened."

"But it felt good to come here, right?"

"Yeah, but that's different. This place is safe. The rest of the world… isn't."

"Well, maybe you should just try it. That's all I'm saying. Go do something fun, something different, go somewhere you've never been. It might help." Then, as an idea struck her, "Hey—Cy and I were supposed to go to Parapluie for my birthday dinner tonight. I guess we'll have to wait until next week, but… would you and Brooke like to join us?"

"I don't know, I'm not sure that would be a good idea…."

"I bet Cy could get the chef to make something vegan for you guys," Andi said. "Please. I want you to be there—it'll give me something to look forward to while I'm lying here all week. And I'm the birthday girl, so, you know. You have to do what I say."

That did it. Coaxed a tiny smile from him. "Well, then, I guess that settles it," he said. "Can't argue with the birthday girl."

Remembering this conversation, especially since the birthday dinner a week later had been so disastrous, made Andi feel even worse. She had refrained from contacting Naveed after his breakup with Brooke; he was always holed up in his room whenever she came over, so she hadn't even seen him since then. It had been so shocking to watch him slam Brooke against the wall behind the restaurant, and even though she'd known he wasn't himself in that moment, even though she'd sensed the panic rising from him, the confusion and fear, it felt like reaching out to check on him would've somehow condoned what he had done. So she'd been texting with Brooke instead, studiously avoiding him—until his hospital admission changed things.

Was that why he was ghosting her now? Because he was holding a grudge against her for ignoring him these past few weeks?

A faint rapping at the door sent Andi's heart racing. She listened, and it happened again. Someone was whispering her name, softly.

Cyrus. Just Cyrus.

Andi shook off her sheets, peeling herself away from them, wishing she could peel that memory away too, because it felt like she had somehow cheated on Cyrus even though that wasn't what had happened at all, *nothing* had happened, and now Naveed couldn't even be bothered to call her back, even though she would have dropped everything to speak to him.

Now, now, now. Focus. She cracked open the door, peeked out.

"Oh good, you're awake." Cyrus was wearing his swim trunks, and a towel was draped around his neck. "I couldn't sleep. Want to go for a midnight swim?"

"Now? In the ocean?"

"Yes now, and of course not in the ocean. I'm not trying to get us killed. I just thought a little soak in the spa would be nice, and wanted some company."

"Oh. Sure. Let me put on my suit." She shut the door on him, briefly considering what it would mean to forego the suit altogether….

No, she wasn't ready for that yet. When she opened the door again to see his grinning face, that sweet, awestruck way he always looked at her, like he felt so lucky just to be in her presence, she grabbed his hand, caught up in the exhilaration of sneaking through the quiet house and darkened grounds. They stumbled their way towards the spa and glided into the still, warm water.

The moon was nothing but a thin crescent, fingernail-sized. Underneath the stars, palm trees swaying above, Andi leaned into Cyrus, overcompensating, perhaps, for the memories he could not know. He took his arm out of the water and draped it around her shoulders. It was so warm, and the sound of the moving water was so loud, and she couldn't help remembering that other time she'd looked up at the stars with him, in the forest after their escape from Dr. Snyder's lab, the terror that had gripped her then, underlying every word, every whisper, every rustle of the trees.

Even though she knew it would kill the mood, she felt the need to confess to him. Not about her earlier thoughts, not exactly, but about something else she couldn't shake from her mind. "I can't help feeling so… guilty about this."

"About what? Brennan said we could use the spa."

"No, I mean, about being here at all."

"Oh. Because of… because of my brother? Because he can't be here too?"

"Well, yeah. Of course I feel bad about that," Andi admitted. "But it's more. I mean, here we are in this place—paradise, really—but I doubt Brennan would have offered to let us stay here if he hadn't felt sorry for us. And, I don't know, part of me feels like it isn't fair. We're getting special treatment when there's still all this terrible stuff going on in the world, because of people like Brennan who have so much money that they'd do anything to get more, anything to keep from losing it all."

"Do you think you'll ever be satisfied, Andi?" From anyone else, the question would have sounded accusatory, but Cyrus said it lightly, affectionately. "I, for one, think we deserve it. We may never get the chance to do something like this again. Who knows what's ahead of us, everything could change tomorrow, we've got to carpe diem and all that."

Andi leaned further into the crook of Cyrus's shoulder, letting her hair pool around him, letting her cold chin dip under the hot water. It was hard to articulate what she was feeling. "But we shouldn't be the only ones," she said. "So many people are struggling with all sorts of things right now. Why can't Brennan and people like him do more to make life better for everyone else?"

Cyrus sloshed his arm around to embrace Andi fully. "Well, well, well. Very subversive. A revolutionary, are you?"

He said it with such admiration that Andi found herself smiling. "No one ever suspects the quiet Asian girl."

Cyrus laughed, that quick, surprised little chuckle that she loved coaxing out of him, and the next words rushed out of his mouth. "Oh God, I love you, Alexandria."

He froze, as if it had slipped out, and Andi felt a strange churning inside. Should she reciprocate? Of course she should, because she loved him, right? Yes, she loved this, the sensation of his body against hers, the softness of his skin; she loved the way he made her feel, beautiful and worthwhile. She'd never said the L-word out loud to the other guys she'd dated, but she hadn't felt this deeply connected to any of them. Plus, it seemed like not saying anything would crush him, and he'd been so good to her, so good to everyone, he deserved to hear it. She squashed the tiny doubt and said, "I love you too, Cyrus."

And then he was kissing her again, so she stopped thinking at all. Their bodies twined together in the water, and they held each other and floated, watching the steam rise into the dark night sky.

Roya

EVEN THOUGH THE POPPET HAD HAUNTED ROYA'S NIGHTMARES and she was a little wary of Kasandra's powers, she still woke up at dawn the next morning and stole away to their meeting spot on the beach.

When she arrived, Kasandra was already there. She greeted Roya with a humongous, lonely smile, which quickly erased Roya's earlier hesitation.

"I can't stay long today," Roya said. It had been close, last time. She had gotten inside just as Auntie Leila emerged from her bedroom.

"That's all right. This shouldn't take much time." Kasandra opened her canvas pouch and pulled out a leather-bound book. A design was stamped into the soft cover, what looked like a thick letter "O" at first, but when Roya looked closer she saw it was a pair of orca whales swimming in a circle. She touched the indentation with her fingers.

"It's the symbol of Orcinia," Kasandra said. "Grandfather said the name comes from the Latin *Orcinus,* 'of the kingdom of the dead.' And from the scientific name of *Orcinus orca,* the killer whale, once thought to be the guardian of the spirit kingdom."

Roya thought about the orcas who had led her to the sea cave. She fingered the key in her pocket. "Can I see the book?"

Kasandra handed it gently to Roya. The book was beautiful, thick and substantial. It was handmade, and the pages inside were written in neat script.

"Be careful with it. There are only a few of these in existence. They were made right here. We make everything by hand—everything." She flexed her feet, shod in soft leather boots. "Goat skin. Anyway, my nan knows a lot about plants. We have two greenhouses that I'm not even allowed to go into, because the plants that grow there are so hard to cultivate. She knows the right combinations to help fix imbalances, and writes down all her recipes and spells in our Book of Shadows. So, let's see what we can do about your brother's problem." Kasandra took the book back from Roya, clutching it protectively. "But, I was wondering… can you do me a favor?"

"Probably. What is it?"

"I want to see some pictures. Of the outside."

Roya hadn't brought any photos with her, but maybe she could borrow Auntie Leila's phone. "Okay. I'll try to bring some tomorrow."

Kasandra flipped through the book. "Here. Why don't we start with the Restorative Blend. I've had it before, one time when I got this fugue that wouldn't go away."

"A fugue? Is that like a fever or something?"

"No. Haven't you ever had a fugue? A soul-sickness? Where everything makes you so sad, and it all feels pointless?"

"Oh. That." Roya hurriedly went on, "He definitely has that. Did it work for you?"

"I guess so. A few days after I took it, I felt much better. Tasted awful, though. Most of them do. You think you can get him to drink it today, while it's still fresh?"

"Oh—he's not here. I guess I never told you that? He's actually… he's in the hospital right now, back in Seattle."

"Hmm. It's that bad? Then we might need to do something stronger."

"No, no, he's okay, that's what my mom says, he should be home soon." But it had been days, and he wasn't. That worried Roya. Especially after what she and Kass had done the day before.

"Well, in any case, that means he can't drink it right away, so that does make it more complicated. It might lose some potency during your journey. Oh wait, I have an idea." She flipped to a later section of the book. "Yes. Here we go. This recipe's better. It improves with age."

Roya peeked over her shoulder. The list included a lot of ingredients she'd never even heard of. Dittany? Extract of gall bladder? "Where are we going to get these things?" she asked.

"We have most of them on hand. There are a few things that you can gather, though. Here's your list."

Kasandra listed ingredients and Roya repeated them in her mind. Four-inch piece of bull kelp. Seven dandelion roots and one stinging nettle root, cleaned and chopped. A teaspoon of sea water.

"Once you find them, put them in a bowl and cover with boiling water, and let it all steep for fifteen minutes. Then strain out the solids and bring it back here tomorrow, and we'll finish it," Kass said.

Roya agreed. This potion felt a lot less risky than the poppet, and she kind of wished they'd started with it instead.

As soon as they said goodbye, Roya got to work gathering her ingredients. She scooped up sea water with an oyster shell, hacked a tube of bull kelp into a piece she thought was about four inches long, and carried them back to the cabin.

But it was still early, and Auntie Leila wasn't stirring yet. Once Roya had put them into a plastic storage container, she decided to keep going.

There was a small shed in one corner of the garden. Inside, she found a red-handled metal spade and a pair of garden gloves. They were too big, but she put them on anyway.

Back to the forest to find the nettle root. Roya headed towards Orcinia, picking her way through the tangle of woods. Even though she had veered off the main path, it felt like her feet knew exactly where they were going.

Or maybe she was just following the sound of the crows. A whole bunch of them were cawing raucously, arguing over something or other, in the droopy top branches of a tall Western hemlock. They flew away as she came nearer, and out of habit she studied their feathers for glints of white, but found none. Not that she expected to see any. The crow who had helped her escape from SILO had never reappeared, and Roya knew, deep down, that he had moved on.

She stepped closer to the tree. The light fell through its branches, thick with life and dust and the foggy morning mist. Right about at her eye level, something was carved into the trunk.

Roya traced the letters with her fingertip. The outlines were fuzzy, but she could just make them out: B + G.

At first she wondered if the carving could have been made by Kass's parents, and got excited about showing the tree to her friend—until she remembered Kass's mother was named Miracle. So that didn't fit after all.

As she turned to leave, she noticed a patch of nettles nearby, so she started digging with her spade. She pulled on the stems, careful not to brush against the leaves even with gloves on, but the root was deep and long. She didn't know if she was supposed to take the whole thing, but kept digging just in case.

Clank. Roya looked up at the tree in surprise: her spade had hit metal.

Roya set the root aside and kept digging, shoveling the forest soil into a mound beside her. Slowly, the earth revealed its secret: a small metal box. When she'd scraped away enough dirt to grab the edges, she plunged her hand in.

But it was in there deep, stuck, and she had to find a thin, hard branch to help jimmy the box out. Eventually, she wrestled it out of the ground. It was old and rusted but still sturdy. On its front face was a lock.

Excited, Roya reached into her pocket for the key. Hands shaking, she tried to force it in—but it didn't fit.

It had to be the right key, though. Why else would she have been led here?

She knew she needed to get back soon, before her auntie woke up, so she tucked the box under her arm and headed toward the cabin. As she approached, she was surprised to hear Auntie Leila calling for her, frantic. She stashed the box under the hedges, along with the gloves and the nettle root and the spade, then ran up to the cabin. "I'm here! I'm right here."

"Oh, thank God. I was so worried! Your mom just called and I couldn't find you—where did you go?"

"I couldn't sleep. Went to the beach."

"The beach?! You should never, ever go to the beach without me. You could have slipped! Fallen into the waves! Been swept out to sea!"

Roya knew that none of these things would have happened, and that she couldn't tell her auntie the real story. She tried to distract her. "Maman called?"

"Oh. Yes. She wanted to talk to you, but I told her you'd have to call her back." She pulled out her phone. "Better do it now! Don't want her to worry. Roya, really, you can't go wandering off on your own, okay?"

"Okay," said Roya, finding the number for "Mahnaz" in Auntie Leila's phone and selecting it. She sat on the front steps. Auntie Leila took the hint and went back inside, but Roya could feel her watching from the window.

The phone only rang once before Maman picked up. "Hi, Maman, it's me," Roya said.

"Roya-jaan! Good timing—we're on our way home now. Naveed just got discharged."

The swoop of relief was so immense that Roya was glad she was sitting down. Maybe it was all right; maybe the poppet hadn't messed things up. Maybe it had even helped.

"So I'll get him settled at home, then I'll be back to pick you up tomorrow," Maman was saying.

"*Tomorrow*?" But Roya still had so much she wanted to do! She couldn't leave Kasandra already....

Maman laughed. "You sound disappointed."

"I didn't mean—I'm glad that you're coming back, it's just—"

"It's all right, azizam. I'm so glad that you've been enjoying yourself. And you know what? I'll stay for a day or two, so we can have a bit more time on the island before we head home together."

"Good. I missed you." Roya was confused by the pang of sadness she felt. Maman sounded happy, but Roya couldn't quite follow her there. "Can I talk to Naveed?"

"Of course. Here he is," Maman said, but Roya could hear a faint response in the background, Naveed's voice: "I don't want to—"

"Talk to your sister." A demand, so muffled that Roya could barely make it out. Maman must be covering the phone's mic. Roya's earlier relief disappeared. She suddenly felt like crying.

Silence. Then, an exhale. "Hey, Roya!" Naveed's tone was cheery, and even though it was good to hear him again, all Roya could think about was how fake he sounded.

"How are you doing?" she asked warily.

"Oh, I'm great. They got me fixed up, and now I'm going home, good as new."

You're lying, Roya thought, but she said, "That's good."

"How are you?"

"I'm fine." Roya paused. "Maman said we'll be coming back in a few days. And Kourosh is coming home too, right? So we'll all be together again. Just in time for your birthday."

"Yeah. That's really… it's gonna be great."

Roya felt like she was talking to a distant relative, someone she barely knew. Naveed kept rambling on. "Are you having a nice vacation? I saw some pictures. It looks like you're having a great time." Who was this Naveed, who had forgotten all his adjectives? Roya was quiet for probably too long, and their silence didn't feel companionable, it felt awkward, the silence of two people at a loss for what to say.

"I found something the other day." Roya wanted to get his attention, to snap him out of whatever weird mood he was in. To make him feel less of a stranger. "A key. I found it by following the orcas. It was underneath some bones in a cave on the beach. And this morning I found a box. An old locked box, buried under a tree. The key must fit, right? But it's so old and rusty. Do you know how to take rust off things? Maybe that would work."

Silence on the other end of the line. She suddenly felt like reaching through the phone, grabbing him by the throat, yelling, *WHY AREN'T YOU LISTENING? JUST LISTEN TO ME FOR ONCE!*

Where had that come from? That anger? Luckily she reined it in. "Naveed?" she prompted instead.

"Sorry, what?" he asked. "I didn't catch that last part."

"I said, do you know how to take rust off things."

"What? Rust? Uh, we're pulling up now. I have to go."

"Oh. Okay. I love you?" Roya winced. She hadn't meant that to sound like a question.

Naveed didn't seem to notice. He blurted a string of words, tripping out of his mouth in a rush, no pauses between them. "Iloveyoutooseeyousoonbye."

He ended the call. Roya set the phone next to her and let her head sink to her knees. She felt emptied out, her initial hope and relief flying away, evaporating into nothingness.

7/31
here i am lying awake (again).
C snores above, rubbing it in.
how is it so easy for him to sleep? to breathe?

so. i think i was wrong, the pins & needles keep coming
but sensation never returned
every night it gets worse
        goes on for hours
        can't figure out how to make it go away
right now it doesn't hurt, but when it comes back
even just sleeping under sheets will be impossible
the slightest brush of my toes against the fabric
will feel like being stabbed by a thousand phantom needles

can't tell anyone about this. you know where that will lead.
still hope it will go away.
just a phase, you'll feel better in the morning, maybe it's the full moon.

i want to blame it on the moon   think it's messing with my head
there are some things   i can't remember
        (does that make me a lunatic?)

or maybe it's my own doing   my head is full of holes
dug them myself   deep, deep holes   crammed them full
of things i don't want to remember   covered them with dirt
packed it down hard   but maybe not hard enough   sometimes
things claw through sometimes   it feels   like
i made the holes so deep   so wide   that they became an abyss

only a matter of time
before everything caves in

my birthday is in a few weeks.
i can't stop thinking about the bridge.
you know, the story maman tells?
the day i was born, almost 18 years ago.
i think about her laboring in the dark
under the drawbridge by the hospital
baba next to her holding her hand
cars whizzing overhead
i think about maman and her een neez bogzarad
and how much pain it must have taken
to expel the creature trapped inside her belly
(AKA me)

maybe that's how i got so fucked up
some troll-spirit got inside me under that bridge
waited all these years to be unleashed

the way she tells it though, it's not about ugliness.
it's about the ringing bell
the turning of gears as the bridge rose to let a boat through
the shrinking of darkness
it's about opening up to let something beautiful in (or out i guess).
and that's where she always ends the story, with that opening bridge.

but that's the wrong place to end.
because the bridge closed again, and the darkness came back.
the darkness always comes back.

will farhad remember me on my birthday? doubt it.
we finally got in touch and turns out he met this girl, zahra.
they're so happy, so in love.
it's sickening.
don't really want to talk to him anymore.

it's bad enough watching C & A whenever they come around.
cyrus and alexandria,
both named after rulers of the ancient world
does that mean they were destined?
who knows—
after all, cyrus represented the beginning of the first persian empire
and alexander its end.

speaking of history i keep putting off registration for fall quarter
just can't picture myself taking the train to the uw
      buying textbooks
      sitting in class
      all those eyes watching me
and it's more than that. don't think i'm smart enough anymore
my head being full of holes and all.
plus the weeks of high fever cooked my brain
and the oxygen deprivation starved it.
reading anything is a struggle
and writing is so taxing
that i always have to nap for hours afterward.

we're going out to dinner tomorrow.
don't want to go, but i'll do it for andi.
it'll be a test.
my return to society.

<u>8/1</u>
a glass of water.
a fucking glass of water.

that's all it took to dislodge me from time.

one minute i'm sitting in the restaurant
        with my girlfriend
        and my brother
        and the birthday girl

and then the waiter slides over a glass of ice water and who knows
why the hell it happened but suddenly i was back in that other place
don't know how i could be in two places at once but i was
and i had to get out of there   out of both places   out of
everywhere   can't even describe it   wasn't like a memory but
like i'd actually gone back in time   like i was reliving it all   but i
couldn't figure out how to get back   couldn't catch my breath
and i thought i wanted   to   die   because dying would be an
escape   but then i was sitting in an alley next to andi
then lying in the back seat telling them no hospital   and then i
forgot again where i was   when i was   and thank god they
took me home instead   now it's late and i think it's the same day
we went to dinner but i don't know   guess i'm back but not really
i feel like a flattened insect   nothing left of me but an
exoskeleton   i don't know where   i   went

<u>8/2</u>
i am nowhere. i am nothing.

<u>8/3</u>
brooke told me what happened.
she showed me the bruises.
i didn't want to believe it
      (still don't want to believe it)
      (i'd never do something like that)
      (right?)
so i yelled at her
called her a liar
she said i needed help so i yelled at her some more
i know her very well.
i know how to make her hurt.
i tore down everything we'd built this past year
      doused it in kerosene
      lit it on fire
      watched it flame up
      and crackle into ash

i don't want her to ever come back.
don't think she will.
it's better this way.

<u>8/4</u>

maman made me an appointment with a therapist.
so you think i'm crazy? i asked her.
there's no shame in getting help, she answered.
i said i didn't want to go.
she said it would be good for me.
doubtful.

she wasn't able to get me in until next thursday
so at least I have some time to figure out how to act normal again

everyone (except baba, who's stuck w/me) is leaving soon
C & A are going to SoCal next week
        bet C won't even visit tehrangeles while he's there
maman and roya are escaping to lopez island.
must be nice for them.

<u>8/5</u>
every night it gets worse   wish i could take some of those
painkillers they sent me home with but of course they're hidden
somewhere under lock & key   to get them i'd have to explain
(def not a good idea)   i hate the way those pills make me feel
hate being out of it   but getting to the point where i just
want it   to stop

<u>8/6</u>

thinking about the bridge.
thinking about the knife.
thinking about the pills.

<u>8/7</u>

have to write during the day now
and sleep, or try to
been so bad these last few nights that i can't
        pick up a pen can't
        wear socks can't
        even move without being engulfed in pain.
try to drift off, it wakes me up.

don't want them to find out
don't want to be poked and prodded
while they do tests and throw more drugs at me
but if it doesn't stop i think i'll go insane
maybe i'm already insane
maybe this is all in my fucked-up head
if i tell them everything they'll probably lock me up
i don't know what to do

i'm so tired of this

i'm so tired of everything

Roya

ROYA WASN'T ABLE TO SEE KASANDRA THE MORNING MAMAN came back. Auntie Leila had awoken early to make waffles for breakfast, ruining Roya's plan to sneak out at dawn.

She tried hard not to think of Kasandra waiting at their meeting spot, walking dejectedly back to Orcinia when Roya didn't show up. But Maman arrived jubilant and smiling, welcoming Roya into such a big hug that Roya didn't ever want to let go. Auntie Leila served the waffles and they all ate until they were stuffed, and afterwards they went walking on the beach.

"I'm sorry about that call yesterday," Maman said as they trudged through the damp pebbles on the shore. "I know Naveed wanted to talk to you, it's just hard for him on the phone. He's really doing much better. Like a new person. You'll see."

The person Roya had talked to on the phone the day before certainly felt like a new person, a stranger, but she didn't want to think about that. She kept scanning the bluff above them for signs of Kasandra. No one was there.

Then it hit her: she should have left a note! Why hadn't she thought of that? She might not have another chance to see Kass before she left. Maman was a light sleeper and often woke up early, so there was no hope of sneaking out anymore. But they needed to finish the potion, that much was clear.

More importantly, though, she needed to see Kass again. She needed to say goodbye.

According to Maman, they were going to leave early the next morning, take the ferry to San Juan Island, and spend the night in Friday Harbor before heading back. Maman had heard of a master woodworker there who made elaborate carvings out of driftwood, and she was hoping to find a good gift to give Naveed. He'd said he didn't want any presents, but Roya had been planning to give him the beautiful amber agate that Auntie Leila had found.

And, secretly, the potion. Roya had already planned how she'd get Naveed to drink it: she could mix it into his morning smoothie and he probably wouldn't notice. The green powder he blended with almond milk smelled gross to Roya, but he always chugged it down without seeming to taste it at all.

If it worked, Roya thought, that would be the biggest birthday gift ever.

In the evening, while Maman and Auntie Leila were busy making dinner, Roya snuck into Auntie Leila's room and took some printer paper, envelopes, and a pen. She rifled through her bag until she found the book of stamps she'd brought for sending postcards, then put all of these in a plastic bag and said she was going to play outside.

"Maman, can I borrow your phone? I want to take some pictures," Roya said.

"Okay. But be careful with it." Maman handed it to her.

Auntie Leila called, "Don't leave the yard!" and Roya said, "I won't!" but she did. And then she ran. She worried that the packet of supplies might be taken by someone else if she left it in their usual meeting spot, so she kept running all the way to the hole in the fence.

Once inside, she stuck to the periphery. Where would Kass be? In the meal tent, maybe? Making dinner, or eating it? Roya saw a couple people out by the greenhouses, but otherwise it seemed deserted. She snuck across the grass, stopping at the meal tent and listening for Kass.

She did hear someone bustling around inside, and smoke was flowing from the chimney of the wood-burning oven, so she peeked in. Sure enough, it was Kass, peeling potatoes with a knife. When she noticed Roya she smiled, revealing her twisted teeth.

She gestured for Roya to come closer, but spoke in a low voice. "My grandfather came home last night. He and Nan are in the main house right now, so you'd better be careful. Where were you this morning?"

"Maman came back. My brother's out of the hospital, and we're leaving tomorrow." Roya fought back tears as she said it. She didn't want to go.

Kass, too, looked crestfallen. But she tried a small smile. "That's good, so he's better?"

Roya shrugged. "I don't know. Did you find all the ingredients? I still want to give him the potion when I get home."

Kass pointed with her kitchen knife towards the corner, where her canvas bag was heaped on the ground. "It's all in there, in a jar. Add it to what you have and let it sit for a day or two. Then strain it and give it to him. Three days, three doses."

Roya found the jar in the pouch. Inside was a brownish liquid speckled with mysterious floating ingredients. Roya was glad *she* didn't have to drink it.

Remembering the deal they'd made, Roya held out Maman's phone. "Oh, yeah. I brought pictures."

Kass scooted closer to Roya as she scrolled back into some old pictures. Various photos of downtown Seattle. The five of them, Roya's whole family, grinning on the waterfront. Cyrus holding up a pie he'd baked. Naveed in the play at Seward Park. Kasandra found that one particularly interesting, but Roya couldn't look anymore. It hurt too much. She clicked the phone off.

"Thanks for showing me." Kass turned back to her potatoes, and Roya was seized with guilt. She hated thinking about Kass in here all by herself, no other kids around ever, no one to talk to.

"I don't want to go," Roya blurted, meaning it completely. She'd rather be here, peeling potatoes in this tent with Kass, than going back home, where everything had been so tense and hard. "Can't I stay here with you? I could help out. I can do lots of things, I'm really good at peeling vegetables, grating them, gathering food, hauling wood. Whatever you need, I can do it."

Something sparked in Kasandra's eyes. "And once we finished our work, we could go to my treehouse, the one my father built, and I could teach you everything you need to know about Orcinia, and then you could tell me about the outside...."

"You have a treehouse? We could bring up some big quilts and spend the night there...."

"And I could show you the pond, we could build a raft and go out to the very middle...."

"And maybe sometimes my family would come visit and you could meet my brothers...."

Kasandra picked up the knife again, carving the peel away from the potato's creamy flesh. "But it would never work, would it. They wouldn't let you live here."

"You never know." But Roya, too, knew it was an impossible dream. Her family was supposed to stick together. Even when they didn't want to.

"You should probably go," said Kass. "I'd get in so much trouble if Grandfather saw you."

Unable to look her friend in the eye, Roya thrust the plastic bag to Kass. "Will you write to me? I put my address on the envelopes. They have stamps too."

Kass took it, but then her face went serious.

"What?" Roya asked, but Kass shushed her. Then Roya heard it too. Footsteps. Voices.

Kass shoved the packet down the front of her dress and took Roya by the arm, leading her to an open flap in the tent. "They're coming. Make sure they don't see you. Don't let them find the hole in the fence or else they'll seal it up and then I'll never be able to leave."

"Okay. Kass, I…." Roya wasn't ready for this.

"We'll see each other again. I know it. Now, go." She shoved Roya toward the flap, and Roya squeezed through, holding tight to the jar in one hand, Maman's phone in the other.

"Kasandra? Who were you talking to?" Roya heard a deep voice say. A man's voice.

"Nobody," squeaked Kass, but Roya didn't hear any more, because she was already running, and someone was following her, but she couldn't let them see the hole in the fence, and was Kass going to get in trouble, oh she'd be in so much trouble, what if they found the envelopes, what if Roya never heard from her again?

She glanced over her shoulder and saw a man with hard, angry eyes and a scraggly gray beard chasing her. "Hey! You! Come back here!"

Roya ran faster. There was no way out but through the fence, and, sending a telepathic apology to Kasandra, she raced as fast as she could towards the hole.

Then she heard someone else. A woman, though her voice was deep and guttural. "Alastor, stop! She's just a child. Let her go." Roya glanced behind her to see an old woman with a thick white braid cascading down her back. It had to be Kasandra's nan.

The man slowed down, but Roya could still hear his heavy breath behind her, fading as she ran from him, as she dove through the fence hole and ran and ran and ran back to the cabin. When she got to the garden she crawled beneath one of the bushes gasping and sobbing and trying to make herself very small, and some dirt got in her mouth and she tried to spit it out but it adhered to her tongue, the grit clinging to her, like it would be stuck there forever.

★

THE FOLLOWING DAY, Roya and Maman said goodbye to Auntie Leila and drove onto the ferry. They parked the car and climbed the stairs to the passenger deck of the ship. Roya held on tightly to Maman's hand, irrationally afraid that Maman had somehow overheard the thoughts she'd had in Orcinia with Kasandra, when she'd been ready, completely willing, to leave everything behind. But Kass's grandfather was scary, and Roya had been so worried about her friend that she'd barely slept the night before. What did Kass mean by getting in trouble? What would they take from her, when she had nothing? Would she be stuck doing the worst jobs, the hardest ones? Would they fix the fence so that she was never able to go the beach again? And the unbearable thought that Roya couldn't stop having: would that man hurt her? She kept thinking about Kasandra's father, about his missing hand. *He shouldn't have made Grandfather angry.*

No. Kasandra's nan wouldn't let him hurt her. Roya didn't even allow herself to question this.

Now, on the ferry, Roya's thoughts of abandoning her family seemed like a betrayal. She had dutifully added Kass's mixture to the potion, filling her water bottle with the foul-smelling concoction. She tucked it into her backpack, right next to the still-unopened metal box. But she couldn't deny that as the ferry quaked beneath her and the loud horn sounded, as they slipped away from the dock and the island grew smaller, she felt an uncanny, building dread. Like she wasn't supposed to go home. Or, worse: like the home that she'd left was not the same one to which she'd return.

"Let's go outside," Maman suggested. Lots of people were gathered inside the front windows, but few were on the outer deck, where the wind was strong.

They stepped through the swinging doors, and a gust of wind hit Roya in the face like a slap. She looked up at Maman, who was smiling, her curly hair billowing around her. They walked to the very edge and leaned against the green metal railing.

Maman spread her arms wide, embracing all the wind, the spray from the water. The gusts seemed so strong, like they were trying to blow Roya back onto the island. But she wanted to stay here now. She wedged herself closer, hugging Maman's waist, burrowing her nose into her belly, the skin there soft as dough. Roya's hair blew against Maman like it was weaving itself into her clothes, so that they'd never be apart, so that Naveed could never come between them again, the way he always did; so that they could go back to being the family they once were. So that Maman would forgive her for wanting to leave. So that they could come back to Lopez again soon and save Kasandra.

"Maman," she said. "I'm sorry, Maman." And even though the wind took the words away so fast that Maman couldn't possibly have heard, she embraced Roya with a powerful squeeze, and they stood there on the deck watching the boat slice through the water, watching the island grow distant. Leaving it behind.

Cyrus

CYRUS'S VACATION COULDN'T LAST FOREVER, OF COURSE. Too soon, it careened to a halt.

He slept late on the morning of their departure, waking only when Andi knocked on the door to ask if he was ready to go. He rushed through the bedroom packing up his clothes, stuffing them into his bag on top of Naveed's notebook, that memento of what awaited upon his return.

He was going to have to face Naveed today. His brother still refused to talk to him on the phone, but according to his parents he was doing better and looking forward to Cyrus's return. Cyrus knew this was just a typical parental peacemaking attempt and didn't buy it for a second. Neither of them knew the full extent of what had gone on that night. He wasn't even sure Naveed did—he'd been pretty out of it—but either way, his brother must have been furious when he found out his notebook was gone.

Cyrus needed to talk to Andi about it. But there was no time. He didn't even get a chance to have breakfast before they left for the tiny Santa

Barbara airport, and he definitely didn't want to talk about it in front of her parents, or anywhere in public.

He bought a greasy breakfast bagel and a smoothie at the airport. Andi went with him, but ordered only a cup of tea since she'd eaten earlier. They sat in silence. He felt like such a slob eating in front of her, but she just smiled at him wistfully.

"This was great, wasn't it?" she said.

Cyrus finished chewing a bite of his bagel and wiped his mouth with a napkin. "Oh, yeah, it was awesome. I'll never forget it, as long as I live."

"Me neither. The beach, the guest house, the hot tub…." She blushed, and it was so freaking adorable that he could hardly stand it. He moved to the seat next to her, the table suddenly seeming like far too much space between them.

"And now we go home," she said, leaning against him.

"Home," he repeated. "Yep."

"It'll be nice to see everyone again, though. I bet you miss your family?"

"Oh, yeah, definitely." He wrapped the rest of his bagel in the napkin, his appetite suddenly gone. "We'd better get back to the gate."

They had to walk onto the tarmac and up a small flight of stairs to get on the plane, like it was the 1950s or something. Before stepping inside, Cyrus took one last deep breath of the ocean-kissed Southern California air.

On the plane they watched a movie on Andi's tablet, but he could hardly pay attention. He hoped Andi couldn't sense the dread seeping out of him. He could practically smell it, the stink of anxiety.

If she did, she didn't say anything. She just leaned into him, her head against his shoulder, content. That made him feel slightly better, like everything would work out in the end.

They landed in Seattle and picked up the car from the long-term parking lot, then drove home. As Joyce turned onto his street, Andi asked, "Should I come over? To say hi to Naveed?"

Cyrus really needed to explain what had happened before she talked to him. "Um, I think for right now it's best if you just drop me off. Maybe you can come over later—I'll feel him out and let you know."

She nodded, seeming a little relieved too, as they pulled up in front of Cyrus's house.

Cyrus fumbled with his seatbelt. "Thanks for the ride. I'll see you later." Before he got out of the car, Andi gave him a peck on the cheek, which calmed him a teensy bit. He took his backpack out of the trunk and waved as he entered the front gate.

Okay. Now to go inside. Inside, where Naveed was waiting. Would he be mad, Cyrus wondered? Maybe he'd worked through some stuff during his time in the psych ward, cooled down a bit? Maybe?

Cyrus's stomach churned around that greasy bagel. What a terrible breakfast choice that had been.

Cautiously, he turned the door handle. It was locked, which he wasn't expecting, so he had to dig his keys out of his bag.

He opened the door. Their cat Pashmak watched him from her perch on the sofa, but the house was silent.

"Hello?" he called, his voice cracking. He sounded so nervous. He *was* so nervous.

No answer.

"Baba? Naveed? Are you here?"

Still nothing. Pashmak stared at him with her green eyes, purring.

"Do *you* know where they are?" he asked the cat. She purred harder when he scratched at the base of her ears. "What about Maman and Roya? They aren't back yet, right?"

Pashmak, of course, offered no answers. Cyrus pulled his hand away. No point in continuing this one-sided conversation.

Cautiously, he creeped upstairs. The bedroom he shared with Naveed was empty. He set down his backpack and took out his phone to make sure he hadn't missed a text or call that would explain where the hell everybody was.

And then he heard it, across the hall, in his parents' room. The door was closed, but through it came an odd, kind of gaspy sound, almost like mirthless laughter.

With an icy, horrified dread, Cyrus cracked open the door. Baba was on the floor—kneeling there, forehead to the ground, on a prayer rug—and the strange sounds, he wasn't laughing, he was—

He was crying.

Baba was *crying*. Which he never did, not even on the night Cyrus had left for LA; Cyrus had been a mess in the waiting room while the doctors pumped Naveed's stomach, but Baba had just put an arm around him, letting Cyrus sob into his shirt, telling him everything would be okay.

"Baba?" Cyrus asked shakily. Crying *and* praying, another thing Cyrus rarely saw him do. This couldn't be good.

"Kourosh!" Baba sprang to his feet, stepping off the prayer rug before gathering Cyrus up in a huge hug. "Kourosh-jaan, I'm sorry, I—I didn't hear you come in."

"What's wrong?"

Baba kept his arms wrapped around Cyrus. Too tight. He didn't say anything for a minute. Cyrus felt unbelievably constricted.

"He… Naveed… he left," Baba finally said. "I think he… ran away."

"Oh." Cyrus was oddly relieved. "But how do you know? Did you try calling him?"

Baba gestured at the dresser. Naveed's phone sat there, blank and inert.

So he didn't take his phone. That seemed like a bad sign to Cyrus. If he had run away… why wouldn't he bring his phone with him?

"He lied to me," Baba said, letting Cyrus go and sinking onto the edge of the bed. "We signed him up for a support group, and I dropped him off at his first meeting this morning. He said he'd made plans for Ethan to pick him up afterwards, that they were going out to lunch to celebrate his birthday. I even called Ethan, just to make sure, and he confirmed that was the plan, sounded so glad that Naveed had finally contacted him. But

I should have asked what time he was planning to pick him up, because Naveed gave him the wrong time, an hour after the meeting ended. Ethan waited a while, but he never showed up."

"Oh" was all Cyrus could manage. His legs didn't feel like they could hold him up anymore. He plopped down next to Baba.

"This is my fault," Baba went on. "I should've waited for him there, should've known something like this might happen... but he seemed so much better...."

"It's not your fault, Baba," Cyrus said. "Should we call the police? Maybe they can help?"

"No." The force of this surprised Cyrus. "No. He's only been gone a few hours and... and they... it's better if they're not involved."

"But they could, like, track him. Trace his credit cards or whatever."

Baba shook his head. "I don't want them digging."

"Digging? Into what? Did something happen?"

"Well..." Baba looked down, picking at a piece of lint on the bedspread. "At the hospital, there was... an incident. With a nurse. You know how he gets, when he's disoriented, when he feels trapped...."

Cyrus felt that bagel churning again. He thought about Brooke, about what had happened in the alley behind Parapluie. "Was the nurse okay?"

"Relatively. He tackled her to the ground and tried to run for it, but he was locked in. Luckily she was able to sedate him... he didn't have any memory of it later, I guess that happens sometimes with PTSD... but they kept him in restraints after that, which only made things worse... and the doctors thought it would be best for him to go to an institution for a while, but your mother and I knew that was more likely to hurt than to help him. He wouldn't go willingly, it would have ruined him, we were sure of that, but I don't know... maybe they were right?"

Baba sounded so weary, so... wrecked. Anger rose to the top of Cyrus's internal stew of emotions. How dare Naveed leave like this, after everything they'd done for him, after everything they'd been through!

If he could just see what he was doing to Baba. And what about Roya? This would destroy her.

"If we tell the police he's missing," Baba continued, "And they find out about the nurse, about his mental state, they're going to think... that he's dangerous, that he might take others out with him... which he wouldn't do, not unless he was backed into a corner... not unless they hunted him down, trapped him... better if they're not involved...." his dad babbled.

"It might not go that way, Baba," Cyrus said.

"It always goes that way, Kourosh. With people like us, it always does."

Although the words made Cyrus uncomfortable, he understood where Baba was coming from. After all, during the Nutrexo debacle, both of his parents had been imprisoned and interrogated as suspected terrorists. They obviously didn't have a lot of faith in law enforcement. But Cyrus didn't like thinking about that, so he changed the subject. "I don't get it—if it was that bad, why did they discharge him?"

"He's been much better for the last few days." Baba still didn't look up. "They started him on some new meds. Tricyclic antidepressants. They're often used for neuralgia, which is hard to treat, regular pain-killers don't work on it. They said it might take a few weeks for the meds to kick in fully, but they helped so much. The pain subsided. His mood lifted. It was like having him back again." He set down the small cluster of lint he'd been collecting in his palm and smoothed the bedspread. "The thing is... they can have some pretty serious side effects, which is part of the reason they wanted him in a treatment center where he could be closely monitored. But your mother and I figured we could keep an eye on him, and didn't want him to spend his eighteenth birthday locked up in an institution. You should have seen him when we suggested going home and continuing treatment as an outpatient. It was like we were giving him the greatest gift in the world."

After hearing all this, Cyrus wasn't sure his parents had made the right decision, though he'd never say so out loud. Instead he asked, "What kinds of side effects?"

"Oh, lots of things. But they were most concerned about the possible mental symptoms. Like delirium, agitation, hallucinations… and… suicidal thoughts and behavior."

"Shit." Cyrus didn't even try to stop the swear word from escaping in front of his dad. "They gave someone who just tried to kill himself drugs that might make him *more* likely to commit suicide? That doesn't seem very smart."

"That side effect is rare. We didn't have many other treatment options—other drugs used to treat neuralgia either aren't as effective, or have similar issues. So we did some research, and in the end we decided that the benefits outweighed the risks."

"It sounds like you made the best choice you could," Cyrus said, because he knew this was what Baba needed to hear.

Baba shook his head again, sighing heavily. "They're all gone, Kourosh. He found the box where I'd locked up all the meds. Everything they gave him, the tricyclics, the sleep aids, the cough medicine, the anti-anxiety meds for his PTSD. They're all gone."

Cyrus understood what Baba was not saying: *that's why he left, Kourosh. He brought all the pills with him because he wants to finish what he started.* It made him feel completely battered, like he'd just been beaten up by some particularly malicious bully. But there could be another explanation. "He might be okay, though. Maybe he's taking the meds like he's supposed to, and he just needs… some time alone, or something? Wait. I'll be right back."

He sprang up and crossed the hall to his room. After caring for his brother these past weeks, he had become very familiar with Naveed's habits and belongings, and quickly spotted the items that were missing. Gone: his messenger bag. A few changes of clothes. His favorite black hoodie.

Next stop, the bathroom. Cyrus opened the medicine cabinet and inhaled sharply: Naveed had taken almost everything. The leftover gauze and ointment, the inhaler he still sometimes used when he had trouble breathing at night, the beard trimmer. His toothbrush, too, was missing.

"His toothbrush!" he exclaimed, running back to his parents' room. "He brought his toothbrush. And the beard trimmer, and a bunch of clothes. So that's it—he probably just needs a break from being here. He moved out, that's all."

"Maybe." Baba didn't seem convinced, though.

Cyrus returned to his room, thinking about the notebook. Maybe he should comb through it later, look for clues. And maybe he could hack into Naveed's phone, maybe he'd find something in there that explained everything.

A text buzzed in from Andi. Hey. Sorry to bug you but I have to know. How's N doing?

Cyrus clicked his phone off, not having a clue how to respond, and flopped onto Naveed's bottom bunk. He was surprised to see that Naveed had taped a bunch of drawings onto the underside of Cyrus's mattress, the Islamic geometric patterns he'd been hunched over so often lately. Baba had suggested working on them because they were drawn using a ruler and compass, and didn't require a lot of fine motor skills. As Cyrus looked closer, he realized he was looking at one recurring pattern, tessellated over multiple sheets of paper and accented with watercolors, a series of interconnecting lines that formed intricate shapes and many-pointed stars. They managed to make what could have been a claustrophobically small space feel expansive instead.

Something about this made Cyrus sad, how he'd never even given a second's thought to what had become of all those drawings. Despite sharing such close quarters, there were so many parts of his brother that he never saw. That he never understood.

Ever since Naveed had first returned home, Cyrus had been vacillating between frustration with his inability to lift his brother out of his funk, worry at Naveed's ongoing poor health, and annoyance at being pulled out of sleep to hear him crying out frantically or coughing up what sounded like half a lung. But these drawings gave him a window into a different side of his brother, a reminder of the old days, of the person who loved making beautiful things.

Tears stung Cyrus's eyes. He needed to distract himself, so he looked at his phone again. Andi's text still hung there, suspended in the white window, asking a question he never wanted to answer.

But he needed to. He took a deep breath and texted Andi the latest news. Naveed ran away. He left his phone here but took a bunch of clothes and other stuff with him. Baba's really upset and Maman & Roya are on their way home so I can't talk now. Maybe tomorrow?

He sent it, then as an afterthought asked, Hey do u have any idea where he might have gone?

Her response came swiftly. Oh my God, that's terrible. Call me as soon as you can.

Then, No, sorry, no idea.

Cyrus thanked her. Tonight, he'd figure out what to say, and tomorrow, he would tell her everything.

An idea struck him as he rolled off the bed. He reached his hand under the pillow. Maybe Naveed had left a note?

Nothing there. He slid his hand under the mattress, where he'd found the notebook. His fingers touched something hard and smooth.

He pulled the object out. It was a book—Maman's tattered edition of *The Blind Owl.* Cyrus had tried to read it once, in English, since it was a classic of Persian literature and all, but couldn't stand the depressed/insane narrator's constant whining, and never got past the first few pages.

A slip of paper stuck out between the pages towards the end of the novel. Cyrus opened the book, but his understanding of written Persian was negligible, so he had no idea what these particular pages said. What did this mean—had Naveed been reading this? Or had he left it here on purpose, for Cyrus to find?

His question was answered when he unfolded the piece of paper used for the bookmark. Naveed had written a very short note. Though it wasn't addressed to anyone in particular, Cyrus had no doubt it was meant for him.

i will never forgive you
goodbye

Andi

TUESDAY, AUGUST 18

ANDI WAS STARING AT HER LAPTOP, TRYING TO WRAP HER BRAIN around a barely-comprehensible video about music theory, when Cyrus texted her the next morning. u home? can I come over?

She quickly responded, Yes, now is good!

Ok, Cyrus replied. Roya's coming with.

Andi closed the laptop, then got up to tidy her bedroom. It was a mess, an absolute disaster zone. After they'd returned home the previous day, she hadn't had the energy to unpack properly, and had let the contents of her bag explode in a small unsightly pile. She dumped it now into the hamper, picked up loose sheets of composition paper that had somehow found their way onto the floor, and pushed her electric keyboard back against the wall.

She had been shocked to get Cyrus's text the day before. When she'd read it, she'd gasped audibly and nearly dropped her phone. Her dad, who had been fixing himself a sandwich in the kitchen, asked what was wrong.

Andi weighed whether to tell them. She had never mentioned the fact that Naveed had been in the hospital most of the time they'd been on vacation, but this was something she wouldn't be able to hide. "Naveed… left. He ran away from home, I guess," she said.

Her mother furrowed her eyebrows. "He did? Why?"

"I don't know! Cyrus didn't say much. It sounds like his family's really upset."

"Are you sure he ran away? It might just be a misunderstanding," her mom said.

Andi doubted that. "No. I'm sure."

"Maybe you could try calling him?" her dad suggested.

"Wouldn't help. He left his phone at their house."

"Well, let's think, then," her dad said. "Where would he go? Maybe he's staying with a friend?"

"I'm sure his parents are calling around," Andi said, even as she wondered what friends he had left.

"Maybe he's at… Seward Park?" her mother said.

"What, you think he's just hiding out in the woods somewhere?"

"I don't know, bǎo bèi. It was the first thing that popped into my mind."

"He's not at Seward." It sprang into her head then, the memory of that conversation with Naveed. The words she'd said to him. *Maybe it would help to go somewhere else… a place you've never been….*

Andi retreated to her room, shaking from the revelation: *she* was the one who told him to leave; *she* was responsible for this.

Her mother knocked, asking if she wanted to talk, but Andi said she had a headache and wanted to sleep. That usually shut them up, even though she knew she'd pay for it later.

She hadn't been able to sleep, of course. So she'd plugged her head-phones into the keyboard and dove back into her composition. It was kind of ridiculous that she felt the need to be so stealthy about making music, but she didn't want her dad finding out that she was dabbling in songwriting and getting all excited, the way he had when she was younger.

The pressure to become the musician daughter that he wanted had led her to choke at recitals, and drained all the joy out of playing piano. But creating her own piece had been something like meditation to her, a way to focus her mind while somehow, at the same time, letting everything go.

Her composition had been simmering in the back of her head the whole time she was on vacation. Sometimes, at night, sounds haunted her, the things she'd heard while at SILO, the pitches of fluorescent lights and humming dishwashers. She had been threading them together in her mind, working out a way to tell her story through music.

On the plane, while she and Cyrus watched a movie together, she'd replayed one particular melody in her mind, thinking she'd work on it when she got home, maybe even record it to give to Naveed for his birthday the following day. And now… now she wouldn't even see him, because he had left….

As she straightened the stack of records piled on the floor, she tried not to think of that day when he'd been here, in her bed. She should tell Cyrus about it. He deserved to know. Only, she wasn't sure if she wanted to yet, especially with Roya there listening.

She emerged from her room to find her father at the front door talking to Cyrus, who looked exhausted and gloomy. Roya clung to him tightly.

"Any news?" her dad was asking.

Cyrus shook his head. "Nothing yet." He smiled when he saw Andi, and she noticed he was wearing his work clothes, a black button-down and slacks.

"Are you headed to work?" she asked, confused.

"Yeah, they called to see if I could come in. Sounded kind of desperate. They had two people call in sick, and they're already short-staffed because the chef's on vacation this week."

"How are your parents holding up?" Andi's dad asked. Cyrus and Roya slipped off their shoes and added them to the pile near the door.

"Bad," said Roya. "Baba's out looking for Naveed but Maman can't get out of bed. It's his birthday today, did you know that? We were supposed to all be together again." Her eyes filled with tears.

"Here, come back to my room," Andi suggested. Once there, she made a little nest for Roya out of pillows and blankets. Roya crawled inside, sniffling.

"Me and Andi are going to talk in the hall for a minute, okay?" Cyrus told her.

"No!" Roya screamed. "Don't leave me! You can't leave."

Cyrus pulled Andi into a hug and whispered, "She's been clinging to me ever since she got home. Even slept in my bed. I hardly got any sleep."

Andi made a sympathetic noise, but Roya said from her nest, "What are you talking about? Andi, do you know where he went?"

Andi really didn't want to tell her that she was the one to encourage Roya's brother to leave. "Um, let's think. So it's his birthday. Where does he like to go on his birthday? Do you guys have a usual tradition? Like going out to dinner somewhere?"

"Not really," Cyrus said. "It's different every year."

Roya poked her head up, suddenly seeming very excited. "The story!"

"What are you talking about?"

"That's the one thing that's the same every year—the story!"

"What—"

"I know where he is!" Roya jumped to her feet.

"You think he's at the...." Cyrus trailed off midsentence. Andi waited for him to go on, but he didn't.

"Andi, can you drive us?" Roya asked.

"Where?"

"The bridge! Kourosh, you know which one, right?"

"The Montlake Bridge," he mumbled.

"Yes, let's go!"

"Um, okay." Andi grabbed her keys and fished her wallet out of her backpack. She peeked her head out of her room and said, "Dad? We're going out for a little bit. And then I guess I'll drop Cy at work. Be back in a couple hours."

"All right," he called. "Good luck."

They piled into her mom's Sentra. Cyrus sat in the front, and Roya slid into the back, buckling into the middle and leaning up against the center console, as if to close the distance between them.

Andi drove along the lake, knowing the route to Montlake well; she often crossed that bridge to get to the University of Washington, where her mother worked. Naveed was supposed to start classes there next month. Would he show up for that? Maybe they just needed to wait it out….

"So, are you going to tell me why we're going to the bridge?" Andi asked, glancing over at Cyrus. But he was staring steadfastly out the window.

Roya leaned further forward. "Every year on our birthdays, Maman tells the story of the day we were born. Like how she was out grocery shopping the day she went into labor with Kourosh, and her water broke. She was so embarrassed. But Naveed was potty-training, and he found the towel she kept in her purse and said, 'It's okay, Maman, don't cry, you just had a accident, I clean it for you.'"

Cyrus sunk lower in his seat, still silent.

"Or how she was at Khaleh Yasmin's house for Shab-e Yalda when I was in her belly, and everyone was reciting poetry and eating pomegranates, and she dozed off and had this dream about being carried over the ocean by a big bird—the Simorgh, it was taking her back home, back to Iran—and when she woke up I was already coming, even though it was too early. I was born a few days later and they kept me in an incubator and let Maman feed me and hold me, even though I was so small that I fit in her palms."

Andi kept her eyes on the winding lakeside road, trailing slowly behind a bicyclist until it was safe enough to pass.

"But, anyway. Naveed's story. She always tells about how she and Baba went walking when she was in labor, before going to the hospital, and how she had to stop under the Montlake Bridge, and how it was so loud with the cars going overhead, and then a big ship came by and they watched the bridge go up from underneath. I bet Naveed went there! I bet he's just sitting under the bridge, waiting for a big ship to come through."

Cyrus was jiggling his leg. Andi rested her hand on his knee, hoping to calm him down. He placed his hand on top and laced his fingers into hers.

"Well, it's worth a try," Andi said. Roya smiled, bouncing a little.

"Don't get your hopes up," said Cyrus flatly.

They wound their way through the arboretum, and saw as they emerged by the water that the drawbridge was raised, causing traffic to stack up for several blocks.

"Park on this side," Cyrus said, so Andi turned down a side street and pulled over next to a beautifully manicured red-brick mansion. They weren't far from the house in which Kurt Cobain killed himself, Andi realized. She'd always wondered what it would've been like to be a neighbor of such a legend, even though she knew it was probably a lot less exciting than it sounded.

Cyrus walked quickly toward the bridge, which now was descending. Roya and Andi followed, but he was moving with uncharacteristic speed and they couldn't quite catch up. They were still a block away when the partitions rose and cars started driving over the metal grating. Cyrus began sprinting along the sidewalk, dashing right up to the edge and peering over the railing.

The second Andi caught up, he was off again, running across the bridge and down a flight of stairs. Andi and Roya followed; as they pounded across the bridge, Andi became dizzy, because she could feel the thing shaking, the whole bridge rattling under the weight of all these cars, and she had to stop to steady herself. By the time she did, Roya was already hurtling down the stairs, onto a narrow walkway leading under the bridge.

They came down to find Cyrus leaning against the concrete wall, looking through the metal grid to see the cars whizzing by right over their heads. The air was filled with a loud buzzing, the roar of cars and trucks and buses.

"He's not here!" he yelled. "I told you, Roya, he's not here!"

He was shaking, Andi noticed, from disappointment, maybe, so she hugged him, allowing him to shudder his breaths into her shoulder.

Something in him seemed to collapse, and she just wanted to keep holding him, but she looked over at Roya, who was leaning against the railing, too close to the dark water.

"He'll come. He will. We just have to wait," Roya said.

They waited a little while, but he didn't. Together they walked slowly back to the car, and drove Cyrus to work in silence. His shift would finish at nine, and Andi asked if he'd like a ride home. "It's no problem," she said, even though it would mean another hour's worth of driving.

He nodded. "Okay. Thank you, Alexandria. I'll see you later."

Then she drove Roya home. She felt a tiny bit bad leaving her all alone, but Roya said she was going to take a nap with her mom.

As Andi pulled up in front of her house, her phone rang. She glanced at the screen, surprised to see that it was Brooke. She accepted the call. "Hello?"

"Andi! How come you didn't tell me?" Brooke sounded like she was crying, her words punctuated by wavery breaths.

"That Naveed ran away? I figured someone told you—"

"*No.* Not that he ran away. That he tried to kill himself last week."

"What?" Andi's throat tightened, and the word came out so quietly that she wasn't even sure Brooke heard.

"My mom told me everything. I can't believe she kept it from me! Just because we broke up—it doesn't mean I don't still care about him."

"Wait, but—no, it can't—why would he—" Andi murmured. It couldn't be true. It just couldn't. Naveed would never do that....

Except, maybe....

Maybe he would.

"Oh, you didn't—did Cy really not—"

"Cyrus didn't tell me anything." Andi was surprised at how angry she sounded. "He said Naveed was in the hospital because he was having issues with nerve pain."

"Well, he lied too, I guess. Or anyway, it wasn't the whole story. Apparently Naveed OD'd on painkillers that night before you guys left for LA, but Cy found him in time and they rushed him to the hospital. They pumped his stomach, admitted him to the psychiatric unit. *Oh fuck, Andi, it just hurts so bad, knowing he's out there somewhere, because what if he's trying to… you know….*" More sobs. But Andi could only sit there, frozen on the side of the road, the car still running. She twisted the keys out of the ignition and dropped them in her lap.

"I'm sorry," Brooke said. "I thought you knew. I didn't mean to lay into you like that. I'm just upset, obviously. We're coming home tomorrow—you wanna hang out when I get back? I really need… to talk to someone…."

"I, um, okay, text me later?" Andi couldn't even think straight.

"Okay, that sounds good. Oh—sorry, gotta go, Dawn's waiting for me. Bye."

Andi walked back into the house as if in a trance, heading directly for her bedroom and flopping on the bed. She got up to have dinner with her parents, numbly forcing down the tasteless food, then saying she didn't feel well, no not a headache this time, maybe something she was fighting off from the plane, and returning to her bed, where she had once pressed the soles of her feet to Naveed's, where he'd said, *do you ever feel like you'll never escape? Like the days are just so endless, and there's nothing to look forward to?* Why hadn't she grasped the true gravity of those words back then?

And Cyrus had lied to her. By allowing him not to talk about what really happened, she'd let him lie to her.

It all made sense now: his unwillingness to discuss his brother, the way he'd frozen up on Lillian's show, his odd behavior at the bridge. The fact that he'd kept this from her for so long filled her with anger. She should stand him up. Forget about giving him a ride home. But—no. In the car, she could confront him about this. And this time, she wouldn't let him dodge her questions.

So she drove to the restaurant and picked him up at nine, where he was waiting with a to-go box of day-old chocolate decadence cake. He smiled at her when he got in the car smelling of wine sauce and caramelized onions. "For you, mon amour," he said in an exaggerated French accent, indicating the cake.

She wanted to open it up and shove his face into it. But she didn't. "How was work?" she asked. It sounded forced.

He went on at length about the kitchen drama of the evening, how someone had used the wrong abbreviation on a ticket so a customer got the wrong entree, and making a new one had completely gummed up the works, so everything got delayed and some people had to wait half an hour between courses. "But they were drinking a lot of wine, so it didn't matter so much," he said. "And at least it wasn't my fault this time. They were so happy I was there. It was nice to feel needed."

Andi didn't reply. She decided to take the freeway instead of surface streets, hoping it would be quicker at this time of night. Suddenly she couldn't wait to get home.

"How was your evening?" he asked.

She couldn't hold back any longer. "I got a call from Brooke."

"Oh? Is she back yet?" he asked, opening the box and pinching off a small piece of chocolate cake with his fingers. He sounded so casual, like everything about today was normal, like it wasn't the day his missing suicidal brother was turning eighteen.

"Her mom filled her in on what's been going on. On *everything* that's been going on," Andi said.

He shut the lid quickly. "What did she say?"

"Why didn't you tell me, Cy?" Andi forced herself to stay calm; she couldn't lose control while they were hurtling along the freeway in this tiny metal box, so powerless to stop anything happening around them.

He sighed. "What did she say, exactly?"

"That you found Naveed after he overdosed on painkillers. That they admitted him to the psych ward. Did they not let him have his phone there? Is that why he never texted me back?"

Cyrus didn't answer.

"And you never bothered to *tell* me this?" she went on, close to tears now. "Why couldn't you just tell me?"

"There was never a good time...." he mumbled.

"There were plenty! You didn't have to lie to me! Things could have been different, maybe he'd still be here! Maybe we could've helped him through this, the way we should, instead of abandoning him!"

Cyrus flinched. Andi changed lanes and took their exit.

"I needed that vacation so bad—both of us did. I didn't want to ruin it," he said softly. "I knew you'd want to go back, but I... I didn't want to."

"What the fuck!" she yelled, surprised at herself, at the endless depth of her anger. "That's not how it works! You don't just care about family when it's convenient! We could have rescheduled our trip, gone another time. We should've been there for him. He must have felt so alone," she said. And there they were, the tears, spilling over before she could hold them back.

"You think I don't care about him? What have I been doing for the last few months? Nothing *but* caring for him! Helping him with everything, and you don't even know, you have no idea how it was, what the nights were like—"

"I can't believe you... how you just... you were so happy there, while he was... and you just wanted to sweep the whole thing under the rug, like it didn't matter...." She wasn't even coherent any more. Blubbering, sobbing.

But she kept her eyes on the road, let it lead her back to their neighborhood. She pulled up in front of Cyrus's house and slowed to a stop.

He had been silent for some time. Finally, he said, "I'm sorry. I should have told you everything from the beginning. But I couldn't. Because I... I didn't want you to think less of me."

"What does that even mean? What does it have to do with you?"

He hung his head. "It has everything to do with me."

"Why?"

"Because… because I…." He looked her in the eyes. "I love you, Alexandria."

Everything just bubbled over then. Too much, it all hurt too much, and she couldn't stand hearing him say her name, the way he had in the hot tub, selfishly keeping her in the dark because he wanted to live out some fantasy instead of dealing with reality. "Stop. I can't do this anymore. Please get out of my car, and don't call me, don't text, I really don't want to talk to you anymore."

"But—"

"GET OUT!" she yelled, reaching over him to open his door. In the process, she knocked the cake off his lap and out of the car, where it toppled into the fading light, a brown stain on the road.

Stunned, he got out after it, and she left him there standing dumbstruck. But instead of going home, she drove to Seward Park, the place where she and Naveed had once reunited, before the course of their lives changed forever.

She pulled along the curb and parked next to the water. In the distance, Mount Rainier reflected the last wisps of sunset. Andi lowered her head into her hands. It felt like her skull was being ripped to pieces, right along with everything else inside her, especially her heart.

August 31

Dear Roya,

I'm sorry it took me so long to write to you. Believe me, I've wanted to. There's been so much going on here. I guess I'll start with the day you left. It's okay that you went back through the fence hole, I'm not mad about that, so don't worry. They sealed it up though. And Grandfather was really really mad. He asked me a lot about you (I told him the wrong name, called you Rose instead) and gave me 12 hours in the Box the next day, but Nan talked him down from 24 so it could've been worse. Plus I got two weeks of latrine duty, which is a horrible stinky job and I'm not going to say anything more about that.

But I hid your envelopes really good. They never found them.

So what else, let's see, we had a ceremony as usual on the night of the new moon. I was really sad because I was thinking about you, and how if you were there we could have taken our lanterns out to the pond and paddled our little raft out to the middle to watch the stars.

I had to help get set up so I hiked with everyone to the clearing, you know the one, with the thirteen birches. We had a procession out there with our lanterns after it finally got dark. It was really pretty and I kept wishing I could show you and I was glad it was all lantern lit because nobody could see how sad I was. Not that they would have noticed. Everyone gets sad on new moon nights because they're thinking of the people they've lost, the ones they're still trying to contact. Well they start out sad, but then they drink the tea and get real mellow. I'm not allowed near the ceremonies anymore because once I snuck a few sips of the tea and it didn't go very well. But it's not fair that I don't get to participate. I just want to see my mother and father again. Why are those tourist acolytes allowed to but I'm not?

Nan always makes me go home after she starts brewing the tea but I like to sneak back out and watch them. I always leave when they start vomiting though. It's a side effect of the tea, it makes you purge all the bad stuff from your body, but I can't stand the sound or the smells. Anyway I knew it was dangerous this time after getting in big trouble plus I was so sore I couldn't sit down but I needed a distraction so I watched.

Grandfather was there, chanting words I couldn't understand, but nobody seemed to be listening, they were all swaying or lying on the ground looking up at the stars or staring at their hands like they were the most interesting things in the world. And then my nan sat up, and she was talking in this strange voice about a cave full of bones, and then she made the saddest sound, and it seemed to rip everybody apart, and I knew I had to go.

I wasn't expecting that. I don't know what she was talking about. But it scared me. And she was sick the next day and the next, and Grandfather tended her and wouldn't let me into her room because he didn't want it catching. But she's doing better now. Grandfather is a good healer. Once when I was young he was on the outside doing one of his missions and he got sick. The doctors told him he had cancer and was going to die. They wanted to pump him full of toxic chemicals to make the disease leave his body, but he said no and he came back here and he healed himself with our medicines. Now he's healthier than ever, the cancer is totally gone. And the journey left him with the power to heal others, too.

Anyway, Grandfather left again this morning after telling all the acolytes that they need to work harder. I followed him down to the dock where he anchors his boat and I watched him load it up with boxes of whatever the acolytes are harvesting. Nan still seems off somehow and everyone is very stressed. It's never been like this before. Everything feels so different. Why does it feel so different?

And now look, I've used up two of my precious sheets of paper already, talking about me. How was your journey home? Did the potion work? Write back to me at the address on the front. Don't worry, I'm the one who always picks up the mail.

Sincerely,

Kass

September 4

Dear Kass,

It has been bad here so I was happy to get your letter I'm sorry
about the fence your grandfather scared me and it was the only
way out I hope you are all done with stinky chores and maybe can
find another break in the fence soon or dig a hole under it I miss
you and I miss the island and the ocean and I miss lots of other
things too. Naveed is gone now he ran away from home while I was
coming back on the ferry I never got to give him the potion and
I forgot all about it in my water bottle and it stinked so bad when
I opened it that I threw up all over the rug in my bedroom (eww.) I
know what you mean that everything feels different These days my
mom doesn't get out of bed and most of the time I just lie with her in
there and we toss and turn together Since I got your letter I keep
dreaming of two little lights bobbing on a raft in a dark pond you
and me out there watching the stars

my other brother is always working or over at his friend's house now
and my dad stays at work late then comes home and locks himself in
the workshop. I think he's making something but he doesn't let me go
in there So I read your letter over and over and think of you peeling
potatos and hiding under stairs where it smells like apples I think of
your shadow book and wonder if maybe it can help me somehow? can
it help bring him back so that we can all stop being sad?
I miss you.

Love,

Roya

Cyrus

CYRUS HURRIED AWAY FROM ROYA'S SCHOOL, SLOWING ONLY when he had rounded the corner and was safely out of sight. He took a long, deep breath of the crisp autumnal air. Golden light filtered through the still-green trees, but soon the leaves would change color, and it would be time to start stocking up on apples and enjoying pumpkin-spice-flavored everything.

It really was a beautiful morning. Too bad he couldn't enjoy it.

Roya's pleas to go back home had gotten more and more insistent as they'd approached the school. One of the third-grade teachers had to literally pry her away from Cyrus. Leaving was hard, because he knew she was going to have a rough day. He wasn't looking forward to going back, himself, after his family's frequent appearances in the news earlier in the summer. He had to promise to take her to the bakery after school *and* play Harvest Time, her favorite cooperative board game, before he could wrestle himself free.

Andi would be starting her senior year today, Cyrus thought with a pang as he walked towards Dev's house. He missed her terribly. At first he had texted her a lot, apologizing over and over, but none of his messages went through. She must have blocked his number.

Sometimes, he thought about the Metafolia website he'd volunteered to make for her. He'd hoped, for a while, that this might get her to talk to him again, and had even gone so far as to register a domain name. But, a couple weeks after their vacation, Brennan Walsh had sent an email to Cyrus, Andi, Jake and Joyce, saying that he'd spoken with his lawyer and they could try to get a class action suit going. Andi had responded to the group with a short reply: *Sorry, but I've given this a lot of thought and I don't want to go through with it anymore. Maybe you can find someone else to testify.*

So apparently that was off the table.

To make matters worse, Cyrus's family had been a mess ever since Naveed's disappearance. The first few days afterward, Cyrus and Dev had tried to figure out where he might have gone. But Naveed had wiped everything. Closed all of his old email and social media accounts. Even his phone was empty; he'd done a factory reset.

Cyrus had to admit that was creepy, all these virtual traces of his brother suddenly wiped out, like he'd never existed at all. So either he really didn't want to be found… or he was just tidying things up before he took that final leap.

All that Cyrus had left of Naveed was his notebook. He'd forced himself to read the whole thing in an attempt to look for clues. But he never showed it to anyone else, not even Dev, because he didn't want to destroy their hopes that Naveed was still alive. The journal entries in that notebook, though, left him convinced that his brother had wanted to die.

So that was it, then. There was nothing more Cyrus could do, and he wasn't going to investigate further, because as the days passed he grew more certain that all he'd find at the end of this horrible worm hole was a dead body. He could see it in his parents, too, their hope in his return deflating, their sorrow moving into grief. And yet, no one else outside of their close circles knew what was going on, since they had agreed to keep his sudden disappearance quiet. Whenever someone asked, Cyrus just said that Naveed had moved out.

Sometimes he wished they could tell Roya the truth. But no one wanted to say it aloud. No one wanted to say: *he ran away so that he could die, Roya.*

But that was what they were stuck with, and it weighed on them heavily. Maman had taken a few weeks off work, during which she'd hardly gotten out of bed, but now she had a looming grant deadline and was constantly at the CFJ office or hiding behind her computer screen. Baba still prayed every morning, noon, and night, and disappeared into the backyard workshop after dinner each day. Roya was unbearably clingy.

For his part, Cyrus had been going over to Dev's at every opportunity to work on their new game and film more videos for their channel. Their subscriber base had grown exponentially after his appearance on Lillian's show, but their success came with an ugly flip side. Lately, their comment strings had erupted into speculation about Cyrus's "reclusive" brother, since people had noticed he was never seen in public, or online, and that Cyrus never mentioned him during their videos. So his wounds were constantly ripped back open as he read and deleted the theories of strangers. (Disgustingly enough, the consensus seemed to be that Naveed was attending some sort of terrorist training camp.)

Now, Cyrus let himself in to Dev's house to find his friend at the dining room table with his laptop. "Hey," he said, swinging his backpack onto the floor and collapsing into a chair across from Dev.

"How did the drop-off go?" Dev asked, still looking at his screen.

"Painful," said Cyrus. "I have to play Harvest Time with her later. I swear that game was invented to torture people. It's so boring."

"Well, at least we have the day off, unlike all the poor suckers who have to go back to school today," Dev said. They still had a few weeks before they started their junior year, since they had enrolled in the Running Start program at South Seattle College, where the quarter didn't begin until late September. "We've got a lot to get done."

"I thought you just said we had the day off!" Cyrus faked annoyance. "We should spend it lying in hammocks and eating bonbons."

"Bonbons? I've never had a bonbon in my entire life. And hammocks are boring. Website maintenance, on the other hand…."

Cyrus opened his laptop. "All right. Let's get to it."

"The commenters are in fine form today," Dev said after clicking around for a bit. "They're really letting their imaginations run wild—according to them, Naveed's a spy for the Iranian government now." He said it lightheartedly, like he found the theory amusing.

Cyrus didn't want to hear it. "Can we turn the comments off? I'm so sick of reading that shit. Why can't they just let it go?"

"People love a good mystery. But—if we get rid of the comments, then we'll miss all the good stuff. That's the whole point of this, connecting with people. Sometimes the trolls come out, but that's why we moderate. I don't mind taking over if you don't want to do that anymore."

"Fine," Cyrus grumbled. He wasn't irritated at Dev, just at the fact that he couldn't get away from Naveed, or from the relentless racist remarks that seemed to follow his brother. How long was this going to go on?

He started wading through his notifications, only to find one about Metafolia. He'd set up news alerts after registering the domain name for the website that was never built, but they came so infrequently that he'd completely forgotten about them.

"Hmm," he said as he started reading. The alert linked to the post of a health blogger who had written a long screed about her experience with Metafolia. Judging from the number of comments it had already collected, despite being posted only an hour earlier, Cyrus judged that she must be pretty well-known.

The blogger had an experience similar to Andi's, but she had taken the supplement right before going to a spinning class and had passed out on the bike, falling to the floor and injuring her arm. "It's taken me a whole month to be able to write about this. Still so angry," she wrote toward the end. "I filed a complaint with the FDA, but they didn't even bother to send a form reply. So take it from me. Just say NO to Metafolia."

Cyrus combed the comments. A few were from people saying that they'd been taking the supplement for ages without having any problems, but he was surprised at how many other complaints he found there.

> This supplement made me sick. So dizzy I couldn't get off the couch all day after taking it. Did you see the shimmering lights too? It was kind of weird, like a mild acid trip, not that I know anything about that lol.
>
> A lot of people say it gives them euphoria, is this thing like a drug or something?
>
> I saw the lights too! Thought I was the only one…
>
> I took a few of these pills and felt super tired & dizzy but tons of other people seemed to like them so I thought it was just me.

Interesting. *Very* interesting.

Cyrus remembered how excited Andi had been about exposing Metafolia, about using it as their "angle." Maybe it wasn't too late? Maybe… if he could help bring justice against this supplement company, he could get back into her good graces….

"What you muttering about over there?" Dev asked.

"Oh. Uh, taking a little detour." Cyrus realized he'd never told Dev about the Metafolia stuff, since it was an unwelcome reminder of the now-tainted Santa Barbara vacation. "Here—I want to show you something."

But before pulling up the blog post, he searched for the Dr. Ben clip, the one where Metafolia's founder, Geoffrey Walker, had been a guest. Might as well start at the beginning.

He and Dev watched the video together. Geoffrey Walker was a clean-shaven, gray-haired old white guy. Somehow, his focused intensity outmatched even Dr. Ben's, which was saying something.

"We use both ancient wisdom and modern technology to bring you this unique product," Geoffrey told Dr. Ben. "Using botanical extracts from all over the world, we create our healing blend to help bring you optimal health."

"Now, I've seen a lot of supplements in my day, but this one really works," Dr. Ben said. "It kick-starts your metabolism, helps immunity and brain function, just makes your body work better. I started taking it months ago and haven't been sick since!"

Cyrus rolled his eyes. He wondered how much Geoffrey had paid Dr. Ben to say that.

After the clip was over, he filled Dev in on what had happened to Andi, what they'd discussed with Brennan Walsh, and the blog post that had just been published. "I'm going to send it to Brennan," Cyrus said. "I wonder if he has any connections at the FDA. If it's coming from him instead of some random blogger, they might be more likely to take action. And maybe we can use our influence to spread the word."

"I don't know," Dev said. "Maybe you should just let it go."

Cyrus had been expecting Dev's support, so this response surprised him. "Um, what? Why?"

Dev sighed. "My mom would kill me if I helped with this, after what happened last time...."

"This isn't Nutrexo, though. It's just a tiny supplement company. And besides, nothing even happened to you—they never found out your mom was the one who hacked into Nutrexo's servers, because *my* mom covered for her." To his surprise, a slight note of resentment crept into his voice.

"I know, but that's why she's so serious about me not getting involved in shit like that ever again. It could've been us." Dev paused. "She can't believe that your mom is still running CFJ. How can she keep doing that, after all the trouble it brought you guys?"

Cyrus had often wondered the same thing, but now here he was, thinking of picking another fight with a different company. "She's not going to back down now, when we're finally making progress," he said, echoing the words he'd heard her saying to others. "You don't have to help me with this, Dev, but I can't just ignore it. People are getting hurt. If Brennan's right about what happened to his mom, they might even be *dying* after taking Metafolia."

"And you're hoping this will win Andi back. Right?"

Cyrus winced. Was he that obvious? "Uh, yeah, I guess that would be a nice consolation prize."

Dev shook his head. "She's a person, not a prize," he said quietly.

"I was only joking," Cyrus said, his annoyance growing. Of course he knew that! Dev shouldn't be calling him out on it. Though Dev had been really sympathetic with all the Naveed stuff, he seemed to have little tolerance for Cyrus's musings about Andi.

"I know," Dev said. "But… that kind of leads into… something I've been wanting to talk to you about. For the game."

Cyrus braced himself. He tried to keep the irritation out of his voice. "What is it?"

"We need to do better. No more defenseless maidens waiting to be rescued. It's sexist, and super cliché. We need to come up with something more original."

"Since when do you care what those whiny feminists in the comments think?" As soon as he said it, Cyrus was aware of how he sounded, and was suddenly disgusted with himself. He slammed his laptop closed. "Okay, *fine*, you're right. Why don't you take over on the game for a while, then, because I've got a supplement company to fight. I'll be back in a minute."

He huffed out to the backyard and pulled out his phone before settling into a lawn chair. This wasn't about winning Andi back, he told himself as he composed an email to Brennan. This wasn't about rescuing her or being gallant or whatever. This was about seeking justice. Preventing innocent people from being harmed.

Once he'd sent Brennan the link to the blog post, he tried searching for the "proprietary blend" Brennan had been curious about, but that went nowhere, and it was kind of boring. Much more interesting was to look for dirt on Geoffrey.

Not that Cyrus could find much about him, either, except for a few vague sentences on the website. It said Geoffrey had been a "longtime student of natural healing practices," but he didn't appear to have any degrees or credentials. Cyrus searched more widely, but the guy had zero online presence. Not much help.

He searched for Dr. Ben instead. Tons about him, but most of it was fawning PR. A few people ranted about him being a shill for the products he touted on his show, but these voices seemed to be small, people on obscure blogs shouting into the void.

After Cyrus had cooled down sufficiently, he went back inside and got to work on the tasks Dev had assigned him for the website. Then they broke for lunch, and were just getting ready to hash out their next episode when Cyrus's phone rang.

The call was from an unknown number with an area code he didn't recognize. He thought about letting it ring through, but decided that wouldn't be wise, what with his brother out on the loose. Assuming he was even alive.

But it wasn't Naveed on the other end of the line. It was Brennan Walsh. "Cyrus! Glad I caught you."

"Oh—hey, what's up?" Cyrus was suddenly tongue-tied. He mouthed, *it's Brennan Walsh!* to the confused-looking Dev, but this only made him look more perplexed.

"I got your email. Jake gave me your number—I hope you don't mind?"

"Of course not." Cyrus was still in disbelief.

"Good timing. I got the Metafolia test results back from the lab this morning. One of the samples I sent—the bottle that had already been opened, the one my mother had been taking when she died—contained traces of a drug that's actually classified as a Schedule I substance. So, it's pretty serious. I just had a conference call with a few people at the FDA— we're talking recalls, criminal investigations, everything. The lawsuit's on the back burner. We'll have to wait and see whether the company gets handed any charges, if the judge orders them to pay restitution to the consumers… it's all up in the air at this point. But this is a move in the right direction."

"Wow. That's… it's pretty incredible."

"Yes. I just wanted to ask you a favor. I know you're pretty well-connected in the online world. Would you mind spreading the word about this? The FDA's going to issue a press release, but I'm not sure how long that will take, and it's important that people stop taking these now. I don't want anyone else getting hurt in the meantime."

"Oh. Um, sure. If you could write up what you want me to say, maybe post that in your own networks, then I'll signal boost in mine and get in contact with that blogger so she can let her followers know...."

They talked for a few minutes about the details, then Cyrus hung up and filled Dev in. "I'll just post it through my personal accounts. Not our shared one," Cyrus assured him.

"Whatever you need to do." Dev sounded resigned.

"I *do* need to do this." Despite the fact that Dev's words of caution still echoed in Cyrus's head, he allowed himself to picture Andi reading his posts and admiring him for the way he refused to back down, the way he kept fighting injustice. He imagined the two of them running in cinematic slow motion towards each other in the alley behind their homes; he imagined them embracing and apologizing and deciding to move on.

Well, at least he could dream.

Roya

THURSDAY, SEPTEMBER 10

EVER SINCE ROYA RECEIVED KASS'S LETTER, SHE HAD BEEN thinking about the box.

It had been shoved under the bed along with the key when she first got home, its importance overshadowed by Naveed's disappearance. But now curiosity burned. What was inside? And what did it have to do with the bones, and what did the bones have to do with Kass's nan? Roya was certain there was a connection now. She would have to tell Kass about it when she wrote again.

It was hard to get motivated to do more writing, though, since third grade had started the day before. Ms. Won had given them a big homework packet already, and Roya was sitting at the dining room table trying to concentrate on a math worksheet.

But this only brought back unpleasant memories about school, where most of her classmates wouldn't even talk to her. The ones who did asked her what it was like to be kidnapped, and she didn't really know what to say so she told them truthfully that it was horrible and ruined everything, and they wanted to know more so Roya told them more, but she must have gone into too much detail because the teacher overheard and she got in trouble for telling "disturbing" stories. Her classmates still regarded her with morbid fascination, but they never wanted to play with her at recess, as if her family's misfortune had been the result of a curse that could be spread by getting too close.

Roya didn't want to think about going back again the next day. So she set down her pencil and let her mind drift back to the box. That was the one thing she actually *wanted* to think about.

She stood up and peeked into the kitchen. Cyrus was home for once, cooking a big stew for them to eat throughout the week. "Kourosh?"

He jumped when she said his name. "Oh! I didn't hear you coming. What's up?"

"I have a question."

"Fire away." He was chopping lamb into big cubes. It looked so bloody.

"I want to know how to dissolve rust."

"Rust? Why?"

Roya didn't want him to know the truth. The box was a secret that belonged only to her. And maybe also to Kass. "I found something at the beach on Lopez. An old coin, maybe? I can't really tell what it is, so I want to get the rust off."

"Hold on a sec." He finished chopping, then rinsed his hands and dried them before pulling out his phone. After a pause, he said, "Lemon juice. Or vinegar. Let it soak 30 minutes and that should dissolve it."

"Okay." She grabbed a big bottle of distilled vinegar from the cupboard. It was very heavy.

"Here, I'll get it." Cyrus poured a few inches into an empty jam jar.

Roya hoped that would be enough. "Thanks," she said.

"Hey, Roya. Are you… okay? You want to, like, walk over to the park with me sometime?"

Roya didn't, really, but it was nice of him to offer. "I don't know. School makes me so tired."

"It would be good for you, though. Trust me, once you got outside, you'd get your energy back."

"Maybe."

"I think the walnut tree misses you," he said, and Roya felt suddenly like a blunt twig was poking at her heart. Once, it had made her so happy, sitting in that tree, playing the flute she now couldn't bring herself to touch. It used to fill her up. But for some reason, it didn't anymore. Being out in the yard was kind of sad now. Everything was overgrown and neglected, the vegetable garden full of withered husks, the elderberries rotting on their stems.

Roya didn't want to think about any of that, so she asked, "Are you going back to Dev's soon?"

"Nah, think I'll stay for dinner. You gonna help me with the dishes? Look at this place. It's a disaster."

It was. No denying that. "I'll think about it."

"Well, I'll take all the help I can get." Cyrus turned back to his cutting board.

Roya took a deep breath. "Why did he leave, Kourosh? Did he think we didn't love him?"

Cyrus's shoulders sagged, but he didn't turn around. "I don't know, Roya. It's impossible to know what anyone else is thinking, and he had so much going on inside his head...."

Roya didn't like his use of past tense. "I think maybe I made the wrong choice. I shouldn't have stayed on Lopez. I should have come home, and then he would have known."

"No. I'm sure he wanted you to stay. It had nothing to do with you, I'm positive of that. If anything, it was me. We weren't, um. We weren't getting along."

He sounded so sad. "Well, he wasn't really getting along with anyone, was he?" Roya asked. "He was kind of... Kourosh, he could be kind of mean and I don't really miss that person, the mean one, and Maman said he was doing better but when I talked to him on the phone after he got out of the hospital it was like talking to a stranger and… and I just… I didn't like it."

She felt horrible admitting those things out loud, but it didn't seem to bother Cyrus. "You talked to him?" he asked.

"He didn't want to, but Maman put him on the phone. He said that they fixed him, that everything was great, but he sounded so fake, and he wasn't listening to me at all."

Cyrus turned around. His nose was red. "Oh, Roya. I'm sorry. Sometimes I got angry with him too."

"Really?"

"I tried to cut him some slack, because I know he was in a lot of pain, but still. Why couldn't he see how hard we were trying to help?"

"Yeah," Roya said. "How could he be so selfish? How could he do this to Maman and Baba, to us? Didn't he know what would happen when he left?"

They both talked quietly now, knowing they were saying things that weren't supposed to be spoken. The meat sizzled in the stock pot. Cyrus stirred it. "I think we need to stop waiting around for him. We need to stop beating ourselves up. We can't let him ruin our lives, and we can't put everything on hold forever. We have to move on."

"But do you think Maman and Baba can ever be happy without him?"

"Of course. Give them time."

That was optimistic. Roya knew what he was really saying. *He's gone, he's not coming back, we have to forget him if we can ever hope to be a family again.*

That blunt twig stabbed at her heart once more. She took the jar and turned away, the acidic smell stinging her nose. "Thanks for the vinegar, Kourosh."

"Anytime." Cyrus poured broth into the pot, sending up a big plume of steam.

Roya walked up the stairs with a new energy. Even if she wasn't ready to move on yet, Cyrus was right about one thing. It was time to stop lazing around. Time to get to work.

She removed the key from her pocket and put it into the jar of vinegar. Maybe she should have asked for more; the liquid only covered half the key, but she figured that would be enough.

Next, she slid the box out from under her bed and examined the lock. It was filled with packed dirt; no wonder the key couldn't get in. So she went to Cyrus's room, found a paper clip, and used it to pick all the gunk out of the lock. Then she poured a tiny bit of vinegar into it and let some pool around the top.

While she waited for the vinegar to do its work, Pashmak wandered into the room. Grateful for the company, Roya patted her lap until the cat curled up there, then stroked Pashmak's soft white fur. She wondered what treasures she might find inside the box.

When the key had soaked long enough, she nudged Pashmak to the floor and headed for the bathroom. The cat must have been curious, too, because she followed Roya and watched as she scrubbed the key off in the bathroom sink, letting the rust fall away. Roya found a cotton swab, then went back into her room and cleaned the lock as best she could.

"What do you think we'll find, Pashi?" she asked the cat, who was batting the discarded cotton swab around on the floor. Roya picked up the key, anticipation burning inside her.

This time, the key slid into the lock easily, and it clicked open when she turned it. She pried the lid off.

On top was a cloth-bound book. She opened it up, flipped through: it looked to be a journal. The handwriting was faded in places, and the pages were yellowed and old.

Roya set it aside. The rest of the box was filled with medical supplies. Needles, syringes, antiseptic wipes. Tiny glass bottles labeled *morphine* and *oxytocin*, pill bottles full of amoxycillin and cephalosporin.

Drugs. She had found a box full of drugs. Instinctively, she recoiled; she didn't want to have anything to do with them. So she took the book out, hoping it would explain, and locked the box up again. Good thing she hadn't told Cyrus about any of this.

Roya shoved the box under her bed, then strung some yarn onto the key, making a necklace of it. After she tucked it underneath her shirt, she settled onto her bed with the cat and the book, and began to read.

January 27, 1979

I made it. I am finally here.

When Z pulled the Bug up to the gate, everyone gave us such an incredible welcome. I expected to stand around as Z was welcomed back, but they hugged me too, kissed my cheeks, like they had always known me.

I have a new name here, as does she, as do we all. Everyone has come to this place to reinvent themselves. To build something better. Here I am Gaia, Earth goddess. She is Zennia, though it's hard for me to get used to calling her that, so I'll stick with Z.

Still adjusting to being back in the States. I'm used to the tropical jungles, to the heat, and I'm constantly shivering here. They all give me a hard time for sitting so close to the fire. But they are grateful for the seeds and plant cuttings I brought with me from Peru, and I am looking forward to setting up my medical tent, to being their healer.

And their midwife, too. Z gave me quite a shock today at the airport, all I saw at first was her shining face, and when I finally noticed the swell of her belly she saw me gaping and laughed, rubbing it with a smile. I asked how long, and she waved a hand, unsure. Seven moon cycles, she thought, meaning just a few months left to go. I'll need to brush up on my pregnancy knowledge. Wish I hadn't sold all my textbooks when I quit med school.

Still jet-lagged from the long days of travel. Off to bed now.

January 31, 1979

Been busy setting up. One of the residents, Beau, helps me in the greenhouses. He says he's not good at building, which is what the others are up to these days, working on our first cabin despite all the rain (so much rain!). Naturally, Z will be living there. Everyone agrees that it's important for the new baby to have a warm place to live. But part of me feels like Alastor is taking over this project, like he's really building the house for himself. He's the baby's father, but still. This is supposed to be an egalitarian society. We're not supposed to elevate one person above all others. And there will be more babies. Maybe, one day, a whole classroom full. The children of the utopia. How lucky they'll be, to grow up in this beautiful place, so near the forest, the bluffs, the ocean.

For now, Beau and I spend our days setting up the drip irrigation, getting the grow lights installed, mixing potting soil and spreading it into trays for the peritassa seeds. (That's not what they called the plant back in Peru, but I always loved its botanical name, Peritassa brevifolia. Besides, we all have new names here anyway, so peritassa it will be.) I hope the seeds germinate. If the peritassa doesn't grow, will they make me leave? I don't ever want to leave.

February 20, 1979

The seedlings are growing well. I've been reading up on obstetrics and working with a local midwife and doctor to get a limited pharmacy set up. Just the essentials, antibiotics and such. Otherwise we will rely on natural healing and preventive care. Beau and I work together all the time now. The others have noticed, I think.

One night at the fire, after Z had gone to bed, Alastor came over and started chatting me up. He was rubbing his hand in circles around my back, telling me how much I looked like Z only prettier—skinnier, he actually said—and that he wanted to show me something in the cabin. I said, right now? And he said, come on, and he didn't mean it as a suggestion.

Beau came over then, and Alastor looked so angry when Beau put his arm around me. I know I shouldn't be such a prude, but I still feel gross thinking about A trying to make a move on me when my lovely sister, the one bearing his child, had no idea.

I told her the next day. She didn't care.

I mean, look at me, she said. I _am_ fat.

Not fat, I said, only pregnant, and I don't like that A's sleeping around. It's disrespectful.

She just shrugged and said, I'm cool with it. He knows I don't want to have him right now. He needs it, he can get it from somebody else.

Well he won't get it from me, I said.

I've been joined at the hip with Beau ever since. Hope A gets the point.

Two more months. The baby seems to be doing well, if a little small.

March 13, 1979

It might as well be official now: Alastor is our leader. I find him so repellent that it's hard for me to understand what it is they see in him, why they look to him for leadership. He is charismatic, I'll give him that. But at least Beau is immune to it. In the greenhouse we have our own sanctuary, a space that's only ours.

Last week, Ukiah came down with a throat infection, probably strep, which luckily didn't spread. I was able to treat it with antibiotics from the supply the doctor gave me, but Alastor found out and confronted me about it. He made it very clear that modern medicine was not welcome within his commune. <u>His</u> commune. I said that I would use it sparingly, only when necessary, and that we should bring it for a vote at the next group meeting. He finally agreed to that much.

Talked to Z about it later. Apparently Alastor nearly died when he was serving in Viet Nam because he had a severe allergic reaction to a medication while being treated for minor shrapnel injuries. This somehow convinced him that ALL medicine is unnatural and evil. Just another example of his inability to see things through any perspective but his own. Hope I can help the others understand this when we meet.

March 31, 1979

The meeting was a joke. Alastor dominated it. All I asked was something completely reasonable, but it devolved somehow into an argument about pharmaceutical companies and their monopolies and how we absolutely should not support them by allowing their toxic products into our Eden. We use only substances derived from nature here, and our healthy lifestyles and natural medicines will keep us strong.

Well, that's fine and all, but I'm not going to trash my medications just yet. Bought a sturdy box while in town yesterday and will hide them somewhere safe, where Alastor can't find them.

I should probably keep this journal there too, in case someone finds it and calls me a "subversive." Which is ridiculous. We all came here to buck the system.

As bizarre as this place is sometimes, I still love it. And I want to be here for Z. I like being near her, and I want to get to know my little niece or nephew, and I want to protect them from A if I need to.

And who am I kidding? It's not like I have anywhere else to go. The family disowned me after the med school debacle, and I spent the last of my savings on the trip to Peru. Besides, I'm completely head over heels for Beau. And my peritassa. . . no, I can't leave. Here I will stay.

April 22, 1979

The last few days have been a whirlwind. Z went into labor on the 20th. She was doing beautifully for a while, but her bag of waters broke early and as labor dragged on I became concerned about infection risk. For a while it was just the two of us, but then Alastor came in, stubbornly insisting that he needed to be present for the birth. Everybody had harvested some really good bud, and he'd been smoking all day and was probably higher than I'd ever seen him. It was making him paranoid, I could tell because he brought such bad vibes with him, but I knew forcing him to leave would make things worse, so I let him stay. Besides, Z seemed to want him there.

But then she stalled out, labor was going nowhere, and when I felt the baby I was shocked. It was breech. I couldn't believe I had missed that, and I wasn't at all prepared for this, didn't know what to do. I tried calling the midwife that I'd trained with, but she was attending another birth on the island and couldn't be reached. Then I heard Z moaning, and she threw up on A, which I probably would have found wonderful any other time, and to his credit he didn't blow up at her, just got out of there to change. I was glad, because I took her temperature and she was running a fever, so I got out my antibiotics from the box, which I'd smuggled in and was hiding under the bed.

Zennia, I said, and she looked at me but I couldn't even tell her what was going on before another wave crested, dragging her attention along with it. They were so powerful now, and she kept asking me where Alastor was, kept saying that she was scared, she couldn't do this, and I was even more afraid, because now I was sure, her baby was stuck.

Alastor burst into the room as I was picking up the phone to call an ambulance. He asked me what I was doing, and I told him, and he took the receiver from me. No, he said. That baby is going to be born here. Not in some horrible sick room where people go to die. Now what's the problem?

I just stood there for a second, then explained the baby was in the wrong position, it was stuck, if it couldn't get out—

He didn't wait for me to finish. He went over to Z and put his hands on her belly, and he started talking gibberish. He was so high, and I was just about to reach for the phone again, consequences be damned; my sister was not going to die giving birth like this was the eighteen-fucking-hundreds.

But she started moaning, in a different way, and I could see it there, like an earthquake inside her belly, the baby inside. . . turning?

I had her move onto her hands and knees, and she looked not at me but at Alastor, and she said his name over and over, like a mantra, and then he helped support her in a squat as the baby started crowning, and a few pushes later it was out.

A baby girl. My little sister's baby girl. But I had no time to be elated, even as that baby squawked and started slurping up her mother's milk; Z was still feverish and was bleeding too much. I had my oxytocin all ready, but couldn't give her a shot while Alastor was there, so I wrapped up the baby real warm after she had gotten her fill of first milk, and I sent A out to show her to the others. Beau was sitting right outside, and he gave me the biggest kiss when he saw that beautiful baby, but I made him follow A and told him to look after the babe and bring her back soon.

Then I was able to tend to Z. She had lost a lot of blood while all this was going on, and she is still very weak, but she is growing stronger, and the little baby is healthy as can be.

She let Alastor name it. He named her Miracle.

May 2, 1979

Even though spring is here, a cold wind blows through camp. The peritassa is ready to harvest. But I'm hesitant to tell anyone.

My vision was to use it the way the shaman did in Peru, as a bridge to healing, a way to bring closure to long-carried wounds. But I get the feeling that my vision does not matter so much here anymore. Z used to have a lot more power with these people, but now she has been reduced in their eyes, ever since she became a mother—even though she has become elevated in mine. When I see her with that babe. . . oh, my heart.

Alastor always ruins it, though. He makes so many demands of her; she meekly complies. And yet she insists that she loves him, and strange as it sounds, they do seem completely committed to each other, even though he continues to sleep with other women. It's not something I try to understand.

He told her that he saved the baby. She doesn't remember what really happened, doesn't know that I saved her life with "evil" modern medicine. She believes him, and I can't convince her otherwise. I'm not sure whose side she's on these days.

Anyway, I am worried about Alastor and my peritassa. As with any drug, it's a balancing act between responsible use and abuse, and if Alastor grows overly fond of its hallucinogenic effects. . .

I'm going to be very strict about the circumstances under which it is allowed to be consumed: once a month, at a ceremony that we'll hold on the night of the new moon. No more frequently than that.

 Beau and Ukiah returned from their visit to the mainland today. B brought me a basket of strawberries. They were magnificent.

May 26, 1979

First ceremony went well tonight. Z and I were the only ones who did not partake. We served as guides, surrounding people with loving energy if their trips got too intense; we made sure everyone stayed safe and helped them during the purging phase.

Alastor was the last one to come down (I suspect that he took a larger bowl of tea than was suggested). Z helped him through, but when everyone else got up to return to camp, he was still lying there by the fire, looking up at the stars. When I came back to finish cleaning up, he was murmuring to Z, quietly but intensely.

The orca, he said. The black whale on the grey stones. It is a sacrifice sent from the gods, the gods of the sea. Tomorrow at dawn. I'll show you.

He seemed to be getting agitated then, but Z has a way of calming him when no one else can. (I think she may well have some magic in her. Starr, who's Wiccan, has been teaching her some things, but Z's abilities to manipulate energy are something beyond reason. If anyone is ever able to tame Alastor, it is she.)

Beau was waiting for me at home. He was crying and smiling at the same time, and he told me what he'd seen. I didn't know that he'd been in Nam, too, he doesn't like to talk about it or think about it ever, he said. But tonight he went back, and this time it was different. This time the jungle was not hostile, it was welcoming. His fellow soldiers, who had been standing next to him talking one moment and blown apart the next, were waiting there, and he was able to tell them the things he'd never gotten to say. He felt so free now, he said.

That's what this is about. So many men here are haunted by the specter of their time in Nam. So many women are haunted by other unspeakable things. The ceremonies are intended to help them bridge their way toward peace. And don't we all need more of that?

May 27, 1979

This morning Alastor called a meeting. We discussed how the ceremony had gone, and he shared his vision with everyone, how the sea gods had spoken of a sacrifice. Afterwards, he led everyone down to the beach he had visualized. I trailed behind, looking forward to seeing him humiliated.

And there, washed up on shore, was a giant orca whale.

I wish we could have done something to help her, but she was already dead.

Alastor's now fully embracing what he's certain is a direct connection to the gods. We've just been calling this place the Lopez Island Commune, but he suggested renaming it Orcinia. (I have to admit, it's an improvement.) And, surprise, surprise: he wants to learn how to tend the peritassa. I made it clear he's not welcome. He hates not being allowed into the greenhouse, but I need to keep at least one spot in our property free of his energy.

June 5, 1979

We have been stricken. A virus is tearing through the camp, a stomach flu that is horribly contagious. Beau and I have been running around cleaning up all the vomit, all the shit, trying to keep everyone hydrated, trying to keep Z and the baby and also Starr and Elsabet, who are both newly pregnant, quarantined in the cabin.

I have to say it was some small satisfaction to see Alastor struck down. But I can't stop worrying that he'll disobey me and break the quarantine, just to show that he can.

Too much to do. Have to stay healthy. We'll beat this. Come back stronger.

June 12, 1979

Hearing rumors. Because I didn't get sick the outbreak was my fault?

I suspect Alastor's behind this story, probably because Miracle became so ill. She wouldn't have caught it if he hadn't gone into the cabin, if he hadn't literally thrown me away from the door, saying that no one could keep him from his woman and child.

I think little M is out of the woods now. She is able to feed again, to keep it down, her fever is gone. But she looks smaller, thinner. Not good adjectives to describe a baby.

I don't know what to do about Alastor. Now that he's actively trying to turn people against me, I'm not sure how much more I can take.

June 24, 1979

We had another ceremony last night. This time Z served as guide alone, because I felt a calling to drink the tea.

When I was in Peru, I always had good experiences. Well—they're never all good, of course, there's always some unpleasantness, but for me that was always outweighed by the transcendent moments of bliss. Not this time.

I was not in the best mood, was feeling shunned as I sat in the circle alone. Beau is still recovering from his flu and decided to sit this one out. No one would talk to me, they all recoiled from me like I was toxic. I should have known better than to enter with a negative mindset, but I wanted to escape from here. And from the moment I took the first sip, everything was all wrong. I walked in darkness. I saw things that I can't even write down, visions I don't want to think about.

The shaman from Peru came to me. He was angry that I took the peritassa seeds without permission. It wasn't a big deal, I insisted, they're seeds, they belong to everyone, but he shook his head. No, he said. Just because you see something you like, that doesn't mean you can take it. You don't have the right to it just because you can tear it away and conceal it in your fist. This is what white people do, he said. They take without listening.

Not all of us, I told him, but he didn't respond. Slowly, I realized what his silence was telling me: my defensive answer showed that I was not hearing him.

Then listen, he said. Don't talk, don't justify, only listen.

And then he showed me all the ways we steal. Showed me the heavy and persistent costs of colonization: trauma, death, disease, fear, misery, continuing for generations on into the present. Even this land that we inhabit here on Lopez—it was never ours for the taking.

These seeds are sacred, he told me. They must be cared for properly and respected. You took them without asking, for your own gain. There will be consequences.

Usually the purging stops by dawn, but I'm still here in bed, sick to my stomach. It was just a vision, I tell myself. A vivid dream, conjured up by my subconscious. Still, even the light looks different this morning. Something has changed. Everything has changed.

June 27, 1979

Starr lost her baby. We are devastated.

Elsabet is still doing all right, but she's so thin, losing weight instead of gaining. Our food supply is getting low. We were counting on a summer of abundance in the fields and orchards, but last week came a series of storms that wiped out many of the vegetable seedlings.

Every morning I wake up sick, but the nausea clears by noon.

Consequences.

I'm terrified.

July 12, 1979

The food shortage is growing dire. We've used nearly all the money in our reserves buying brown rice and beans and lentils, but this isn't enough to feed us all. Several people have left, Starr and Elsabet among them. I was sad to see them go, but wish them well on the outside.

The only people remaining, a dozen or so of us, are those who are completely committed to Orcinia, and those who have nowhere else to go.

I guess I fit into the latter camp, because I'm not so sure I believe in our vision anymore.

I'm seeing everything differently these days. This supposed utopia now seems exclusionary. We're a bunch of white people trying to figure out how to subsist on this land without ever talking to, or even acknowledging, the natives who called this place home for thousands of years before us. We isolate ourselves, saying that we're building a better world—but are we, really? And is it a better world for everyone, or just us?

Beau says that he's happier here than he ever has been in his life. Even though I am still shunned, still seen with suspicion by the others, especially after I failed to perform some unknown miracle that would have saved Starr's babe, he manages to get along with everyone. I'm just happy that he's staying.

I think he suspects why I've been sick, but I haven't admitted it to anyone yet, can barely admit it even to myself. I can feel her, I know she's there, it's just that I'm afraid she's like a birthday wish, if you say it out loud it won't come true.

July 20, 1979

A blight has been spreading through the orchards. The leaves are crisp and dry, there's not an apple to be seen. The other day, some creature (a wolf?) got into the chicken coop and killed the whole flock. At this rate, we will have no food left for the winter.

Alastor has a plan to save us. (Of course he does.) Apparently he's been pitching it throughout camp for several days, but it only now filtered down to me. He wants to make Orcinia into some sort of retreat, where people pay us to experience our new moon ceremonies and live off the land for a few weeks before returning to their normal lives.

The idea disgusts me so intensely that I had to fight to keep from throwing up when Beau told me. I reminded him that peritassa is illegal in the US, but apparently Alastor knows of some loopholes that would allow its consumption for religious purposes. The worst part is that everyone else is excited about the idea. I suppose I understand, they're desperate, looking for a savior.

I don't know how to stop this. All I know is that I cannot let it happen.

August 4, 1979

Last night I was up late, thinking about the peritassa plants again. Knowing that I must destroy them, trying to work up the courage. Then I heard footsteps approaching: it was Z, supporting Ukiah, who was barely conscious. A building accident, she said. They were building in the dark? I asked. She shrugged.

Sure doesn't look like an accident to me.

Ukiah's in bad shape. He must have broken his ribs, punctured a lung, but worse, he has a head injury, hasn't woken up since. He needs a hospital, badly.

The Bug broke down the other day and hasn't been repaired. We no longer have phone service. I need to stay with Ukiah. I'm trying to keep him comfortable, though I'm almost out of morphine. I haven't seen Beau all day, but Z stopped to check in and I told her how bad it was, told her to walk down the road and borrow someone's phone, but that was hours ago. I suspect Alastor found out and didn't let her leave.

Beau will be able to sneak his way out, I hope. As soon as he gets help, as soon as Ukiah is taken care of, I'm going to the greenhouse to get rid of my peritassa. It's the only way to end this misfortune. If I don't, it's obvious that the consequences are coming for me next, and I can't lose her, my tiny seed of a daughter.

Beau. I need to tell him. But where is he?

Where did he go?

Andi

ANDI AND BROOKE SAT ON THE SHORE OF LAKE WASHINGTON. They had hiked up the trail from the main beach so that they could have their own private spot. The gentle waves lapped at their ankles while they watched Roya float in the sparkling water.

"Did you listen to the interview yet?" Brooke sipped her green juice. She had just finished up at work, but had been tasked with watching Roya since her mom and Mahnaz were busy working to submit a grant before the deadline.

"No. I can't—I don't even want to hear his voice, you know?" Andi burrowed her feet under the smooth stones. The top layer was warm, but the rocks beneath radiated a definite chill.

"You should listen, though. He mentions you. I'm surprised no one's asked you about it yet."

People *had* been looking at Andi extra oddly at school the day before, after the NPR interview with Brennan and Cyrus had aired, but she continued ignoring them and their hushed whispers. During dinner later, her dad had fawned over both Brennan and Cyrus for their role in the Metafolia recall, but for some reason, her mom had seemed as unenthusiastic about it as Andi. She quickly changed the subject to Andi re-taking the SAT in October. Which didn't much help Andi's mood, or the headache that had been pulsing at her temples all day.

"Oh—here." Brooke rifled around in her gigantic canvas tote. She pulled out a crinkly plastic bag filled with gummi bears. "Have a couple cannabears first, that'll take the edge off."

"Cannabears?"

"They're infused with cannabis. One of my co-workers is a budtender too. He hooked me up." Brooke squinted at the water. "Help yourself. I can keep an eye on Roya."

"No, that's okay. I'm good." It was tempting, but Andi had grown up witnessing her dad's struggles with addiction, and didn't want to fall into the same traps he had.

Brooke shrugged and returned the bag to her tote. "Just makes it easier, sometimes," she said. "To deal with these shit-tastic situations we keep finding ourselves in."

Andi couldn't hold back a small smile. Exactly two things had been keeping her from plunging into despair lately: working in secret on her piano composition at night, and hanging out with Brooke.

The two of them had been spending time together nearly every day. At first, they had traveled all over the city searching for Naveed, whom they both hoped was still alive somewhere. Andi had aired her conflicted feelings about him to Brooke, and it came as a relief to know they both felt the same way. Brooke had hated him right after they broke up, but said she understood his behavior a little better after hearing about his PTSD diagnosis. Not that it excused what he'd done to her, what he'd said to her. Just that it made it easier to understand, and to stop blaming herself so much.

They explored every corner of the city, but eventually their hopes of finding Naveed dimmed, and they stopped talking about him, stopped talking about Cyrus. It didn't mean Andi stopped thinking about them, of course, but her time with Brooke morphed into more pleasant diversions of hanging out in cafes, going to shows together, spending the entirety of Labor Day weekend at the Bumbershoot Music Festival.

And now here Cyrus was, intruding in her life once more. Andi had to admit, though, that she was curious about what he'd said in the interview.

"Okay, you're right," she told Brooke grudgingly. "I should know what he said about me. I'll listen."

Brooke tapped at her phone. "Here, I'll pull it up."

Andi scooted closer as Brooke googled *metafolia cyrus*. Before she'd even typed in his last name, the interview popped up in the search results. Brooke found the audio archive and pressed Play.

The host started by summarizing the Metafolia recall. "The company's founder, Geoffrey Walker, could not be reached for comment—federal authorities are searching for him, but his whereabouts are currently unknown. Today we're joined by two people who were involved in publicizing the supplement's harmful effects: Brennan Walsh, CEO of Bountiful Earth Market, and Cyrus Mirzapour, the young man who also played a key role in exposing wrongdoings at Nutrexo this past summer. Thank you both for being here."

"Thank you for having us." That was Brennan. Good thing, because Andi's blood pressure was already rising, and Cyrus hadn't even said a single word.

"Mr. Walsh, how did you initially become aware of Metafolia?"

Brennan went on for a while about his mother, about how he'd decided to have the supplements tested after hearing that other people had suffered similar health problems.

"And Cyrus. You've been gathering lots of attention for this case on social media. What motivated you to get involved?"

"Well—" There was a hint of hesitation in Cyrus's voice, but he continued, "I was in Southern California last month with Andi and her family—Andi Lin, her dad is friends with Brennan—uh, Mr. Walsh—and he told us what happened with his mom and we were like, whoa, that's weird, because something happened to Andi too, she ended up in the ER after taking it."

"Oh—Andi Lin, who was also a victim in the Nutrexo scandal? I hope she was all right."

"Yeah. She was okay, I mean, it was kind of serious I guess, she was in bed for like a week afterward, so, yeah, it made me want to know if something else was going on. And once we found out what it was, I had to help spread the word. I didn't want anyone else to get hurt. Didn't want the company to get away with that."

"How old are you, Cyrus?"

"I turn sixteen in a few weeks."

"Not even sixteen yet." Andi could practically hear the interviewer shaking his head in disbelief. "Well—you are one remarkable teenager. So, Mr. Walsh—"

Andi turned it off. Had it not been Brooke's phone, she would have thrown it as far as she could.

"Yeah, that was pretty much the end anyway," Brooke said.

"Wow. Just, wow." Andi's voice came out tight and cold. Cyrus knew how much she hated talking about that night, and here he was telling the whole world about it, making her sound like a helpless victim, not even mentioning that *she* had been the one who actually wanted to fight the company in the first place.

She felt like yelling. Screaming. Running.

Brooke must have sensed this, because she slid her phone into her tote and stood up. She extended her hand to Andi, who took it.

"Empty your pockets," Brooke said as she pulled Andi up.

"Why? Are you robbing me?"

Brooke snorted. "Of course not." But she stood there, palms outstretched, waiting. Andi surrendered her phone and keys, which Brooke tucked into her tote bag. "We're going for a swim."

"But—I didn't bring a suit—"

"Tank top and shorts look like perfectly fine swimming clothes to me."

Andi glanced out at Roya, still floating there in the water. She looked so peaceful.

Brooke grabbed her hand, but she didn't need to pull Andi along, because Andi ran willingly alongside her, their feet gingerly picking their way across the stones, and then they plunged in, gasping at the initial chill, and Andi didn't let herself think about the day she and Cyrus had gone swimming in the ocean, she only looked at Roya, at the delight shining on her usually-morose little face when she saw that Brooke and Andi were joining her; she only heard Brooke whooping and Roya squealing with glee.

Brooke plunged underwater. When she came up, her blue hair was plastered to her head and mascara ran in thick tracks under her eyes.

Andi smiled. "Brooke… you look like… like a deranged witch."

"Witches don't look like that," said Roya, and she sounded so serious that both Andi and Brooke burst out laughing. It felt so *good* to laugh, to really laugh, out here in the sun-warmed shallows of the lake.

They swam. Andi floated on her back for a while, then paddled over next to Brooke. "It's nice in the water. I'm glad we're here."

"Me, too. Seems like I've hardly seen you this week."

"I know. I wish you went to my school. I hate it there," Andi said.

"Why don't you just do the online thing, like me?"

"My parents don't think it looks as good on college applications. Plus, honestly, I don't know that I could stay motivated to keep up with it."

"Yeah. It's not very fun. I miss my old school," Brooke said quietly. She had been attending a Waldorf high school, but her dad, who had worked with Tara Snyder at Nutrexo, was in prison now, and her mom couldn't afford the tuition anymore.

Andi never knew what to say when Brooke's dad peripherally entered their conversations, so she just laced her fingers with Brooke's in the water and gave her hand a squeeze. Brooke squeezed back.

"Why don't you come to our house anymore, Andi?" Roya asked. "I miss you. So does Kourosh. Everyone was always happier when you came over."

It gripped Andi then, that sense of sudden, overwhelming grief, the kind that came out of nowhere and tightened rapidly around her heart. And if that was how *she* felt, what was Roya going through? Poor Roya, who was so in the dark about the many undercurrents flowing around her.

"Cyrus and I... we... we decided it would be better not to see each other anymore." It wasn't a very good answer, Andi knew, but it was all she could think to say.

Roya spun around in the water. "Well, it's not better. He's always so grumpy. Not that he's around much anyway."

Andi felt a fresh surge of anger at Cyrus. How could he just leave his little sister to fend for herself? "Roya, if you ever want to come over after school, you're welcome anytime. I don't want you to feel like you're alone."

She thought she saw the glimmer of a smile on Roya's face. "Okay. Maybe."

"Hop on my back," Brooke told Roya. "Let's go out further."

Roya wrapped her wet arms around Brooke's neck, and together they swam through the shallows into the deeper water.

"Ack, don't strangle me," Brooke said to Roya. "Here, why don't you float on your back for a while. I'll hold you up."

Roya relaxed into Brooke's outstretched arms, and Andi swam past them, rolling onto her back and closing her eyes, letting the gentle waves rock her. Cyrus had wormed his way back into her brain, the NPR interview irritating her anew. It bothered her so much: all Cyrus was doing, really, was picking on one little company. Rightfully so, she would give him that—but what good was this going to do in the long run? It wasn't fixing the larger problems. This was something she'd tried to tell him before; he'd never listened.

It got her thinking. Remembering back to Brennan's house, to him talking about trying to get a bill through to fix the broken FDA regulations.

What if she could help to do *that*? To make sure that not only this supplement company, but every company who tried to exploit loopholes and put harmful products on the market, would be properly regulated so that these things could be prevented in the future?

True to his word, Brennan had sent Andi and her parents tickets to the benefit gala for his foundation, which was coming up the following weekend. Andi steeled herself, knowing now what she needed to do.

She would go to that gala. Even if Cyrus was there, too, even if she had to face him. She would sit at the table with Brennan Walsh and Senator Bittner. She would do her homework beforehand and figure out exactly what to say, and she would work as hard as she could to change things for real.

September 16

Dear Roya,

I'm sorry to hear about your brother. And I have to apologize because I think I might have made it worse. That day with the poppet, things didn't go right at all, it's hard to explain but I felt an evil presence even though I had cast a circle, and then I got scared and left the circle without making a proper doorway, and I'm worried that made all the bad energy flow in. I was hoping that the sea water would cleanse him of it, but I think it was already too deep inside.

It took me a while to get back to you because I've been going through our Book of Shadows to see if there is anything I can do to help you bring him home. But you need to ask yourself before you begin if that's what you really want, because he won't come back fixed. It's hard to say whether he lost part of his soul while he was on the threshold, or if something latched onto him and dug in its claws, or maybe both, but either way the healing is going to be hard work. On the other hand, there's a lot more you can do if he's close to you. I've copied down some spells you can try. I put in a few simple ones, so try those first even though I don't think they'll do the trick. There are larger forces at work here and you will probably need to use the more powerful ones. Nan always says to be cautious about doing blood magic, but sometimes it's the only way. Just be careful not to cut too deep.

Again, I am very sorry if I made things worse. I never wanted to hurt you. Really all I want is for you to come back. Or maybe someday I can visit you. Know what's strange? Nan is actually leaving the island, for the first time I can remember. Grandfather received a message from the gods at our ceremony the other night. He and Nan need to make some important sacrifices to Hekate. If they don't, the passage between the human world and the spirit one is in danger of closing forever.

Nan doesn't seem excited about leaving though. Something has changed in her after the last ceremony. She's been avoiding Grandfather, and seems confused when she looks at him, almost like she doesn't know who he is anymore. Still, she's going, and I am tempted to figure out a way to hide in the boat so that I can see what's off the island too. But it would never work. They'd all notice if I wasn't there to send them off. I'll have to find another way.

Love,

Kass

Cyrus

CYRUS WAS WIPING THE RESTAURANT COUNTERS WITH SANITIZER when Chef Thierry called him to the office. He finished up and headed back there, figuring it had something to do with the menu for the Walsh Foundation gala the following evening. Thierry had asked him to help with the catering and Cyrus had jumped at the chance for extra hours.

But when he entered, Chef Thierry looked upset. He gestured at the chair opposite him. "I have some bad news."

Cyrus sank into the chair, his thoughts immediately going to his family—had something happened? Naveed's body finally found? Or, an accident at home? Maman doing something self-destructive? Baba getting hurt out there in the workshop? Roya? Please let it not be Roya, he thought, and was so wrapped up in his worry that he almost didn't notice when Thierry added, "It's about Brennan Walsh."

Cyrus was thrown. He had not expected that at all. Though he was slightly relieved that this had nothing to do with his family, he gripped the armrest tightly, bracing himself.

"I just saw it on the news. Brennan… he's…" Thierry picked up the glass tumbler of whiskey that had been sitting on his desk. "He's dead."

"But… how… are you sure?" Cyrus had talked to him a few days before about setting up another Metafolia-related interview. And the benefit was tomorrow. Somehow it seemed impossible that Brennan, who had so many things planned, could actually die.

Thierry gulped his whiskey. "They found him—his body—behind a restaurant in the Yakima Valley. They're saying it was a homicide."

Cyrus was still in shock. It made no sense. "What was he doing out in Yakima? And why would someone kill him? Do they have a suspect?"

"I don't know. It only happened a few hours ago."

"Oh God," Cyrus said. "It's just… it's horrible. I don't even know what to say."

"He was one of the good guys," said Thierry. "Fighting the good fight. Why does it always happen to the good ones?"

Cyrus had no response for that. He was thinking of Brennan, of his house in paradise, of Cyrus's short-lived fantasies of moving in, becoming Brennan's personal chef, living with Andi….

All of it descended on him perilously, the suddenness of all these paths closing, the knowledge that *never again* would he talk to Brennan, never again would he go back to that place with Andi or anyone else, and it was enough to turn him leaden, too heavy to move—but at the same time, he didn't want to sit here in front of Thierry much longer, because he was dangerously close to bawling.

"I'm sorry, I'm really… can I… clock out please…." Cyrus said.

Thierry poured himself another drink. "Of course. Oh, and the gala's still on for tomorrow, as far as I know. But if you need to take the day off, I understand."

Cyrus nodded and left. His phone had died at some point during his restaurant shift, so drained of battery power that it wouldn't even turn on. He forced himself to stay composed during the ride home with his co-worker Steven, trying to participate in a conversation about Steven's quest to find the best burger in Seattle, all the while thinking, *keep it together, keep it together.*

When he opened the front door it was dark in the house, as usual. No one ever waited up for him. But tonight he heard a noise: Baba was in the kitchen, pulling the recycling bin from under the sink.

Cyrus plugged in his phone at the charging station on the counter. "Baba? It's not garbage day tomorrow." He had been bringing the trash to the curb for weeks.

Baba straightened up, startled. "Kourosh! Home already?" He seemed to think for a moment, then added, "Come with me? I've finished my project. It's outside."

Confused, Cyrus followed him out to the fire pit. And there he saw it, inside the iron ring, glowing pale in the moonlight: a narrow wooden box, about a foot long. It looked like a tiny coffin.

The lid was closed. Carved into the top was a many-petaled flower.

Baba saw him looking. "There are eighteen," he said softly. "One for each year."

"What's inside?" Cyrus asked, more than a little creeped out now.

Baba shrugged. "Things he left behind. Things that remind me of him. Sketches he made. Sawdust. Dead leaves."

Baba crinkled paper from the recycling bin and nestled it into the firewood beneath the box. Cyrus, unsure what to do, hung back.

"I thought you might understand." Baba sounded a little disappointed, a lot crazy. "I just don't want to see it anymore. I don't want to think about it, about him, about what I did or didn't do, I want to let him go. Let it all go. Let it burn."

He lit a match and threw it into the kindling. The paper started to curl back, and Cyrus felt the heaviness pressing down on him again. Oh God. They all needed so much help.

Remembering something, Cyrus said, "Hold on—I'll be right back." He ran up to his room to get Naveed's notebook, and when he returned, he tore out all the pages, crumpling them one by one and tossing them into the growing flames. Once they were all gone, he tossed in the paper cover. The thick cardboard puckered and twisted as it caught fire. Baba's face in the firelight was an unreadable mask.

"I understand, Baba," Cyrus said quietly. "You know, though, this wasn't your fault. Nobody blames you."

"It's not just that," Baba said. "Your mother. I don't know what to do for her. I don't want to lose her, too, I see her fading, but I don't know what else I can do."

This confession knocked Cyrus unexpectedly off-kilter: even his capable, strong father didn't know how to get through this any better than Cyrus did.

He wasn't even going to try to stay composed in the face of all this. It all came down as he watched the fire burn, crashing over him, everything he'd shoved out of his mind rushing back in. Everything. Naveed slumped in the bathroom, the heavy boots clomping up the stairs, flashing lights and ambulance doors closing, texting Andi from the waiting room, the airplane, the avocado tree, the dinner with Brennan, the waves, the salty kiss, the hot tub, the guilt, the guilt, the guilt.

Cyrus watched the flames consume the box. When the fire died down, Baba hugged him and said he was going to bed. Cyrus, though, had something else to do before he would be able to rest.

He found some paper and a pen, then sat down at the dining room table to write the letter he should have written a long time ago.

Dear Andi,

I'm sorry. I shouldn't have waited so long to say this, but maybe you'll understand by the time you finish reading. Did you hear about Brennan? I can't believe it. I guess you never know when your number's up. Who knows, I could be gone tomorrow, too, but I don't want to go without finally doing the right thing: telling you the truth. You'll probably still hate me, but at least maybe you'll see why I had to run from it. Well, I guess

you can't run forever, because it caught up with me
tonight, and this confession is the only way I can
move past it. Or something.

Okay. Here's what happened. Here's the worst thing
I've ever done, written down on paper, so I sincerely
hope you'll burn this or shred it or whatever when
you finish reading. Nobody else knows all this, not
even my parents, not even Dev. I've never been able to
tell anyone.

So. That Night. I came home from work and it took
me forever to get to sleep because I knew I only
had a few hours before our flight to LA. I had
to be quiet when I came in because Naveed was
sleeping, or at least I thought he was. But once I
finally drifted off, he shook me awake.

He asked me where the pills were. Said he couldn't
sleep, sounded really desperate. I was so tired, I
didn't want to get up, so I told him where the box
was, that if he brought it to me I would unlock it
and give him one of the sleeping pills.

Then I must have drifted off, but part of me was
fretting in my sleep, and I woke up again and realized
Naveed wasn't in the room. So I got up and looked
for him, and when I found him in the bathroom he
was sitting on the floor, leaning against the wall. He
must have known where I hid the key, because there
were pills all over the place, painkillers, the empty
bottle on its side next to him, and he looked really
out of it.

Obviously, I was freaked out, but tried to be rational
and asked how many he'd taken, and he didn't really
answer, just said his feet were hurting really bad,
his hands too, and he couldn't get up. I was so

scared he'd OD'd, so I turned to get my phone but he grabbed me and begged me not to go. He said he'd rather die than go to the hospital. And I could tell that he meant it.

He kept begging. But I shook free, found my phone and called an ambulance, and when I got back to the bathroom he was hunched over, gathering up a big handful of pills and muttering to himself about how much he hated me, how he'd never trust me again, never forgive me.

And it just made me so mad, just completely fed up. I was sick of dealing with him. Sick of not being able to sleep at night, waking up to him coughing or screaming or freaking out and having to talk him down. Dealing with his moods and tantrums during the day, always being nice to him even when he was a total jerk. It was exhausting. And here I was trying to keep him from swallowing all those pills...

I kind of blew up. I said some terrible things, the worst things I could have possibly said, and immediately wished I could take them back. He stared at me for a second with these eyes, shocked, hurt, terrified, furious, all at the same time. And he shoveled all the pills into his mouth, and I tried to stop him but he chewed them up and then just kind of faceplanted onto the floor, and my dad was there all of a sudden and then the firefighters came running up the stairs, they were the first to get there, and they pushed me out of the way and I couldn't stop thinking it was all my fault, I was the one who told him where the pills were, I was the one who pushed him to do this to himself, I was the one who gave up on him just because I was tired of dealing with everything.

I'm a horrible person.

I found his journal later. It was full of disturbing shit. He thought about dying a lot. Once we got to Santa Barbara, I convinced myself that it was good I found him, because if it hadn't happened then, it would have been some other night. He would have found some other way. At least while he was in the hospital I knew he'd be safe. They wouldn't let anything happen to him there, and that gave me the freedom not to worry, and I felt—still feel— so completely sick over the whole thing, and I just wanted to never think about it ever again. But somehow that only made things worse.

I'm sorry I didn't tell you the whole truth. It was only because I was afraid of losing you, but I lost you anyway, and it's been just as awful as I thought it would be. I don't fool myself into believing we can ever have what we once did, but I hope that someday we can at least be friends again, because I miss you so much, and losing a brother has been really hard, not just for me but for all of us, and I think we've all gone a little nuts here in our isolation. We need more people like you around, Andi. Kind and thoughtful, willing to forgive. (I hope.)

Yours, C.

Before he could second-guess himself, he sealed it inside an envelope, grabbed his now-charged phone, and walked to her house through the back alley connecting their homes. It looked like she might still be awake; the light was on in her room. But he felt like a bit of a creeper sneaking through her backyard after midnight, and wasn't about to freak her out by knocking on her window. Instead, he jogged to the front door and stuck the letter through the mail slot before returning to the alley as quickly as possible.

As he walked back home, he decided to let her know it was there. He couldn't text her, since she'd apparently blocked him, but he might as well try email. He powered his phone back on and waited for it to wake up.

Cyrus entered the back gate as his phone buzzed, showing that he had a missed call. He stopped in shock when he saw who it was from: Brennan Walsh.

He looked behind him, as if expecting Brennan's ghost to be following. No, of course, that was ridiculous. The time stamp showed that the call had been made hours before, shortly after 8pm. When did Chef Thierry say Brennan had died? "A few hours ago," and that had been around ten, so….

So Brennan had tried to call Cyrus right before he died?

He hadn't left a voicemail, but when Cyrus waded through the rest of his notifications, he saw that Brennan had sent a follow-up text. With trepidation, Cyrus opened it.

Hi Cyrus, just met with your brother. He says he hasn't talked to you in a while so I hope you're ok. I'm headed to Seattle and there's something I need to talk to you about in person. Are you free tomorrow at 10am?

Cyrus sank into a chair on the dark patio. Wait, so this meant… his brother was alive? His brother was *alive*. And he had met with Brennan Walsh just before the CEO was killed.

The questions kept coming. What had Brennan needed to tell Cyrus, and why did he seem concerned about Cyrus being okay?

And Naveed. Why had *he* met with Brennan?

What happened after their meeting?

What had Naveed done?

II.

The Apple Orchard

Naveed

ON THE MORNING OF HIS EIGHTEENTH BIRTHDAY, NAVEED AWOKE to sun shining through the metal grate of the bridge above him. Cars buzzed overhead, a dense vibration that had been playing in his ears all night, probably the reason this bridge wasn't a refuge for other homeless people: it was loud here.

He pulled a deep breath into his lungs. Let it out slowly, smoothly. No catch in his throat, no cough. None last night, either.

He smiled.

The air was still chilly, and he pulled the sleeves of his hoodie over his hands. He opened his bag and took out the orange pill bottles, twisting the lids off with his palm, careful not to let them spill. He swallowed his morning meds, then packed himself up, feeling the sudden need to be far from this place.

Naveed was the only one in the streets, save for the sleeping-bag huddles on the Ave, which made him feel like he was wandering through a world in which he was one of the only humans left. And in that light he saw everything anew, noticing the way ivy snaked up buildings on the UW campus like carnivorous plants devouring brick, the foil-lined energy bar wrapper that caught the sun as if it were a precious jewel, the wads of chewing gum pressed against a wall in the shape of a heart. Beauty and filth, life and destruction, everywhere.

If he did what everyone wanted him to do, he'd be returning here in just over a month to start his freshman year of college. But the emptiness he felt while walking through campus only cemented what he already knew: he didn't belong here. He wouldn't be coming back.

He wished for coffee. He was tired, as always, but wasn't supposed to have too much caffeine because of his meds. So he found the closest café and bought himself an almond milk chai latte and a bagel. The sleepy barista barely even glanced at him, and when she asked for his name to write on the cup, he told her it was Nate.

He sat in a corner and sipped his drink, grateful for the way it warmed him on the inside. He was constantly cold now that his hair was gone. He'd buzzed it off in a park bathroom the day before, collecting the long curls in a nest of brown paper towels in the sink, then tossing them unceremoniously in the garbage. Funny, considering how long he'd been growing it out, how he wouldn't let anyone else cut it even though it had been a frizzy mess for months; he could still feel Brooke behind him, trying to comb out the tangles, saying nothing when big clumps came out as easily as pulling a drought-shriveled plant.

Nothing left of that now. Nothing left of any of it.

The bagel was too dry, so he only ate half before finishing the rest of his drink and leaving the cafe. Had to keep moving, though he doubted anyone cared he was gone. It wasn't exactly a secret that everyone was fed up with him.

Cyrus's words threatened to repeat themselves in his head, but he wouldn't let them. He drowned them out by reciting that passage from *The Blind Owl*, the one about the butcher that he couldn't get out of his mind. *The pleasure of cutting up the raw meat... the heads of the sheep with the dust of*

death on their eyes… they too had seen this, they too knew what the butcher felt.
He imagined himself as that butcher sometimes, wiping his bone-handled
knife on the legs of the sheep, embracing the decay, embracing his role
as a master of Death.

If only it had been like that. If only he'd had some power back in that
tiny room in Tara Snyder's lab, if he had been the one with the knife, maybe
it would be different. He wouldn't be this strange skittish creature who
passed out at the sight of a single drop of blood, who couldn't stomach
dairy or meat, who panicked and lashed out and hurt people, sometimes
without even remembering what he had done.

But now he was starting over. Now he was Nate, and Nate didn't have
any of this baggage, Nate had never even met Cyrus, he didn't know
anything about *The Blind Owl*. Nate was just beginning.

Naveed ducked into the nearest public library branch as soon as it
opened, then signed onto a computer to check his email. He held his breath,
hoping he'd find an unread message in the account he'd opened for Nate.

But it was empty. She hadn't written back.

Naveed exhaled, disappointed. He clicked into his Sent folder and
opened the message he'd written several days earlier to make sure it had
gone to the correct email address.

Documentary Film Help?

Aug 15 at 12:47am

N.M. <beyondthewindowpane@gmail.com>
to Vanesa Rosales <vanesa@rosalesfilms.com>

Dear Vanesa:

I just finished watching your first film and loved everything about it. I was
wondering if you have any openings for interns/volunteers to help out on
your new documentary. I'm happy to do whatever you need, no matter
how tedious, and am available to start right away.

Thank you for considering,
nate.

Pretty much the whole time Naveed had been in the psych unit, he'd been combing through mental lists of acquaintances who might offer routes out of his life in Seattle. As soon as he'd remembered a text conversation he'd had with his friend Ethan several months earlier, in which Ethan mentioned a local filmmaker who frequently offered internships for high school and college students, he felt the unfamiliar stirrings of excitement through his numb haze. That was a good sign, he thought. A signal that he was headed in the right direction.

He'd watched Vanesa Rosales's first documentary the night he got home. It was heart-wrenchingly beautiful, and as soon as it was over, he'd looked up the website of her independent film production company. Vanesa had smiled at him on the *About* page; she was maybe in her early thirties, with friendly brown eyes, dark skin, and a short Afro. Her first film had explored her family's longstanding roots in agriculture, going back to her mother's ancestors who worked as slaves in Mississippi plantations, and her new film would be a sequel of sorts, exploring the other half of her heritage. In collaboration with her father Fernando, who had grown up in the fields, this documentary would focus on modern-day indigenous Mexican farmworkers.

Yes, Naveed had thought. *This is it.* Being involved with this film would give him exactly what he needed: a project, a purpose.

But three days had passed with no response. Maybe she was busy filming?

A quick glance at her social media pages showed him that his hunch was correct. Vanesa had posted a selfie the night before. Behind her, a bruise-colored sunset framed the dusty brown hills in the distance. *Just arrived in Sunnyside, WA,* the caption read. *With any luck we'll soon be filming in the same organic apple orchard where my dad worked when I was a teenager.*

Naveed's excitement rose. There was nothing tying him to Seattle— maybe he could head out there, so that when she emailed back he could offer to help with filming. He'd never been to that part of Central Washington before, but Sunnyside sounded nice, and no one would ever think to look for him there. The break would be complete.

He looked up the bus schedule and found that there was a Greyhound leaving for the Yakima Valley from downtown Seattle in the evening. Perfect.

After logging off, he cleaned up in the library bathroom, forcing himself to look in the mirror at the face he barely recognized. He wasn't sure if buzzing his hair had been the right move. Without it, his face looked craggy, the ridges of his eyebrows and cheekbones so pronounced, his nose rising in the middle like a mountain peak. The beard trimmer had run out of charge before he'd gotten to his facial hair, though, so he'd left the scruffy black stubble. It made him worry about how they'd perceive him when he walked into the bank. After all, he could change his hair and his clothes and even his name, but he couldn't change his brown skin. He couldn't shake the label that had chased him all summer. *Terrorist.*

But this was the last task before he could leave this place, so he steeled himself and walked the few blocks to his credit union, making sure to keep his hands visible as he entered, trying to arrange his face into Nate's easygoing expression.

But to his surprise, the teller was friendly, though she called him "Mr. Mirzapour," which threw him off a little. She allowed him to take the maximum withdrawal from his account, no questions asked, and even wished him a happy birthday on his way out.

Before putting his wallet away, he took out his driver's license. His sixteen-year-old face grinned up at him. That carefree, oblivious face.

Naveed kept the ID in his hand while he hiked back down to the water. Then he tossed it in, relieved to be rid of it, ready to leave that person behind.

The card didn't sink, though. It floated on the surface, that tiny photo still smiling up at the sun.

Naveed hurled a handful of gravel into the water, pelting it with small stones, then finding larger rocks when that didn't work, heaving them in over and over again, not stopping until the ID finally disappeared into the depths, swallowed up by the muddy waves.

Naveed

AT FIRST, NAVEED LOVED SUNNYSIDE. THE CLIMATE WAS COMPLETELY different, hot and dry, and he could breathe so much easier. Sure, the small rural town was not a place he'd usually have chosen to live, with its shopping centers full of big-box stores, its many churches, its squat faded houses and fields of sagebrush. But he liked all of that, its unpretentiousness.

Under Nate's name, he booked himself a weekly rental in a motel, a middle-of-the-road accommodation with a comfortable enough bed and a mostly-functional swamp cooler. Since he paid in cash, they didn't even care about his lack of ID.

The land here was mostly flat, so he bought a cheap used bike, fixed it up, then took it out for a spin. After his long illness, he was woefully out of shape, and only made it five blocks before he had to turn back. But every day he pushed himself to go a little further.

After a few days he settled into a routine. First thing after waking up was to take his morning dose of the tricyclic antidepressant that made him drowsy and dry-mouthed but helped keep the nerve pain away.

(He refused to call it by the brand name that Genbiotix had dreamed up for it, not wanting to give them any publicity, even in his own head.) Then he'd go for a bike ride, and come home to have his breakfast shake and read for a while. None of that Persian literature or depressing poetry for Nate; he preferred escaping into fantasy worlds where good inevitably triumphed over evil.

Once he'd rested up, he took one of his daytime benzodiazepines—benzos, he called them in his mind—because being out in public still made him anxious. He hopped on his bike again and headed to the gym to lift weights, then to the library to check his email, which had so far remained empty. After that, back home for lunch, usually beans straight from the can with a few tortillas he bought from the mercado near his motel, then a siesta during the heat of the day when he tried to sleep. More often than not, he couldn't, despite his constant drowsiness. Sometimes he was tempted to take a sleeping pill, but he never did. Those, he was saving.

Instead, he'd lie there listening to Spanish-language radio, soaking up "the voice of the campesino" on KDNA. He had gotten all the way through second-year college Spanish before graduating from the Running Start program, and this was a good distraction for his brain. Even though it took a lot of energy to focus, working on translation kept him from dwelling on how very alone he was out here, or drifting into other dangerous territory.

In the evenings it grew cool as the sun descended, and he would get back on his bike, circling the farms and orchards surrounding Sunnyside, hoping to catch a glimpse of the film crew he would be working with as soon as Vanesa got back to him.

A week passed, and he heard nothing. He didn't want to believe that this silence meant *no*, so he paid for another week at the motel. He'd been trying to conserve money, but only had enough to live here for a few more weeks, so he began to look for other work. The problem was that he couldn't apply for a normal job without an ID. Plus, he didn't have a phone number, which made things more difficult.

Sometimes, he considered trying to find work in the fields. He was feeling a lot better now, and could probably handle it physically. But what if they sprayed pesticides on the crops while he was out working? All the anti-anxiety meds in the world couldn't stop him from losing his head if chemical mist began raining down, polluting his skin, filling up his lungs.

One day, he worked up the courage to stand with the day laborers outside the hardware store. He'd always been good at building things, so why not?

They were confused when they saw him approach, thinking he was offering them a job, but he explained in halting Spanish that he, too, was looking for work. They let him stand with them, but talked amongst themselves in dialects that were hard for him to follow. In his previous life, he'd often been mistaken for Hispanic, but he was so obviously not one of them, tall and wiry where they were stocky and muscular.

Eventually, a white guy who had just loaded up his truck with lumber approached and asked, loudly and slowly, for help building a fence. He only needed two people, he said.

Naveed stepped forward. The man glanced at him and shook his head. He selected two of the stronger-looking guys, who left to help him finish loading up.

Why had he even bothered trying? Naveed's face grew hot. He walked away from the others without a word and biked back home.

He turned on the radio and filled the bathtub nearly all the way up. Before he got in, he added a generous squirt of dish soap, since the bubbles kept him from looking at his scrawny body, at the unsightly scars on his wrists and the backs of his hands where the skin had grown back wrinkled and discolored, at the surgical scar on his chest, still an angry red slash.

Normally, being in the water calmed him. The way it held him up and reduced the sensations in his limbs helped him forget the constant numbness in his hands and feet, at least temporarily. He tried to listen to the men talking on the radio, but they couldn't drown out the thoughts that kept rising to the front of his mind.

You don't belong here.

Vanesa is never going to email you back. She doesn't want you.

Pretty soon you'll run out of money. And meds—they only gave you a month's supply. What'll you do when they're gone?

No one wants you here. No one wants you anywhere.

You are worthless.

The sleeping pills were on the nightstand. A whole bottle of them. He could down them all, drift to sleep right here in the nice cool water, slip underneath the surface and never come back up.

It would be so easy.

In a way, it felt good to imagine death and the forever-escape that it brought. Earlier in the summer, he'd never allowed himself to even consider suicide. All of his energy was focused on staying alive, on dragging himself through because he was promised that the misery would end, that he would get better eventually. He believed that. He wanted to make it through, prove that he could do this, prove that he could be normal again. Sometimes he'd lose resolve, but then he'd see Roya peeking shyly into his room or snuggling next to him in his chair on the back patio, and he knew he needed to stay.

But Cyrus had changed all that. Cyrus had changed everything.

Naveed squeezed his eyes shut, trying to shove the memories into the shadowy depths of his mind where he'd buried all the things that hurt. But it was no use. They came rushing back with violence, pummeling him, forcing him to remember those endless nights in the psych unit when he had struggled against his restraints, screaming for hours on end, pleading for someone to take off his socks because the neuralgia had flared up and the weight of the fabric made the pain unbearable, growing so desperate that panic grabbed him by the throat and he had to struggle for every breath, every cry for help. Still, no one stopped. They all bustled past his closed door without a glance. After a while he wasn't even sure if he existed anymore. It felt like a hellish purgatory, a place where time was suspended, where he might be trapped forever and ever.

The inpatient psychiatrist, a prim blonde lady in a white coat, eventually stopped by to inform him that they had locked him up and strapped him down because he was "a danger to himself and others." She spoke with him for all of five minutes before formulating a diagnosis that was laughable in its obviousness: PTSD. That only made him more disgusted with her, more convinced that she couldn't be trusted, since she apparently couldn't see that tying him up and keeping him here against his will was only driving him deeper into madness.

She'd asked him what had happened the night of the overdose, but he'd refused to tell her anything. He couldn't tell anyone. It was impossible to convey just how miserable he'd felt that night, how his feet had hurt so badly he couldn't even stand up, and all he wanted was relief, but he'd dropped the bottle of painkillers and couldn't pick up those slippery tiny pills. Of course Cyrus had barged in at that moment, assuming he knew what was going on, calling an ambulance even though Naveed begged him not to. Only then had Naveed started scooping up the pills, pressing them against his sweaty palm and scraping them off with his teeth even though the pain was excruciating, chewing them up so that it would be faster, mouth filling with bitterness as Cyrus said the words Naveed would never, ever, be able to purge from his brain.

Fine. You want to die so bad? Go right ahead! Our lives would be so much easier if we didn't have to worry about you anymore.

Naveed hadn't wanted to wake up at all, but the next thing he knew he was strapped to a hospital bed in the psych unit. After what felt like weeks, his parents were finally allowed to visit, but they only came because they had to pretend to be supportive. He could see it in their eyes. They were sick of him ending up here. Ashamed of their unstable son and all the trouble he kept bringing them.

He'd hoped—irrationally, since he knew everybody was out of town— that someone else would come to see him. Once, while drifting in and out of a half-sleep, he'd heard Andi's voice so clearly, like she was sitting there next to the bed. *Hey,* she had whispered, quietly, gently. *I just wanted you to know that I'm here.*

He had opened his eyes, suddenly hopeful. But the room was empty. Andi was not there. She had not come back. Those words were only a memory; darkness closed in again as he remembered when she'd said them, in that alley behind Parapluie. She'd been crouching beside him, not touching him though, her voice so calm. She'd played something from her phone's speakers, a beautiful piano melody that temporarily distracted him. A kindness he didn't deserve, not after what he'd done to Brooke.

He still didn't want to believe it had really happened, that he'd actually slammed her against a brick wall. But she had showed him the proof, the bruises inflicted by his hands, purple-black against her pale wrists. Her accusation had terrified him: he had hurt Brooke, physically hurt her, yet he didn't even remember doing it. He shouldn't have lashed out so defensively, shouldn't have said the horrible things he'd said, piling cruelty upon cruelty. Once she was gone, though, he told himself it was better that he'd driven her away. He didn't want to hurt her again.

Their relationship had been dying a slow death all summer anyway. It had gone sharply downhill after that first day they were finally alone, when she'd taken him back to her empty house and they had undressed each other, and he searched desperately for the spark of arousal but it just was not there, and they kissed and he felt nothing, the sensation of her naked skin pressing against his own turned his stomach instead of turning him on, and when she reached up to grab onto his hair her fingertips brushed against his forehead and he lost it, he bolted for the bathroom and threw up. After that, even thinking about sex made him queasy. Yet another way that he barely recognized himself these days.

Still, Brooke had been good to him, and the way he'd treated her was unacceptable. The guilt gnawed at him constantly.

That was the thing, though. All of this had been eating away at him, but not consuming him completely, leaving just enough for him to keep going on and on. He had been on the brink of death many times, and had never succeeded in crossing over. Even now, he couldn't trust that a bottle of sleeping pills and a tub full of water would take care of the job. Thinking about killing himself was kind of like dreaming of traveling to Iran: just another journey he could never take.

Naveed let his head sink deeper beneath the water, so that only his nose was above the surface. It wasn't only that he was afraid of failing. Something stronger was keeping him here: he needed to prove that he wasn't going to act out the script they expected him to follow, that their assumptions about him were wrong. He wasn't going to hurt himself or anyone else; he could function as a productive member of society. He could do this.

He dipped underwater, wanting to see how long he could hold his breath, and trying to cleanse his mind of these thoughts. He only made it to the count of eleven before coming back up. Once the water had cleared from his ears, he could hear the radio again, and snapped to attention when he heard the name of the speaker they were introducing: Vanesa Rosales.

"Thank you for joining us today, Vanesa," one of the hosts was saying. "You're currently working on a new film—can you tell us what it's about?"

"Yes, I've been following several migrant families as they move to various farms throughout the seasons. Some of them are U.S.-based, and others are in the guest worker program," Vanesa said. She was a fast talker, and Naveed wasn't able to translate every word, but the passion with which she spoke would be plain in any language.

Naveed understood most of what Vanesa was saying as she went on, how poorly the workers were often treated, how little they were paid, how the conditions in the farmworker camps were so bad—full of filth and disease and unsafe drinking water—that her crew hadn't even been given permission to film there. The workers weren't able to do anything about it, since they had been brought to the U.S. on H-2A guest worker visas to work for a specific employer who could fire them and have them deported if they spoke up.

Listening to this made Naveed mad, but it was refreshing to have his anger directed at something that didn't have to do with him. Hearing the interview only solidified his resolve: he was going to work on this film. Tomorrow, he would email Vanesa again. He'd show her how badly he wanted this.

And if she still didn't get back to him… then he'd have to take matters into his own hands.

Naveed

ONE MORNING SEVERAL WEEKS AFTER MOVING TO SUNNYSIDE, Naveed awoke to an unpleasant yet familiar sensation. It felt like someone was stabbing his hands and feet relentlessly, shoving the blades in deeper and deeper. He wanted to cry, or swear, or both: this was the first time he'd felt the nerve pain since they started him on the tricyclics. He had skipped last night's dose, though. He'd decided to go down to one a day. Buying himself time.

He was tempted to take a tricyclic now, but it would be better to wait until the evening. The pain was bearable as long as he didn't move around too much, and usually subsided during the daytime anyway.

Nothing he could do but wait for it to pass. While trying to ignore the *stab-stab-stab* of sharp objects that didn't actually exist, he watched a sunbeam slice through the curtains, illuminating the carpet. Something was off about it, though; it was the wrong color, an orangey-red instead of the usual bright sunshine. It felt so much like the light of dusk that he actually checked the time to see if he'd slept through the whole day, but the clock showed that it was 9:38 am.

When the pain finally subsided, he threw back the curtains, only to find a red sun high in the sky, a thick haze in the air. It looked like the world was ending, but, according to the news, it was only smoke from wildfires burning in Wenatchee. People with respiratory conditions were warned not to go outside.

Naveed had been breathing fine, but he still paused to wonder if he should continue with his plan. Despite all the antibiotics he'd been blasted with, he worried, sometimes, that the MRK bacteria had taken up permanent residence in his lungs. But the bug had also infected the skin on his wrists and hands, and even his blood. It could be anywhere, surviving in colonies all over his body, lying in wait.

He had no choice, though. He only had $18 left, which wasn't enough to pay for another night at the motel. Today, he had to make his move.

So he went through the motions of dressing, eating, brushing teeth. He packed everything he owned into his messenger bag and a small box that he tethered to the back of his bike. Then he turned in his key card at the office. The air outside was so smoky it smelled like a barbecue. Before hitting the library, he dug through his backpack for his inhaler, taking a hit and moving it to his front pocket.

He could feel ash from the fires being sucked into his lungs with each breath. But he had to do this. It was his only hope.

At the library, he checked his email. Nothing from Vanesa.

So it was official, then: she didn't want him. He'd been stupid to try, stupid to hang his hopes on that ridiculous long shot. It was time to close the door on that possibility. Time for Plan B.

He pedaled slowly down the road, heading for the only organic apple orchard in town, the only one he'd been able to find online anyway, where he planned to ask for a job in the fields. It didn't sound so bad to spend his days picking apples, and since it was organic he wouldn't have to worry about pesticide spray. Maybe, if he succeeded in getting the job, he could stay in the farmworker camps. Not that they sounded very appealing from Vanesa's interview, but at least he wouldn't have to worry about finding a job *and* housing.

There was, of course, the matter of his hands not working as well as they should. But what could be better physical therapy? Repetitive motion, building strength and agility.

The red sun hung heavy in the sky. Heavy like his breath, which felt like a weight, a thing he had to lift. At least the haze diffused the heat a little.

He took a left at the street he'd mapped, and was relieved when he noticed the small sign at the entrance to the property. *MORTENSEN FRUIT*, it proclaimed in block letters. He was in the right place.

Naveed walked up to the office trailer at the entrance to the property and opened the door. Inside, the air conditioning cooled his sweaty skin. No one was in the seating area in front, and he paused to examine a framed article on the wall. It featured a photograph of two smiling white guys shaking hands under an apple tree. *New partnership with Bountiful Earth Market makes Mortensen Fruit a major player in growing organics industry*, the headline read. Naveed looked away, disgusted at the thought of those guys getting rich while their exploited workers were stuck in dire poverty. He was tempted to turn around and leave, but at this point he didn't have much choice.

"Can I help you?" A man peeked his head out of his office: Luis Romero, according to the sign on his door.

Naveed stood up straighter. "Hi, I'm looking for a job. Could I fill out an application?"

Luis laughed, like Naveed had just told a particularly hilarious joke. Then he looked him up and down, shaking his head. "I don't think you'd be a good fit," he said.

Naveed squared his shoulders. Put his anger into his eyes instead of his mouth. "Why not? I'm willing to work hard. I need this—"

"You don't want to work out here. This job isn't for people like you. Why don't you go back to town, find something at the Walmart."

"No. *This* is what I want to do."

Luis met his eyes, scrutinized them. He seemed to see something there, a glimpse of Naveed's determination. "Habla español?"

"Sí," replied Naveed, without missing a beat. "Usted me puede dar el trabajo?"

Luis sighed. "Uno momento." He retreated to his office for a minute, and Naveed heard him talking to someone else over the radio. They spoke in Spanish, but Naveed got the gist of what the other voice was saying. *We've got a bunch of people out sick today. Sure, we can take him.*

Luis returned. "Can you start right now?"

Naveed smiled. "Absolutamente."

"But only as a trial period. You'll get paid in cash at the end of the day, the piece rate based on how much you pick. If you don't work fast enough, or we don't need you anymore, you're out."

"Deal. And if it works out, can I stay in the farmworker camp?"

Luis looked at him in disbelief. "No. Housing is for guest workers only."

"Oh, of course." Dammit. Where was he going to sleep tonight? At least he'd be getting cash at the end of the day. A half-day's work should be enough to cover one night at a cheap motel.

Luis walked him out to the orchard. Endless, perfect rows of apple trees stretched out before them. The noon sun, still cloaked in the haze of smoke, hung high in the sky. Workers, most of them men, hurried between the trees and gigantic plastic bins, emptying the bulging barrel-like bags slung around their chests.

"Ramón!" Luis called to one of them.

Ramón jogged over. He had a bandana tied around his face, probably to protect against the smoke. "Yeah, boss?" he asked in Spanish.

"Got a new one here. Show him what to do."

Ramón pulled down his bandana and extended his hand. "First day?"

Naveed nodded, accepting the handshake. "I'm Nate."

"Ramón. Nice to meet you." His eyes crinkled as he smiled, revealing a gap between his front teeth. "Let's go get you a ladder."

As they walked, Ramón introduced him to the bosses, none of whom seemed to take much interest. They handed Naveed a bag and a tripod ladder, then showed him the bin where he would be unloading his harvest.

Naveed stared into it. Though it was white, it was like looking into an abyss. According to Ramón, it held about 1,000 pounds of apples.

"Every time you fill a bin, you get a chip," Ramón explained as they carried their ladders into the orchard. "Hold onto it, because—"

"Wait, wait," Naveed said. "You fill more than one of these every day?"

Ramón laughed. "You'd better. I can do fifteen on a good day."

Naveed swallowed. *Fifteen?* Ramón could pick *fifteen thousand pounds* of apples in a single day?

Ramón set up his ladder next to a tree, marking it as his. The branches bent under the weight of all the red apples. "They'll cut you some slack because it's your first day. But you'd better get at least three full, or else they'll fire you. Here, watch." He scrambled up the ladder. "The trick is to never, ever just pick one apple per hand. Do two, or better yet, three." It only took Ramón a minute to fill his bag, then he darted down the ladder and over to the container, depositing the apples into his bin.

He gestured at Naveed. "Now, go."

It took Naveed a while to pick his first bag. Everyone else casually climbed their ladders all the way to the top, but he had to be extra careful not to lose his balance, and to watch his feet while descending so that he didn't miss a rung. His hands were clumsy at first, dropping the occasional apple, but he soon got into a rhythm. When he dumped his first bag, he felt a brief burst of triumph—it was an accomplishment for him, anyway—until the supervisor who handed out the chips berated him for his slowness.

Naveed walked briskly back to his tree, and repeated the same cycle over and over again for the next six hours. He wished he'd remembered to bring a protein bar out to the orchard, and found himself at the top of his ladder secretly devouring an apple midway through the afternoon. It struck him that this was the first time he'd eaten fresh food in weeks. He always passed up the fruits and vegetables at the mercado because they were too expensive.

Occasionally, he had to sit in the shade for a few minutes and take a hit from his inhaler, knowing that he was losing precious picking time, but needing a break from the endless tedium. All the while, the other workers barely paused in their *up the ladder - fill the bag - down the ladder - fill the bin* loop.

By the time the day was over, he had picked almost three bins. Several buses had pulled up, but Naveed wanted to finish his, get his last chip. He was about to head back to his tree when he ran into Ramón, who had a full bag of apples.

"Take mine," he said. "I already got to fifteen today."

Thankful, Naveed switched bags with Ramón behind a tree when no bosses were looking, and Naveed brought back the apples, adding them to the bin. He looked expectantly at the supervisor.

"It's not full yet," the supervisor said.

"C'mon, man, it's close enough," Ramón spoke up from behind Naveed.

"Nope, sorry."

"I guess I should… do a few more…." Naveed turned around to look back at his tree, but this made him dizzy and he had to steady himself on the edge of the container. Every muscle ached; the idea of picking even one more apple made him want to slit his own throat.

Another worker came up to Ramón and said something in a language Naveed didn't understand. Ramón answered, then looked at Naveed and said in Spanish, "This is my friend Javier. Javier, Nate."

Naveed shook Javier's extended hand and they exchanged holas. "Sorry, Nate, I've gotta go catch the bus," Ramón said. "See you tomorrow." He walked off with Javier.

The dizziness didn't subside as Naveed made his way back to the tree he'd been working on. He probably shouldn't be climbing ladders right now. That last bin would have to go unfilled.

He turned in his ladder, then spotted Luis, who gestured for him to return to the office. Once inside, Luis asked, "Got your chips?"

"Sí." Naveed handed over his two precious chips.

"Where are the rest?"

"This is all."

Luis shook his head as he opened a small cash box. "Piece rate is half a cent per pound. So two bins, 2,000 pounds…" He handed Naveed a $10 bill.

Naveed was speechless. He'd worked harder this afternoon than he ever had in his life, all for ten bucks?

"If you want to come back tomorrow, harvest starts at 6 a.m."

"Are you fucking serious?" Naveed said in English, his anger spilling over.

Luis stared at him. "This is how it works out here. You don't like it, you don't have to come back."

Naveed turned and left. Despite his exhaustion, he hopped on his bike, which was still parked outside the office. He needed to get out of here, get away from Luis, because all he could think about as he pedaled away was how good it would feel to strangle him.

Naveed

NAVEED DIDN'T BIKE FOR LONG BEFORE HE NEEDED TO STOP. Dizziness and anger swirled confusingly together, each feeding the other somehow, and the path ahead of him was all distorted and his heart was beating too fast and he felt like he was no longer in control of anything that was happening in his body or his head.

He trampled into the brush alongside the road and sat down to rummage through his bag. He quickly ate a protein bar, then swallowed a benzo with the last dribble of liquid from his water bottle.

Naveed lay back, hoping he was invisible from the road, waiting for the pill to take effect. His body was worn out but his mind was on fire, he imagined it combusting, smoke pouring out from his ears, adding to the murk in the air, so much taut rage wound up like a spring inside him, fists curled, teeth clenched, ready to fight not flee, wanting to beat something to a pulp, not that he'd be able to do that without passing out, haha, what a wreck, what a *fucking wreck* this was, not just this situation but his life, his life was a total complete absolute wreck.

He had nowhere to go. He couldn't afford even the cheapest motel.

Ten dollars. All that work for ten dollars! How did the farmworkers stand it? How did they survive?

He didn't know *how*, but he knew that they *did*. They survived, and they kept coming back day after day. He focused on this truth, guiding his thoughts away, once again, from the bottle full of sleeping pills nestled at the bottom of his backpack. No. All those workers, they could handle this. He could handle it, too.

Blood pulsing in his ears. The thump of his heart. The smoke in his lungs. The cough coming back. Well, three weeks was a pretty good run. What did he expect, to keep getting better, to get strong enough to leave illness behind forever? That wasn't how it worked at all. It would get better for a while before getting worse again. This endless cycle! The futility of everything!

He lay there, his thoughts wheeling in escalating spirals, for what seemed a very long time, until the drugs kicked in and smoothed them out. He was finally able to relax his hands, and stared at the half-moon indents his fingernails had made in his palms. No broken skin, though, that was good, and at least he'd been able to stay within himself, he knew that he'd been lying here motionless, hadn't dissociated and lost a chunk of time where he acted on impulses without conscious knowledge. That needed to be avoided at all costs.

He got back on his bike. He could go buy a sleeping bag. Find some quiet field to sleep in, maybe. But he was all turned around now and wasn't sure how to get back to the main road. He headed down the one he thought was correct, pedaling slowly. The heat had let up a little, but the air was stagnant. He pushed through it.

And then the girl ran out in front of him.

He saw her dart out onto the road, tripping on a raised lip of pavement and sprawling right in his path. He swerved out of the way, hitting the gravel shoulder, the tires skidding out from under him. He managed to catch himself before falling completely, but stumbled clumsily into the brush, clutching his heart, it was beating so fast but the benzo was trying to slow it down, and it was a supremely uncomfortable feeling, a war inside his chest.

From where he was kneeling, he could see the girl, who had thankfully moved out of the middle of the road, but was sitting on the other side crying quietly.

Once he'd calmed down a bit, he walked across the road, approaching her cautiously.

"Are you okay?" he asked in English, but at her blank expression repeated it in Spanish. She looked up at him as he spoke, and for a second his heart sped up again: she looked so much like Roya. Her eyes were wide, her hair long and dark, and she seemed very young, maybe five or six.

She shook her head, still sniffling, and pointed at her knee. It was purple-red, a big bruise already forming there. Not skinned, no blood, thankfully.

"You are with someone?" Naveed asked. "Your mother?"

The girl said nothing.

He wanted to help, but it was obvious from the wary way she regarded him that she knew he was an outsider and didn't trust him. Smart.

She tried to get up, but winced when she put weight on her leg. That knee definitely could use some ice. "Can I find someone?" he offered. "To help you get home?"

"No. I'll be okay. You can go," she responded in Spanish.

He couldn't, though. She was hurt, and it seemed to him like they were far from everything. "Here, hop on my bike. I will push you home. If you feel better and want to walk, tell me and I will help you down."

She nodded hesitantly. "Okay. That sounds okay."

He held the bike steady as she climbed on, then pushed it from the front handlebars. She balanced pretty well, and the road was flat and devoid of traffic. Still, it was an uncomfortable position, and he was relieved when she told him to turn down a side road and said she could walk from there.

He was about to leave when he heard someone yelling. "Gabriela!"

"Papi!" she yelled back, limping down the road. Naveed watched as a man emerged from around a bend and gathered her up in a big hug—and a second later, realized he knew who it was.

Ramón noticed Naveed at the same time. "Nate. Hola."

"Cómo estás," Naveed said, but Ramón didn't answer. Gabriela was chattering in his ear. Naveed turned around to leave them to it, but Ramón stopped him.

"Thank you for helping my daughter. We were about to have dinner—would you like to join us?"

"Oh, I—I don't know, I should go now."

Gabriela regarded him with her big eyes. "Please stay."

Who was he kidding—he was starving, and desperately thirsty. "Okay, yes, I would like to eat with you, please. Gracias."

He followed them around the bend to a cluster of ramshackle buildings, long rows of them studded with frequent doors. *The farmworker camp*, he thought.

Ramón led them to the end of one of the buildings, where a round-faced woman stood in the doorway, her tank top straining against the globe of her belly. Her dark hair was pulled back, her full lips flicking up in a tentative smile.

After Ramón introduced "Nate" to his wife, Marisol, and told her about what had happened to Gabriela, she welcomed Naveed in, then removed a can of soda from the mini-fridge and held it to her daughter's knee.

Naveed scrubbed his hands off in the sink before joining them at the small table. He sat on the cardboard box they offered him for a chair and waited for the oscillating fan to blow in his direction. Their cabin had several windows, so at least there was a cross breeze, but it was still sweltering inside.

Marisol moved as if her body was a great burden. She shuffled across the floors, her belly getting in the way of everything. Naveed didn't recall seeing her in the orchard. He hoped she had been able to spend the day resting instead of scurrying up and down ladders.

As she carried over a plate of tortillas and started spooning some sort of stew into bowls, Naveed took in the tiny living space, the bedroom area with a mattress on the floor and a separate nest of pillows off to the side, wet clothes hanging from a makeshift clothesline that bisected the room, the toilet barely hidden from view by a mildewy shower curtain.

Ramón brought Naveed a plastic cup of water that he ladled out of a stock pot on the counter. Naveed thanked him, trying to drink it slowly. He didn't want to think about what might be in the stew, but the calm buzz from the benzo kept him safely zoned out.

"So, Nate, where are you from?" Ramón asked, settling himself back onto his box-chair.

"Seattle," Naveed answered.

"But where is your family from?"

He knew what Ramón meant. Naveed's Spanish was far from perfect; he understood the language a lot better than he spoke it. He was obviously not a native speaker. He stared at his bowl and said, "I have no family." He couldn't tell the truth, but even this tacit denial of his Iranian heritage was painful somehow.

"What brings you here? Have you worked in the fields before?" Marisol asked as she sat down.

"I have been looking for work. I have not done this kind of work before. Today was my first day. It was very very hard." He took a bite of the stew. There were some chewy, meaty bits, but as long as he didn't think about it, they were easy to ignore. Whether he'd be able to keep it down was another issue, but he'd deal with that later. Wanting to get the focus off himself, Naveed asked, "So, where are you from?"

As they ate, Ramón and Marisol explained that they'd come to the States from Oaxaca when Marisol was pregnant with Gabriela six years earlier. Naveed had assumed that they were part of the guest worker program, but their downcast eyes and quiet voices led him to wonder if their journey had been a different kind. The conversation moved on, and he didn't ask for details.

Ramón was trying to learn English, so Naveed practiced with him for a bit. Marisol taught him a few words of their native language, Mixtec, which was spoken in many regional variations by lots of the other farm-workers. Once Gabriela had finished eating and headed back outside to play, Ramón leaned back in his chair and said something to Marisol in Mixtec. Naveed took the opportunity to let his tired mind drift. They had been so kind to him, but he couldn't ask to stay with them. There was so little space here as it was. Now that he was sitting down, though, he didn't want to get back on his bike to buy a sleeping bag and look for a good spot to spend the night.

His attention was jerked back to the present when Ramón addressed him in Spanish. "Hey Nate, tomorrow there's going to be a film crew at the farm with us. They're going to ask you to sign some papers so that you can be in the film. You should sign them."

"Really?" was all Naveed could think to say. His heart was beating faster again. It had to be Vanesa's project, right?

"Yeah, it's important. Marisol and I have been working with them for a while, but it took a long time to get permission to film at the farm. I just hope that if people see what our lives are like, they might understand. Most of the time it feels like we're invisible—no one cares about us, and I want…" Ramón paused. "I want a life better than this for my children. And it's been bad lately. The heat, the smoke, the sickness going around… I hope that the film gets people's attention. Because otherwise, what's it going to take? Does someone have to die out here before they'll finally listen to us?"

Naveed felt a little breathless. "Yes. Of course. I will sign." Then, judging that the time was right, he added, "I am wondering how I can stay here in the camp? I need a place to stay. My own place." He stumbled over the words, hoping that they understood he wasn't trying to invite himself over.

Ramón and Marisol exchanged a look. "Javier mentioned—I think there's an empty cabin over near him," Ramón said. "You could probably get away with staying there a week or two."

"Oh, thank you! Yes, I will take it," Naveed said. He got up and thanked Marisol for the meal using the Mixtec word she'd just taught him, tatsa'vi, then followed Ramón outside. They walked through the rows of houses, stopping only briefly to knock on Javier's door and ask which cabin was vacant. Naveed thanked him when he pointed the way to Cabin 29, a few doors down. Javier just shook his head and retreated back inside.

The door wasn't even locked. Ramón opened it for Naveed, who trailed behind him with his bicycle. The first thing he noticed was the stuffy air, heavy with the stench of decaying garbage. And it was small, much smaller than Ramón's place, with only one window and a twin mattress on the floor, a heap of twisted sheets and blankets on top. It looked like someone had just left.

Naveed stood frozen in the doorway. Once again, he was thankful for the benzo sending its calming buzz through his brain.

Ramón opened the window and wrestled the garbage bag out of the can, letting loose a cloud of flies as he did so. "I'll take this out. Oh, and don't drink the water. You have to boil it first. See you tomorrow." With that, he was gone, and Naveed forced himself to wheel his bike inside cabin 29, his new home.

Naveed

WEDNESDAY, SEPTEMBER 9

NAVEED LEFT THE DOOR OPEN SO HIS CABIN COULD AIR OUT.
He did his best to ignore the questions sprouting in his mind: *why did someone leave here without taking out the garbage? Or packing up the blankets?* Everything about the situation felt wrong, but what other option did he have?

The stench of rot made his stomach tighten, so he breathed through his mouth. Even though he wanted to lie down, he needed water to take his evening meds, so he dumped out the cloudy contents of the stock pot. The bottom was all rusty—how long had the water been sitting in there?—so he scrubbed out what he could and filled it up with water from the sink. Then he put it on the hot plate and cranked the heat to bring it to a boil.

The air was too stuffy. He opened the only window, which looked out on the row of buildings opposite him. Somewhere, a radio played. The music was energetic and lively, but it was somehow the loneliest sound in the world.

A fly buzzed by him, bolting for freedom through the open door, but that only made the remaining ones seem louder. The dense vibration of tiny beating wings filled up his ears, trying to pull him into the shadowy abyss nestled deep inside his mind where horrifying memories lurked.

Oh God. He was going to throw up. It was creeping up on him again, the suffocating dread, the paralyzing panic. *No. Don't let it out. Keep it buried. Pack the dirt back down. You're okay. Everything's okay.*

It wasn't, of course, but he distracted himself by rifling through his bag for the ginger candies he had brought from his nightstand at home, and found them zipped in a front compartment next to his house keys. The silver star charm Roya had given him caught the light. Winking at him. Reminding him of what he had left behind.

He unwrapped a ginger chew and sucked on it, hugging his knees, resting his forehead on them. His keys. They were still in his bag, all of them, even the key to the minivan, which he hadn't been able to take off the chain even though the van had exploded to bits, even though it was also a constant reminder that his parents had never given him a key to their new car, since they wouldn't let him drive yet. His house key, though. That one he could use. He pictured himself walking up to the front door, turning the key in the lock—

No. He was never going back there. Never.

After the ginger candy was gone, he managed to let go of his knees. A shower, that's what he needed.

He closed the front door, locked it, drew the curtains, stripped off his sweaty clothes and stepped underneath the cool water, which helped a lot. He always felt better when he was clean. By the time he'd slipped on his boxers, the pot of water had finished boiling, so he took his tricyclic with a tiny sip of hot water.

He pushed aside the funky-smelling blankets on the bed and lay down. As soon as he did, the cough started up again, so persistent that he could barely get a breath in. This was how it had been for months, tolerable during the day but getting worse the second he tried to go to sleep. He couldn't stand this. Not tonight.

What he needed was that cough syrup, the codeine-laced stuff they'd sent him home with earlier in the summer, which he'd found in the medicine box. He took two doses, then swallowed a sleeping pill for good measure. He didn't want to think. Just wanted oblivion. And, hopefully, the meds would prevent him from crying out in his sleep. The window was still open. Everyone would hear.

This is miserable, he thought while waiting for them to kick in. *Why am I here? Why am I doing this to myself?*

The keys. The silver star charm. He had a way back in. He could walk away from all this, go right back home....

No. He couldn't go back to his exasperated parents, couldn't go back to Cyrus, who had probably been telling everyone how he'd heroically saved his brother from committing suicide. The whole world probably knew about it by now, and the ghost of that moment would follow Naveed forever; if he came back they'd probably lock him up in a mental institution, the way the doctors had wanted in the first place. Meanwhile Cyrus got to be the sane gallant hero and hold Andi's hand and feel her skin beneath his fingertips and love her without complication, without crushing darkness always trying to close in, without the constant struggle to be happy and normal. Cyrus just *was* happy and normal. The way Naveed was, once.

No. Not going back. He wasn't even Naveed anymore, right? He was Nate. Nate, Nate, Nate. He had to remember. Nate didn't even know... he knew none of this... Nate was not going back to Seattle, never... never... never....

The next thing he knew, the door was rattling. Naveed struggled to wake up. Where was he? What time was it? Why was the door shaking?

"Nate, you in there?" Ramón. That was Ramón's voice.

Naveed sat up stiffly, then stumbled to the door and opened it.

Ramón's eyes widened, and only then did Naveed remember he was wearing nothing but his boxers. It was still dark outside, but floodlights from the next row of cabins washed him in yellow light. He saw what Ramón was staring at. That smooth scar between his ribs, thick and long, pink against his brown skin. He moved to cover it up, but then he remembered his hand was scarred, too, so he ran his fingers through his nonexistent hair instead, hoping the gesture looked casual. "What is going on?"

Ramón blinked. "Oh—the bus comes in ten minutes. Sorry, should've warned you last night that it gets here early."

"Yeah. Okay. Yeah. Thanks." Naveed closed the door.

Was he really doing this? Going back for another day in the fields where he might earn another ten fucking dollars, if he was lucky?

Well, what else was he going to do? Lie here all day in this foul-smelling room, a prisoner to his dark thoughts? No, thank you.

There was another alternative, one that had been blooming in the back of his head while he slept, leaking out from the deep dark hole where he'd buried it and solidifying rapidly, equal parts terrifying and difficult to ignore.

He pushed it out of his mind now, though, and got ready as fast as he could, but the sedatives made him feel like he was moving through an underwater world. He hoped the bus would wait.

Before leaving, he grabbed a couple of protein bars from his dwindling stash, filled up his water bottle from the stock pot, and dumped all his meds into a plastic bag that he could keep in his pocket. Then he closed the door behind him, hoping the rest of his stuff would be safe, since he couldn't lock it up.

Tiny flakes of ash brushed against his face as he walked. Looked like today was going to be even smokier. Good thing he'd remembered his inhaler.

He arrived in the parking lot just as the bus pulled up. Ramón was standing next to Javier, speaking with him in Mixtec, and both of them nodded at Naveed when he approached. He nodded back, stifling a cough with a swig from his water bottle, and sat in the back of the bus right behind Ramón. He leaned his head against the window. The meds wanted to drag him back down to sleep again, but he forced himself to stay awake by chewing on one of his protein bars.

The ride didn't take long, no more than five minutes. They drove along the perimeter of the orchard, then passed through the main gates and down a small road before coming to a stop alongside several other buses filled with workers.

No one moved to get off the bus. Everyone sat there, some sipping from thermoses of coffee, a few talking, but everyone mostly quiet, looking out windows or lying down in their seats.

Ramón turned around. "We have to wait till the bosses get here. Might be a while."

Naveed couldn't believe it: he'd gotten up before dawn to catch a bus just so he could sit around and wait until the bosses decided to show up?

Ramón rested his head against the back of the seat, pulling his hat over his eyes.

Naveed felt a distant surge of anger against the bosses for this blatant power play, the message that it sent: *Our time is valuable. Yours is not.* He couldn't believe the workers put up with this day after day. But no one else seemed to care, so he settled in against the window. At least this would give him a chance to finish sleeping off the meds.

He woke up when he heard the door open. Two people were climbing the stairs onto the bus. Naveed recognized one of them instantly.

Vanesa was dressed casually in a sweatshirt and skinny jeans, but even so, she had a commanding presence that made it hard to look away. Behind her, an older man whom Naveed assumed must be her father, Fernando, leaned on a cane.

Naveed's heart hammered away. He could go right up to them now, say he was Nate, the guy who had emailed about the job, and beg them take him away from this life, away to the one that Naveed had wanted when he invented Nate in the first place.

But that was a stupid, impossible idea. Vanesa had ignored his emails. He had been rejected, simple as that. The option to work with them no longer existed.

"Buenos días," Fernando said, then switched to Mixtec for a while before explaining about the documentary in Spanish. After taking a few questions, he distributed the film release forms. Naveed quickly signed an illegible scribble.

Vanesa came through to collect the forms. Naveed pulled his sleeves down to cover his hands, so that she wouldn't see his scars when she took it. But she barely glanced at him. "Gracias," she said, and moved on to the next person, because he was one of them now, just another worker on the bus, waiting to start another day of toil.

Naveed

THURSDAY, SEPTEMBER 10

THE DAY PASSED IN A BLUR. NAVEED DID HIS BEST TO AVOID being caught by the filmmakers' cameras. It wasn't hard to do, since they spent a lot of time filming Ramón, who was working the next row down. Naveed watched them from his vantage point in the tree tops as he picked. He listened to Vanesa's conversations, in English, as she and her small crew—two camera guys and a sound lady—discussed lighting and camera angles and a bunch of other technical stuff that, at one time, might have intrigued him. None of that was of much use to him anymore, though.

During their lunch break, Naveed wandered off by himself to eat a protein bar while Vanesa spoke with Ramón and some of the other workers. The bosses stood nearby, watching intently. It was obvious that the filmmakers' presence here was not welcome, but Vanesa didn't seem bothered by the bosses' silent hostility. She ignored it, focusing all of her attention on the workers instead, listening to their stories and capturing them on film, with Fernando sitting beside them acting as a translator.

The afternoon was the hardest. At least the smoke kept the sun from beating down on them, but it irritated Naveed more and more; he climbed his ladder slower and slower as he grew shorter and shorter of breath. He had filled three bins, which was already better than yesterday, but the bosses mocked him every time he came back with another bag, spitting words at him that he didn't understand. Didn't matter. Their intent was clear enough.

Naveed hurried away, determined to speed up, to make it to at least five bins today. He climbed into the branches, stuffing apples into his bag faster than he ever had before, filling it within minutes.

But he was so focused on moving quickly that he forgot to look at his feet while descending the ladder, and one millisecond of carelessness was all it took: he missed the next rung, couldn't find his balance, suddenly the world was tilting—

He was falling—

Hard ground beneath his cheek. An ache in his left shoulder.

With a swoop of nausea, he tumbled backwards in time, as the shadow-creatures clawed through the dirt and swirled around him thicker than smoke, surrounding him, dragging him into their horrible abyss… his shoulder digging into the floor… and he couldn't move, because he was tied up… the rope, had to break the rope….

"What the fuck was that about?" came an angry voice that didn't belong. The words were in Spanish. The ground was not made of smooth metal. It was dirt. His hands weren't tied up, they were free.

He grabbed onto the voice like it was a hook, pulling him out of that other place. "Get up," the voice was commanding. "Get up, right now."

Spanish. He was Nate now, and Nate didn't remember any of those things. Nate wasn't stalked by shadows. When Nate fell off a ladder, he sprang back up again.

Naveed pushed himself up with his right hand, letting his left arm hang by his side. The whole thing was numb. There were apples all over the ground. His bag was empty. He'd have to start over.

"Sit in the shade and drink this." The boss practically threw the bottle of water at Naveed. "Then get back to work."

As he walked away, he called out, "He's fine. Anyone else need water? Keep drinking, it's hot."

It seemed odd that the bosses suddenly cared whether they were getting enough water, but when Naveed raised his eyes to look around, he saw why: Fernando and one of the camera people stood about twenty feet away from him. Capturing the whole thing on video.

Fernando called out something that Naveed didn't quite catch—probably asking if he was all right. Naveed nodded and turned away, too shaken to do anything but stumble into the shade with his water. Once Fernando had moved on, he hunched into a ball to take a secret breath from his inhaler. Then he got up as if nothing had happened and climbed back up the ladder.

It took a while before he could use his left hand again, and by the end of the day he was still working on filling his fifth bin. He wanted so badly to get at least five chips, so he worked frantically, even though his body was screaming at him to stop. He kept picking as the other workers filled their last bins and lined up to turn in their ladders and buckets and chips. Ramón had stopped by to check on him, but Naveed waved him off. "See you on the bus."

"One more bucket," the supervisor said. Naveed glanced at the line, at the waiting buses, and gauged that he could get one more in before the bus left. So he ran back to the tree, picked his last bag, dumped it into the bin, and got his fifth chip.

But he still needed to stop by the office, so he walked as quickly as he could to see Luis, who arched his eyebrows at the five chips. "You picked all day and this is all you got?"

Naveed wanted to defend himself, but what could he say? *I fell off a ladder and can still barely move my left arm?* No chance in hell. "I'll do better tomorrow."

Luis shrugged, because what did it matter to him? He handed Naveed his $25—a real windfall!—and sent him on his way.

He stepped outside just in time to see the last bus pulling away. Goddammit. Looked like he'd be walking home.

He trudged along the road. It was a few miles around the perimeter of the orchard back to the camp. Would've been so much faster with a bike.

The swaying tall grasses, bleached as bones, rustled menacingly. For a second he swore he saw a white figure moving through them, advancing on him rapidly, and he froze as his heart seized in panic, but the figure vanished as soon as he tried to focus on it.

Just a mirage. From the heat.

Everything's fine, he told himself. *Just get home. Take a cold shower, drink some water, down a couple of sleeping pills. Then you won't have to think anymore.*

Yes. That sounded nice.

Why stop at a couple? The question rose from nowhere, from everywhere, floating to the top again.

Then, Ramón's voice. *What's it going to take? Does someone have to die out here before they'll finally listen to us?*

STOP. He couldn't let himself go down that track, no, no, no. He would get home and sleep, then pick eight bins tomorrow. Eight bins. How much would that earn him? Five dollars a bin. Five times eight. What was five times eight?

The tall grasses bent in the wind. Their shadows seemed to move independently from them, thickening and pulling away from the ground. Naveed blinked and they returned to their rightful places.

He shook his head. Mirages. That was all.

Just ahead, he noticed a trail someone had beaten into the grass. He veered toward it, wanting to be alone for a minute to gather his wits, which felt like they were rapidly disappearing.

He was so focused on the blades of grass, looking for any shadows that were too thick, that he didn't notice when the path widened into a small clearing. As soon as he stepped into it, someone shrieked.

He stopped, startled to see the little girl crouched in the weeds. Gabriela.

"You almost wrecked my village," she said in Spanish.

Now that he looked down, he could see that he'd nearly stepped on something: a cluster of tiny stick-houses.

"Lo siento," Naveed said. Grateful for the distraction, he kneeled next to her. "It is a pretty village. Who lives here?"

Gabriela picked up two small sticks and laid them in her palm, very gently. "This is the mami." She pointed to one. "And the papi."

"Oh. Where are their kids?"

"They don't have kids yet. The mami has one coming, but she's afraid."

"Afraid? Why?"

Gabriela pulled a long reed of dry grass out of the ground and laid it on the dirt beside her village. "The babies keep dying. The first was too early, it came out in black lumps. The second baby had a hole in its heart. The third baby had no face." Here she paused, and Naveed was grateful, because he wasn't sure he was translating correctly, it couldn't be right, Gabriela was so little, too little to be saying this.

She pointed to the middle of the mami stick, at a small swelling in the bark. "The fourth baby, who knows?"

Naveed's dizziness returned. "I—I am sorry. I hope she is healthy."

She held out the papi stick to him. "Want to play?"

"Lo siento," Naveed said again. "I must go."

Gabriela turned back to her stick world, and he bolted away along the path. *The third baby had no face.*

Had Marisol… had she tried to have other children, after Gabriela?

Maybe Gabriela just had a very active imagination, maybe she'd come up with all of that on her own. But Naveed doubted it. Earlier in the summer, he had done way too much googling on the long-term effects of herbicide and pesticide exposure. He'd read about the health problems of agricultural workers, who would often stand gladly in the fields while they were sprayed, welcoming the cool mist on a hot day. He could list all of the afflictions: the cancers, the diseases of kidneys and lungs. The miscarriages. The harrowing birth defects.

Naveed ran the rest of the way back to camp. He had no idea where he found the energy, just kept hoping that if he moved fast enough he'd be able to outrun the things that were stalking him. But as he closed the door to his cabin, he knew he hadn't escaped. Because even though he'd tried to keep everything contained, smoky fog kept rising from those deep dark holes in his mind, wisping through the packed dirt, emerging, spreading everywhere. He'd come to a place where shadows grow, and something enormous and destructive was gathering strength inside of him, and there was nothing he could do to get rid of it now.

Naveed

THE NEXT MORNING, NAVEED WOKE UP TO RAMÓN KNOCKING on the door. "Nate, you up yet? The bus leaves in five minutes."

"Coming." Pain rolled through Naveed's sore shoulder as he got up. It had woken him several times in the night when he'd shifted positions, breaking through even that winning codeine/sleeping pill combination. At least the nerve pain hadn't bugged him the last few nights.

He moved through the underwater daze, pulling on his last clean shirt, not allowing himself to think about how much he dreaded going back to the orchard. He filled up his water bottle and grabbed two more protein bars for his breakfast and lunch. There were only a few left; they were all he'd eaten the day before. Once he'd gotten back to the camp, Ramón had stopped by to make sure he'd found his way home. He apologized that he hadn't been able to make the driver wait for Naveed to get on the bus, and invited him for dinner again. Naveed declined, not wanting to face Marisol. *The second baby had a hole in its heart.* No, he couldn't deal with that right then. He went to his cabin, showered, ate his protein bar dinner, and crashed instead.

When he opened the door now, Ramón and Javier were standing nearby, waiting for the bus. Ramón shot Naveed his gap-toothed smile, but Javier looked tired, his eyes dull. He quickly turned away, coughing. It was a cough that Naveed was intimately familiar with, the heavy, productive, chest-rattling type. He'd heard it several times during the night when his shoulder woke him up, and hadn't been sure if it was someone else's cough, or his own, or if he was imagining it entirely.

"You okay?" Naveed asked, then remembered Javier didn't speak much Spanish. But he must have understood that phrase, because he nodded.

"He's all right. Just the smoke," Ramón said.

When the bus arrived, Naveed followed Ramón and Javier to the back and sat behind them, as tired and beaten down as everyone else. But he was much more awake this morning and found it impossible to doze, especially since every time Javier coughed Naveed wanted to run away and wash off in the shower. Instead, he stared out the window, thinking about the day stretching ahead of him. How would he find the energy to pick all those apples?

He wondered if Vanesa and Fernando would be there again. Hopefully they'd stay away from him today. He needed to focus if he wanted to get to eight bins.

Would their film really change things? Naveed wondered as he watched the sun rise over the orchard. Would it have the effect that Ramón hoped, making the farmworkers visible instead of ignored, so that people who watched it would be moved to help? Or would they just think, *wow, too bad for them*, and breathe a secret sigh of relief as they turned off another bummer documentary and went back to their comfortable lives?

Naveed was pretty sure he knew which way it would go, based on how quickly everything had gotten back to business as usual after the Nutrexo debacle. It was going to take a lot more than a single documentary to jolt people out of their inertia, to make them stand up and fight against injustices that didn't affect them personally. Something bigger was needed—people didn't bother paying attention unless death was involved. But ordinary death wouldn't do. It had to be special in some way. Violent. Spectacular. Devastating.

This was something that had haunted him frequently over the summer. If he had died, would people still be talking about Nutrexo? About MRK? Maybe, although the death of a brown person was never weighted as highly as the death of a white one. It still might have made it harder for everyone to look away.

He could do it today. He could take all of his pills, every single one of them, climb up high into a tree and wait to fall asleep forever. The filmmakers would probably keep an eye on him anyway, after his fall yesterday, and maybe they would catch it on film… his final plunge from the tree, the horrified workers gathering around his corpse. He could even make a sign to hang around his neck so they would know why he had done it, like that Korean farmer Maman used to talk about, the one who had died by suicide during WTO protests in Cancún years ago. If he was going to kill himself, he wanted it to *mean* something. Becoming a martyr for a cause he believed in would be infinitely better than taking his life just because he was tired of living it.

That is, if he even managed to die. With his luck, they'd call paramedics who would bring him back to life somehow, and he'd probably end up adding a serious brain injury to his growing list of health problems.

Why are you even considering this? he asked himself. *It's a horrible idea, and it's not going to work. Stop thinking about it.*

That was the thing, though. Once his brain started going down that track, it was impossible to steer it anywhere else.

It's not a bad idea, actually, Nate chimed in. *I mean, where do you go from here? Don't you see how you've dug yourself into a hole? You came here to be free, and all you managed to do was trap yourself inside a new miserable life. What are you going to do when your meds run out and the nerve pain comes back? You won't be able to get out of bed, let alone stand on a ladder picking apples all day.*

I'll figure something out, Naveed answered. *I need to be here. I need to help Marisol somehow. And Gabriela.*

You're doing this for Marisol? You barely even know her.

Doesn't matter. I care about her.

Are you sure you aren't just doing it for yourself? You don't think you have a little hero complex going on?

I have all sorts of complexes. I'm a complex person.

Ha. I just think it's funny, is all. That you'd go through so much trouble for someone you just met, but you abandoned your own mother without a second glance.

It's not like that. Besides, Maman doesn't care. She's probably glad to be rid of me. I'm sure she'll get over it.

Oh, yeah, like you got over what happened to you. That was pretty easy, right?

Shut up.

And your sister—

Shut up—

She understood you, didn't she? But you left her, too.

Shut up shut up SHUT UP

Don't you see? There's nothing here for you. No way out. You're crazy, talking to yourself, seeing shadows where they shouldn't be. No one needs you, no one cares about you, so stop being a coward and get this done.

Fuck you, Nate. You were supposed to help me.

I am helping you. I'm trying to get you to see sense.

Well, I'm not listening, so just fuck off, all right?

No. I'm not going anywhere.

"Nate?"

Naveed looked up to find that everyone on the bus was gone, except for Ramón, who was running his hand in front of Naveed's eyes in a semi-joking way. "Hola, Nate? Are you there?"

Naveed stood up and forced a smile to cover his embarrassment. "Sorry. I am a little tired today. Let's go."

The air was much clearer this morning, and the sun beat down on them mercilessly as they picked. Although Naveed was grateful to breathe normally again and not need to sneak hits from his inhaler, he almost missed the haze of smoke as the temperature climbed and climbed. It must have been close to a hundred degrees by the time they broke for lunch. As they worked, the bosses roamed the fields distributing bottles of water. Naveed guessed they didn't want anyone passing out while Vanesa was still there filming. The water wasn't cold, but it still tasted much better than the metallic-tinged stuff he had brought from home.

For a while, Naveed hoped that he could escape into work, that the tedious job would numb his mind. But he couldn't stop focusing on the physical discomforts, the soreness of his picking and climbing muscles and of course his still-aching shoulder, and this made Nate's voice stronger. *Why do you keep doing this to yourself?*

The heat made everything worse. His long-sleeved shirt was drenched in sweat. The portable bathrooms smelled so awful that Naveed couldn't even set foot inside them. There wasn't anywhere to take a piss in the orchards without others seeing, so instead of sitting with Ramón during lunch he walked all the way out to the tall bushes at the far edge of the fields to relieve himself in private, only to get yelled at by one of the bosses. He decided not to drink much throughout the afternoon. Just enough to keep from getting too dehydrated. He plucked apples from their branches, ignoring the camera's gaze when it occasionally panned his way. He put the apples in his bag. Dumped the bag in the bin. Climbed back up for more. Over and over and over again. Four bins. Five. Six.

Every time he climbed the ladder, the baggie of pills pressed against his leg. They felt so heavy. They wouldn't let him forget. Neither would Nate, who egged him on relentlessly. *Come on, aren't you sick of this yet? Just end it.*

No. I'm going to stick this out. Today, I'll get eight bins. Tomorrow, ten.

Soon after he had received his seventh chip, he heard several workers shouting from a far corner of the orchard. Vanesa, whom Naveed could see through the branches, motioned for the camera guy to follow her. Naveed craned his neck, but couldn't see what was causing the commotion. He kept picking despite the dread twisting in his stomach. Something was wrong.

When he dumped his bag, he asked one of the bosses what had happened. "It was nothing. Get back to work," he said gruffly.

Naveed kept his head down. He kept working, as did the others around him, although he didn't see the filmmakers again for the rest of the day. Maybe they had been asked to leave? But he didn't see Ramón either, which worried him more than he wanted to admit.

At the end of the day, he dumped the final bag into his eighth bin. He had done it. He wasn't a failure. He had picked eight thousand pounds of apples in hundred-degree weather. And he'd also managed to avoid killing himself. It might not be saving the world, but at least it was something.

He turned in his chips to Luis, who was on the phone when he entered the office and distractedly counted out $40 before shooing Naveed away.

One bus was still in the parking lot. Naveed walked on and scanned the seats for Ramón or Javier. He didn't see either of them, so he asked if it was the right bus. The driver said they'd be leaving for the camps in a few minutes.

Naveed slumped into a seat and closed his eyes. His heart beat loudly in his ears. He needed to bike to the grocery store and laundromat tonight, but had no idea where he'd find the strength. Somehow, though, he would. Just needed to rest first.

He must have dozed off for a minute, because the next thing he knew the bus was on the road. He sat up and looked around, but still didn't see Ramón or Javier. Around him, the other workers talked amongst themselves in low, serious voices. Naveed wished he could understand what they were saying. But, at the same time, he didn't need to. He'd been correct: something was wrong.

As they filed off the bus, he watched a small group of workers walking towards Marisol, who was sitting in the shade fanning herself with a scrap of cardboard. Even though he was afraid, he followed them. He needed to know what was going on.

He watched them tell her something. Watched her eyes widen in surprise, watched her ask them questions and nod at their solemn answers.

She rubbed her belly with her right hand, eyebrows furrowed. After a while, the other men moved away, and she waved goodbye.

She caught Naveed's eye before he could turn to leave, so he cautiously stepped forward and asked her, "Is everything all right? I do not know what happened."

Marisol didn't nod this time. "It's Javier," she told him in Spanish. "He collapsed in the fields today. It's lucky the filmmakers were there. They drove him to the clinic right away. Ramón is with him now." She shivered. "I hope he's okay."

"I am sure he will be fine." It didn't sound as bad as he'd feared, and he was glad it wasn't Ramón. But he thought about how unwell Javier had looked in the morning... the sound of that cough....

He walked back to his cabin, which felt like an oven. He packed all his clothes into his messenger bag and wheeled his bike outside. There was no way he could rest right now, so he might as well get his errands done.

Several hours later, he returned with a bag of clean clothes, a fresh box of protein bars, a big jug of filtered water, and enough tamales from the taqueria where he'd eaten dinner to share with Marisol and her family. It felt good to prove Nate wrong. Sure, he'd just spent nearly everything he'd earned today, but look at all the normal things he'd accomplished.

He had made only one concession to Nate. He'd tried to breeze by the pharmacy at the grocery store, but some strange pull kept leading him back there. Every time he circled through, he slowed to look at the rows and rows of pills. *No,* he told himself. *Yes,* Nate said, and wouldn't shut up until Naveed finally gave in and tossed a bottle of extra-strength pain relievers into the cart.

After he'd unpacked and taken a quick shower, he brought the bag of tamales over to Ramón and Marisol's. It was already dark, but the light was on inside, so he figured it wasn't too late to knock on their door. When he did, Ramón answered. He looked exhausted.

"Hola!" Naveed said, relieved to see his friend again. "I brought you...."

But he didn't finish, because he saw Marisol behind him, crying. Ramón's eyes shimmered.

"What happened?" Naveed said, even though he was afraid of the answer.

"He's gone," Ramón said. "Javier. We took him to the clinic but… we were in the waiting room and he… he could barely breathe, and he passed out again but we couldn't wake him up, he couldn't get the air in. They couldn't help him. And now he's gone."

Naveed felt like he'd been doused with ice.

Javier's dead.

He's dead. But it wasn't supposed to happen like this.

It should have been me.

"He's gone," Ramón repeated. "And now it's time for us to fight back."

Naveed

FRIDAY, SEPTEMBER 11

NAVEED AND RAMÓN SAT OUTSIDE, LEANING AGAINST THE cabin wall. Ramón had taken off his baseball hat and was turning it around and around in his hands.

"This shouldn't have happened," Ramón said. "He was in bad shape by lunch. I told him to go home, but he couldn't. He hasn't been feeling well for a while, and wasn't picking as much as normal. The bosses were threatening to fire him. He didn't want to end up like the others." He made a sound that was almost like clearing his throat, but it turned into a definite cough at the end.

Naveed pretended not to notice. "What do you mean, the others?"

"Javier is—was—a guest worker." Ramón paused to clear his throat again. "They can only stay as long as they work for this company. If they lose their job, they get deported. It's been happening a lot lately. That's why there are so many empty cabins. We're not supposed to be here, either," he said, lowering his voice. "Marisol and I. We're not guest workers, but we had to leave our old place when the landlord jacked up the rent. Couldn't find anywhere else to live, but Javier helped us move into the camp. Nobody really checks up on it. We figured it would only be temporary, but we've been here a few weeks now. Still looking for a better place. For when the baby comes."

Naveed swallowed. "Is that what happened to the man of my cabin? He was deported because he got sick and could not work?"

"Yes."

"This… it is not right. The way they make you live," Naveed said.

"I know. I've had enough. I'm tired of them riding our asses trying to get us to work harder than we already do. You saw how they are, when you fell yesterday. They don't care. But this time, it's different. Vanesa and Fernando, they were there at the clinic. It's all on film. I don't know if that will make a difference, but… I'm not going back out there. Not until things change."

Despite his horror at the general situation, Naveed felt a growing excitement. "Do you think the other workers might join you? You would be stronger together. You could—" He didn't know the Spanish word for *strike*, so he finished, "how do you say, walk out. Refuse to work until they give you what you want."

Ramón leaned his head against the wall and closed his eyes. "I don't know. If the company fires them, they'll get turned over to la migra to be deported. We could too, if they find out we don't have papers. It might not be worth the risk."

"Justice is always worth the risk." But as Naveed said this, he couldn't help thinking about Maman, and what it had cost her—what it had cost *him*—to bring Tara Snyder to justice. Had *that* been worth it? He couldn't even answer that question.

Ramón sat for another few minutes, then slowly pulled himself up. "Then it looks like I've got some doors to knock on."

"How can I help?" Naveed asked, even though he knew he wouldn't be too successful with door-knocking. Most of the others were more comfortable speaking Mixtec, but even without a language barrier, they probably wouldn't listen to Naveed anyway. He was an outsider here; they didn't trust him the way they did Ramón.

"You can refuse to work tomorrow," Ramón said with a sad smile.

"Yes. I can definitely do that."

"There might be something else. I'll come by later and let you know."

Naveed walked back to his cabin. He didn't want to drug himself to oblivion, though. Not when Ramón might come back in need of his help.

Instead, he stared at the ceiling and thought about death and disease. This infection going around… it seemed a lot like MRK. But then again, the symptoms of MRK were similar to a lot of other respiratory infections, with the exception of that awful blood-red phlegm. The main difference was in how hard it was to treat. Besides, MRK had supposedly been eradicated at Harborview. Naveed had been Patient Zero, the first one infected, but due to their effective quarantine, it hadn't spread beyond the hospital.

At least, that's what they'd told him. But the homeless men who had given him a ride to Seattle had never been quarantined. Naveed had been thinking about them a lot lately; Blackbeard appeared in his dreams from time to time. In a way, that man had saved his life, and what had Naveed done in return? He'd been so delirious that he couldn't remember many details, but he'd probably coughed all over their car.

What if? What if they had come down with it, too, and what if it had spread to others, what if it was making its way all over the place now, all over the world, even, if those workers had been deported to Mexico carrying MRK….

Maybe no one knew because no one was looking for it. Or, maybe people did know, maybe it was a budding epidemic, but it hadn't made his radar. Considering how little time he spent on the internet these days, it seemed possible—and if this horrible disease really had been unleashed on the world, it was all his fault.

He took a deep breath. Tonight, thanks to the improved air quality, his lungs felt clear, which was a relief. But he was worried about Ramón, and he still couldn't believe Javier was dead, that he wouldn't be there standing with the rest of the workers in the morning.

Your fault. He rubbed his chest, thinking about that suspicion he still couldn't shake, that MRK had been hiding in his lungs all this time. That first day of work, he had shaken Javier's hand. And Ramón's. What if he was a carrier, spreading MRK everywhere he went?

No, he told himself. *The disease was going around before you got here. Stop blaming yourself.*

Even so, Nate couldn't help but add, *You were Patient Zero—and that makes you responsible. How can you live with yourself, knowing that someone else is dead because of you?*

"Shut the fuck up!" Naveed said, only realizing that he'd said it out loud when he heard his own voice echoing in his ears. And suddenly, for no reason at all, a strange ugly laughter came spilling out of his mouth. He laughed and laughed and didn't know why, nothing about any of this was funny, and he wondered if the laughter belonged to Nate, and the sound of it was so unfamiliar that it scared him, what if Nate was pushing him out, getting stronger and stronger, Nate was going to take over his body and there would be none of Naveed left.

He laughed so hard that he cried, tears rolling from his eyes onto the bed, the bed of a sick worker who had been forced to leave it all behind. Where was he now? Had he recovered? Or was he dead, too?

Naveed had just managed to quiet down when a knock sounded at the door. It was Ramón, looking pale and worn out, leaning against the doorframe.

"Are you feeling all right?" Naveed asked, hoping that Ramón hadn't heard that bizarre laughing fit.

"Not really," Ramón admitted. "I'm going to bed. But, Nate, in the morning… I'm going to need your help. We're all going to take the buses to work like usual, but when we get there we're going to wait in front of the offices. When the bosses arrive, you and I are going to tell them what's going on."

"Why me?" Naveed asked.

"No one else wants to risk leading the strike. They're worried they'll be blacklisted. Plus, we're both comfortable speaking Spanish."

"Marisol could come too. She speaks very well."

Ramón eyed him. "The bosses don't know her—she's been working in packing plants, not in the fields. Besides, they're not going to take our demands seriously if they come from a woman."

Naveed opened his mouth to protest, but Ramón went on, "And you speak English too. That could come in handy if they bring in the managers."

"Okay. Can we make signs also? We could march out to the main road. Get the support of the public."

Ramón looked surprised. "Uh, I guess, but it's late...."

"I will get supplies." Naveed could probably make protest signs in his sleep. "So what do we want?"

"Want?" Ramón's eyes were a little unfocused.

"Our demands," Naveed prompted.

"Oh. Fair wages... we want... clean drinking water and... regular breaks... there was something else... oh, being able to take sick days without worrying about getting fired...."

"Okay. I've got it from here," Naveed said. "You go get some sleep. I'll see you in the morning."

Naveed headed back out on his bike, thankful to have a job to do. He spent the next few hours gathering supplies for protest signs. Back to the store for Sharpies, a box cutter, and duct tape (that shit was expensive—but this was important). A quick swing behind a thrift store yielded a bunch of perfect cardboard boxes stacked up near the Dumpsters. He carried them off the property before cutting the boxes into manageable sign-sized pieces and tucking them under one arm for the bike ride home. Since he couldn't easily find any sticks or scraps of wood, he spent several hours in his cabin duct-taping lengths of cardboard together into handles and writing out slogans as neatly as he could. By the time he was done, he had a nice array of signs, some in English, some in Spanish, and some still blank to be filled in by others. He wanted to get the attention of any passing drivers who could show their support.

Maman would be proud, he thought with a pang before shutting her out of his head again. She wasn't here, none of them were, he was all by himself in this tiny desolate cabin, alone but for the flies buzzing through the air and the shadows strengthening inside him.

Naveed

SLEEP WAS IMPOSSIBLE TO FIND THAT NIGHT. NAVEED'S NERVE PAIN made an unwelcome reappearance. Nate chattered at him incessantly. But a sleeping pill was out of the question if he wanted his brain to be functional first thing in the morning, so he just had to lie there and wait for the hours to pass.

Once the other workers started getting up, Naveed showered, scrubbing extra hard as he thought about the illness going around, and was dressed and gathering up signs by the time he heard the knock at the door. But when he opened it, he was surprised to see that it was not Ramón. It was Marisol. She had a blanket draped around her shoulders.

"What's wrong?" Naveed asked.

She pulled the blanket tighter. "You'll have to go alone to see the bosses. Ramón needs to stay at home. He is too sick. He needs to rest."

"Oh, no. I'm sorry. Yes, I will meet with the bosses," he said, but as she was turning to go, he added, "Wait. Is he coughing a lot?"

She nodded, her lip trembling slightly.

"I have something for you," he said. "Hold on."

He found the bottle of cough syrup, which was still about half full. "Here. Take this. It is strong medicine. He needs lots of water too. I hope he will feel better. Oh, and one more thing." He found the pain relievers he'd just bought and handed the bottle to her. "For the fever. You and Gabriela, be sure to wash your hands."

She looked confused, but thanked him and left.

You shouldn't have done that, Nate said. *Those pills could have been our way out.*

I'll do whatever the hell I want, Naveed retorted. *Do you even get it? We share the same body. If I die, you die.*

I'm willing to sacrifice myself for the greater good, Nate said.

Naveed felt like punching the wall. He would've, too, except that his fist would probably go straight through to someone else's room, the walls were so thin here.

He was going to have to do this alone. What if he fucked it up? What if they laughed him out of there? They had no reason to take him seriously. Luis had only given him a job three days ago.

Oh God. This was going to be a disaster.

Damn right it will, Nate said.

Naveed tried to slow his breath, which was coming too fast. His heart fluttered wildly. He felt like he was going to throw up.

Breathe in. Breathe out.

It's going to be a disaster.

Frantically, he shoved his hand in his pocket. Took out his baggie of meds, dumped them all out on the bed. He sifted through the sleeping pills, passing over the handful of tricyclics he still had left, heart sinking when he saw it.

One more. He only had one more benzo.

There was no question that he needed it now, so he took it. This meeting had to go well. These workers, all of them, deserved so much more than this, and he would do whatever he could to help them. But he didn't know what would happen once it wore off, which only made him more anxious; it was like standing on the edge of a cliff at night, looking down and not knowing the depth of all that darkness.

He sucked on a ginger chew, closed his eyes and breathed as deeply as he could, until he finally felt that calm descending like a cool cloth on his overheated brain.

Then he got back up. He grabbed the stack of signs and walked over to the cluster of waiting workers, holding them high, trying to nonverbally transmit the message, *I made signs! Come and get one if you want!*

One of the workers, a man he hadn't met with a leathery face and pleasant smile, took a sign and said, "Tatsa'vi." That got it started: others came, too, understanding what he was trying to do. Several of them asked about Ramón in halting Spanish. Naveed told them that Ramón wasn't feeling well and needed to stay home.

The mood of the crowd was different this morning. The beaten-down resignation of the day before was gone. Today, there was a nervous excitement in the air. Naveed guessed he wasn't the only one who was looking forward to a day off, even if the outcome of their strike was uncertain.

After the short bus ride, most of the workers filed off the bus, then looked to Naveed, as if wondering what to do next. Some of the people with signs stayed behind, explaining that they would spread the word to the other buses yet to arrive. Naveed led the rest of the group to the front of the office, where they formed a human chain stretching out in front of the entrance. As more buses arrived, the chain grew longer and longer. They held their signs and waited.

The first car that pulled up, though, didn't belong to one of the bosses. It was the white van the filmmakers drove. He watched Vanesa get out of the driver's seat.

She chatted with a few of the workers and began setting up. Naveed's anxiety rose. He had been working on a short speech inside his head, running through the list of demands that Ramón had dictated, but now that he knew it would be filmed, he needed to make it better. His Spanish would have to be perfect.

Fernando approached a nearby cluster of workers. Several of them glanced in Naveed's direction as they talked. Great—they must be telling him that, in Ramón's stead, he was the unofficial leader of the protest. The last thing he wanted was Fernando coming over to ask him his name.

But he didn't have to worry about that, because Luis arrived in his red pickup then, and the filmmakers headed his way to capture his reaction.

He got out of the truck, slamming the door. "What's going on here?" Luis demanded in Spanish.

Naveed stepped forward, squaring his shoulders. All eyes were focused on him, the cameras too, but this time it didn't bother him in the least. His earlier nervousness vanished. It was like being on stage, and he got that same thrill he used to get when acting: he had their attention, and he intended to keep it. "We're not going to work today," he said in Spanish. "Javier Ibarra died yesterday. He was sick, but he was forced to keep working even in the extreme heat, and it killed him. We aren't going to let this happen to anyone else. We will not return to the fields until you meet our demands: Fair wages. Sick leave. Access to clean water. Improved housing conditions."

As he'd feared, Luis laughed dismissively. "You just got here. You don't know anything about this. I don't even have the authority to meet those demands. So, you—all of you—get back to work." He said something in another language that might have been Mixtec. Naveed wondered if Luis was trash-talking him to the other workers, but not one of them moved.

"If you don't have the authority, then call your managers. I will speak to them when they are ready to speak to me," Naveed said in the steeliest voice he could muster. It wasn't hard. This felt glorious.

Luis stormed past them, breaking the human chain. No matter. It reformed as soon as he slammed the office door.

The workers all had huge smiles on their faces now. Luis was rattled. That was good.

Vanesa approached Naveed. "Can I speak with you for a moment?" she asked in Spanish. "I'd like to do a quick interview. For the film."

"I'm sorry," Naveed said. "Not right now. I am not the leader anyway. Ramón organized everything, but he could not come today. You should talk to him instead. Excuse me." He slipped away from her, grateful that another bus had just showed up so that he could pretend to be busy. She didn't follow.

Naveed mingled with the newly-arrived workers, most of whom decided to join the picket line. They all stood in front of the office until Luis reappeared in the doorway, standing there with his hands on his hips, like an angry father. "I've spoken to the managers. They say that if you don't get back to work, you will all be fired for insubordination."

Even though he'd said it in Spanish, everyone seemed to understand. This was what they had expected. Still, no one moved. Some raised their signs higher.

"And you"—he gestured at Vanesa—"no longer have permission to film on this property. Turn off your cameras and leave. Now."

Naveed took a deep breath and stepped towards the office. Luis watched him approach, a wary expression on his face.

Naveed tried his best to look friendly, not confrontational, like he was trying to help Luis out. This time, he didn't speak too loudly. This conversation was between him and Luis. "You should not fire them. It is not a good idea."

"It's out of my hands," Luis said.

"Maybe. But the managers need to understand that this will have consequences. It is too late, so much has been filmed. A worker is dead. And if you fire the rest, people will be very, very angry at the company. It is in their best interests to listen to us. To work with us."

Luis said nothing.

"I would like to speak with them."

"I'm not sure that will be possible."

"Tomorrow. Ramón and I will come tomorrow morning so we can all sit down and talk." Naveed hoped Ramón would be well enough by then. "We want to get back to work too. We want to work together to find a solution."

Luis ran his hands through his hair. Naveed could hardly believe it: this was working. By showing restraint instead of losing his temper the way he wanted to, he looked like the sensible one, and it was hard to argue with that.

"All right. Tomorrow. Be here at 9am," Luis said.

Naveed walked back into the crowd, smiling. This was going to work. He caught Fernando's eye and asked him to translate. "Tomorrow morning we will meet with the managers. Today, we march."

Naveed

NAVEED MARCHED DOWN TO THE MAIN ROAD WITH EVERYONE, including the filmmakers, whose cameras were back on the second they left the property. They stopped near a small stand of trees where people could take turns resting in the shade. A fair number of cars drove by. Which was good. Their struggle needed to be visible.

But it wasn't enough, Naveed thought as another car whizzed past without so much as a wave of acknowledgment. And he knew exactly what to do about it.

He tapped on the shoulder of someone on the film crew—the sound lady, a muscular white woman wearing a wide-brimmed hat. When she turned, he made a rectangular shape with his fingers and pretended to click a shutter. "Photo?" he asked, gesturing at the workers.

She understood the pantomime, and reached for her phone. "Do you want to be in it?" she asked, pointing at him, then at the line of protesters.

He shook his head and held out his hand. "I take? Please?" Even though Naveed felt slightly disgusting imitating a thick accent, he couldn't blow his cover and let the filmmakers know he spoke English.

She hesitated for a second, but opened the camera app and handed it to him.

He took her phone and crossed the street, noticing how intently she watched him—did she think he was going to steal it?—and took several photos of the protesters. It was, he thought, an impressive turnout. At least two dozen workers were there. He should have made more signs.

A few of them grinned when they saw him taking the picture, and he felt a burst of pride. All of those people with their signs—it looked so *official.* It looked like a movement.

As soon as he finished, he chose the best two photos and emailed them to Nate's account. He hoped that the sound lady didn't notice what he was doing, that she wouldn't go into her sent emails later. Not that she'd recognize Nate's address, but still, it was sloppier than he would have liked.

Once the photos had successfully sent, he crossed the street again and returned her phone. "Gracias," he said. She smiled at him and tucked it back into her pocket.

But he wasn't about to get away so easily. Vanesa had appeared out of nowhere. "Looks like we all have some spare time right now," she said to him in Spanish. "We'd really like to talk to you. Hear your story."

Not gonna happen, thought Naveed, but he said, "I am sorry. I need to go now. To town. To spread the word." Once again, he pushed past her, and walked on down the road.

As he walked, he actually found himself whistling. Whistling! It was so strange, how he felt. Buoyant, like floating in a salty sea. For so long, he had been fighting just to stay above water, but now he felt like he was swimming along with the current.

The sun was hot, but it didn't bother him. He was used to that by now. He wasn't toiling in the fields. He was strolling down the road, and he knew where he was going.

Nate, for whatever reason, was silent. It felt so good, so peaceful inside his head. He could get used to this.

Naveed turned the corner into the farmworker camp, which was quiet during the day, dusty and forlorn under the bright sunshine. He headed for Ramón and Marisol's cabin, but before he got there, he spotted Gabriela playing in the shade of one of the buildings. She sat cross-legged on the concrete, deep in concentration, several characters from her stick family in either hand. *The third baby had no face....*

Naveed shook the memory away just as she noticed him. "What are you doing here?" she asked in Spanish.

"I have to ask your parents something." He was about to continue on his way when she stopped him.

"They're sleeping," she said. "Papi is sick, and Mami says she's tired and needs to take a nap. You shouldn't wake them up."

"Oh. Okay," he said, trying to tamp down a sharp spike of worry. "Can you help me? I wonder if they have a picture of Javier."

She looked at the ground. "We have no pictures."

Dammit. It had been a long shot, he supposed.

"But he has one in his cabin," she added, still not looking at Naveed. "He showed me. So I could see his children."

Naveed breathed out, feeling like little pieces of his heart were being extracted from his chest. Did Gabriela understand the finality of death? Had she realized that those children were never going to see their father again?

"Why do you need it?" she asked.

"I do not want him to be forgotten," Naveed said. "And it will be harder for people to forget if they see his picture." If they know what he left behind, he thought but did not say.

She nodded and stood up. "This way."

When they reached the cabin, Gabriela twisted open the door handle with ease: Javier had not locked it.

For some reason this only made Naveed's hesitation stronger. It felt so very wrong going in there, but this was important. For people to care about this, Javier needed to be more than just a name.

He went inside, but Gabriela did not follow. Finding the photograph she had mentioned wasn't difficult: it was tacked up on the wall above the small sink. There was Javier, with two young girls on one side of him and a woman holding a toddler on the other. They were all smiling so brightly that Naveed had to turn it over as soon as he got it off the wall, tucking it into his back pocket. He wondered if anyone had told them yet.

The next stop was his own cabin. Gabriela followed him there. "Where are you going?"

"To the library," he said, wheeling his bike out.

"I want to come," said Gabriela.

He was about to tell her no, but stopped himself. How often had Gabriela left these camps, other than to wander through the nearby fields? It probably didn't happen often. And she could easily ride behind him, now that he'd cleared everything off the rack.

"If your mother says it is okay," he said.

Her smile was so wide that he found himself mirroring it. He folded up a clean towel to make the wire rack more comfortable for her to sit on, then they walked the bike over to her cabin together.

Naveed hung back while she burst inside. Her parents were two shapeless forms underneath the blankets on the bed. He stepped backward, uneasy, as Gabriela shook Marisol awake and whispered into her ear.

Marisol sat up. "Is it really okay if she goes with you? It would be a big help. I'm just so tired."

Naveed swallowed, worry spiking again. "It is no trouble at all."

"Okay, then, have fun."

Gabriela kissed her on the cheek and skipped back to Naveed. "Let's go!"

They rode away. She sat behind him, clutching his waist tightly, and he tried to find that goodness he'd felt earlier, the sense of purpose. It was still there, but it felt like he had to dig past a lot of heavy stuff to find it now.

At the library, she looked at picture books while he explained to the librarians what he needed. They helped him scan Javier's photograph and send it to himself, then he sat down at a computer and checked his email.

His heart jumped when he saw his new messages. One of them was from Vanesa. It had been sent the evening Naveed moved into the farmworker camp.

Re: Documentary Film Help?

Sep 9 at 8:43pm

Vanesa Rosales <vanesa@rosalesfilms.com>
to N. M. <beyondthewindowpane@gmail.com>

Hi Nate,

Thanks for your emails. I haven't been sure of our timeline since we've been waiting for permission to film out here in Central WA, but we should be wrapping up in the next week or two. We have a tight deadline to meet and will need a lot of help with post-production. Please send along your resume, and I'll be in touch when we get back to Seattle to see if you are still interested/available.

Best,
Vanesa

Naveed deleted the email, not understanding why he felt so uneasy about it. He had already made his choice, but this cemented it. He had no possible future with them. There was no way he was going back to Seattle.

Instead of dwelling on that any further, he got right to work. He wrote up a short summary explaining the events of the past few days, including the photograph of Javier with his family, and another showing the workers picketing on the side of the road. He mentioned that Bountiful Earth was a major buyer of Mortensen Fruit, hinting at a possible boycott.

Once that was done, it didn't take him long to disseminate the information. After all those years of listening to Maman's dinner-table conversations and volunteering at CFJ events, he knew exactly which orgs were most likely to take up arms in the struggle, and which of those had the highest reach. He opened some new accounts so that he could send it to them as "Anonimo." It meant "Anonymous" in Spanish, but had a much better ring to it, almost like a superhero name or something.

He briefly considered sending it to CFJ too, but decided against it. Best to keep his distance. They'd probably hear about it eventually, but it wouldn't be from him.

Gabriela appeared next to him. "What are you doing?"

"I am nearly done. One moment," he told her. Then he sent the brief to the local newspaper and TV news station, as well as their Seattle counterparts for good measure. Once that was done, he signed out of everything and turned to face her just as her stomach rumbled loudly.

"Should we go eat lunch?" he asked, and she nodded eagerly.

On their way back outside, she slipped her hand into his. He didn't feel the brush of her fingers, but he had been paying attention to her movements, and closed his hand around hers. He led her toward his favorite taqueria near Central Park.

As they waited to cross the street, she asked, "Why do your hands look like that?"

Naveed winced. How could he possibly answer that question? "It is just how they look," he answered.

She studied his wrinkled skin. It made him uncomfortable, and he wanted to pull his sleeves down to hide it, but he restrained himself. "They've been like that since you were born?" she asked.

"No. It was... a sickness."

The walk sign flashed, so they began crossing. "I didn't know sicknesses could do that," she said.

"Sometimes. What would you like for lunch?" he asked. Luckily she started asking him about the menu instead, so that he could stop thinking—or at least *try* to stop thinking—about MRK. *What if, what if....*

It smelled so good inside the restaurant that Naveed realized how hungry he was after subsisting mostly on protein bars for the past several days. He ordered taco plates for himself and Gabriela, cold horchata to drink, and a container of menudo for Ramón and Marisol. But when they gave him his total, he realized that he didn't have quite enough cash and hastily changed one of the horchatas to water instead. That left him with one dollar and some change.

Shit. He should have been more careful with his money, he supposed, especially now that he no longer had a job. But once they got to the park and sat opposite each other on a picnic table in the shade, he changed his mind. It was worth every penny to see Gabriela's face when she took her first sip of horchata. "It's so sweet! And so cold!" she exclaimed with glee.

They were so busy eating that they didn't talk much after that. He watched her shovel down her entire lunch, all three tacos plus the sides of rice and beans, before polishing off her horchata. Her appetite was so astounding that he wondered if she'd had anything to eat for breakfast.

As he sat across from her, listening to the watery sounds she made as she tried to suck up the last bits of horchata through her straw, those dark brown eyes staring up at him, he found himself gripped by a sudden, immense sadness so enormous that he felt crushed underneath it.

"Can I go to the playground?" she asked. He nodded, and as soon as she left he put his head down on the picnic table and fought to keep himself from crying. What was happening to him? He couldn't even pinpoint what was making him so sad, but the intensity of it was almost unbearable.

You care about her, don't you? Nate asked. *But she doesn't care about you, not really. She's like an animal starved for food. Only following you around because you feed her.*

So it was Nate. That explained his sudden change in mood. *Shut up, Nate. I'm stronger than you. I'm not listening. So go the fuck away.*

I don't know how long it's going to take you to understand this, Nate retorted. *You made me. You can't get rid of me. As long as you're here, I'll be here.*

It was true. That was the problem. Nate wasn't going away, and Naveed didn't know how much more of this he could endure.

Naveed

THE BICYCLE KEPT WOBBLING. GABRIELA DIDN'T WEIGH MUCH, but she changed the center of gravity, and with every turn of the pedals, Naveed found it harder and harder to stay balanced. The lack of sleep and the days of exhausting labor in the fields had caught up with him, and it took all his concentration to keep the bike upright and moving forward.

He eventually had to accept that he wasn't going to make it all the way back to the camp. Instead, he changed his route, and pedaled over to the road where the workers were still picketing.

The moment he stopped, Gabriela dismounted and ran up to one of the women standing in the shade. "Norma!" she said, and started speaking animatedly in Mixtec.

After Naveed finally got the kickstand down—he was a bit dizzy so it was harder than it should have been—he walked slowly over to them. One of the other workers clapped him on the back and handed him a bottle of water. He tried for a smile, but it wasn't happening. Though he really didn't want to get back on that bike until he had rested a bit, staying here would mean he'd have to pretend to be normal, which would take energy he just did not have right now.

So he asked Gabriela, "Can you stay here? I bring soup to your mother and father. I will return soon." Maybe he'd have enough time for a short siesta in his cabin. Once he got some rest, his brain would work better, and Nate would be quieter.

Gabriela said a few words to Norma, who looked at Naveed and nodded. Gabriela shot another smile at him. "Okay. See you later, Tío Nate."

Out of the corner of his eye, he noticed Vanesa approaching—still looking for that interview, probably—so he quickly got back on his bike and headed towards the camp.

Once there, he removed the plastic bag holding the container of soup from his handlebars and knocked on Marisol and Ramón's door.

No answer.

Maybe they were still asleep? He knocked louder, but they still didn't come, so he cautiously opened the door.

At first he was confused when he looked inside the room. Ramón's blanket-covered shape was still huddled on the bed, but the air was hazy inside, and it smelled strongly of toast. He looked toward the kitchen and saw why: the burner on the hot plate was glowing red, and the stock pot of water bubbled away, filling the room with steam. Marisol sat slumped against the mini-fridge, eyes closed, a dish towel in her hand.

Naveed set the soup on the table, turned off the burner and kneeled down so that he was at eye level with her. Her hair was plastered to her forehead, and her breathing was wheezy, labored.

"Marisol!" Naveed shook her shoulder. "Are you okay?"

Her eyes fluttered open before closing again. "Oh," she said drowsily. "I must have fallen asleep."

"You should go back to bed—" Naveed started, but then she started coughing, holding the dish cloth to her mouth. When she pulled it away, he saw it. The sticky red phlegm, bright with blood—

There was nothing he could do: the instant his brain recognized it, he blacked out. When he came to he was on the floor in front of her, but he turned away immediately, he had to get out, had to get out of here NOW, had to get help—

He bolted out the door, heading back to where he'd parked his bike. The kickstand was stuck, and he swore at it as he tried to get it to move, every second of wasted time compounding his anxiety, and even worse his skin was crawling, he needed to take a shower and scrub himself, or wash his hands at the very least, but there was no time, no time.

The kickstand finally snapped up, but as he was about to mount his bike, he heard someone yelling at him in English. "Hey, you! What do you think you're doing?"

He looked over his shoulder and saw two heavyset white security guards standing in the parking lot, sunglasses on, batons raised.

"This is private property, kid. No trespassing," one of them said, stepping closer.

Naveed's head was so crowded that he could barely grab onto a single thought. *They found me. They're going to take me away. I can't stay here anymore, I have nowhere to go, they're going to take me, but they can't, I need to get help, need to get out of here.*

Stay calm. Breathe. Just relax and breathe.

Impossible. There was no air here. None that he could find, anyway.

But then he remembered the bike, he was still holding on to the bike, and he hopped on and pedaled as fast as he could, even though he was wobbly at first, still unable to draw in a good breath, they were chasing him, still yelling, the security guards, he couldn't let them catch him, no no no none of this was happening no everything was happening again, the guards, the protest, the coughing, the blood, and where had the air gone? Where was it, where was it?

Keep it together. For Marisol. You have to get help. Yes. Help. If he found someone fast enough, if he told them it was MRK, they'd be able to get her the right treatment before it was too late.

He wanted to glance backward to see if the security guards were still chasing him, but he forced himself to keep looking ahead. Had to keep it together. For Marisol. Ramón. Gabriela. The baby. Everyone. It all depended on him doing this one thing right.

And he might have made it, but he hadn't gotten far from the camp when it happened: he lost his balance, and suddenly he was swerving off the road, he was flying over the handlebars somehow, it was impossible to know what was happening or why but the next thing he knew he was on the ground, a sharp pain in his shoulder again, tall grasses swaying above him, he recognized this place, this moonlit wheat field, he had to keep running, had to run or she would find him, but he couldn't move, and he couldn't breathe, and she was coming, he could see her moving through the grasses, a white figure stalking him always, and he was desperate to escape, but that was the thing. Time kept moving in circles. You could run and run and run, but all of this would keep coming back. It would always come back to this.

Time slipped by. Eventually he managed to calm down and regain control of his breathing, though getting back on the bike was out of the question; he was too exhausted to even sit up.

Nate, of course, took the opportunity to taunt him. *You failed, and now it's too late. Because you brought MRK to this place, because you couldn't get it together and find help in time, Marisol struggled for breath until she couldn't find it anymore, and Gabriela came skipping home only to find her mother and her unborn sibling dead. All because of you.*

At first Naveed tried to fight back. *No, she might be okay, maybe someone else found her, the security guards?* But Nate wasn't having it. He kept flooding Naveed's brain with images that he didn't want to see, he was watching Marisol die over and over again, Gabriela finding her, Ramón collapsing over her body.

You bring nothing but misery everywhere you go. Why are you still here?

Slowly, Naveed brought the baggie out of his pocket. He had made a dent in his sleeping pill stash over the past few nights, but still had about ten left. Probably enough to be lethal. Five more tricyclics. That was it. All he had.

He started with the tricyclic, hoping it would shut Nate up, but it didn't. What was the point in going on, Naveed wondered. It was so hard to keep fighting every single day. He was worn out, and didn't want to deal with any of this anymore. Besides, Nate was right: he had no future here, or anywhere; he had nowhere left to go, nothing but a dollar in his pocket and a baggie full of sleeping pills.

Really, there was only one sensible solution, and he was already holding it in his hands.

Naveed

NAVEED SWAM IN A DEEP VAST OCEAN ALONGSIDE AN ORCA WHALE. They skimmed near the surface, but always stayed under. Maybe he was one of them, too, he couldn't be sure. He couldn't see himself. His own borders had vanished, so maybe he wasn't human or orca at all, maybe he was only the water, pulled along by the creature beside him. He was not afraid. There was no room for fear here. He wasn't cold or uncomfortable or in pain, he just floated along, trusting that the orca knew where it was going.

Naveed walked along a road. He knew this road, had traveled it many times in the week leading up to this moment. The sun was high in the sky. It must be noon. Not as hot today as it had been. No mirages drifting up from the black pavement. He turned the corner, slowly, everything he did was slow. He wasn't sure what he might find, but he was not expecting this: a tall chain-link fence now bordered the dilapidated buildings of the farmworker camp. It was one of those temporary ones, attached to concrete blocks. NO TRESPASSING/ PROHIBIDO TRASPASAR signs were affixed to nearly every panel. On the ground near the door to one of the cabins, a stack of multicolored plastic cups lay on its side. There were other items on the ground, a rumpled pair of jeans, something that looked like a tablecloth. Then a movement caught his eye: he saw them, the security guards, and was off and running again....

Naveed was lying in a bed. It was a ridiculously comfortable bed, with a real pillow and a heavy comforter that smelled like fabric softener. It felt so good, he just wanted to pull the covers over his head and keep on sleeping. He didn't dare open his eyes: if this was a dream, he wanted it to last forever.

But he was awake now, awake for real, and naturally he wondered where he was. The last time he'd been on a bed this comfortable, he realized, was that time he'd fallen asleep in Andi's room.

Overcome with curiosity and a strange hope, he peeked out of the covers and looked around. It wasn't her room, of course it wasn't, but it wasn't a hospital either, and it wasn't a motel or a jail cell or a farmworker camp or a secret research facility where he was being held against his will, at least not that he could tell. The walls were beige, empty except for a framed poster of the Eiffel tower and a little placard proclaiming, "Live. Laugh. Love." The bedspread was covered with purple lilies, and a small vase filled with silk roses was arranged atop a doily on the nightstand. By some miracle, his stuffed-full messenger bag sat on a chair in the corner of the room.

What was this place? And how had he gotten here? He didn't feel alarmed, exactly, just unsettled. But he did have to use the bathroom, urgently, so he forced himself upright. His body was still sluggish, thanks to all the sleeping pills he'd taken. Nate had been goading him on to keep going, but he'd managed to stop at three. Then he'd sorted through his remaining meds, keeping the tricyclics but using the rest of his energy to toss the sleeping pills one by one into the dark field.

Hopefully that hadn't been a mistake. But he hated carrying that temptation in his pocket all the time. If he was going to stay alive, he needed to make it harder to do himself in.

Naveed stepped toward the door. The knob turned easily: he wasn't locked in. He exhaled in relief. Down the hall, past other closed doors, to a bathroom with a pink toilet and bathtub. Sure, why not.

The counter was a mess of toiletries, makeup bags, travel-sized tubes of toothpaste. Wet towels everywhere, some wadded on the floor, others slung over towel bars. It looked like a bunch of people were living here. Once he'd finished up, he washed his hands thoroughly with the sliver of soap, scrubbing under the hot water until they were red. He wiped them on the driest towel, and was about to head back to his bedroom, but decided to turn toward the kitchen instead. He felt like he hadn't had anything to drink in days, and the tickle of thirst at the back of his throat would drive him crazy if he didn't do something about it.

He padded down the hall to the kitchen, stopping short when he saw that someone was sitting at the dining table behind a laptop.

Vanesa.

She set down the container of ramen she'd been eating. There was a window behind her, sun shining onto her back, her natural curls illuminated halo-like. "Decided to finally join the world of the waking, huh?" she asked.

He took an involuntary step backward, but didn't know what to say to that. How long had he been here?

"Want some ramen? Breakfast of champions," she said with a cautious smile.

"I just came to get some water," he said.

"Help yourself." She scrutinized him in a way that made him very uncomfortable, and it was only after he found a glass and began filling it with tap water—not even bothering to boil it first!—that he realized their entire conversation had been in English.

Shit.

He gulped down one glass of water right there at the sink, not having any clue where to go from here. As he filled it up a second time, she said, "What are you doing here, Naveed?"

His chest tightened painfully. *She knew.* Had she been the one to bring him to this place? But how had she found him, and where? What kind of mood had he been in at the time? Had he yelled at her? Hurt her?

The water was overflowing, so much clean water, running out of the glass onto his hands. He reached for the tap to turn it off, but it felt like everything was moving in slow motion. She was still watching him, she missed nothing, she knew she'd caught him and that he was rattled, probably knew that he wanted to run straight out of here and never face her again.

But she didn't seem angry with him, or in a rush to send him away, so maybe he'd been lucky; maybe he hadn't let his crazy show, not too much anyway. He needed to know what was going on. He needed to know what she knew.

He took a sip from the glass and walked slowly to the table, where he sat down across from her. No more running. "I don't know, Vanesa. What *am* I doing here? What is this place?"

She closed her laptop. "It's our rental house," she said. "We were out driving yesterday, on our way to get some footage by the farmworker camp, and who do we see crouched near the side of the road but the mysterious guy who led the workers' strike. Nate, they called him, though no one knew where he came from. No one knew where he disappeared to, or why he didn't come back to speak with the managers like he said he would, or where he was when the bosses announced that everyone was fired and had one hour to move out of the camp."

Naveed swallowed hard. He had completely forgotten about his promise to return to negotiate with the managers. He hadn't even told Ramón. "The workers… they got deported?"

"Not yet. One of the local churches is letting them set up camp on their property for now."

He didn't want to ask, but he had to. "What about Ramón? And Marisol?"

Vanesa's expression was grim. "They're in the hospital. Ramón's okay, they'll probably discharge him today, and one of the families from the church agreed to let him and Gabriela stay with them. Marisol, though… she's not doing so well."

But she was still alive. That was something.

"They've tried a whole bunch of medications, but she isn't responding to treatment," Vanesa said.

"Of course she isn't. She has MRK."

Vanesa tilted her head. "Murk?"

"Multi-drug resistant *Klebsiella*. MRK," Naveed said. "She needs to be on rindamycin. It's the only thing that will work."

"How do you know this?" Vanesa asked.

He didn't answer her question, but she was smart. She would figure it out soon enough. "This is important. She needs to start treatment as soon as possible. Can you talk to her doctor or something?"

Vanesa picked up her phone. "I'll text my dad—he's at the hospital with them right now. What's the drug called again?"

"Rindamycin," Naveed repeated. "Is Gabriela okay?"

"Relatively speaking. She's not sick, if that's what you mean."

Naveed released his hands, which had been gripping the cup too tightly. Now he just had to hope that Marisol would respond to rindamycin, that it wasn't too late…

Once she finished texting, Vanesa set the phone down and focused her stare on him again. "When we found out the farmworker camp was closing, Ramón asked if we could pack up his cabin," she said. "Gabriela came with us, but she kept running out to check the other cabins, yelling her little head off for Tío Nate. But he never came, and she didn't want him to lose his stuff, so she went into his cabin and got his bag. A messenger bag—interesting choice for a laborer. And while we were packing up Ramón's cabin, we found this. Gabriela said that Nate gave it to them." She took something down from a kitchen cupboard, then set it on the table between them. A bottle of codeine-containing cough syrup, with the name MIRZAPOUR, NAVEED printed clearly on the prescription sticker.

Naveed pressed his lips together. Goddammit.

"I followed the Nutrexo situation closely," Vanesa said. "I know who you are. But I don't understand why you came here, why you didn't tell us who you were from the beginning. I don't understand why you skipped the negotiations that all those workers were counting on you to attend." For the first time, her voice had an edge to it, but it softened slightly as she said, "I don't know why we found you sobbing in a field on the side of the road. But I want to know. I want you to tell me."

Naveed couldn't hold her gaze anymore. He stared at his ugly scar-webbed hands. He supposed it was lucky that he'd been crying when they found him. Better to be sad and sleepy than scared and violent. That was probably why they had taken pity on him and brought him here, but it didn't make him any less embarrassed about it.

"I'd like to interview you," she said. "On camera. Doesn't have to be right this minute. You can wait until you're ready."

Naveed kept his eyes low as a sudden understanding washed over him. They hadn't taken him here because they wanted to help him. They'd done it because they knew who he was, and thought he might be valuable. They'd caught him like a little golden fish in a fairy tale, thinking that he was enchanted and would bring them riches. Not knowing, not yet, that he was cursed instead.

"The interview. It's for the documentary?" he asked.

"Of course. Like it or not, you're part of the story, Naveed."

The story. Is that what this was to them, just a narrative playing out while they hid behind the safety of their cameras? But no, it was obvious that Vanesa cared about what was happening to the workers. He wasn't so sure that she cared about what was happening with him, but why should she?

"Okay. I'll do the interview." He raised his eyes to meet hers. "On two conditions. One, I don't want anyone else to know that I'm here working with you on this until the film comes out. The focus needs to be on the workers and their story. I don't want to make it all about me."

Vanesa searched him with her eyes. "Don't have to worry about that. All right, that one's easy. What's the other condition?"

"I need a place to stay."

She didn't look at all surprised. "We have the rental for another week. Not a problem for you to stay here. But I want my room back—you can have the couch. And you'll need to make yourself useful."

Naveed didn't really want to give up that comfortable bed, but he was relieved that he'd be able to remain in this house. "Sure. What do you need me to do?"

"The documentary's missing something. A key perspective." She paused for another fork-twirl of ramen.

He had no idea what she was getting at, so he waited until she finished chewing her noodles and spoke again. "Every time I try, I get shot down. But maybe you can use your connections to help me. I would really, *really* love to include an interview with Brennan Walsh."

Who the hell was Brennan Walsh? Naveed had no idea what she was talking about, so he remained quiet. Somewhat helpfully, she continued, "He's been working with your brother, right? I heard them on NPR the other day. I was hoping you might know a better way to get in contact with him."

"I'm not following. What does Brennan Walsh have to do with anything?" Naveed asked. The mention of Cyrus had stirred up a torrent of discomfort, like dry leaves in a sudden wind. If this involved him speaking with his brother, he was going to have to find a way to wriggle out of it. Though he had to admit, he was curious—why had Cyrus been on NPR?

She set down her ramen cup. "It just so happens that Mortensen Fruit supplies most of their product to a single buyer. Bountiful Earth."

Naveed remembered the photograph hanging outside Luis's office, those smiling executives shaking hands in the orchard, and this zinged together in his brain with another memory: he was in the psych unit, Maman sitting in the chair next to his bed, talking on the phone while he pretended to sleep. "He's staying with Brennan Walsh. The CEO of Bountiful Earth! Can you believe that?" There was a pause while the other person reacted with surprise. "No, I had no idea," Maman went on a moment later. "Jake just said they'd be staying with an old friend. But Kourosh seems to be enjoying himself. And I suppose the connection could be useful for CFJ...."

That explained why Vanesa wanted to talk to Brennan Walsh, but Naveed also realized something else: if he played this right, Walsh could fix everything. As the CEO of a company that prided itself on sustainability and fair treatment of its workers, he could put pressure on Mortensen Fruit to settle their labor dispute or risk losing their largest buyer. Maybe Walsh could even arrange for them to rehire the farmworkers who were unfairly fired and prevent their deportation.

Naveed sat up straight. "I'll see what I can do. But I'll need a computer."

"We have a spare laptop. I'll go find it." Vanesa's mouth twitched, as if she were restraining a larger grin.

"Wait. First—can we go ahead and do my interview now?" Naveed wanted to get it over with.

"You bet. It'll just take me a few minutes to set up. Why don't you go get ready? I need about half an hour."

Naveed wasn't looking forward to the interview, but it would be best to get it done while the last drops of sedative were still flowing through his system to counteract the anxiety. He could already feel the nervous anticipation growing within him, expanding throughout his chest like an inflating balloon. There was hope: he could still fix this.

But he could also still fuck it up.

The Death of Javier Ibarra

Sep 14 at 10:42pm

N. M. <beyondthewindowpane@gmail.com>
to Brennan Walsh <walsh.b@bountifulearth.com>

Mr. Walsh:

I hear that my brother Cyrus had a very nice stay at your estate in Santa Barbara last month. Despite the fact that our family doesn't have the best track record with corporate executives, you welcomed him into your home. So I want to believe you're different. I want to believe that you aren't like the rest of them, letting your pursuit of profit destroy people's lives while spouting meaningless slogans about how socially responsible your business is.

And that's why I'm writing today, because I want to know: Are you aware of the death of Javier Ibarra, a farmworker who lost his life picking organic apples—the same apples found in all of your Bountiful Earth stores?

Maybe you know about this already. Maybe you don't let it bother you, maybe you can't even remember his name because you file it in your head under *just another Mexican immigrant*. But Javier was a person. Javier was a husband, a father of three, a kind man whom I had the pleasure of meeting before his tragic death. A death that was directly caused by the extreme working conditions in the fields.

Do you have any idea how hard this work is? Do you know that each of these workers pick thousands of pounds of apples every day and still barely make a living wage? Can you imagine how it would feel to spend a twelve-hour day climbing up and down ladders picking fruit in the scorching heat, every muscle aching, unable to slow down without being berated and threatened with the loss of your job? And can you imagine how it would feel to do all that while sick with the worst flu you've ever had, unable to take a single day off work for fear that it would cost you everything?

Bountiful Earth's mission is to improve the health of its customers, its employees, and the planet. And yet, the people who work the hardest to supply your stores with its fruits and vegetables are suffering horribly. This work breaks their bodies and their spirits every single day.

After Javier's death, the Mortensen Fruit farmworkers here in Sunnyside attempted to organize in order to demand better working conditions. In return, they were fired and forced out of their housing. Now, they are homeless, jobless, camping at a sanctuary church as the weather turns and the threat of deportation looms.

If you didn't know before, you know now. So, the question becomes: what are you going to do about it?

Sincerely,
Naveed Mirzapour

Re: The Death of Javier Ibarra

Sep 17 at 3:31pm

Brennan Walsh <walsh.b@bountifulearth.com>
to N. M. <beyondthewindowpane@gmail.com>

Naveed,

Thank you for writing. I do take these issues very seriously. I'm sure you understand that they are complex, endemic to the industry, and not easy to change, especially since the work force is mostly undocumented. But yes, I am very aware of the death of Javier Ibarra, and am traveling to the area tomorrow to meet with my suppliers and discuss these issues. My schedule is packed during the day, but would you like to meet up for dinner?

Cheers,
BW

Re: The Death of Javier Ibarra

Sep 17 at 8:42pm

N. M. <beyondthewindowpane@gmail.com>
to Brennan Walsh <walsh.b@bountifulearth.com>

Dinner tomorrow works for me. 7pm at Dolce Vita on 6th St?

Re: The Death of Javier Ibarra

Sep 17 at 8:58 pm

Brennan Walsh <walsh.b@bountifulearth.com>
to N. M. <beyondthewindowpane@gmail.com>

Naveed,

It's on my calendar. See you tomorrow at 7pm.

Cheers,
BW

Naveed

NAVEED SAT AT DOLCE VITA, WAITING. HIS INSIDES WERE TRYING to jump out of his skin, and he couldn't stop fidgeting: folding and unfolding a napkin on the table, straightening and rearranging the silverware, running his thumb against the edge of the butter knife. He dipped a slice of stale bread into olive oil and took a bite, but it tasted like nothing.

He had to keep it together just a little bit longer. Everything depended on how this dinner went. If he succeeded in persuading Walsh to help the workers and give Vanesa the interview she wanted, this would be proof that he belonged here, on this earth, that he wasn't a useless waste of space. But if he didn't….

If he didn't, that was it. He was done.

It had not been a good week. Luckily he'd done the interview when he did, because it was the last time he had felt truly coherent. He'd sat down in front of the camera and felt himself slipping into that protective shell that he could retreat into while acting, where he became someone else. Only, this time, he was playing himself, a version of himself anyway.

But it didn't feel true at all, it felt like a caricature of normality, because although he mostly told the truth, he left out the circumstances that led up to him leaving Seattle; he sat there pretending to be a healthy, sane person, and the whole thing left him feeling profoundly weird and depleted.

He wrote the letter to Walsh that night, after finding his email address on the website of a corporate watchdog group that had published the contact information of various executives, and sent it off.

But it had all been downhill from there. Now that his sedatives were gone, Nate was stronger than ever, and he was out for blood. All day and all night, Naveed's thoughts were cluttered with images of decaying bodies, of bright red coughed-up phlegm, of slaughtered animals. *I am the butcher.* The bone-handled knife. Naveed could feel the weight of it in his hands, feel the cool blade against the tentative new skin of his wrists.

To make matters worse, the filmmakers were watching him. They had set up hidden cameras throughout the house, recording all of his movements. Not that Naveed ever saw them, that was the thing about technology these days, they could make cameras small enough to be virtually invisible. He wasn't angry about it; it made sense that they wanted to capture everything about their precious golden fish. It just meant that he had to waste a whole bunch of energy making sure that he didn't slip up.

He was never able to sleep on the couch with those cameras rolling, especially since it was so close to the kitchen, the drawer full of knives. After the rest of them had gone to sleep each night, he wrapped his blankets around him and sat on the concrete patio in the backyard, dozing intermittently through the dark hours, returning inside at the first sign of daybreak. Out there he could feel the seasons changing, the tilting of the earth, the shift towards the crisp autumn days that he had once so enjoyed. Now he dreaded the colder weather, the lengthening darkness.

Sometimes, in the shadows, he glimpsed that white apparition that still stalked him, but it dissolved to nothingness every time he looked directly at it.

The only good thing was that he'd managed not to catch MRK again. And somehow he kept it together during the days, trying to stay focused as Vanesa and the crew taught him how to catalog the hundreds of hours of footage they had collected, glad to have a mind-numbing job to distract him. But it never worked for long. Each night, Vanesa returned with news of Marisol, who, along with Ramón and a growing number of other workers who had fallen ill, had been diagnosed with MRK. The doctors had so far been unable to treat Marisol with rindamycin due to a shortage of the antibiotic, and her illness had been growing worse. One night, Vanesa told them that she had been intubated and transferred to the ICU. The prognosis was not good, for her or for the baby.

The night before his meeting with Walsh, Naveed had taken his last tricyclic. He still hated taking them, but knew, by now, that the antidepressants were the only reason he was able to endure Nate's endless chatter while appearing relatively normal to the others. He dreaded what was to come now that they were gone.

If he succeeded tonight, he would figure something out. He had no idea how he'd get his prescriptions refilled with no money, no ID, and no proof of health insurance, but maybe he could tell Vanesa what was going on and she could help him.

If he failed, then there was no point in going on. He would leave, start walking out of town, follow the highway for a while, maybe throw himself off a cliff or in front of a car. A meaningless end to a meaningless life.

Now, Naveed felt the small weight of the digital audio recorder under the napkin on his lap, which was already capturing the sounds of the restaurant. Thanks to his numb fingers, he wouldn't have been able to press Record without looking at the thing, so he'd started it early. He had "borrowed" it from Hailey, the sound lady—he hadn't asked, and doubted Vanesa would have approved since he wasn't planning on getting consent, but it was important that he have an objective record of this conversation. Especially if Walsh made any promises he didn't end up keeping.

Finally Walsh arrived, fifteen minutes late. Though Naveed had seen photos of him, he was still surprised by his big smile, his unassuming appearance. Walsh walked over to his table, extending his hand. Naveed didn't stand up, but reluctantly shook it anyway.

"Nice to meet you, Naveed. Sorry I'm late—did you get my email?"

Naveed blinked, confused. How would he have gotten emails while sitting here in the restaurant? Then he remembered about smartphones. He'd been living without one for so long that he'd almost forgotten what they could do. "No. I didn't."

Walsh sat down, looking at his phone. "Been a crazy day. Will you excuse me a moment? I just have to wrap a few things up."

The server came over a minute later. "Are you ready to order?"

Walsh glanced at the menu and ordered lasagna and a bottle of wine. Naveed ordered himself spaghetti, no meat, no parmesan. Then he sat there, watching Walsh chew on bread while tapping at his phone. Just like the bosses at the farm, making him wait, sending the message that his time was not valuable.

Suddenly everything about the man seemed repulsive, his pale skin and artfully disheveled hair, the sheen of olive oil on his lips. Naveed hated him, hated everything he represented.

Finally, Walsh set his phone down and took a sip of his wine. "Sorry about that. So. I'm curious, what are you doing out here in Sunnyside?"

Naveed pushed down the hatred so that no animosity leaked into his voice when he responded. "I'm helping out with a documentary about farmworkers. Actually, we'd love to interview you for the film, if you'd be interested." He hadn't meant to lead with that, but there it was.

"Maybe. It would have to go through my publicist, though." Another bite of bread. "I had no idea you were involved with a project like that. Cyrus didn't mention it."

"What did he tell you about me?" Naveed tried not to sound too bitter, but wasn't sure he was successful.

"Not much. He didn't really talk about you."

Naveed silently fumed, but reminded himself why he was here. To stand up for the farmworkers. "Anyway. Like I said in my letter—"

Walsh interrupted. "Trust me, Naveed, I know what it's like for these workers. In fact, I met with the owner of Mortensen Fruit today. They pay the workers more than any other farm in the area, did you know that?"

"Well, it's still not enough. They're barely making minimum wage, even when they're fast pickers. And their living conditions are terrible—"

"Maybe by typical American standards, but they're not bad as farmworker camps go. A lot of other places have bunkhouses where a dozen workers share the same cramped space. Plus, at Mortensen they don't have to worry about pesticide spray, since the orchard's organic. The owner's doing the best he can. He feels terrible about what happened to Javier."

"Oh, does he? Yet he doesn't even want to listen to his workers' concerns, or lift a finger to help them."

Walsh took another piece of bread. "According to him, he came to the orchard last weekend, on his day off, ready to talk with the workers and see if they could come to an agreement. But nobody showed up."

"Ramón was sick." Naveed watched Walsh's hands tear the bread into smaller pieces. "He couldn't be there. It wasn't his fault."

"Yes, I heard about the bug going around," Walsh said, looking at Naveed pointedly. He didn't say anything more, but Naveed knew what he was thinking: *Yes, I know about MRK, I know you were Patient Zero, I know that this is all your fault. Stop blaming Mortensen for the troubles you've caused.*

Thankfully, the server arrived with their orders then. The sweat-socky parmesan smell of Walsh's lasagna wafted over to Naveed. He tried to ignore it as he took a bite of his spaghetti. The sauce was runny, too tart, and the noodles looked like a heap of entrails. He put his fork down.

Walsh didn't say anything for a while. He sliced at the lasagna with his knife, eating big forkfuls and chewing them thoughtfully. Finally, Naveed asked him, "Why did you want to meet with me? It sounds like you just want to defend the status quo. I get that these are complicated problems, but you have the power to do something about them. You could refuse to buy from Mortensen until they give the workers their jobs back and come to an agreement that everyone's happy with."

"I'm not sure I can do that," Walsh said. "Mortensen's the most affordably priced organic fruit supplier out here, and we have a good relationship with them. I'm under a lot of pressure right now to increase our profits. It's not a good time to pick battles."

"But it needs to happen, and it needs to be *now*." Naveed took a deep breath. "Someone we've been following for the documentary, she's about to have a baby, and she's really sick. Critical condition. They're not sure if she's going to make it."

Walsh swallowed some wine. "I'm sorry to hear that." It didn't sound like he meant it. He probably didn't care at all. Didn't even know Marisol, her history, her daughter.

"She can't die. She can't," Naveed said. "But there's a shortage of the antibiotic they need to treat it. Wait, do you know anyone at Genbiotix? Maybe you could pull some strings? Get a shipment of rindamycin sent out here?"

Walsh looked at him questioningly. "I don't have any connections with pharmaceutical companies."

"I'm sure you know someone...."

"It sounds to me like something *you* could do."

"Me?" Naveed scoffed. "Yeah, right. They'd never listen to me."

"Why not? Genbiotix kind of owes you, don't they?"

A memory jolted into Naveed from earlier in the summer, when he was still in the hospital recovering from MRK. Genbiotix had sent a rep to apologize to him, a dark-eyed young woman wearing a very low-cut top. He had seen through her immediately, knew that she was only there to make nice with him and his parents so they wouldn't sue, and the whole thing had disgusted him so entirely that he refused to take the business card she'd held out to him. *If you ever need anything,* she had said. What was her name? It was something unusual that had caught in his brain at the time. If he could only remember it... maybe she could help Marisol....

He was still searching for the name—something that started with a C, but what was it?—when Walsh leaned forward. "I'm sorry about all of this, really I am, and I promise to think about it."

Naveed felt so stupid. Why had he agreed to this meeting in the first place? Why had he ever thought that a rich old white guy would care about anything but his own self-interest? "Thoughts are worthless," Naveed said, his voice full of disdain. "Actions are what matter. I want you to *do* something about it."

"I'll try. Don't know if it'll do any good, but I'll talk to some people at the benefit gala in Seattle tomorrow." Walsh leaned back again, and swished the wine in his glass. "Why did you come here, Naveed?"

"I told you. To work on the documentary."

Walsh stared at him, and Naveed could see he wasn't buying it. And then he understood: he'd been surprised that Walsh suggested a meeting in the first place, but now he knew why. Naveed was the freak show that everyone wanted to watch.

When Walsh spoke again, his voice was quieter. "I get it. I've been through some rough times too, and I know what it's like to be desperate to get away. But there's nowhere to run, because, like they say: wherever you go, there you are."

Naveed wished he could yell, *You have no idea how it is!* What was Walsh trying to prove, feeding him old platitudes and acting like he knew exactly what Naveed was going through?

Walsh lowered his eyes, rubbing at his forearm which, Naveed now noticed, was bisected by a thick finger of scar tissue. "I fought in the Vietnam War, did you know that? And it fucked me up. For a really long time. My buddies from high school and I, we all got drafted, and out there in the jungle I lost them all. They were blown to pieces right in front of me, and I was the only one who came back. I came home and I gave my condolences to their mothers, and I knew they would have given anything to have their sons walking through that door instead of me. And every night, I saw it again, I watched them die. I couldn't stay there, in that place where we had all grown up together. So I left."

Naveed didn't really want to hear any of this, but he didn't interrupt the monologue either. Part of him, he had to admit, was curious where this was going.

"I heard about this commune on Lopez Island and went to check it out. And the moment I met Gaia, everything changed."

Naveed rolled his eyes internally. So now Walsh was going to tell him that all his problems could be solved by falling in love. Because love cures all—goodbye, mental illness and chronic pain! Hell, maybe love was even effective in treating MRK. Someone should tell Genbiotix.

"She was like no one I've ever met, before or since. Life was hard in Orcinia—don't get me wrong, it was rewarding, but we worked all the time. With Gaia, everything felt manageable, and we had these new moon ceremonies that really helped me deal with the ghosts of 'Nam and come to peace with what happened out there...."

He trailed off, staring into space. After a minute, Naveed said, "Well, good for you. Guess all I have to do is escape to a commune and find a woman whose sole purpose in life is to heal me. Thanks for the tip."

"No, no," said Walsh. "That's not what I meant. And that isn't the end of the story, not by a long shot." He breathed in. "I hadn't thought about her in years, but I've been dreaming of her every night for a month now. Ever since your sister found the bones in that sea cave."

Wait, what? He wasn't sure he'd heard that right—was Walsh talking about Roya? It seemed so random... but then again, she and Maman had been vacationing on Lopez... and hadn't Roya said something about bones during their phone call? He wished he could remember.

"It didn't end well between us." Now Walsh looked genuinely sad. He stared at his empty wine glass. "It might have worked out okay, if it weren't for Alastor. The commune was supposed to be egalitarian, but he became the de facto leader. He had been in 'Nam, too, and he came back furious at the world. He was charismatic, but he wasn't the kind of person you'd want to disagree with.

"Gaia was the only one who pushed back. And she was punished for it. She was our healer, and one night she was tending to a man who had been in a building accident. At least, that's what she was told, but I found out much later that one of the others had seen Alastor whaling on the guy after an argument. Anyway, I was out in the greenhouse watering Gaia's peritassa plants, the ones we used for the ceremony. To her, they were sacred. She was so protective of them—they were like—they were like her children." Walsh paused, swallowing hard. "She never allowed Alastor inside. But he knocked on the door and told me that Gaia had sent him, that she needed leaves to make tea for the sick man. I didn't believe it, but I was afraid to challenge him. I stalled, but finally he barged inside and started picking. And that's when Gaia came in.

"I tried to stop her, tried to explain, but she ran away. By letting him in, letting him touch and desecrate those plants she loved so much, I had betrayed her. Alastor went after her, yelling at me to stay out of it. Like a spineless fucking idiot, I did. And when she never came back, when he told everyone that she'd abandoned Orcinia, I believed him. I thought it was my fault. That she'd been so upset by my betrayal that she'd left us all. I looked for her, through the years. But we'd all changed our names at the commune. Gaia didn't exist in the real world. I never knew what happened to her. Or maybe I did. Maybe I just never wanted to face it. But she's not letting me forget it now."

Naveed didn't know what to say. He doubted Walsh even remembered he was there. His phone chimed, but he didn't even glance at it.

"Fuck," Walsh said under his breath a moment later. "Alastor. The peritassa." He fixed his eyes on Naveed. "When's the last time you talked to your brother?"

What did that have to do with anything? "It's… it's been a while," Naveed said, wishing he knew what the hell was going on.

Abruptly, Walsh stood up and took out his wallet, setting a $100 bill on the table under his wine glass. "Nice meeting you, Naveed, but I've got to go."

He started walking toward the door, dialing someone on his phone and holding it to his ear. Naveed shoved the audio recorder into his pocket and rushed after him, perplexed about the odd turn the conversation had taken.

Walsh hung up, and typed away on his phone as Naveed followed him outside. Night was setting in quickly. Walsh turned the corner into the small parking lot in back, eyes still glued to the screen as he stepped towards a maroon rental car. Another car, a black sedan, was parked beside it, but other than that the lot was deserted.

"What about the workers?" Naveed asked, but Walsh didn't even turn. He had forgotten about the farmworkers, and he had forgotten about Naveed: none of that mattered to him, he was just going to stand there tapping at the expensive device that connected him to the whole world but sucked his attention away from the person standing right in front of him.

It overtook Naveed then, a tidal wave of frustration and rage. Everything had a hazy red glow, like the sun through smoke, as Nate rose up in him. Out for blood. And not his own this time.

"The workers. You can't forget about the workers," Naveed said, clamping a hand on Walsh's shoulder.

Walsh turned to face Naveed, his eyes widening in terror.

And then something in Naveed's head exploded. He felt it, he heard it, the loud boom, the red haze blossoming like a burst blood vessel, spreading across his vision until it was all he could see. Nate had done it, he thought as the world disappeared. Nate had broken free, and nothing could hold him back now.

Naveed

FRIDAY, SEPTEMBER 18

WHAT A BEAUTIFUL SKY, NAVEED THOUGHT DAZEDLY WHEN HE opened his eyes. The light bleeding up from the horizon, fading to darkness; those first stars, the brightest ones, already winking on. The waning moon a tiny sliver of light against the black.

Quiet. Dark and quiet. It felt like someone was leaving, or perhaps had just left. But when Naveed turned his head, he saw that he was not alone.

Walsh was lying next to him, blank eyes staring at the moon above. The white skin of his neck cut in a similar curve. His throat. Open. Blood still flowing out.

Time skipped. Naveed was sitting up, his head throbbed, he was afraid to open his eyes. All he could think was *run run run*. Something clattered out of his hand onto the pavement, which surprised him. He glanced at it before he could stop himself.

An ivory-handled knife, its metal blade slick with blood.

The next thing he knew, he was backing out of the parking lot in Walsh's rental car. He wasn't even sure how he'd gotten the keys. Maybe

Walsh had dropped them, that was probably it. The knife was wrapped up in the bottom hem of his shirt, he didn't want blood to get on the seat, had to concentrate on driving. Though he expected to run into the cops at every turn, none had shown up yet. It must have just happened, though what exactly *had* happened?

Brennan Walsh was dead, and Naveed had a bloody knife in his lap.

Had he—had Nate—killed Walsh? That was the only thing that made sense—but where had that knife come from?

There was something inside his head, a big shadowy gap that his brain would not let him access. An image he did not want to see. It was all mixed up with snippets of conversation, random flashes of memory, everything jumbled together in a way that made no sense.

Naveed slowed as he approached a red light. *Concentrate.* He hadn't been behind the wheel since he'd lost sensation in his feet. Muscle memory made it easy for him to find the pedals, but it was hard to get the pressure right, and he came to a jerky stop. Shouldn't be doing this. Any of it. None of this was right. His head was pulsing, *boom boom boom,* like a second heart. Something kept dripping down the back of his neck. *Just breathe. Don't panic.*

The only thing he could think to do was get back to the house, clean up, try to figure out what had happened. No one had been there when he left. Hopefully they wouldn't be back yet, and he could have a moment's peace while he collected himself.

He reached the house. Put the car in park. Kept his head down as he walked inside, the knife still in his hand. His shoes made sticky sounds against the floor. Had to grab onto the wall when a sudden rush of dizziness took him. Everything inside was dark, and when he ducked into the bathroom, he kept the light off. It would be better not to see.

That was when he remembered the cameras that were undoubtedly watching him as he moved through the house. It had been a mistake to come here, but he couldn't do much about it now. He would clean up, grab his stuff, and get out.

He washed his hands, washed the knife, wrapped it in a hand towel. After he turned the water off, he became aware of murmuring voices. Then, as he stepped into the hallway, he heard something else. It was the sound of sobbing, deep ugly sounds that almost could have been laughter, were they not soaked in obvious misery.

The sound was coming from Vanesa's room, where the door was cracked open. A silvery light glowed within; the sobbing sound was kind of tinny. They must be watching footage. He took a step closer, and the sound stopped abruptly.

Naveed paused, wondering if they'd heard him, but then Vanesa let out a long sigh. "I just don't know about this."

"You're worried it's not ethical?" That was Hailey, the sound lady.

"I'm not talking about the film. There's something really wrong. I don't want to kick him out, but… not sure I want him to stay here anymore, either."

"So he's got problems. Don't we all? He's a lot better than when we found him. Seems harmless enough."

Vanesa was quiet for a minute, long enough for it to dawn on Naveed: they were talking about him.

"I hear him at night," Vanesa said. "I used to keep my window open, and I'd hear him out there, in the backyard. He just sits there. All night long. He's always disappearing for long walks, he's supposed to be categorizing clips during the day but barely gets anything done. And yesterday, when I came home, I saw him in the kitchen. He was taking the knives out of the drawer, one by one, holding each one up and staring at it for a long time before putting it back. This went on for probably ten minutes—he had no idea that I was there. I couldn't sleep at all last night. I don't know what to do about him."

Naveed's veins went cold. He'd thought he'd been doing a good job of hiding, but Vanesa had seen right through his act. And she was afraid of him.

Well, she probably should be.

The silvery light flickered, and the sobbing started up again. "Are you all right?" came Vanesa's voice through the laptop speakers.

Naveed crept closer, until he could just make out the figure on the screen. There he was, in mud-streaked clothes, hugging his knees, rocking forward and back and sobbing, sobbing, sobbing.

"Naveed?" Vanesa was off-camera, but her voice was soft.

The person on the screen pulled back, lifting his head. Anger was plain on his tear-streaked face. "Don't call me that. It's not my name. I'm Nate. Naveed's dead." He lowered his forehead back onto his knees. "He's dead, he's dead, he's dead. And I'm the one who killed him."

Naveed stumbled backward, the hallway spinning around him. He had to get out. But he fell into one of the walls, the thump of his body announcing his presence. He could hear Vanesa and Hailey's footsteps behind him, but he didn't turn around. The knife was still in his hands, wrapped up in the towel. He cradled it against his stomach as he scooped up his messenger bag from the living room floor. They were saying things to him: *Wait, where are you going?—Did something happen?—Just calm down, have a seat, tell us what's going on, we want to help—*

The words bounced off him. He didn't want to hear anything they had to say. But he also felt the same blinding rage that had filled him up as he'd stood facing Walsh, and he didn't want whatever had happened back there to happen again.

Vanesa stepped closer, reaching out as if to touch him, but Naveed dodged her hand. "Get the fuck away from me. You think I don't know what's going on? There never was a documentary, was there? It was all a setup, so you could trap me here in this house with your hidden cameras and turn it into some sort of sick reality show. You just wanted everyone to watch me squirm, watch me fail, give them front row seats to the slow-motion train wreck that is my fucked-up life."

They both stared at him, open-mouthed, shock on their faces. It felt kind of good to call them out, but he forced himself to turn away. "I heard you, Vanesa. You wanted me gone. So—here I go. I promise you'll never see me again." He left, slamming the front door behind him.

In the car, he twisted the key in the ignition, pulled away from the curb, too fast this time, tires squealing on the pavement. Hands shaking. Head aching. Now what?

Just drive, said Nate.

Drive where? Go where?

Away.

Go away go away go away.

III.

The Final Sacrifice

Cyrus

CYRUS SAT FROZEN ON THE BACK PATIO, UNABLE TO EVEN STAND up yet. He was just so shocked, examining and re-examining Brennan Walsh's text from all possible angles.

Just met with your brother....

There's something I need to talk to you about in person. Are you free tomorrow at 10am?

None of it made any sense. Naveed, alive? Meeting with Brennan in Yakima right before the CEO's death?

Cyrus had a weird moment where he actually started typing, Yeah I can meet at 10am, before stopping himself. The person who'd written that message was never going to check his phone again. It was hard for Cyrus to wrap his brain around.

Okay. First step: go inside. He opened the kitchen door, closing it softly behind him.

Now what? Should he tell his parents?

Of course. They needed to know.

First, though, he did a quick google of his brother's name, breathing a short sigh of relief when nothing related to Brennan Walsh came up. Annoyingly, though, the top hits were posts from various trolls speculating on his terrorist ways.

He climbed the stairs, so exhausted, wishing he'd never turned on his phone. He glanced at the clock. 1:16 a.m. It had taken him longer than he'd thought to write that letter to Andi.

Timidly, he knocked on the door to his parents' room and cracked open the door. Baba bolted upright. "What is it? Is everything okay?"

"Um, I have some good news and some bad news." Cyrus wished he didn't sound like such a cliché, but his brain was not working very well anymore. "Which do you want first?"

Maman was sitting up, too. "Just tell us," she said in a pained voice, as if guessing that the good news was not very good.

"Okay, so I found out Naveed is alive."

"That is good news," Maman said suspiciously, waiting for the catch, because of course there was one.

"Yeah. But. I only found out because Brennan Walsh, he—he died earlier tonight, he was murdered out in Yakima, but I got this text from him and it turns out he met with Naveed right before he was killed."

They just stared at him. Bleary-eyed, still sitting in bed. Maman's curly hair was tangled on the side she'd been sleeping on, so that part of her hair stuck out in a frizzy mess, while the rest was limp and drooping.

She turned to Baba and muttered something in Persian that Cyrus didn't quite catch, but probably translated to some equivalent of *oh fuck.* Baba looked equally grim.

"It might be okay," Cyrus said. "Could be a coincidence. They met, they went their separate ways, Brennan ended up dead for some random reason."

"Maybe," Baba said. "But that's not what the police are going to think."

Cyrus remembered the conversation they'd had after Naveed's disappearance, and Baba's conviction that they shouldn't get the police involved. "But… shouldn't we tell them?" Cyrus asked. "I mean, I don't want to throw Naveed under the bus or anything, but what if they find out about that text? Won't it look worse if we don't come forward?"

"Kourosh-jaan," Maman said. "What kind of person would kill Brennan Walsh? I don't mean that rhetorically—I want you to tell me what you think. Who would do such a thing?"

The question took him off guard. It seemed a little philosophical for the situation. He'd expected she would be panicking as much as he was, but instead she just looked resigned.

Cyrus's throat constricted. He swallowed hard. "Uh, I don't know. Some psycho? A crazy person who went off their meds and lost control?"

"That's the knee-jerk response, but mentally ill people are more likely to be the victims of violence than the perpetrators," Maman said. "Don't fall into the trap of making them the scapegoat. Go deeper."

Everything about this conversation was uncomfortable, but indulging her was better than arguing. "Okay, I guess… someone who was out for revenge? I don't know who would want to hurt Brennan, though. Maybe it was someone who couldn't control their temper, who got caught up in the heat of the moment. Or somebody who hated what he stood for, who had something to prove."

"And what kind of person do you think they are? What's their life like?"

"Well, they probably don't have a lot of friends. It's probably some isolated loner who spends all their time hating the world."

"And why is that? What happened to make them that way?"

"I don't know. Maybe they have a hard time forming connections with people. Or maybe they have some tragic shit in their past that they never got over." Oops. He just kept swearing in front of his parents.

But Maman didn't seem to care. She only stared at him pointedly, until the cold realization swept over him: he might as well have been describing Naveed.

Cyrus was shocked. "Maman! You don't think he did this, do you?"

"I think that other people might. He fits the profile." Her voice was heavy. "Kourosh-jaan, your brother tried to kill himself. He was really struggling, and his PTSD was serious enough that they wanted to institutionalize him. We should have listened to the psychiatrist, but we didn't, and now he's out there alone, trying to cope with everything all by himself." Her voice broke, and she took a deep breath.

Baba reached for her hand, but kept his eyes on Cyrus. "The CEO of a food company turns up dead shortly after Naveed meets with him. How do you think that's going to look to the detectives?"

Cyrus thought about all of the internet chatter that the trolls had generated. It was a bunch of racist bluster, Cyrus knew; if there was one thing Naveed was not, it was a jihadist. Still, he could see the police seizing onto it, because it fit with the story they expected of him. The whole thing made Cyrus want to throw up.

"It's not going to look good," he admitted. A creak in the hallway startled them and they froze. Cyrus peeked out the door, which was still ajar, and relaxed when he saw no one was there. Just the old house settling, that was all.

"But we still need to tell them, right?" Cyrus continued. "They'll find out about the meeting eventually, and if they find Brennan's message to me, they'll think we were trying to hide something from them."

Baba stood up. "Let me see that text."

Cyrus handed over his phone, wishing that he didn't have to keep dealing with middle-of-the-night crises involving his brother. It almost made him nostalgic for the relative quiet of the past month.

Baba read it, then showed it to Maman, who was pulling on her robe.

"Do you have any idea what Walsh wanted to tell you?" Baba asked.

"No clue."

"And you're sure Brennan Walsh is the only victim? No others were mentioned in the news?" Maman asked quietly.

Cyrus's throat tightened again. He'd just assumed that Naveed was still alive, since he had been at the time that text was written. But the man who'd sent it was gone now. What if Naveed was, too?

But a quick search on his phone confirmed that his assumption was correct. "None of the articles mention other victims. There's a number to call with information, though."

"What do you think, Mahnaz-jaan?" Baba said. "Should we call them?"

Maman crossed the room to the window, which looked down on the front yard. She pushed the blinds gently to the side, moving them almost imperceptibly to peek through the crack. "I think they already know," she said. "A police car just pulled up across the street. No one's getting out, though." She stepped away from the window. "They're watching. Maybe waiting for a search warrant to be issued."

"Then we should call," Baba said. "If we approach them first, we show that we're willing to cooperate. And if they're here, they must be aware that Naveed met with Brennan Walsh, so we wouldn't be giving them any information they don't already know. We won't be able to tell them how to find him, anyway."

"I wish we could talk to a lawyer first, but... I think you're right."

Cyrus read Baba the number for the information hotline, and sat on their bed as his dad made the call and his mother brushed her hair. After Baba hung up the phone, he rolled up his prayer rug and stowed it at the back of the closet.

The three of them descended to the kitchen together, where Maman started a pot of cardamom-scented black tea and Baba nervously arranged the fruit bowl at the center of the table, leaving the honeycrisp apples and prune plums and Persian cucumbers, but taking away the paring knives they usually left nearby.

A few minutes later, they were startled by a loud knock at the door.

"Let us do the talking, Kourosh-jaan," said Maman, tightening the loop on her blue silk robe. "You can show them the text, but don't let them see anything else on your phone. We'll take it from there."

Cyrus nodded. He didn't want to mess anything up.

Maman took a deep breath, squared her shoulders, and reached for

Baba's hand. They walked to the door together. Cyrus wasn't sure what he was supposed to do, so he remained at the table.

"Mr. and Mrs. Mirzapour?" the officer said when the door opened. "We're following up on a tip regarding the murder of Brennan Walsh."

"Yes, of course. Come in—I was just making some tea," Maman said.

Their boots thumped loudly on the floor as they walked inside. Cyrus hoped they wouldn't wake Roya up.

The officers, a buff Asian man and a husky white woman, took the seats Maman offered at the table. She poured them cups of tea, even offered them sugar cubes. It seemed to Cyrus like she was laying it on a little thick, but he wasn't about to say anything.

First, the officers looked at the text and grilled Cyrus about it. What was the nature of his relationship with Walsh? Well, that was kind of a gross way to put it. After the slight nod from his parents, Cyrus explained about Jake's connection—instantly regretting it, what if they went and knocked on his door next?—and about how they'd stayed at Brennan's house, about the Metafolia supplement. That was the only reason Cyrus thought Brennan might have contacted him, but he had no idea what was so urgent that Brennan had suggested a meeting with him.

"Why was Naveed meeting with Walsh in Sunnyside?" the female officer asked.

Cyrus, once again, looked to his parents. They didn't nod this time, so he didn't say anything.

"We don't know," Baba answered. "He moved out a month ago, and hasn't been in contact."

"No contact at all? Why's that—did you have a falling out?"

"We haven't heard from him. We don't know what brought him to Sunnyside," Maman said firmly.

"I see. And what was his mental state like the last time you spoke?"

Cyrus winced, but luckily the officers were looking at his parents, both of whom had poker faces on. "I don't see why that's relevant," Maman said. "A lot can change in a month."

"All we know is that Walsh is dead and Naveed had a meeting with him beforehand," said Baba. "But there's no reason to believe that Naveed was involved in any way. Is there?"

The officers looked at each other. Then the male officer said, "According to the restaurant staff, Walsh met with a young man for dinner. They had what appeared to be an intense conversation. They said that Walsh left in a rush sometime between 8:15 and 8:30, and that the young man followed him outside, seeming upset. Walsh's body was found in the parking lot shortly afterward. Time of death was about 8:25, according to the medical examiner."

Shit. So, the text Brennan had sent Cyrus at 8:19 confirmed that the "young man"—the last person seen with Brennan Walsh when he was still alive—was Naveed. Basically, they'd just turned him into the lead suspect.

"Two others came forward with some additional information," the other officer said. "Naveed had been staying with them while they worked on a documentary together. They confirmed that he had gone to meet with Walsh. But he came back to their place around 8:40. Looked like he'd been in a fight, blood all over his clothes. Very agitated. He grabbed his stuff and sped off in a car that neither of them recognized."

Cyrus was stricken with dread at how bad it all sounded. Maman sat across from him, her expression stony. Baba stared determinedly into his tea.

"So. Do you have any idea where he went?"

"No. Not a clue."

"Any friends he might stay with here, or out of state?"

"Not that we know of," Maman said.

"Mind if we look around for a minute?" asked the female officer.

"Do you have a warrant?" Maman fired back. Cyrus found himself amazed at her, at the way she stood up to them. Even though she was probably terrified inside, reliving memories of previous interrogations, she didn't let them see.

He was also very glad that he'd burned Naveed's notebook earlier that evening. That poem… *I am the butcher*… thank God they would never read that.

The officers didn't answer. Instead, the male officer leaned forward in his seat, warming his hands on his mug of tea, but not raising it to his lips. "The people he was staying with in Sunnyside said he's been having some mental health issues. Has he had any recent violent outbursts? Any suggestions that he might harm others?"

"We've told you what we know," Maman said in a way that clearly communicated, *this conversation is over.* "And as we've said, we don't have any idea where he's gone. If you need to ask any additional questions, we'd be happy to answer them when our lawyer is here."

The officers stood up, and the woman put her card on the table. "If you hear from him, get in touch with us right away."

They showed the officers out, and Maman started cleaning up the teacups, the pot of undrunk tea. As if to try to restore some normalcy to their once-again ruined lives.

"Go get some sleep," Baba said to Cyrus. It almost seemed like a joke, because how could he sleep with all this going on? How could anyone?

Nevertheless, he climbed the stairs. When he got to the top, he noticed that Roya's door was ajar.

Shit. They hadn't been very careful to keep quiet. Especially not the officers, with their loud voices. What if Roya had heard all of that? He crept closer to the door and peered into the darkness.

Roya was not in her bed.

And her window was wide open.

Andi

ANDI AWOKE TO A QUIET, INSISTENT TAPPING ON HER WINDOW. She sat up, disoriented, to find that she'd fallen asleep at the piano. The inspiration had been flying into her that evening, and she'd been so immersed that she'd turned off her phone and closed her door so that she could stay up late to work on her piece. But she'd put her head down to think about how it should end, and must have nodded off. It still bugged her now. What kind of ending should it have: grand and climactic, or quiet and understated?

Not that this was a remotely relevant question when someone was knocking on your window in the middle of the night.

She peeked through the blinds, heart beating fast. It raced even harder when she saw who was out there. Roya.

Andi motioned toward the front door and crept through the house, quietly, to open it for her. She was surprised to see that someone had slipped a letter through the mail slot, and picked it up. Her name was written on the envelope. In Cyrus's handwriting.

What was going on? She opened the door for Roya, who was standing barefoot in her pajamas with her satchel slung across her chest, crying.

"Come back to my room," Andi whispered, not wanting to wake her parents.

Roya followed her, as if in a daze. Andi set the letter on her desk. Now was not the time to open it.

"What's wrong?" she asked once her door was closed.

Roya sniffled. "Why does it have to be like this?" she asked. "All the bad things happening all the time."

"What's going on? Are you okay?"

"They think Naveed murdered someone. Or, at least they think everyone will think he did, and…" Her sobs grew stronger. "Maman said… she said Naveed tried to kill himself. Is that why he was in the hospital? They all knew, but they never told me?"

"Oh, Roya," Andi had no idea what to say. She was confused and shocked and all she could do was hold the little girl.

After a few minutes of letting Roya sob away, Andi asked, "Why did you come here?"

"Because they lied to me. They all lied to me. I couldn't stay there."

"They don't know you're here?"

Roya shook her head. "No."

"Okay," Andi said. "I have to tell them. So they know you're safe. They'll be worried about you."

"They won't even notice I'm gone. Nobody ever notices me anymore."

Andi moved pillows around on her bed, making a nest for Roya, just like she had the day Naveed disappeared. "Here, get cozy. I'll be right back." She briefly considered calling Cyrus, but wasn't ready to talk to him yet. Especially since she hadn't read the mysterious letter he'd left. What did it say? No time for that now. She had Mahnaz's number in her phone, so she sent a quick text. Mahnaz responded that she'd be over in a few minutes.

When she arrived, Andi invited her in. "Roya's in my room. She overheard… some things you were saying about Naveed… but I don't understand. What happened?"

Mahnaz exhaled slowly. It was the first time Andi had seen her in over a month, and she looked older, wearier. "Andi-jaan, Brennan Walsh was killed a few hours ago. He had dinner with Naveed at a restaurant out in the Yakima Valley, they had a heated conversation and left together, and Walsh was found dead in the parking lot shortly afterward."

Andi gripped the doorway to fend off a wave of dizziness. "What? Brennan's dead? But why would Naveed…."

Mahnaz shivered. "How much did Roya hear?"

"She heard you talking about—about what happened last month, when Naveed tried to—" Andi couldn't quite bring herself to speak those words to his mother. "When he tried to. You know," she finished.

"Did Roya hear what the police said?"

Police? This was bad. It was so bad. "I don't know. She didn't mention them."

"Where is she?" Mahnaz asked.

"In my room. This way."

Roya had burrowed so far into the nest that only a tiny circle of her black hair was visible.

Mahnaz kissed it. "Roya-jaan, I'm so sorry. Let's go home, and we can talk about it."

"NO!" Roya yelled, loud enough that it echoed off the walls. Andi heard her parents' bed creaking. Great. Now they were up too. "Nah deegeh, Maman, I'm not going anywhere with you. You all lied to me!"

Andi didn't want to point out that she, too, had been complicit in the lying. She stepped out of her bedroom and opened her parents' door, heard herself explaining what was going on. Saw both their faces go slack with shock when she told them Brennan was dead. And that Naveed was apparently the main suspect.

Roya was screaming in Andi's room. "NO! I'M NOT GOING HOME! I HATE YOU AND I HATE BABA AND I HATE KOUROSH AND I'M STAYING RIGHT HERE FOREVER AND EVER AND EVER!"

Andi's mom got out of bed. "Let's go to the living room," she told Andi. They sat next to each other on the couch, a throw blanket wrapped around them both. Andi was still too shocked to cry, but she couldn't stop shaking. She was thinking of that night behind Parapluie, the sound that Brooke's body had made as Naveed slammed her against the brick wall, the fear radiating from him, the distance in his eyes, like he didn't know where he was or what he was doing.

Had something like that happened with Brennan? *No*, Andi thought. No. Naveed would never murder someone.

Then again, she hadn't thought he would try to kill himself, either.

Andi leaned in closer, letting her mother stroke her hair and rub her back, thankful to not be alone.

Eventually, Mahnaz came out of the bedroom. She looked close to tears.

Andi's mom said, "Roya's welcome to stay here. She doesn't mean it. She just needs to cool down."

"Thank you," Mahnaz said, a slight tremble in her voice. "The police will be back to search our house once they get their warrant, and I'd rather she wasn't there."

"Of course. She can stay as long as she—as long as you both—need," Andi's mother said.

Andi returned to her room after Mahnaz left. Roya peeked out of the covers, saw it was only Andi, and burrowed back down.

"Can I join you?" Andi asked as she climbed in. Roya didn't stop her.

"I hate them," said Roya after a pause. "I hate them for keeping secrets, but I know I shouldn't hate them for that, because I...." She trailed off.

Andi squeezed her hand. "I know how you feel."

"No, you don't understand." Roya pulled her hand away. "I want them to pay attention to me. I want them to leave me alone. Two opposite things that I want at the same time, and I don't know which one I want more."

Andi didn't want to make her more upset, so she just said, "It's been hard, hasn't it, Roya?"

"Mmm hmm," Roya squeaked while tears streamed down her face. Andi's heart tightened. This wasn't the simple, explosive tantrum a little kid would throw; Andi recognized the messy, conflicted emotions of an older girl. A girl who was learning how to cry silently.

"If he tried to die on purpose," Roya whispered after a minute, "That means he wanted to leave me forever."

"I'm sure he didn't think about it that way." Andi couldn't believe she was having this conversation with an eight-year-old. "He loves you. He didn't do it to hurt you."

"Well, it *does* hurt," Roya said. "It feels *horrible*."

There was nothing more to say. After Roya cried herself to sleep, Andi did too.

It was not a restful sleep; it was like those days when she used to have slumber parties with her friend Marina, constantly waking up in the night when the other person shifted or turned over. Plus, there was the whole matter of Brennan Walsh. Dead. How could he be dead, when she'd just been at his house a month ago? That place had been so beautiful. Until Cyrus had ruined it.

And where was Naveed now? Where had he gone?

Around ten in the morning, there was a soft knock at her door. "The police are here," her dad said, like it was a perfectly normal thing. "Can you come out and talk with them for a few minutes?"

Roya was still fast asleep. Andi threw on a hoodie and stepped into the kitchen, where her mother greeted her with a mug of tea and a piece of toast. The officers were eating toast also. If it hadn't been for their dark suits, their batons and guns—why did they have to bring those in here anyway?—it would have been like they were just hosting a couple of exceptionally muscular acquaintances for breakfast.

They asked Andi when she'd last seen Naveed, whether she knew what he was doing in Sunnyside, if she had any idea where he might have gone. She answered their questions, but didn't mention the suicide attempt or the incident at Parapluie. From the way they talked about him, it seemed obvious that they believed he was the murderer. Andi did her best to convince them otherwise, even though she wasn't entirely sure of his innocence. All she knew was that he wouldn't react well if they hunted him down, and she wanted him to have a chance.

They left after what seemed like a very long time. As she watched the front door close, Andi put down her mug. "Wait, what about the gala for the Walsh Foundation? It was supposed to be tonight. Is it still happening?"

"Yes. They sent out confirmation that the event's still on," her father said. "To be honest, though, I'm not really up for it. If Brennan was going, I'd want to, but." That was the end of the sentence. He looked down at his phone, and the unspoken words hung in the air.

"But I need to be there." Andi had been planning to speak with Senator Bittner about working on a bill to tighten FDA regulations, and had put a lot of research into it over the past week. Now, it seemed more important than ever. Brennan wouldn't have wanted her to give up the fight.

Roya wandered into the kitchen looking slightly lost, and Andi's mom sat her down at the table with orange juice and a piece of toast. Roya picked at it.

"Why do you want to go?" Andi's father asked. "It's not going to be very interesting. A bunch of rich people milling around, eating canapés and drinking champagne."

"Because. I just have to. I kind of… I promised Brennan I would do something, and I don't want to… you know. Let him down." It sounded ridiculous, but it was true. "I can go by myself. You guys can stay home and watch a movie or something."

"You're not going by yourself," her father said.

"What are you talking about?" Roya asked.

"Oh, just a fancy party we were supposed to go to tonight," Andi said.

"Is that the one Kourosh is working at?"

"He's helping with the catering, I think."

Roya sat back. "He said the hotel is really cool. The ballroom's right over the water."

"So are you coming with me?" Andi asked her parents.

"We don't have a ticket for Roya," her mother said without answering her question. "Someone will need to stay with her. Unless she's ready to go home by then."

"I'm never going home," Roya declared. They all avoided looking at her, and each other. "And I want to go to the ball, too. I want to stay with Andi."

"It's not a ball," Andi said. "I don't think there's going to be any dancing."

"But it's in a ballroom, isn't it?" A faint smile played on Roya's lips. "I've always wanted to go to a ball."

"She could have my ticket," Andi's father said from behind his phone.

"If we take you to the ball," Andi's mom started in her bargaining voice, "Do you think you might be willing to go home afterward? We love having you, of course, but your family misses you."

"No, they don't."

"They do. They want you to come back home."

Roya chewed her toast. "I'll think about it."

By afternoon, she had decided to take the deal. Andi's mother went over to Roya's house to get a dress and shoes for her and fill Mahnaz in on the plan.

While Roya was getting dressed, Andi finally got a chance to read Cyrus's letter. But as soon as she'd finished, she wished she'd never opened it. Reading about what had happened the night Naveed tried to kill himself stirred up even more emotional turmoil. She wasn't sure how much more of this she could take in one day.

Cyrus was probably waiting for her response, but by now he'd be at work, chopping vegetables and prepping food for the gala. She wouldn't reply yet, she decided. She would wait until the event and approach him in person.

The problem was, she had no idea what she was going to say when she saw him.

Naveed

SOMEHOW NAVEED ENDED UP IN THE MOUNTAINS. HE FOLLOWED the curve of the highway as it gained in elevation, eyes darting to the rearview mirror every few seconds. No cops yet.

It seemed a miracle that they hadn't found him. He'd figured that Vanesa would have called them as soon as he left. But maybe she hadn't. Maybe she'd just been happy to get rid of him and didn't have any clue, yet, that Walsh was dead.

Naveed drove. The throbbing in his head slowed to a dull ache. Something kept trickling down his neck, and he grew increasingly certain that it wasn't sweat. The car smelled like blood. *Don't think about the blood.*

He couldn't stop thinking about the blood. Eventually he grew so light-headed that he had to pull over. He wanted to keep moving, didn't feel safe sitting there on the side of the road, so conspicuous to Highway Patrol, but he didn't want to pass out behind the wheel and hurtle off a cliff. Not yet, anyway. He still had things to do first.

Naveed waited until the road was clear before he cautiously stepped out of the car, getting up slowly and waiting for the inevitable head rush to pass. He opened the trunk to find all of Walsh's luggage, including a soft leather briefcase containing a slim silver laptop. And an envelope with several guest passes to that benefit dinner he had mentioned, along with a copy of the seating arrangements. Several familiar names at Table 1 caught his eye: Joyce Lin. Jake Powell. Andi Lin. Cyrus Mirzapour.

Naveed hastily shoved the envelope back into the briefcase and rummaged through the other bag, the rolling carry-on suitcase. Clothes, lots of clothes. Good—he needed to change. Along with the briefcase, he grabbed a few shirts, a suit jacket and pants, plus a pair of shiny dress shoes, and moved them to the passenger seat.

Once he'd sat down in the front seat again, he unbuttoned his top layer, the plaid button-down shirt one of the camera guys had let him borrow, then reclined his seat all the way and forced himself to look at the back of the collar. As he'd feared, it was soaked with blood.

It wasn't so bad passing out while lying down, a bit like falling into a sudden sleep. Coming back groggy and disoriented was the annoying part.

Naveed wiped off his neck, then tied the button-down shirt around his head nice and tight. Hopefully it would stop the bleeding.

He reached for the knife in the passenger seat. It was still wrapped up in the hand towel, and he was afraid to look at it. What Vanesa said about him going through the kitchen knives had rattled him. He had no recollection of doing that. No doubt the hidden cameras had caught it on film, and they'd be showing the police, and if the knife wrapped in that towel matched the ones at the rental house....

Did you do this, Nate? You smuggled a knife out of that house without me knowing? How is that possible?

For once, Nate was silent.

Naveed took the bundle into his hands and began to unwrap it, expecting to see a standard kitchen knife. But that wasn't what he found at all.

The blade was thick and sharp. The handle was ivory-colored, and covered with intricate carvings.

A bone-handled knife. A serious knife.

The kind of knife used for butchering.

This was worse, much worse, than finding out he'd taken one from the rental house without knowing. Somehow, he had conjured this... this *thing* into reality. He had been so fixated on blood and knives and *I am the butcher* that his thoughts had become solid and materialized in real life. He had killed a man—and not just any man, a wealthy and powerful corporate executive—with a weapon created by his own mind.

Part of him wanted to throw the knife out the window and be done with it. But what good would that do? It wasn't bound to normal physical laws; it might resurface somewhere else when he, or Nate, called for it. The bone-handled knife would follow him forever.

Instead, he studied the carvings. The central design showed two orca whales swimming in a circle. He must have gotten the idea from that dream he'd had after taking all those sleeping pills, swimming deep in the ocean alongside the killer whale. He'd felt so peaceful then, so interconnected with the universe. He wished he could find his way back there now.

Enough of this. He had to get back on the road. But as he shifted his legs, attempting to get comfortable, he remembered the audio recorder in his right front pocket. When he took it out, he was surprised to see the minutes still ticking by on the screen display. The length of time elapsed was two hours, eleven minutes.

It had been recording all this time.

He stopped it, hesitating for only a second before pressing Play. Then he pulled back onto the highway.

Of course, there was a chance that the recording would be crap, uselessly muffled by the rustling of his jeans. But he'd shoved it into his pocket with the mic at the top, so it was possible that it had picked up some of the sounds while he'd been out... maybe it could give him some answers about what had happened with Walsh....

The first fifteen minutes at the restaurant were mostly silence, except for the occasional questions of the server who came by his table and the clanking of his silverware as he fidgeted with it. He didn't want to mess with the recorder while driving, so he just let it play out.

Naveed listened to the whole conversation with Walsh again, but it was different than it had been the first time. He felt detached from it now, emotionless about the things that had previously irritated or enraged him.

Except when he got to the part about Marisol. That part still weighed on him heavily. He wasn't going to leave this world without doing something to help her. He just needed to find that Genbiotix rep. What had her name been? Something that had fit her a little too perfectly, so much that it had almost seemed like she'd made it up.

He couldn't remember. His brain felt like it was liquefying. Every time he tried to hold onto a thought, it poured right through his fingers. Focusing his attention on it wasn't helping, so he let it slosh around in the back of his mind as he listened.

The stuff Walsh was saying about the commune seemed even weirder the second time around. Orcinia. Wasn't that, or something like it, the scientific name for orca whales? Strange how it all kept coming around again. Circles and circles. Endless loops that he could never seem to break.

He sat up straighter as the end of the meeting neared. There were the random bursts of static as he shoved the recorder into his pocket. But he could still hear himself pleading with Walsh as they walked outside. *What about the workers?* His voice desperate, verging on pathetic. *You can't forget about the workers.*

What he heard next surprised him. A deafening thud, so loud that he jumped, followed by the sound of something heavy dropping to the ground, and a loud scrape against the recorder's mic.

There was a moment of stillness, with faint movement in the background, footsteps, maybe. Then came a grotesque gasping sound, and something else falling to the pavement. A body, Naveed realized. So the first body to fall had been Walsh, and the second his own? But that didn't make sense; the mic scrape would have come when *he* hit the ground—

Then someone spoke. No: two people, one voice very deep, the other less so. They whispered to each other, so he couldn't understand what they were saying. It didn't even matter to him at this point. What mattered was this: he and Walsh had not been alone.

Someone else—two other someones—had been there, too.

Maybe he hadn't killed Walsh after all.

It was almost too much for his mushy brain to handle. He barely had time to process all this before he heard footfalls on the recording, very loud, like they were right next to the mic. A voice saying, "No—stay there. I need to finish this one."

"There's no time," the deeper voice said. "We need to leave."

"He was an unintended sacrifice," the other one said. Something about the voice, its rippling softness, made him guess it was an older woman. "I need to finish the ritual. Maybe these two will be enough."

"No. There's still one more we need. In Seattle, at the charity event tomorrow."

The other voice seemed impatient. "I'm not leaving until he's taken care of. Go, start the car. I'll be right behind you."

Grumbling. Footsteps. A car door closing very quietly. Naveed tried to imagine what was going on. Was the woman kneeling over his body? Maybe she'd pressed the knife into his hand and was about to make him stab himself before something scared her off just in time?

But she only murmured, "Still breathing. Good. It wasn't your night to go."

The next thing he heard was the sound of the car pulling out of the parking lot. Shortly after that came lots of rustling, followed by another door slamming and a car starting, then some wounded-animal-like whimpering sounds that he must have made as he drove away from the restaurant.

Naveed stopped the playback, letting it all sink in. He was so confused, and weirdly disappointed: none of this fit with what he'd thought had happened.

Trying to sort it all out felt completely overwhelming. So he turned what little attention he had left to the road, and before he knew it he was crossing the bridge into Seattle. He hadn't even intended to come here, not consciously anyway, but it was a relief to be somewhere familiar. He needed to stop and rest for a minute, so he exited off I-90 and descended into the Mount Baker neighborhood. He found a residential street that looked well populated with cars, the quiet, dark houses towering around him.

There was so much that he still needed to figure out, but as soon as he put the car in park, a wave of exhaustion overtook him, so intense that he couldn't even try to fight it. He crawled into the back seat and fell into a dreamless sleep.

He awoke with a word in his head. *Charisma.* It was still dark outside. According to the dashboard clock, it was 4:03 a.m. Though his head ached dully, his brain felt like it had solidified again, allowing him to think more clearly. And that word kept repeating. *Charisma. Charisma.*

Astonished, he sat up.

That was the name of the Genbiotix rep! Charisma… what was it… Carter? No, not Carter… Cooper. Yes! Charisma Cooper. So now all he had to do was find her online, write an email explaining the situation, beg her to send the antibiotics to Sunnyside's community hospital. Even if there was a shortage, they had to be able to spare enough to save the life of a pregnant woman and her baby. Especially because of the documentary. If they provided the antibiotic and Marisol survived, Genbiotix would come out looking like heroes. If they didn't, they'd look like cold corporate bastards.

That ought to be enough to motivate them.

Without looking at his shirt-bandage, he took it off and gently touched the back of his head. He couldn't feel if his fingers were wet or not, but when he looked at them, bracing himself, he saw no blood. He balled up the shirt and stowed it under the passenger seat.

Naveed grabbed the briefcase from the front seat, and opened Walsh's laptop. Naturally, it was password-protected. But he was able to log on as a guest, and as soon as he was in, he checked for nearby unsecure WiFi signals. He didn't find one, so he drove to the next street. This time, he was in luck: one of the available networks didn't require a password.

Once connected, he typed out his email to Charisma Cooper, begging Genbiotix to send an immediate shipment of rindamycin to the hospital in Sunnyside, where Marisol was in the ICU. He told them about the documentary, and copied several other people—including the hospital itself as well as Genbiotix's head of PR, whose contact info had been published on the same list as Brennan Walsh's. After a brief internal debate, he also copied Vanesa. She could take it from there, since he wouldn't be able to check his email again. He would need to ditch the laptop and find a place to hide while he figured out his next move.

But he didn't send the email quite yet. Something else was itching at him, another connection that had eluded him before. He kept thinking about how paranoid Walsh had seemed as they left the restaurant. The fear in his voice when he'd mentioned the guy from the commune all those years ago. *Alastor. The peritassa.*

Had Walsh thought Alastor was after him for some reason?

When's the last time you talked to your brother?

And, possibly, after Cyrus too....

More importantly, was he right?

Still one more we need. In Seattle, at the charity event tomorrow.

Not that it made a difference. It didn't matter to Cyrus whether Naveed lived or died, so why should Naveed care if his brother was in danger?

But... Cyrus wasn't the only one going to that event.

Andi would be there, too.

No. Everything was fine. Wasn't it? The whole thing was just so... unlikely. But Walsh had seemed so convinced....

On a whim, Naveed searched "orcinia." He was stunned to find a website among the search results proving that it actually existed, though not as a commune anymore, as a "spiritual discovery retreat." There wasn't much information on the site other than a few pictures. Naveed stopped cycling through them when he saw the photograph of the smiling older couple standing in front of a yurt. The caption noted that they were the owners of Orcinia, but their names were not mentioned anywhere on the site. The woman's white hair was tied into a braid. The man—Alastor, could that be Alastor?—had a long grey beard. But what caught Naveed's eye was the symbol painted on the canvas wall behind them: two orca whales swimming in a circle.

In disbelief, he rummaged around until he found the bone-handled knife. He examined the symbol, looking back and forth.

They matched. Exactly.

So was *that* what had happened? Alastor, or the old woman, had killed Walsh, and left Naveed with their knife. Why the woman had let him live, why she would leave him with this key clue to her identity, he didn't understand.

Too bad he couldn't take this to the police and let them handle it, but they would never believe him. Besides, even if he hadn't killed Walsh, Naveed had still stolen his car and fled the murder scene. That made him a criminal in their eyes. Going to the police for help was out of the question. He would have to take care of this himself.

There was one more thing he wondered about, though. Naveed searched for "bones lopez island" and found an article about how a young tourist had made the accidental discovery of a human skeleton, thought to belong to a woman who died thirty years ago. But no one had come forward with any leads on her identity, so it would likely remain an unsolved mystery.

Naveed wished he'd been paying more attention to Roya when they had talked on the phone. Of course his parents hadn't told her why he had been in the hospital, but she picked up on stuff like that. He'd been so nervous, trying to think of normal things to talk about, that he hadn't really heard what she'd said. Hadn't she mentioned something about bones? She'd asked him something... about rust. Wait, yes, she was talking about a key, a rusty key that she'd found near some bones; a box that could not be opened.

What was in that box? Was it something Alastor wanted?

He hadn't noticed her name on the seating chart... but was Roya going to be at the dinner, too?

Naveed's gut twisted. He sent the email to Genbiotix, wiped his browser history, and clicked the laptop shut, though there was much more he wanted to know. It was so tempting to drive to his house. Just to check on Roya. To make sure she was all right. But now that he was in the city, police were everywhere. He wasn't safe here, needed to abandon this car. He'd have to leave on foot.

He wet the hand towel with his water bottle and scrubbed off his face and neck. His hair was long enough now to have a slight curl to it. Hopefully, the wound on the back of his head wouldn't be noticeable.

Then he changed into Walsh's suit and dress shoes. He would need to leave most of the contents of his messenger bag behind, but he opened the briefcase and tossed in the rest of his ginger chews, his water bottle, and the keys to his old house. The silver star charm winked at him under the street lights, reminding him of what was at stake. He slid the knife into the briefcase's front pocket.

Naveed stowed the laptop under the driver's seat and stepped out of the car, looking, he hoped, like an overworked businessman about to start a long day at the office, briefcase in hand. He glanced one last time at the car, parked in front of a stately mansion like it belonged there, before stealing away into the darkness.

Andi

ANDI SNAPPED HER BEADED CLUTCH OPEN AS HER MOTHER pulled the car into valet parking at the hotel. She checked her phone for the millionth time, re-reading the texts she'd been exchanging with Brooke throughout the day, as once again the Mirzapour brothers muscled back into their lives. She was ridiculously nervous about meeting up with Cyrus again, not to mention talking with Senator Bittner, but the irreverent GIFs that Brooke had scattered throughout their conversation made her smile.

Roya sat next to her, gazing through the car windows. She was wearing a light blue summer dress—her nicest one, according to Mahnaz—and had insisted on bringing her satchel. Even though it looked heavy and awkward, no one was in the mood to argue with her.

After parking their car and checking their coats, they stepped into the ballroom. Roya had been right: the view was amazing. It was on the third floor of the hotel, which was located on the downtown Seattle waterfront. Walls of windows looked out over the waves of Puget Sound.

A white ferry chugged towards the sunset, heading for the faint pine outline of Bainbridge Island.

Inside the room, elegant people stood in small clusters holding glasses of champagne. The mood was somber, and everyone was wearing black. Andi felt self-conscious in her dress, a nearly full-length dark maroon that she'd worn to junior prom the spring before. At least Roya stood out too, not that this was much comfort; she would have anyway, as the only young child there. Large round tables were laid out with centerpieces of multicolored apples and autumn leaves. There were name cards at each spot.

"Roya, can you find our table?" Andi asked. She wished with every passing second that she hadn't come. If Brennan had been here, he would have welcomed them in, started introducing them to people, taken her right over to Senator Bittner. But he wasn't, and she keenly felt his absence. She didn't belong here. At all.

Her mother had seen someone she recognized, and said she'd meet them at the table. Andi glanced around the room, looking for the senator, whose picture she'd looked up online.

A waiter passed with a tray full of hors d'oeuvres: lettuce leaves that looked like little boats stuffed with some sort of savory mousse. Andi stopped him, taking two. She'd intended one to be for Roya, but they were so delicious that she ate them both. She wondered if Cyrus had helped make them.

Roya tapped her shoulder. "Our table's over there. Do you have anything to write with? I want to cross out your dad's name and put mine in."

Andi finally spotted Senator Bittner across the room. She was talking to a short-ish man with thinning auburn hair who gave off a distinct *I'm a very important person* vibe.

"No, I don't think so," Andi said distractedly. "Hey Roya, why don't you sit at the table for a minute. I'll be right back." She summoned all her courage. She was going to do this. She owed it to Brennan.

When she approached, the senator and the man didn't seem to notice. They were deep in conversation, but after a moment the man glanced at her. It looked like he did not appreciate being interrupted.

But she was already here, and they were both staring at her now. "Senator Bittner?" Andi asked. "I'm Andi Lin. Brennan Walsh is—um, was—a friend of my dad's, and he mentioned you would be here and there's something I wanted to talk to you about." Ugh. Not very smooth.

The senator smiled and held out her hand. Andi shook it, hoping hers wasn't too clammy. "Andi Lin. I know who you are, of course. It's a pleasure to meet you. Mr. Whitaker, can we continue our conversation later?"

Mr. Whitaker scrutinized Andi for a moment before turning away. Andi felt a burst of admiration for the senator: the courage it took to give such an obviously powerful man the brush-off like that.

"You know Brennan?" the senator said once he'd left. "Knew him, I mean. I can't… I just can't believe he's gone. I keep expecting him to walk through the door any minute."

"I know. I can't believe it either," Andi said.

"And then the vultures swoop in," Senator Bittner muttered to herself, casting a quick glance in Mr. Whitaker's direction. Andi's interest pricked up—what did that mean? But no, she'd had enough corporate intrigue for one lifetime. She had different things on her mind now.

The senator was saying, "So. Andi. What did you want to talk to me about?"

"Well, I don't know if Brennan mentioned the Metafolia supplement to you? Or maybe you heard about it on the news." The senator nodded, so Andi figured she didn't need to explain any further. "Anyway, the whole thing got me thinking about the way that supplements are approved for sale. I've done some research, and it's kind of shocking how easy it is to get them on the market. And it isn't just supplements, it's all sorts of food additives. Like Blazin Bitz Crave—the FDA actually approved those too. Brennan said that you might be interested in putting a bill through to tighten up regulations."

Senator Bittner frowned. "Believe me, I'd love to. But it's a difficult climate for that right now, politically. A bill like that would never go through. There would be too much backlash from food industry lobbyists."

Andi's heart sank. "So you're saying it's a lost cause?"

"I'm afraid so."

"But Brennan would have wanted—"

"Brennan would have wanted a lot of things." She sighed. "I'm sorry, Andi. But I'll keep it in mind. Maybe someday, when the pendulum swings back again."

"Okay. Thanks anyway." Andi turned away, completely disappointed. She never should have come. Suddenly she wanted to talk to Cyrus, to vent her frustration, because he would understand. She remembered how she'd scoffed at him for what he'd done to that supplement company, thinking it didn't solve the real problems, but at least he'd done *something*. And he'd gotten results.

One of the waiters passed by and offered her a different appetizer, small toasts topped with a dollop of artichoke dip and a dusting of fresh herbs. Her stomach growled. She wondered if he'd heard it. "I'd better take two," she said.

"Have as many as you want. I've been around this room three times, and nobody's taking any. These people," he said conspiratorially, as if he knew Andi was not one of them, "They don't eat. The champagne, on the other hand? We've probably gone through a hundred bottles already."

Andi smiled and accepted the napkin he handed her, loading it up with the delicate toasts. "Do you work at Parapluie? I know one of the caterers... I was just looking for him."

"No, I work for the hotel. Sometimes we have outside caterers come in to do these events."

"Would you mind if I peeked inside the kitchen? I need to talk to him for a second."

He shrugged. "This way."

She followed him down a short hallway. Several rolling racks were parked by the kitchen door, with trays full of plates stacked inside. Each plate contained a mound of microgreens topped with shaved carrots and toasted pumpkin seeds, a creamy dressing drizzled on top.

"Looks like it's almost time to serve the first course," the waiter muttered, sliding his tray into a pass-through window. He nodded at the door. "Go ahead."

Andi stuck her head in. The room looked like a battle zone, carrot shreds all over the floor, Chef Thierry barking out orders to the cooks on the line, several people standing at stainless steel tables chopping potatoes as fast as they could. But Cyrus was not there.

One of the potato choppers turned and saw her. "What are you doing back here?" he asked, eyeing her evening gown.

She stepped in the door. "Um, I'm looking for Cyrus? I thought he was supposed to be working tonight."

He sniffed. "He called in. So now *I* get potato duty."

"Oh. Okay. Sorry." She backed out, unexpectedly rattled by the news. She'd been so sure that Cyrus would be here, and though she was nervous about talking to him, she wanted to get it over with. Maybe she'd have to drop by his house later instead.

When she returned to the ballroom, everyone was making their way to their tables as the salad was served. Andi's mother was sitting at the table, but Roya was not there.

"Where's Roya?" she asked.

"I thought she was with you," her mother said.

"I'm sure she's around here somewhere." Andi mentally berated herself for not paying better attention. "I'll go look for her."

She checked the bathroom first. No sign of Roya there. So she checked all the halls around the ballroom and back by the kitchen, where there was a flurry of activity as the waiters rushed to get everyone's salads out.

Andi walked back to the ballroom, hoping that she'd just missed Roya somehow, and she'd be sitting at their table like she should be. But she realized there was one place she hadn't checked: the outdoor terrace. She'd avoided it because there was a cold wind blowing tonight. But maybe Roya had gone outside. She liked to be outside.

And then Andi saw, out of the corner of her eye, something that shocked her.

No, she must be imagining things. Right? It made no sense. He must be another party guest; he looked like them from the back, the dark suit and close-cropped hair. But she recognized the way he moved, his lanky body, his slightly clumsy shuffling walk.

Naveed. He was here.

Roya

ROYA SAT AT THE DINNER TABLE ALONE, STARING AT THE APPLES in the centerpiece arrangement. She wished she could eat one, but knew it wouldn't be polite.

The ball wasn't any fun. She didn't know what she'd expected, but people always wanted to go to balls, so she'd thought there must be *something* exciting about them. This was just a bunch of grown-ups milling around looking sad. She didn't really need any more of that.

Andi and Joyce had both left to talk to people, so Roya took one of the name cards from the table and stuffed it into her satchel before heading towards the bathroom.

She'd made up her mind. She needed to talk to Naveed, and the only option left was to use the blood magic that Kass had suggested. She'd tried the other spells, but they hadn't done a thing. It was time to get serious.

Roya washed her hands with hot water and soap, thinking about where she should perform the ritual. She could go into one of the stalls, but it didn't feel right to do it in here, with these fluorescent lights blaring down on her.

As she was drying her hands, a group of ladies walked in, stopping their chatter abruptly when they noticed her. That settled it: she couldn't stay. She nodded at them and stepped out of the bathroom, still holding the paper towel. Behind her, she could hear their low voices. "That was her, wasn't it? Naveed's sister, I can't remember her name. Is the rest of her family here too? The nerve…."

Roya couldn't listen anymore, and now she didn't want to go back to the table at all. She wanted to be somewhere dark and quiet, where no one was looking at her. Outside, maybe? It looked like there was a deck. But it was cold tonight, and they had taken her coat, hidden it away somewhere.

She headed back to the entrance. The girl who'd taken their coats was standing at the open door oblivious to everything except her phone, so Roya easily snuck past her into the coat closet.

It was bigger than she thought it'd be, stretching far back into darkness. In the front area, coats dangled from racks with little tags hanging from them. Roya quickly spotted hers, its bright colors contrasting against the dark wools of the grown-ups' coats, but she didn't take it off its hanger. This room would be perfect.

She walked into the shadows. It was very quiet, but she thought she heard something, a rustling in the dark. *Just your imagination*, she told herself, but stopped before going too far back. She sat against the wall underneath one of the coat racks and took the name card out from her satchel.

It had "Jake Powell" written on the front, but she tore it along the fold so that she was left with the blank back. She wished she'd brought a pen that she could write Naveed's name with. Too late now. She'd have to improvise.

The first thing she was supposed to do was cast a circle, but she didn't really know how, so she just traced an invisible line around herself while thinking about how badly she wanted to find her brother.

Then she sat down, took a deep breath, and ran her finger against the edge of the paper name card.

She didn't manage to draw blood the first time, but after a few more tries, she figured out the right angle and sliced a thin slit across her fingertip.

The blood didn't come out very fast. She began writing Naveed's name in Persian on the card, since it was shorter that way, but had to stop often to squeeze her fingertip. While she wrote, she whispered the incantation that Kass had found in the Book of Shadows. *"Keeper of what disappears, hear me now, open your ears. Find for me what I now seek, following the wisdom the spirits speak. The spell is cast between the worlds, beyond the borders of time and space. Keeper of what disappears, let what I seek come to this place."*

Roya repeated it two more times, but it was over before she finished writing the last letter of his name. While she worked, she found herself humming Naveed's finding song very quietly.

Right as she was making the final line, squeezing her finger hard to coax out another drop, the rustling grew louder. A shape materialized out of the darkness. It walked closer. It spoke.

"Roya?"

The voice startled her so badly that she let go of the name card, and the last drop of blood splashed onto the floor.

A face appeared in the dim light. In astonishment, Roya realized that it was Naveed. But he almost didn't look like her brother at all. His hair was very short, and his eyes had a strange glow to them. His mouth was grinning in a way that was not quite right.

Was this really happening, or had the blood magic brought her some broken, shadow-version of him? Roya wasn't sure. It all felt very real, her back against the hard wall, her throbbing finger. Her brother's monster-eyes glinting in the dark.

"I'm glad you're okay," he said. Which didn't really sound like something a monster would say. But then he kneeled next to her, a little too close. His breath smelled like rotting things. She drew back. "Did you open the box?" he asked. "What was in it?"

The question caught her off guard. Reflexively, she clutched at her satchel, where the box was safely wrapped up in an old scarf. It was a burden to carry it around everywhere, but she didn't want anyone else finding it. She wanted to get it back to Kass, back to Lopez, where it belonged.

He noticed her movement and reached for the bag. She snatched it away. "I'm not going to give you the box! It has nothing to do with you, and that isn't why I wanted to talk to you at all, I just can't believe… I can't believe you wanted to die, you wanted to leave me *forever*, leave all of us forever, even though we loved you. We loved you, and you wrecked it, you have no idea how bad it's been, all because of what you did."

For a second Naveed looked stunned. Then he narrowed his eyes, which had turned hard and flat. She thought of that seed she'd tried to plant within the poppet's heart, slippery with goat blood; she thought of the churning waves dragging it under, never to surface again.

She wanted to take back what she'd said, because really she'd only meant to ask him what was going on, give him a chance to explain himself, but she was scared now, and angry, so many feelings jumbled up inside her that she didn't know what to say or do.

"I should've known they'd turn you against me, too." He stood up. "You know what? I'm done with this. Done with all of it."

"No, wait," she protested feebly as he strode through the dark closet and out the door. She wanted to go after him, but then again she didn't, and besides she was feeling weird, like all the mixed-up feelings inside were making her head spin or float or something. She figured she'd better stay where she was for a minute.

When she closed her eyes she saw those bones in that cave. The orcas, the bones, the key, the girl, the forest, the book, all leading her to this moment, but where did she go from here?

She put the name card back into her satchel, wrapped her finger in the paper towel she'd taken from the bathroom, and stood up. She couldn't believe that the spell had worked—but it hadn't helped at all. Everything was still ruined.

Roya made up her mind: she would find Andi and tell her that she wanted to go home. To her *real* home. She felt really bad about how she'd treated Maman the night before. Maybe she couldn't make things right with Naveed, but she could with the rest of her family.

She peeked out of the closet. The coat check girl was still distracted, and Roya slipped by her again. But as she did, she saw someone else walking quickly out the doors of the ballroom. Someone with a long white braid trailing down her back.

Kasandra's Nan! What was she doing here? There was no time to think. Roya hurried after her, an idea forming in her mind. Nan had arrived at the elevator bank and was pushing the down arrow repeatedly. Roya walked up to her, heart pounding.

"Nan," she said, then corrected herself. "I mean, Zennia?"

Zennia looked surprised and frightened at the same time. "It's you. Kass's friend."

Roya nodded. "I found something in the woods when I was on Lopez. It was your sister's. I think you should have it." She removed the box from her satchel. Then she pulled the key, still attached to the cord around her neck, over her head and held it out.

Zennia took the box, then balanced the key carefully on top. "My sister's?"

There was some sort of commotion in the ballroom behind them. Zennia glanced over her shoulder. The elevator dinged, and the doors slid open.

Without warning, Zennia pulled Roya close and gave her a kiss on the top of her head. "Thank you." She stepped into the elevator and punched the buttons inside. Roya stayed rooted in place, watching Zennia's face shine with amazement, until the doors closed and she was gone.

Andi

ANDI WAS SO STUNNED TO SEE NAVEED THAT SHE ACTUALLY dropped her purse. When she bent to pick it up, she lost sight of him in the crowded dining room. She scanned the faces around her. No sign of him. Where had he gone? Had he even been there at all, or was her mind playing tricks on her?

Then she noticed that one of the doors to the terrace was slightly ajar.

She made her way over to it and stepped outside, closing the door behind her. Dusk had swiftly settled, but she could see him in the dim light. He sat on the railing, his back to her, his legs dangling three stories above the cold water of Puget Sound.

"Hey," she said quietly, not wanting to startle him, but he stiffened anyway. "Hey. Don't worry—it's just me."

"Hey, Andi." His words seemed to have little weights attached. She imagined them sinking through the air, splashing into the water below.

"Why are you here?" she asked, then regretted it when he tensed up again. It looked like he was about to launch himself off the balcony any second.

"The question I ask myself every day." He said it woodenly, without a hint of emotion.

"No, I didn't mean… it's just… you know that they're looking for you, right? It was dangerous for you to come here. How did you get in, anyway?"

"I had a ticket. I made them think I belonged. People never see what they aren't expecting."

She wanted to ask him how he'd gotten the ticket, but something stopped her. His suit. Where had that suit come from? It looked expensive, like it had been tailored, but it was baggy on Naveed. A sickening thought occurred to her: had it belonged to Brennan Walsh?

Andi's heart almost stopped beating a second later when he let go of the railing with his right hand, but he only gestured at the horizon, the faint glow of the dying sun silhouetting the mountains, the sea sparkling beneath. "Look at this. All of this. Beautiful, right? Perfection. It isn't real, though. None of this is real, it's just the fantasy they've created with their money, so that they can come here and enjoy their sunset and sit around their tables with fucking apple centerpieces and pretend like it was all created effortlessly for them, like no one suffered for it."

He returned his hand to the railing, gripping it tightly. His skin looked darker than it had been the last time she'd seen him, and his hair was so short. His voice sounded different than she'd remembered, too. All she could think was that she had to get him down from there. It would all be over if he let go.

Andi stepped closer to the railing. She hugged her bare arms, rubbing them vigorously against the chill that had nothing to do with the wind. "I missed you," she said.

He didn't look at her, but mumbled something that got whisked away in the breeze. She stepped as near as she could without touching him.

"I'm glad to see you," Andi continued, trying to pretend she'd run into him under normal circumstances at a social event. Like he wasn't sitting there so precariously balanced on the thin railing, like he wasn't a murder suspect being pursued by the police, like he wasn't possibly wearing a dead man's suit, like none of that was happening and they were just picking up where they left off. "I've been wanting to tell you I'm sorry," she continued. "For not visiting when you were in the hospital. Cyrus didn't tell me—he didn't tell me what really happened. I would've come back if I'd known."

Naveed turned towards her, a pained expression on his face. Then something in the dining room window behind them caught his eye. Andi followed his gaze, noticing that Cyrus had sat down at their table and was talking to her mom, distractedly scanning the room. Looking for her, probably. Oh no, what would happen if he—or anyone else—came out here now? She prayed silently that no one would interrupt them.

When she looked back at Naveed, his expression had hardened. "You're just saying that. It's not true. You're just saying it so that I don't do this."

He let go, with both hands, and she gasped and lunged forward to catch him, but he hadn't moved, he was still balanced there, and he was grinning, but it was not his grin at all, it was like someone else's had been grafted onto his face.

She drew back, afraid that if she touched him, he really would fall. He held his arms straight out, like an acrobat on a tightrope. "You don't care about me," he said in that voice that was not his. "You just don't want this to be your fault."

"Naveed, look at me," she said softly, staring at him, trying to will him to look her in the eye. At first he resisted, but she didn't stop. She held him there with the force of her gaze until he finally turned. "Look at me. I'm not lying." Her voice broke, and she could barely see through the shimmer of tears, but still she didn't take her eyes away from him. "I would never lie about something like that, and you know it. You know who I am. And I know who you are, I know you're a good person, and I know you care about us, just like we care about you. We love you, Naveed. We all do. Even Cyrus. Even Brooke. Every single one of us."

She wished she could have managed something more eloquent, but she was freaking out so completely that it was the best she could do.

She remembered that moment they'd shared in her bedroom, how she'd imagined transferring her love into him, and she did it again now, even though they weren't touching this time, even though she knew that such a thing wasn't actually possible. But somehow she sensed he could feel it, and she imagined it filling him up. Maybe not all the way, because love from just one person could never fill another up entirely, but enough to get him through.

They looked at each other for one long, eternal moment. Then, to her relief, he lowered his arms, returning his hands to the railing. "I don't think Nate's going to rest until I'm dead." His voice, now, was quiet and weary.

Andi started to ask who Nate was—maybe that's who killed Brennan?—but Naveed continued, "I'm sorry, Andi, but this has to end tonight."

He swung his legs around to her side of the railing and slid down. He landed clumsily, taking a few dizzy steps sideways before steadying himself against the rail. Something heavy in his suit pocket thudded against it.

Her heart began hammering again—what was in there?—and he was reaching inside, pulling something out, something small and black—

"No, Naveed, you don't have to do this—" she began, but stopped when she saw what he had in his hand. A narrow black electronic device. Some kind of mp3 player?

He pressed it into her palm. His hands were very cold. "Take this, and listen to it alone. You're the only one I can trust to—"

She waited for him to finish, but he looked beyond her now, into the dining room, his eyes wide. "It's her. The old woman." He turned back to face Andi. "You need to get out of here. And Roya. Kourosh too. I don't know what they're planning, but something's about to go down, so leave now and be really careful, watch out for her, and for a man with a long beard. Alastor. Or maybe he won't have a beard, maybe he's using another name, I don't know."

He started toward the ballroom doors, but Andi stepped in front of him, blocking his path. "Wait, what's going on? What are you talking about?"

He shook his head and pushed past her, throwing open the door and striding across the ballroom. She followed him, aware of the stares of the other diners—realizing, too late, that someone was standing at the podium, giving a speech. "Brennan would have wanted us to carry on tonight," the speaker was saying. "Bringing people together, that's what he did best...."

Cyrus was taking a bite of his soup, his eyes on the speaker. Naveed grabbed his brother's wrist and Cyrus dropped his spoon, startled. Andi watched her mom bend to pick it up from the floor as if on autopilot, though she looked just as bewildered as Cyrus.

"Did she give you this?" Naveed asked in a loud whisper, gesturing toward Cyrus's soup bowl.

"What are you doing here?" Cyrus whispered back.

"The old woman, with the white braid," Naveed said. "Did she give you this?"

"Um, I think so? I'm not—"

Naveed flipped over the soup bowl, the plate of salad. Then he spilled Cyrus's glass of sparkling cider on top. "Don't eat it! She's trying to kill you!" He straightened up, looking around the dining room. "Where did she go?"

A security guard had appeared, and Naveed saw him at the same time Andi did. He took off running, dashing for a side exit and barreling through the door, leaving the entire room in stunned silence.

Cyrus

CYRUS STARED AT THE MESS ON THE TABLE IN FRONT OF HIM, dumbfounded. His soup—that delicious creamy porcini mushroom soup, one of his favorite dishes at Parapluie—was seeping into the white tablecloth. Oddly enough, his first reaction wasn't to wonder what the hell his brother was doing here, or to be embarrassed by all the eyes on him. He wanted to find his spoon and keep eating. He'd just arrived, and he was so hungry, and he'd only gotten to eat a couple bites of soup before his obviously-unbalanced brother had showed up out of nowhere and ruined his meal.

But Andi was standing near his seat, fiddling with something in her purse before closing it and offering Cyrus her hand. "Let's get out of here," she whispered. "Everyone's staring. Come on."

Her mom stood up too, and they made their way out as the speaker tried to get everyone's attention. He clinked a fork against his glass. "Pardon the interruption," he said. "Not to worry, security is on top of it.

And Chef Thierry is plating up a truly inspired main course for us all to enjoy during the auction. Now, as I was saying...."

"Are you okay?" Andi asked Cyrus as they walked. She kept turning her head, glancing through the room.

"Yeah. Luckily the soup didn't spill on my lap. It was still pretty hot. That would've been unpleasant."

"No, I mean, do you feel all right?"

"Of course. What, you really think some old lady poisoned me? That would be crazy."

"Did you see who served you?"

"No. I was listening to the speaker." He had been paying enough attention to realize the impoliteness of starting to eat his soup before anyone else at the table got theirs. He'd done it anyway.

"The food was just sitting out in the hallway," Andi mused. "Everything was so chaotic back there by the kitchen. She easily could've taken one of the soups and...."

"Stop. Nothing happened, except that my brother has gone completely insane." They were walking past the entrance doors now. "Oh shit, I guess we have to call the police, huh?"

"I think my mom's already on it," Andi said glumly, and Cyrus noticed that Joyce had her phone pressed to her ear. "Oh—thank God, there's Roya," Andi added. Cyrus saw his sister standing by the elevator bank. He wasn't quite ready to talk to her yet, though. First, he wanted Andi's attention.

"Hey, can we talk?" he asked. Joyce had hung up the phone and was rushing over to Roya. Maybe Cyrus wouldn't have to tell her what had just happened. The thought filled him with relief.

"Now?" Andi asked.

"Yes, now. It's been a long day, what with the police interrogating us and searching our house. I had to miss work because of all the... activity. I almost didn't come at all. But I knew you'd be here, and I wanted to see you. I wanted to talk. So." The enormity of it hung over him. "Did you get my letter?"

She looked at him, her expression inscrutable. "Yes."

"So, what do you think? Can you ever forgive me?"

He'd waited all day for the answer, and maybe that was why it happened, maybe he was just so nervous that he felt very strange for a second. It was like he could see the air, like it was made of layers of golden dust that settled in shimmery waves all around her face. It was kind of beautiful, he thought. Then he blinked, and it was gone.

Andi sighed. "Of course I forgive you. You aren't a horrible person, by the way. We all lose it sometimes. But you really should have told me, and it's going to take a while before I can trust you again."

"Okay," he said. "That's fair. I'm still really sorry. And I missed you so much. Like, unbelievably much."

"I missed you, too." Andi combed her hair with her fingers. "But things got so complicated when we were going out. I don't think either of us needs more complication in our lives right now. We should just be friends, I think."

Even though this conversation was important, he was finding it hard to pay attention. It was happening again: the golden dust, and flashes of greenery now, like there was some transmission from the jungle interrupting his usual thoughts. He wanted to sit down, but couldn't quite figure out where he was in relation to the benches he was sure he'd seen against the walls.

Andi was looking at him questioningly. "You sure you're feeling okay?"

"I'm fine, I'm fine. You just got kind of shimmery for a second," he said, then wished he hadn't, because it wasn't a normal thing to say at all. Luckily, Roya interrupted; she ran over and gave him a big hug around his waist.

"Kourosh! I'm so sorry. Are Maman and Baba mad at me? I want to go home. Can we go now?"

"Of course they're not mad," he said. What was the other question she'd asked? The flashes of green and gold were coming faster now, in a way that unsettled his stomach.

Then, a ding that sounded harsh and distant. The elevators. "We'll take you home as soon as we can, Roya," said Joyce. "Let's go down to the lobby. The police are on their way, and we'll need to talk to them for a minute first."

She sounded so calm. Was that where Andi got it, her eternal serenity?

"Cyrus? Are you coming?" Somehow everyone else was in the elevator already. Cyrus pressed a hand to his stomach. He suddenly didn't feel well at all.

Andi stepped out of the elevator, led him inside. As the doors closed and the metal box started moving downward, his legs went all wobbly. "I think I need to sit down," he said, or maybe he only thought it. The next thing he knew he was on the ground and everyone was crouching around him, concerned.

"I'm okay," he said, but he wasn't so sure anymore, because their faces were cutting out. They were getting blurrier, the golden dust starting to obscure them, but the greenery was sliding into focus, and he recognized the subtropical plants of Brennan Walsh's garden back in Santa Barbara. That had been such a beautiful place. He wished he could go back.

They helped Cyrus up and guided him out of the elevator, and he felt like he needed to reassure Roya. She didn't need any more drama right now, that was for sure. And his parents, oh his poor parents, they didn't need this either, especially not after the day they'd just had. He opened his mouth to say something, but instead of comforting words coming out, he doubled over and threw up.

And not just once. He couldn't stop. Where was it all coming from, he wondered distantly. So much vomit. He was vaguely aware that a lot of activity was going on around him, Joyce asking someone to call an ambulance, Roya sobbing, Andi's cool hand on his cheek, saying, "you're okay, you're okay, you're okay," like she was trying to convince herself. She had looked so beautiful in that dress. He didn't want to get too close and throw up all over her. Or maybe he already had.

The garden was pressing up against him, overlaying itself on his vision, and he thought he'd much rather be there. He whispered to Andi, during a brief moment of stillness when his stomach wasn't in spasms, "Stay with me?"

"Of course," she said. "I'm not going anywhere."

Reassured, Cyrus slipped back into Brennan's garden. He walked out to the patio in back of the guest house, and was unsurprised to find Naveed sitting there looking like his old self, utterly at ease, carving a piece of wood. Cyrus stood at the outdoor counter, where a big pile of vegetables waited, ready for him to cut. He set to chopping.

Cyrus looked over at Naveed, who was whittling away. "You shouldn't be doing that. Remember? You're not supposed to use knives."

"Well, you probably shouldn't be handling food when you're puking every five seconds. And yet, here we are," Naveed said.

"Here we are," Cyrus repeated. Somewhere far away, his other body, his real one, was vomiting again. But not here. Here, everything was warm and peaceful. A breeze stirred the leaves of the avocado tree overhead. Cyrus picked one of the green fruits and added it to the pile.

"I'm sorry I thought you were crazy," Cyrus said. "I guess you knew what you were talking about. Someone must have poisoned my soup. Pretty random, right?"

"Yeah. It's weird."

"Well, thanks for saving my life and all," Cyrus said.

Naveed looked at him grimly. "Don't thank me yet."

Cyrus didn't want to dwell on that. "Does this mean you forgive me? For what I said? I didn't mean it, you know. I was just tired of everything and I kind of blew up."

"I don't blame you. I was tired of everything too. And I was kind of a dick sometimes."

"No. Well, yeah, you were, but I get it now, I see where you were coming from. I wish I'd been better at helping you, especially that night... but instead I said those horrible things. I'm probably the worst crisis counselor in the history of the world."

"Probably. Nothing you can do about it now, though. Except avoid a career in counseling."

"Done and done."

They lapsed into silence. How many times, in the days and years before, had a variation of this scene played out? Cyrus and Baba chopping in the kitchen, Naveed carving something or other, Maman flitting through and chiding him for all the wood shavings on the floor, Naveed insisting he would sweep them up, Roya scooping them into her hands instead, making them into beds for the family of mice she was sure lived in her walls. Back then, it had all felt so ordinary. Boring, even. But now he wanted it back.

"Remember when we used to do this?" Cyrus asked.

"I was thinking the same thing. I miss those days a lot."

"Me, too. You think we can ever go back?"

Andi's voice leaked in from the other world. "Cyrus? Stay with me. Stay awake—" She stopped abruptly, her voice rising in sudden alarm. "Oh no, oh no, please help, someone help, what's happening to him?"

"Stand back," a deep voice said. It startled Cyrus, the man's stern tone, and he retreated to the garden, rattled. What was going on out there? He wasn't sure he wanted to know. Andi had sounded so frantic. Which was not like her at all. If she sounded that worried… it couldn't be good….

It was still pleasant enough when he returned, but something had changed. Naveed didn't look so happy anymore.

"Sorry about that," Cyrus said, as if he'd just interrupted their conversation to answer a text. He shoved away his worry and asked, "So, what are you carving?"

That seemed to perk his brother up. "I don't know yet. This was always my favorite part, the discovery. When there are so many possibilities, before you have to choose a path." He looked at Cyrus. "So. Which way do you think this will go?"

Cyrus got the sense he was talking about more than the wood. He started to answer, but paused in his vegetable chopping. The edges of things were starting to disappear, and his chest felt weird. Like something wasn't quite right in his heart.

"Do you hear Andi? She's calling you. You'd better go to her," Naveed said.

"No, I don't want to go yet! I still have so much to chop. And I have a ton of questions. Like, where have you been? And what happened with Brennan?"

"You know I can't answer that." Naveed set down his knife and stood up. "Goodbye, Kourosh. I have to go."

"Wait," Cyrus called, but he was gone, just like that, and the garden was disappearing, leaves flickering into darkness. Somewhere Andi was saying his name, but Cyrus felt lost. It was all around him, her voice, but he couldn't quite tell where it was coming from. He couldn't find his way back to her.

Naveed

SATURDAY, SEPTEMBER 19

NAVEED EMERGED OUTSIDE THE HOTEL BEFORE THE SECURITY guard could catch him. Even though another guard watched from the periphery, he did not follow—they must not have recognized Naveed, and probably didn't care what happened to him now, as long as he was off their property.

He slowed. Security, or someone else, may have called the police, and he'd attract more attention if he was running. The nerve pain had recently reignited in his feet, making it feel like he was crossing a bed of needles, but somehow the hurt felt far away. He was strangely exhilarated. This was almost over. Everything was finally ending.

To think that things could end! That loops could be severed, made linear again!

Nate had been growing louder all day. The interaction with Roya had amplified him so much he'd almost taken over completely. He would have, too, had it not been for that brief conversation with Andi. Of course, Nate was there whispering that all her words were lies, but even Nate had withered beneath her tearful stare. There was something miraculous in the way she'd looked at him, unflinching, like she was seeing everything he had inside, all of his many stupendous flaws, and caring about him regardless.

Of course, she might feel differently after listening to the recording, once she knew how messed up he really was. That was of little concern to him now, though. All he needed was that moment, that memory of her standing next to him on the deck, listening to him, treating him like a normal human being. That gave him enough strength to tune out Nate just a tiny bit longer. One more task, and he'd be done.

Naveed kept walking along the side of the street closest to the water, but slowed when he came to his destination. A wooden staircase led down to a short pier with a single boat tied to its far end. Earlier in the day, he'd spent a lot of time wandering the waterfront around the hotel, knowing that Alastor and the old woman would probably escape by boat—the easiest and least conspicuous way to return to Lopez Island. His hunch was correct: he'd eventually found their sailboat, thanks to the small Orcinia symbol painted on the bow.

He had quietly made his way on board, knife in hand, hoping to ambush them so that they'd never be able to carry out whatever plans they had for the benefit dinner. But they were not there. So he decided to stake the area out, in hopes they would come back during the day. He hid in the nook underneath the staircase, his back against the retaining wall, but they never showed. They must have either slipped by him—maybe he'd nodded off again and missed them—or they had been out all day.

Now, he descended the stairs and found Walsh's briefcase stowed in the shadows where he'd left it. He put his house keys and the silver star charm in his pocket, wanting those to be with him until the end. Then he unwrapped the knife.

He stepped onto the pier, walking its whole length, down towards the boat at the very end. The wind whipped at his face; the clouds were still bright with the memory of sunset. Beneath him, the sea churned, agitated by faraway black whales rippling through the water.

As he watched, a shape materialized in front of him. Someone had just gotten off the boat and was crouching near the rope that tied it to the dock, his long beard blowing in the wind.

Naveed rushed forward, knife in hand. Alastor saw him coming and started to stand up, but Naveed rammed into him when he was still semi-crouched, knocking him on his side, right at the edge of the dock. As they came down, though, Alastor shoved his elbow hard into Naveed's wrist, and he lost his grip on the knife. It skittered out of his hand and off the edge, splashing into the water.

Didn't matter. Naveed didn't need it anyway: he had the upper hand. He grabbed hold of the man's neck and climbed on top of him to immobilize his arms.

"Alastor," he said. "You killed him. You killed him, and you wanted everyone to think I did it, but I didn't. *You* did."

Alastor was trying to fight back. He managed to get his hands free, and began clawing at Naveed's hands. Naveed could see him digging his nails in—nails that were kind of long, really, he noted with curiosity before looking away to avoid seeing any blood. But he couldn't feel a thing, and he wanted to laugh, to taunt Alastor, to let him know that he could do this *all day* if he needed to.

A strange realization swept over him: this felt *good*. To have the power of choosing what happened next. To watch a killer struggle for breath, to watch the color drain from his face. It wasn't quite Tara Snyder, but it would do. It would do.

The light was starting to go out in Alastor's eyes. Only one of his hands was grasping at Naveed's anymore. Naveed could end it here, finish him off—

But Andi's voice came into his head then. *I know who you are. I know you're a good person.* He wasn't, though. A good person would not be doing this, would not take pleasure in killing someone. Even if they deserved it.

He loosened his grip at the same instant that Alastor flicked open a pocketknife and slashed him on the cheek.

Naveed cried out in surprise, and suddenly Alastor was on top of him, and all of Naveed's anger and frustration rose up inside. No. He wasn't going to keep getting beaten down. He was sick of that.

He rolled to his side, Alastor still holding on, and then there was a sense of vertigo, of ground giving way.

Hitting the water was so shocking that Naveed didn't even know what had happened at first. One second he was on the dock, and the next he was submerged. The burning cold water of Puget Sound surrounding him; the heaviness of his jacket, his shoes, the keys in his pocket; the sting of salt in the cuts on his cheek and the back of his head; the air, where was the air? Which way was up?

He kicked and rose to the surface, bursting out of the water and taking in a big breath, turning around frantically, looking for Alastor. From here Naveed couldn't see to the top of the dock, but he did notice a short barnacle-crusted ladder that led back up. He had to get out of this water, which was cold, it was so, *so* cold, had to swim to the ladder, had to keep moving even though his arms already felt frozen.

Then he heard it behind him, the disturbance as Alastor broke the surface, water cascading all around. Naveed only had a second to gulp air into his lungs before Alastor was upon him again, forcing Naveed's head beneath the water and holding it down.

Naveed tried to get back up, but Alastor's hands were steady and relentless. Naveed kicked at him, flailed, but the water cushioned his limbs, as if they were encased in pillows, blunting their impact. He could not get away.

His lungs burned. His waterlogged shoes felt like anchors.

Just give up. Just breathe the water in, said Nate. *This what you wanted. This is the end. Might as well stop fighting.*

No, Naveed countered. *Alastor doesn't get to choose. It's my choice to make, and I don't want to die.*

I don't want to die.

For a second Naveed wasn't sure where he was. The loop had started over again, maybe, as it so often did, with this struggle for breath; it seemed like that was all his life was, a search for air. Anxiety swelled within him. The water closing in from all sides. The wet fabric swirling around him. Those hands on his head, weighing him down. All he wanted was to breathe.

Don't panic, he told himself. *If you panic, you will die. Calm down. You have to stay calm.*

He thought of Andi again. Her unflinching eyes, refusing to let him go. He thought of Roya, not the Roya in the coat closet, but the one who used to snuggle next to him in his chair, her head resting against his shoulder. He thought of Cyrus bringing a plate of vegan pistachio cookies up to their bedroom and putting on a playlist of ridiculous cat videos for them to watch while they ate. He thought of Baba carrying his old drafting table out to the patio and teaching Naveed how to draw the geometric patterns that decorated mosques all over the world. He thought of Maman, often sleepless in the night, just like him, brewing a pot of mint tea for them to share in the dark living room.

He thought of these things, he thought of these people, and he went still.

And then he dove down, deeper into the water.

His brain screamed at him—*no, no, up, not down!*—but he kept swimming. The pressure from Alastor's hands was gone, replaced by a new one, the pressure of depth. The water pressing on him. The need to breathe now, now, NOW.

He stopped diving and swam as far away from Alastor as he could before he finally came up for air. He'd wanted to do this quietly, but his gasping desperate breaths were loud. And a profound relief.

Once he'd refilled his lungs, he tried to get his bearings. He was close to the pier, near one of the pilings anchoring it to the floor of the sea. He swam to it and grabbed on. His teeth were chattering, he realized, his limbs completely numb.

Alastor was swimming, too—but not toward Naveed, toward the boat, calling to Zennia. Naveed looked up and saw the old woman leaning over the side. Alastor reached to her, and she helped pull him out of the water.

Naveed wondered if they'd noticed him, but they didn't look in his direction. "Don't just stand there, get me a blanket," Alastor was saying. His teeth were chattering too. "Then untie the boat. We have to get out of here."

"Not yet. We need to talk," Zennia said.

"Plenty of time for that later. Go. Now."

"Not until you tell me what really happened the night Gaia left."

"Zennia, that was decades ago. You expect me to remember? Your sister abandoned us and let a man die. That's all there is to know."

"Stop." Zennia's voice was filled with cold fury. "All these years, you've been lying to me."

Slowly, Naveed let go of the piling and swam toward the ladder as quietly as he could. He grabbed onto the bottom rung.

"I'd never lie to you. Why are you even thinking about this?" Alastor's voice became quieter, more threatening. "Get me a blanket. Now. You want me to freeze to death?"

Zennia didn't answer that. "Every new moon. Every single one, I tried to find her. She never came, and now I know why. You were keeping her from me, because you didn't want me to figure out that the entire life we constructed, that we built around *you,* was all a lie."

Naveed pulled himself to the second rung. The water dripping from Walsh's suit was very loud, but still they did not seem to hear.

"I don't—"

"Gaia never wanted to leave. Those bones they found, they were hers. Someone fractured her skull and dumped her in the ocean."

"You're not suggesting that I—"

"You hated her. And you probably think I don't remember that night, but I do." Zennia sounded now like she was fighting back tears. "I remember you came back home so late, and I was up with Miracle, and you were surprised I was awake. And you started washing up because your hands were bloody, and you said it was because of the dying man, that you'd gone to visit and he was so delirious he scratched up your hands. You asked if I'd seen Gaia, because she wasn't with him and you couldn't find her anywhere. But you knew exactly where she was. *She* did that to your hands, because she was trying to fight back. Before you killed her."

Naveed kept climbing the ladder. The icy wind made him shiver so hard he could barely grip the bars.

"And the night Miracle was born. I would've bled to death if Gaia hadn't had the right drugs to save me! And you would have let me die. A sacrifice for your ideals."

Naveed pulled himself onto the pier. He could hear a helicopter now. Sirens. They must be looking for him. Couldn't outrun them now. But if he could lead the police to straight to Alastor, the real killer....

It was the only shot he had left. All he had to do was make it down the pier. Climb the stairs. Make it to the street. Standing up was difficult, though. His clothes were too heavy. He shrugged off the suit jacket.

Zennia was still talking. "You dragged me into this... but Hekate never would have demanded human sacrifices. Who really told you to do this? Why was it so important to kill them?"

"You have no idea what Hekate wants. I'm the prophet, Zennia. The gods speak through me."

"No. This was something else. What was it, Alastor? Who are you, really?"

The sound of the helicopter grew louder. Naveed saw it hovering nearby and waved his arms. Could it see him? His white shirt probably looked bright against the dark pier.

He stood up, shakily. With every step, the house keys in his pocket pressed against his leg. He thought of the silver star charm attached to them, of the magic Roya thought it contained. Might as well start wishing now.

All he had to do was get to the road. Quietly, so Alastor didn't notice. But he couldn't stand the feeling of the clammy wet fabric against his skin, the way it refrigerated the wind and threatened to send him back to another time, and he couldn't leave right now. Everything depended on this.

He couldn't undo the buttons of his shirt without looking down at his fingers—but under the glow of the lights above, he could see blood streaming down his hand, leaking from the places where Alastor's nails had torn open his skin.

The next thing he knew, he was on the ground. The dock beneath him was rocking in the gentle waves that lapped at the shore. He was freezing cold. He looked up at the sky and there it was again, the moon, barely visible now; it was waning, continuing along its endless cycle. The loop. The moon was in a loop, too. And the sun, the tides, the seasons. Always ending, always beginning again.

What was his life? A line, or a circle? Or a line with many looping circles, curlicues like Roya used to draw when she was pretending to write in cursive? Her hand on the paper, her tongue sticking out with the effort it took to keep them neat and even.

Get up. Get up, his instincts were saying. But he didn't want to listen. He was so tired, and so cold, and he probably would have stayed there, had the sound of heavy footsteps not jolted him back to reality.

He turned onto his side in time to see the glint of Alastor's knife as he brought it down right where Naveed had just been. Alastor quickly corrected, though, and pinned Naveed on his back.

Naveed tried to yell for help, but the world seemed soundless. Then, as Alastor lowered the blade, touching it to Naveed's neck, stinging against his skin, something happened.

A loud thump. The knife clattering to the ground. Alastor staggering, falling back into the water. Zennia standing where he had just been. In her hands, the metal box that she'd slammed into his skull.

After the final splash, silence. Alastor did not resurface.

Naveed was so stunned he didn't even try to move, but Zennia didn't seem concerned with him. She took something out of the box, a little book, which she held in her hands. Then she pulled something else out of her pocket. A small vial. She twisted the lid off and drank.

"No," Naveed said, but it was too late. She fell to her knees, and her body began to shake. He tried to get up, wanting to hold her head steady so she wouldn't slam it against the pier, but it felt like he was carving his way through a block of ice. By the time he sat up, it was already over. Her hands relaxed, and the book slid onto the dock. Her breathing stuttered to a stop.

The ground beneath him shook. Naveed turned, barely registering the red and blue flashing lights, the many guns pointed at him, before a searing electric shock hit him between the shoulder blades and he went down.

"I said, put your hands up! You're under arrest," a police officer yelled as he slammed Naveed's head into the damp wood of the dock, detonating another explosion inside his skull, and the salt stung his cheek so he tried to lift his head to turn it, but the officer rammed it back down instead, bright bursts of light shooting across Naveed's eyelids, everything so loud suddenly that he wanted to cover his ears but he couldn't move his hands, couldn't move anything now, his body twitching uncontrollably as they forced him against the rocking ground, and all the sounds crowded into his head: sirens blaring, voices shouting, waves crashing, and beneath them all, an agonized howl that he distantly recognized as his own.

Andi

ANDI SAT IN THE AMBULANCE NEXT TO CYRUS. THE MEDICS HAD given her two jobs: hold the bowl by his mouth in case he threw up again, and try to keep him awake. The first job was easy enough, especially since not much was coming up anymore, but she was not very successful at keeping him conscious. They had him on his side on the gurney, facing her, while they put in IV's and gave him oxygen. Even though she kept talking to him, he hadn't opened his eyes for some time now. She was holding his glasses in one hand; it felt oddly intimate to see him without them.

She still couldn't believe how quickly he'd deteriorated. Less than twenty minutes ago, she'd been talking to him outside the ballroom, telling him they should just be friends. And then he'd gone all pale and glassy-eyed, had passed out in the elevator, had started vomiting. At some point he'd resurfaced long enough to ask her to stay with him, but right after the medics had arrived he'd gone into convulsions—she was thankful they were there, because it nearly gave her a heart attack, the way his limbs jerked so wildly.

As they loaded him into the ambulance, there was a brief discussion between the medics and her mother about which hospital they should take him to. Andi couldn't really follow it. All she cared about was keeping her promise: she needed to stay with him. She climbed into the ambulance before anyone could protest, and they didn't make her leave. Andi's mother said that she and Roya would meet them at the hospital after talking with the police.

Off they went, screaming down the streets toward Harborview. Andi kept her focus on Cyrus, but she was also aware of what the medics were doing, what they were saying; they were worried about his heart rhythm. She listened to them with a distant curiosity. It gave her something to hold onto, besides the thing that kept coming into her head, which was Cyrus's letter. The words in the first paragraph haunted her. *I guess you never know when your number's up. Who knows, I could be gone tomorrow, too.* Sitting here next to him now, she thought about the weight he'd been living underneath, and was seized by an intense stab of love for him. More than anything, she wanted those words not to become true.

Andi was also still rattled from her conversation with Naveed, and irrationally angry at her mom for calling the police. Of course she had to, but... couldn't she have given him a little longer to get away first? She could already see it, Naveed running, the police yelling at him to stop, Naveed not hearing or not caring; the gunshots, the blood seeping through his dark suit—

And Roya, poor Roya. Both of her brothers... oh God, what about Sam and Mahnaz? Had anyone told them what was going on?

Andi was trembling. She'd left her coat in the cloakroom, which now seemed so far away. Shakily, she set down the bowl and opened her clutch to put Cyrus's glasses inside so that she could hold onto both of his hands. Maybe he wouldn't be able to leave if she was holding on.

Her eyes fell upon the black device that Naveed had given her. A voice recorder, she saw now. She was suddenly relieved not to be back at the hotel, having to tell the cops about their conversation. They'd probably make her hand it over, but she needed to know what was on it first. *You're the only person I can trust….*

All she could do now, though, was hope that Naveed would be safe from the police, and safe from Nate, whoever he was. Right now, Cyrus needed her. She balanced the clutch on her lap and squeezed both of his hands, focusing on their warmth.

When the ambulance arrived at the hospital, the driver opened up the back door, and they wheeled Cyrus out. Andi had to let go. One of the medics helped her out of the ambulance as the other brought him inside. "You'll need to stay in the waiting room now," he was saying. "They're going to need to—"

He didn't finish, because his partner was yelling, "Drew! Quick, the crash cart—"

The medic ran over, and they rushed Cyrus through the hospital doors. Andi tried to follow them, but she was having a hard time getting her legs to move normally, and by the time she stepped inside she didn't see any trace of them.

"Cy, oh Cy, please stay awake," she found herself whispering, forgetting that she didn't need to keep talking; he couldn't hear her anymore. She felt incredibly dizzy all of a sudden, flooded with memories, and had to steady herself against the wall.

A passing nurse saw her and asked if she was all right. "I just need to sit down for a minute," Andi said.

The nurse produced a chair from somewhere and set it against the wall. "Take your time."

Andi was finding it hard to catch her breath. And her dress smelled like vomit. It made her want to throw up.

She managed not to, and sat there shivering. She didn't know where to go, which waiting room to sit in; the hospital was huge, and besides she wasn't quite sure where she was now, in some back hallway where the ambulances arrived.

The medics passed through again some time later, wheeling an empty gurney, and she sat up straighter. One of them walked right past her and out the door, but she called out to the other one before he left. "Wait! How is he?"

Maddeningly, he shrugged. "They're working on him now. He's going to the cardiac ICU, they'll let you know when there's any news. Want someone to walk you there?"

"I need a minute first," Andi said. Working on him? What did that mean? They knew which unit he was going to, so at least he was still alive, but… the cardiac ICU, that wasn't good….

The medic nodded and continued down the hall, but returned moments later to wrap a warm blanket around her.

"Thank you," she said, suddenly close to tears at the small gesture of kindness.

"Just grab a nurse when you're ready. They'll show you to the waiting room."

Andi nodded as his partner appeared at the door. "Drew, come on! We've got another call."

They rushed out, and their sirens blared, then grew fainter as they drove away. She supposed she should get up, but wasn't sure her legs would hold her yet. Instead, she pulled her phone out of her clutch, reading through the texts from her mother. Still at the hotel, be there as soon as we can, how is Cyrus doing? His parents are on their way.

Andi couldn't think about that. Now she really didn't want to go to the waiting room, didn't want to be the first to talk to Mahnaz and Sam.

She texted back, relaying what the medics had said, then returned her phone to her clutch. Even though she wanted to hide from it all, to curl up under the blanket and ignore everything, she forced herself to take out the voice recorder. She rummaged around until she found the earbuds she brought with her everywhere, and started to play back the recording.

The first few minutes were silence. What was that about? she wondered. This was explaining nothing.

Only when an unfamiliar voice said, "Can I get you anything to start with?" and Naveed's voice, considerably louder than the other one, responded, "Not yet, I'm waiting for someone," did she begin to understand. A few moments later, she heard Brennan's voice.

Andi pulled her blanket tighter. This must be a recording of their conversation at the restaurant.

She closed her eyes and leaned back against the wall, trying to visualize the scene as it played out through her ears.

Andi found herself surprised over and over again. Naveed had been working on a documentary all that time? And rindamycin, he'd mentioned rindamycin, the antibiotic they'd taken for their MRK infections. Was MRK the bug that Brennan mentioned was going around? That would mean Lillian Page had been right, that it actually was spreading. And what was all this stuff about Alastor, the guy who led the commune on Lopez Island? Brennan had seemed worried about Cyrus after mentioning him, but Andi didn't understand why.

Then Brennan said he had to go, and there were rustling noises, a door opening and closing. She kept listening, feeling sick, knowing what was coming next. She tuned out some of the more disturbing sounds, but her interest perked up again when she heard two new voices.

Andi had to stop the playback for a few minutes afterward to let it all sink in. So. This meant that several others had apparently been there. They had killed Brennan and planned to kill someone else, probably Cyrus, at the "charity event." Who were they, though? They were talking about rituals, about sacrifices… could one of those voices have belonged to Alastor? But why would he kill Brennan after all this time? And why would he go after Cyrus? That made no sense at all. And Naveed had mentioned that Nate was after him too, but who was Nate?

She learned that answer a few minutes later. *I'm Nate. Naveed's dead… and I'm the one who killed him.*

Oh God. Naveed… she'd known there was something off about him, but she'd had no idea it was this bad. She could still hear his weary voice on the hotel balcony. *I don't think Nate's going to rest until I'm dead.*

Andi listened for a few minutes longer, but the rest of the recording was mostly silence, with occasional quiet muttering. She stopped the playback and returned the voice recorder to her clutch. What was she supposed to do with all this?

You're the only person I can trust.

Andi was tempted to call Brooke for some much-needed moral support, but the thought of having to explain everything to her was too much right now. Numbly, she got up and asked someone to show her to the cardiac ICU.

When she walked into the waiting room, her mother jumped up and gathered her into a hug.

"Where is everyone?" Andi asked. Cyrus's parents and Roya were nowhere to be seen.

"Cyrus just woke up, so they went inside to see him. The doctors gave him something to counteract the poison, and it seems to be working. You can go inside in a minute, but… there's something I need to tell you first." Her mother gestured at the row of chairs.

Andi knew what that meant. *You'll need to sit down for this.* She settled into a chair. "Okay. What is it?"

Her mother put her arm around Andi, pulled her close. "There were… Andi, there were a couple of fatalities."

Andi braced herself, knowing that Naveed was one of them. He was having some kind of mental breakdown while on the run from the police—when did that ever end well? She wondered if that was why he'd given her the recorder. So that she would understand, after he was gone.

"Two people died out on a pier not far from the hotel. They're still piecing things together, but Naveed—he was there. The police took him into custody."

"Oh" was all Andi said. So he was still alive? She could barely even keep up anymore. It felt like her thoughts and emotions were chugging along several miles behind her.

"Nobody knows exactly what happened," her mother said. "But Naveed fell into the water, apparently, so they brought him here to be treated for hypothermia and some other minor injuries. They need to get him warmed up and do their evaluations before they question him."

Andi ran her fingers through her hair. "Can I go see him?"

"No, bǎo bèi. They arrested him—he can't have visitors." Her mom sounded kind of annoyed that Andi was even asking. She probably didn't want her daughter hanging out with a murder suspect.

Mahnaz and Roya appeared at the waiting room door, hand in hand. Andi was glad to see that Roya appeared to have forgiven her mother. Sam was right behind them, and when the three of them saw Andi, they pulled her into a group hug.

"How is he?" Andi asked.

Mahnaz gave her a tired smile. "He'll be okay. Although he did say he would never eat soup again."

"He was asking about you," Sam added. "They want him to rest now, but we told him you were here. He wanted to know if you have his glasses."

"Oh, yeah, I do." Andi rummaged in her clutch for them, tilting the opening toward herself so that they wouldn't see the recorder inside, though she wasn't quite sure why she was trying to hide it. She handed the glasses over, slightly relieved that she didn't have to visit Cyrus right away. She felt like she was close to making a connection, and needed to figure that out first.

"Roya, do you want to go down to the cafeteria with me for some hot chocolate?" Andi asked. She could tell from the quick grin Mahnaz shot her that the gesture was appreciated. Andi had no idea how she was keeping it together.

"Okay," Roya said. She slipped her hand into Andi's, and the two of them left the waiting room. As they stepped into the elevator, Andi remembered the descent with Cyrus earlier that evening. What had he said to her? *You got kind of shimmery for a second.*

Shimmery. Like the television had looked when Andi had taken the Metafolia supplement.

Come to think of it, her experience—though much less serious, of course—had followed the same pattern. The shimmering lights, the fainting, the vomiting.

Maybe that was it. That was the connection.

It made a strange sort of sense. Cyrus and Brennan had been on NPR together talking about Metafolia, discussing how they'd been responsible for the company coming under investigation....

Was that what Brennan had realized during dinner with Naveed? That Alastor, from the commune on Lopez Island, was somehow connected with Metafolia, and wanted them both dead because they'd exposed the fact that it contained an illegal drug?

It all seemed so bizarre, but at the same time, very possible.

And someone else had been involved, too. The old woman with the braid, the one who had served Cyrus's soup.

When Andi and Roya arrived at the cafeteria, it was already closed for the night. So Andi bought a couple bags of chips from the vending machine, and they sat opposite each other at a table in the dining area.

"Roya," Andi said, "I want you to think back to the hotel. You were standing by the elevators when we walked out. But before we came—did you see an old woman with a white braid come by?"

Roya looked at her suspiciously. "Why?"

"I think she might have poisoned your brother."

Roya shook her head. "Nan wouldn't—" She stopped abruptly.

"Who's Nan?"

Roya looked uncomfortable, but she finally answered. "I made a friend on Lopez Island. Nan's her grandma. But that's not her real name. Her real name is Zennia."

Andi rubbed her goosebumpy arms, remembering something Naveed had said on the terrace. "Did you see anyone else? Alastor?"

Roya's face went hard. "I didn't see him there. But he's a bad man. How do you know about him?"

"Long story," Andi said. "But, I think he might be going by another name. Do you know what it is?"

"No. But it makes sense. People take different names when they go to Orcinia."

"Maybe your friend would know, then? We could ask—"

"What if Alastor made Nan do it?" Roya blurted. "Kass said there was going to be a sacrifice. But why would they want to hurt Kourosh?"

"Hold on." Andi pulled out her phone and found a screen cap of the Dr. Ben show on which Geoffrey Walker had appeared promoting Metafolia. She held it out to Roya. "The one on the left. Do you recognize him?"

Roya squinted at the photo. She shuddered. "He looks different without his beard. But that's definitely him. That's Alastor."

Andi clicked off her phone and slid it back into her clutch. She really didn't want to turn in the audio recorder to the police, but it was important evidence: Alastor and Zennia had murdered Brennan, and they'd tried to kill Cyrus too. Whatever Naveed had done on the pier, he had likely been acting in self-defense. It might be enough proof to save him yet. But she should probably have a lawyer weigh in first.

"Come on, Roya," she said. "I need to go talk to your parents."

Cyrus

CYRUS WATCHED THE HOSPITAL WALLS SLIDE BY. HE'D TRIED TO argue that the wheelchair wasn't necessary, but the nurses insisted. Andi had offered to push him. "It's kind of a long walk to the psych unit. So just sit back and enjoy the ride."

Deep down, he was grateful, since he was still pretty worn out. Although his heart issues had resolved after they gave him treatment for the poison, the nausea had remained for days. Just looking at food made him want to throw up. He tried to act like that was no big deal and made lots of jokes about it, but it really bothered him. He loved food so much, and people kept bringing him things he normally would have found delicious, but he couldn't stomach anything. It was horrible.

He'd finally made some progress, and had been able to keep enough down yesterday and this morning that they felt he was ready to be discharged. Cyrus held out hope that maybe it had something to do with the hospital, that once he got home things would get back to normal again.

He wished he could find more humor in his rather surreal circumstances. Luckily, Dev could, and he'd spent a bunch of time in Cyrus's hospital room working with him on a fast-paced animated video that told the whole sordid story. It had been a huge success, netting over a million views and counting, along with thousands of kind comments wishing him well. Even better, the commenters were now coming to Naveed's defense whenever the trolls came out. (He had made a brief appearance in the video, in cartoon form, with a caption Dev added: "not a terrorist.") It had gained them so many subscribers that they'd decided to put their game on the back burner and focus on videos instead.

Still, none of it was funny to Cyrus. A deep sense of unease had settled. Someone had wanted him dead, had nearly succeeded in killing him. And he'd been so unsuspecting. This frightened him more than anything: what other enemies did he have out there that he didn't even know about?

He talked over all this with the psychologist, who helped him understand that this was an isolated incident, that there wasn't a shadowy army waiting in the wings to off him. Cyrus went over the details time and time again in his mind. Geoffrey Walker, or Alastor, or whatever his real name was, and his wife Zennia had owned a "retreat center" that used a hallucinogenic plant called peritassa in their religious ceremonies. Using his Geoffrey Walker alias, Alastor had started a separate business to sell Metafolia, a mixture of "health promoting" herbs that included tiny amounts of the hallucinogen. One particular batch—the one Andi had been unlucky enough to try—had mistakenly contained it in much higher levels.

In high enough doses, it was lethal. Zennia had prepared a super-concentrated extract and added it to Cyrus's soup. Cyrus couldn't stop thinking of Naveed bounding into that room just in time. If he'd taken one more bite, he probably wouldn't have survived.

Cyrus was on his way to talk to his brother for the first time now. Naveed was still in the psychiatric unit, still under guard while the police and FBI investigated. Between the audio recording that Andi had given them and the evidence they'd found on Alastor's boat—clothes stained with Brennan Walsh's blood, written details of the "sacrifices" Alastor had planned, plus a string of emails on his laptop in which he'd denounced Brennan and Cyrus for bringing his company under investigation—Naveed was no longer a suspect in Brennan's death. And, for once, he'd been lucky: on the night of the benefit gala, some passer-by had captured a video of the scene at the pier on their phone, clearly showing Zennia whacking Alastor in the head before killing herself. Naveed was still facing felony charges for stealing Brennan's rental car, but Cyrus's parents and their lawyer were hopeful that they'd be able to avoid prison time for him. Nothing was certain yet, though.

Andi wheeled Cyrus along. Maman and Roya had come to pick him up, but they'd gone down to the cafeteria for a snack since Cyrus wanted to see his brother before he went home. This hospital seemed so massive, so labyrinthine—Cyrus was relieved they'd insisted on the wheelchair, and glad Andi was there to guide him. She knew the way; Naveed only had a few authorized visitors, and Andi was one of them.

"How's he doing?" Cyrus had asked after her first visit with him.

"He's fine. He says hello," Andi said, but she wouldn't look at him. She was staring fixedly at one of his monitors.

"No, really," Cyrus said. "Tell me the truth."

"Really, he's okay."

"Andi. Please."

She sighed. "It's been a rough week for him. To say the least. He says the new meds are helping a lot, but… you know. He was there when Brennan got killed, then Alastor almost drowned him, and just when he thought he was safe, the police tased and arrested him. Now he's stuck in a locked room in the psych unit. He's terrified he'll end up in prison. So yeah, he could be better."

Andi visited them both every day after school. An hour with Naveed, an hour with Cyrus. Though Cyrus tried to fight it, an old jealousy crept up in him. Not like they were getting up to anything with an armed guard right there, but still. He wondered what they talked about in their time together. She never went into detail.

So, when they were buzzed into the psychiatric unit, Cyrus wasn't sure what to expect. What kind of mood would his brother be in? Was he still angry with Cyrus, even after all this time?

They pulled up to Naveed's room and had to wait a minute before they were allowed to go inside. Andi parked Cyrus's wheelchair and sat down next to him. This unit felt so different from the floor where he'd just been. It was in an older, darker part of the hospital. All the doors were closed, giving the narrow hallway a very claustrophobic vibe.

She must have noticed he was jiggling his leg, because she said, "Don't be nervous."

"I'm not nervous." He made a conscious effort to stay still. They sat in silence for a while, but finally he couldn't take it anymore and glanced over at Andi. She had a faraway expression on her face.

"What are you thinking about?" he asked.

"Oh, nothing."

"Tell me. This place is creeping me out. It's too quiet up here."

"Just figuring out some music stuff. For the piece I'm working on. Nothing interesting."

"Then tell me something else. Got any funny stories from school today?"

"Nothing funny happened today," she said.

Okay, then. Apparently she didn't have any distracting anecdotes up her sleeve. Which was unfortunate, because thinking about school only reminded Cyrus that he'd be starting the community college program next week, which he most definitely was not looking forward to. He had decided not to request any more hours at Parapluie since he knew he'd be super busy once school started, but Chef Thierry said he was welcome to pick up shifts during breaks. Cyrus wasn't sure he'd go back, though. Working with food was no longer remotely appetizing.

Cyrus started jiggling his leg again. He couldn't help it.

Andi put her hand on his knee. "Really, Cy, he was in a good mood when I saw him earlier. It's going to be fine."

"So, what's the deal with you guys?" Cyrus blurted. "I mean, some days he doesn't even let my family visit, but he still wants you. Why's that?"

"I don't know, okay? But he needs support right now, so I want to be there for him. Because I'm his friend. That's all we are, just like you and me, we're friends, it doesn't have to be some competition."

"All right, all right." Cyrus was just glad she was talking to him again. He'd take whatever he could get. "Friends it is."

She squeezed his knee, and the door to Naveed's room opened. A nurse peeked out and said Cyrus could come in now.

He stood up. "Are you going to head home?" he asked Andi.

"No, I'll wait. I took the bus here from school, and your mom said she'd give me a ride home with you guys."

"Okay. I'll be out in a minute."

"Take as long as you need." Andi pulled out the copy of *Crime and Punishment* that she was reading for her English class.

The nurse held the door for Cyrus. He was irrationally afraid to look inside, but when he did, he saw a normal-looking hospital room, only with much less equipment—no IV poles by the bed, no beeping monitors. The guard stood in the corner. When Cyrus walked in, Naveed was sitting at a small table, writing something on a sheet of loose-leaf notebook paper. He quickly turned the page over when he saw Cyrus.

"Hey, Kourosh. I was just writing some letters. Part of my therapy," Naveed said. "Anyway, I'm glad you're here! Have a seat, make yourself comfortable. Mi casa es su casa, haha. You feeling better? Just got discharged?"

Cyrus realized that his brother was just as nervous as he was. For some reason, this made him a little more at ease, even though the guard was watching them closely. He lowered himself into an armchair. "To be honest, it's better than it was, but I still feel like crap." He was about to add something about how he was happy to be going home, but stopped himself just in time. It would be a bit cruel to rub that in. "I mean, I'm glad to be alive and all, but you know. Sometimes it takes a while."

Naveed nodded, even though it wasn't a complete thought. If anyone understood, he did. "I'm glad you're okay," he said.

"I'm glad you're okay, too." Cyrus paused. "You know, I was really pissed when you spilled my soup. But you were like some superhero on a mission to save your brother from the evil hippie cult."

Naveed tipped an imaginary hat. "Just doing my job, sir."

Cyrus laughed, absurdly touched to see this hint of normalcy. Although he felt like he'd already apologized to his brother, he knew he needed to do it in real life. He had to say it out loud. "I'm so sorry, Naveed. About what I said that night. I didn't mean it."

Naveed regarded him intensely. "You did, though. You meant it when you said it. And that's the thing, Kourosh. When things get bad, those words are all I can hear, and that makes it way too easy to convince myself that everybody would be better off if I was dead. You took my notebook, too, read all my private stuff. So you can't just say you're sorry and I can't just say I forgive you and it will all be good. It's not that easy."

Cyrus looked down. His stomach was all twisted up again. He was hoping it wouldn't be this hard. "Well, what am I supposed to do, then?"

"I don't know. I guess... just promise me that if there's ever a time when I—or someone else—needs help, you'll try to do better."

"Well, that won't be hard, considering how spectacularly I failed last time." Cyrus hoped that would get a smile out of him. No such luck. "But... it's not going to happen again, right?"

"I hope not. But it could," Naveed said softly. "PTSD isn't something that just runs its course and goes away forever. I have to learn how to deal with it. And that's why... I have something to ask you."

"Okay, what is it?"

Naveed exhaled. "So I have this new psychiatrist, Dr. Imari," he said. "I just started working with her, but we really clicked. I feel like her approach is helping already."

"That's great," Cyrus said. "But you look kind of starry-eyed. I hope you're not trying to tell me that you're in love with your psychiatrist or something."

Naveed laughed, surprised. "No! No. It's just, I've been thinking. I don't know what's going to happen yet, if they're going to send me to prison or whatever, but the lawyer seems to think she can get me out of it. I know Maman and Baba are kind of hoping that I'll start at the UW with a small course load if it works out, especially since I can't defer my admission. If I don't show up, I'll have to reapply. But I just can't do it. I'm not even sure I'm ready to go home."

"Why not?"

"Because…" Naveed looked down at his hands, avoiding Cyrus's eyes. "Things got… pretty bad in Sunnyside. Inside my head, I mean. The doctors don't really know why, it's too early to tell if it was a sign of something more serious, or if it was just a side effect of the tricyclics I was taking… and there's also this thing called post-sepsis syndrome that can apparently mess with your brain… but I just… I need to figure out how to deal with all of this somewhere else. Somewhere that's not home."

"Okay." Cyrus didn't really know what else to say. "So… if you didn't go home… where would you go?"

"Yeah, so Dr. Imari told me about this place up north, off Highway 20. A residential treatment center called Englewood that actually sounds kind of awesome. I mean, the therapy part would be pretty intense, but I think it would really help. Their philosophy's based on mindfulness, and it's out by the mountains in the forest—"

Cyrus interrupted. "Hold up. Didn't they want to send you somewhere like that before?"

"No, that was a different place, more of a traditional mental institution. This one sounds so much better. They even do equine therapy. You know, with horses."

"Horses, huh?" Cyrus thought about that. "Remember, like a few years ago, when you were scheming to go to Iran? How you and Farhad were going to go out to his grandpa's pistachio orchard and ride around the countryside on horseback?"

"I remember." Naveed had the tiniest hint of a smile on his face.

"I always knew you would," Cyrus said. "I could totally picture you, training falcons and shit, galloping across the desert on a fine steed."

Naveed's smile faded. "It'll never happen. I mean, look at me, look at—at all this." He gestured at the room, the guard.

"It won't always be like this," Cyrus said quietly.

A few moments passed before Naveed finally said anything. "I don't think we actually get to ride horses in therapy. It's more like, you know, caring for them and stuff."

"Like mucking out stalls?" Cyrus said. "Sounds like a riot."

Naveed shrugged that off. "There's usually a long waiting list, but they just started this new transitional program, and Dr. Imari thinks they might have an opening."

"Have you talked to anyone else about this?"

"Not yet. I mean, obviously, we'll have to check it out first. But, what do you think? Would Roya be okay with it if I left for a while?"

Frankly, Cyrus was wary of the idea, but he said, "I don't know, Naveed. I think it's your decision to make, and really we just want you to be safe. Roya would understand. She'd probably be fine with it, as long as you come back home when you're done. And as long as she gets to see those horses."

"Of course I'd come back," Naveed said. "Can't make any promises about the horses, though."

There was a knock at the door, and the guard told Cyrus, "Time's up."

Cyrus was pretty sure they weren't supposed to touch, and Naveed made no move to hug him, so he awkwardly waved instead. "Um, see you later, I guess."

"Yeah. Come back and visit sometime?"

"Sure. Maybe in a couple days."

"I'll be here." Naveed looked so sad that Cyrus had to turn away.

Andi smiled at him when he stepped outside. Roya was there too, sitting in the wheelchair.

"Hey, that's mine," he told her.

She scooted over. "Sit next to me. There's plenty of room."

He squeezed in beside her as Andi asked, "How'd it go?"

"Fine. I'll tell you about it later. Where's my mom?"

"She went down to get the car." Andi zipped up her backpack. "We're going to make our getaway through a back entrance."

She pushed them through the corridors, and they took the elevator up to the top floor. "Where are we going?" Cyrus asked.

"You'll see." Andi kept wheeling them until they reached a narrow corridor with windows on both sides: a sky bridge between the buildings.

"Wow," Cyrus said. The view was both amazing and dizzy-making. The streets below, the city buildings, the hill sloping down to Puget Sound, so blue against the setting sun.

She wheeled them right to the window. "It's so pretty," Roya said. "So pretty."

They paused there for a long moment, taking it all in. Andi put her hands on Cyrus's shoulders. He held her left hand with his right, and draped his other arm around Roya. Something about it, the way they were all tangled up together, felt strangely perfect, and he remembered the way he'd felt in his hallucination, his dream, whatever it was, when he'd wished for everything to go back to the way it used to be. This was different, though. It was similar to nostalgia, but it wasn't quite the same thing, because he was feeling it for a moment that was happening right now. He wondered if Roya would remember this someday. If she'd say to him, when they were grown-ups living their own lives, when they got together for Yalda or Nowruz: *do you remember that time at Harborview when we watched the sun set over the water?*

This was his life, Cyrus realized, in all its complicated messiness. No sense wishing for those days that had long ago passed. All around them, in this building they knew far too well, lives were being upended, breaking apart, snapping back together again. But he was here, with people who loved him; he was going home. He was alive.

Cyrus's phone buzzed. I just pulled up at the curb. Where are you?

"Uh-oh, Maman's waiting for us," he said.

"Oops. Better hurry." Andi gripped the wheelchair handles. "Okay, guys, hold on!"

And then she ran. As the wheelchair picked up speed, Roya squealed with joy. She spread her arms wide, turning her head toward the window. "I'm flying! I'm flying!"

Cyrus held tight to her waist, and behind him Andi laughed. The thrill of speed, the sudden lightness in his heart. Remember this, he thought. Remember it, and hold on.

Your Letter

Sep 26 at 3:42pm

Vanesa Rosales <vanesa@rosalesfilms.com>
to N. M. <beyondthewindowpane@gmail.com>

Dear Naveed,

Thank you for your letter. I'm glad to hear that you're seeking help for your mental health issues and wish you the best with your treatment.

I do have some news about Marisol. I was in touch with Genbiotix after that email you sent. Long story short, they ended up shipping out enough antibiotics for a full course of treatment, and even donated some more to the hospital to help deal with the outbreak. Marisol pulled through and was recently discharged. Her baby was delivered by emergency C-section the night after you left. He was premature and will be in the hospital for a while longer, but he's a strong little guy. They named him Javier.

As for the film, we moved into post-production after the strike was resolved. Not sure if you've seen the media coverage, but if not: thanks to some fantastic lawyers giving their time to the cause and lots of community involvement, the workers were all given their jobs back and Mortensen Fruit agreed to their demands. The camp didn't meet federal requirements for H-2A workers, so they've arranged temporary lodging for the rest of the picking season, and will begin construction of a new building for next year.

We're planning to submit to the Seattle International Film Festival for a premiere next spring. The focus remains on the workers, but your involvement in their struggle has made this a much richer film. To bring things full circle, we'd love to include a follow-up interview with you, so that you can explain the events from your perspective. Let me know if you'd be interested in getting together in the near future.

Best,
Vanesa

September 27

Dear Kass,

I'm so sorry about your Nan I want you to know that I'm not mad
at her well maybe I'm a little mad because she did try to poison one
of my brothers but he's doing okay now and it was your grandfather
who put her up to it anyway   But I wish she hadn't taken the poison
herself. That's what makes me sad I think about you all alone and it
hurts who are you going to live with now? What will happen to Orcinia?
there's a lot I want to tell you but it would be easier to talk can you
call me sometime?

I love you.
Roya

October 3

Dear Roya,

Do you remember when I told you it felt like everything was changing? Well, that was nothing compared to this.

We waited for the boat, but it never came. We didn't know what happened to Nan and Grandfather.

The men came the next day. They were dressed all in black and they had guns bigger than any I've ever seen and they were very scary. As soon as Summer (the acolyte taking care of me) saw them, she told me to hide under the front steps. They stormed the gates, trampled our plants, went straight for the greenhouses. They took Summer away. I saw her getting into a van wearing bracelets that held her hands behind her back.

Even though she told me to stay hidden, I ran out and tried to keep them from taking her. It didn't work.

I'm not on the island anymore, so if you've written to me, I didn't receive your letter. It's a good thing I memorized your address. They took me to a place on the mainland. Some kind of hospital. They seem worried about how small I am. No one can believe that I'm eleven. They feed me a lot, but Nan was right, the food on the outside is terrible. It's too salty and doesn't taste real somehow. I don't like it.

They told me that Nan and Grandfather are dead. I hope they are lying. It's hard for me to believe what they say sometimes.

They are teaching me that everything I knew was wrong. Nan was a bad person because peritassa is illegal. It doesn't help you, it is bad for you and it is dangerous. There is no way to talk to people who have died. I'll never get to talk to Mother or Father. I'll never talk to Nan again.

I don't understand it, Roya. I saw it all the time with the acolytes. We helped so many of them. The new moon ceremonies changed their lives, they said. Gave them peace. I just don't see how that's evil.

They try to make me think that this is the right world. That I will be happy here. But this world is white and boring and everything smells like chemicals, even my clothes! I miss the green and the dirt, and no matter how much they try to tell me otherwise, I'll never believe that this is better.

I think they're going to keep me here for a while. Please write to me! Send me your number and maybe I can convince them to let me use the phone.

Write back soon,

Love,
Kass

Andi

FRIDAY, OCTOBER 9

ANDI SKIPPED SCHOOL THE DAY NAVEED APPEARED IN COURT for his sentencing. It was hard to watch him walk into the courtroom with rigid posture and an emotionless face. She'd gotten to know all of his moods pretty well during her many visits to the psych unit these past weeks, and she could feel it seeping from him, the panic he was trying hard to keep at bay.

But it was over quickly; the judge had taken the defense attorney's recommendations and charged Naveed with misdemeanor theft of rental property. He was released on probation, sentenced to complete 100 hours of community service and continue his mental health counseling.

When the verdict was read, Naveed turned around and gave them the biggest, brightest smile they'd seen in months.

Andi had joined the Mirzapours for their celebratory lunch afterwards. She didn't stay long, figuring he'd want time alone with his family. But before she left, he asked if she could give him a ride to Englewood the following day. It would be a long drive, taking up most of her Saturday, but she didn't mind at all. In fact, she was glad he'd asked, because she wasn't ready to say goodbye yet.

The next morning, Andi parked in front and rang the doorbell. Naveed opened the door and gestured for her to come inside. She and Cyrus talked in the kitchen while Naveed had a long, tearful goodbye with his parents. Then Roya jumped onto him, circling her legs around his waist and nuzzling her head into his neck.

"You sure you don't need me to come along?" Cyrus asked Andi.

"We'll be fine. I think it's really hard for him to leave you guys. He wants to say goodbye here, not drag it out."

Cyrus sighed. "I know. Will you stop by afterward, though? Tell me how it went?"

"Of course."

"And make sure you scout out the place a little. Just to make sure there aren't any nefarious secret research projects going on."

A surprised laugh escaped Andi's mouth before she could stop it. She shoved his shoulder. "Don't even joke about that."

They made their way to the front door, where Naveed and Cyrus exchanged a brief hug. "Stay out of trouble," Cyrus told him.

Naveed pulled away. "You got it."

"Promise you'll come back," Roya said.

Naveed bent down to embrace her one more time, then pulled something out of his pocket: a ring of keys. Dangling among them was the silver star charm that had once been attached to Roya's flute. "Of course I will—got my keys right here. I'll be back in a few months. Promise you'll come visit?"

Roya nodded, smiling. He picked up his suitcase, tucking the keys into the front pocket. Andi held the door open as he carried it through, then closed it behind them. She couldn't bring herself to look back at the window to see his family standing on the other side of the glass, watching him go. But Naveed flashed them a grin and waved one more time as he closed the gate.

As soon as Andi pulled away from the curb, though, he folded in on himself, lowering his head and hugging his knees to his chest. She didn't try to make conversation, just turned up the music and kept driving.

Once on the freeway, they settled into the lull of the road. Naveed straightened up, stretching his legs into the footwell, and stared out the window for a while before finally saying, "Thanks for taking me."

"Sure thing," Andi said. "I think this is what I needed, actually. A good long drive to clear my head. Better than studying for the SAT. Plus my mom's been hounding me to get started on college applications, but I'm having a hard time thinking about that right now."

Plenty of things had been competing for her attention: researching colleges, keeping up with her ever-escalating school workload, visiting Naveed, arguing with her mother about visiting Naveed, dealing with the headaches that came frequently, trying to make time to work on her music. But she still felt like there was more she should be doing. It bothered her that, once again, the part of the Metafolia story she thought was most important—the poor regulation of dietary supplements and lack of consumer protections—wasn't even being discussed, since it had been completely overshadowed by the sensational deaths of Brennan, Alastor, and Zennia. Andi often vented her frustrations to Brooke, who kept telling her she was welcome to start attending CFJ meetings whenever she was ready. Maybe she would be, soon.

"Do you know where you're applying?" Naveed was saying.

"My parents—well, my mom and grandparents anyway—have their hearts set on Stanford. Berkeley would be acceptable. They probably wouldn't mind if I ended up at UW, though."

"But which one do *you* want?"

"I don't know. I've been looking into it, and they all have good musical composition programs."

"That's what you want to study?"

"Kind of, but my mom would never go for it. She wants me to have a practical major. Doesn't want me to end up in a mind-numbing job as a receptionist, like she did. Actually, I've been thinking of going the pre-med track. Maybe doing music comp as a minor."

"Pre-med, huh?"

"I know. So stereotypical. But… I don't know, I've kind of started getting interested in psychiatry lately."

"You have? All that time hanging out on the depressing psych floor didn't make you want to kill yourself?"

She glanced at him. He was half-smiling, but she didn't find it funny at all. "*No.* Of course it didn't. I don't know, I can't really explain why. Just that it interests me, and seems like a good way to help people."

There were other reasons she'd been considering the profession, deeper ones that she could barely articulate. She wanted to understand, *really* understand, people like Alastor and Tara Snyder. What if they'd gotten the right help somewhere along the way? Would that have put their lives on a completely different trajectory? And it would be nice to understand what was going on inside her own head, too, which had been a pretty chaotic place lately. Naveed wasn't the only person with a whole lot of stuff to work through.

"Well, if that's what you want to do, you should go for it. You'd make a great therapist." Naveed paused, then started breathing the way he did when he was about to say something, a series of short quick inhalations through his nostrils. She waited for him to go on, but he remained quiet for a while.

As they drove slowly through the congested traffic in Everett, he finally spoke again. "Hey, so there's something I wanted to ask you about. I talked to Vanesa yesterday. You know, from the documentary? She's going to meet up with me at Englewood soon to do a follow-up interview. It sounds like they're totally swamped with post-production work since they have a January deadline to submit to SIFF. Anyway, I asked if they have anyone working on the music, and she mentioned that they're kind of scrambling because the person they had lined up just backed out. So I wanted to see if that's something you might be interested in doing."

Andi was stunned. "You mean, compose a score? I don't know, I've never done anything like that before, and I'm not really that good, Naveed...."

"I think it would be more along the lines of choosing songs for the background music. Which you most definitely would be good at, by the way. It doesn't need to have a lot of music, just a few touches here and there. They have access to a bunch of royalty-free stuff that you could choose from. But if you wanted to write something original, I'm sure they'd love it."

"Wow," Andi said. The thought of selecting music for an actual movie was simultaneously thrilling and terrifying. "Wow, I... yes. I'd love to."

"I'll let her know," Naveed said.

Andi's brain was already starting to buzz. Being involved in the documentary could be exactly what she'd been looking for, contributing her own talents to help make the important story they were telling even more powerful, finding the perfect music to add more emotional heft. And maybe she *could* try to write something original for them—but what kind of mood would she try to evoke? Something melancholy, or uplifting? Or a little of both....

Don't get carried away, she told herself. *It's not a sure thing.* But even if it didn't work out, the possibility had awakened something in her. Maybe all those hours spent hunched over the piano at night weren't frivolous after all. Maybe they were leading her somewhere.

She thought about the song she'd been working on for the past several months. It was getting closer to the way she heard it in her head, but she was still not sure what to do about the ending. Endings were so hard.

"Do you think I'm doing the right thing, Andi?" Naveed asked a few minutes later. "I feel bad about leaving so soon after I just got home. I mean, I love them, but... I'm not ready to be around them all the time yet. I'm still such a mess in here." He touched his right temple.

"You seem better than you were."

"On the outside, maybe. Inside's a different story. I mean, it *is* a lot better—I think those tricyclics were really messing with my head. The

SSRI's are working so much better for me. Well, sort of, they're not doing much for the nerve pain, but I'll try some other options for that once I get settled at Englewood. It's just, I depend on the meds so much right now—I need to figure out other ways to deal with this too. And I've been given this amazing opportunity for a second chance. Lots of people aren't that lucky. So I can't screw it up. This is the only way to break the loop."

Andi kept her eyes on the road. It always hurt to hear about the struggles he went through inside his head, but she knew he needed her to listen. "I think it's a good move. We'll miss you, but it sounds like Englewood is where you need to be right now."

"I guess so." He drummed his fingers on his knee. "Andi, you know… I wouldn't have made it through this without you."

"Oh, I'm sure you would've—"

"No. Really. You've been there for me, and I'll never forget it. So if there's anything you need, ever…."

"Thank you," she said, touched. To keep tears from welling up in her eyes, she added, "Next time I'm in mortal peril, I know who to call."

He laughed, then they lapsed into silence, watching the trees slide by the windows outside. Too soon, it was time to exit the freeway.

They turned onto the winding roads leading through the woods, missing Englewood's entrance gate the first time and having to double-back to find it. Andi followed the long driveway lined by fiery-leaved trees, their red-gold foliage lighting the way like flaming torches. The main building, with its cedar siding, looked kind of like a mountain resort.

Andi pulled up in front before noticing the small parking lot off to one side. "Do you want me to go in with you?"

"No, this is fine. Thanks so much for the ride."

She put the car in park. "Here, at least let me help with your luggage."

As Naveed slowly got out of the passenger seat, she walked around the car, pulled his suitcase from the back seat and set it on the sidewalk.

He turned to face her. "You'll come visit?"

"Of course." They were standing close enough to the front doors to set off the sensors. The doors slid open, but closed again when he didn't go inside. "I'll be here next weekend, with Cyrus. And maybe Roya, if she wants to come."

The doors opened, but still he didn't go in.

"Can I hug you goodbye?" she asked, and he nodded. She wrapped her arms around him. He hugged her back. Andi drank it all in: the sweet, mulchy smell of wet leaves, the sharp tang of woodsmoke, the cedar panels radiating the sun's warmth; the heat of Naveed's throat, the loud whoosh of breath flowing in and out of his chest, the fluttering vibration of his pulse. The doors closed and opened, closed and opened, but neither of them let go.

Finally, he pulled away and picked up his suitcase. He smiled tentatively. "Okay. Here goes."

"Bye, Naveed," she said. "See you next weekend."

He stepped inside the doorway, then turned back to face her. For a second she thought he was going to say something more, but he only nodded and waved with his free hand. Then he disappeared through the door.

In a daze, Andi walked back to her car and started it, but she wasn't quite ready to get back on the road yet. She pulled into a parking space and leaned back in her seat, letting it all hit her, the turbulent emotions pulling and pushing like waves. Her mind wandered back to the song she was working on, to that ending she just couldn't get right. Then she remembered something Naveed had said, about breaking the loop, and it hit her.

Maybe there was no ending. Maybe, just when you thought it was over, it would begin again, this time with a new layer. A new motif, or a new harmony, some percussion in the background; maybe it could gather and gather in complexity, morphing organically with every cycle.

She quickly dismissed the idea, because obviously it was impossible to write a song that went on forever. Who would want to listen to that, anyway? But as she drove home, she couldn't help revisiting the thought. Something about it seemed so elegant, so *true*. A melody that kept going and going, turning like the seasons, like the phases of the moon: circling back forever in an endless loop.

AFTERWORD

This was a difficult book to write—and an even harder one to publish. In many ways it was a very personal story, one that continually surprised me as long-buried events from my past kept finding their way onto the page. And as I revised it in spring and summer 2020, many details from the story began jumping into the present as well. Perhaps that speaks to the cycles that flow into and around our lives, on an individual and societal scale. Still, the parallels often felt uncomfortably eerie.

But this story was therapeutic for me to write, and I can only hope that it is so for readers, too. The year of this book's publication has been full of dark times, but also moments of beauty and promise. And yet—if you're finding it hard to see that glimmer in the distance, if your inner Nate is trying to take over, please reach out for help. Believe me, I know that's much easier said than done, but you matter. You are needed, here in this world, right now in this moment. So, tell a trusted person how you're really doing, or chat with the helpful and supportive people at suicidepreventionlifeline.org. The Lifeline phone numbers in the U.S. are 1-800-273-8255 for English and 1-888-628-9454 for Spanish. Or, the Crisis Text Line can be reached by texting HOME to 741741. I've compiled additional resources (including international suicide prevention hotlines) on my website at alannapeterson.com/resources/mental-health.

As usual, many others have helped shape this book. Always, much gratitude goes to Pam O'Shaughnessy and Melanie Peterson for their excellent editorial guidance and all-around support, and to Jacob Covey for the beautiful cover and book design. For helping me explore the multitude of sensitive subjects in this book and providing insight into cultural details, I'm very grateful to Alejandra Oliva, Janice Kao, Kristel Peterson, Liz Covey, and Pontia Fallahi. Every book is a new learning experience, and I'm indebted to your generosity and expertise as I try to do these topics justice. Any mistakes, however, are my own.

On a similar note, I have learned much from Community to Community Development and from members of Familias Unidas por la Justicia, the farmworker union whose formation inspired part of this story. Thank you for continually fighting to give agricultural workers the same basic rights afforded to those in other industries. If you're interested in learning more or getting involved, head over to alannapeterson.com/resources.

To my #TeamCrowbie squad: thank you for all your help spreading the word about these books! You have no idea how much I love seeing your enthusiastic posts and reviews. And if you're not a member yet but would like to learn more, go to alannapeterson.com/newsletter for details on how to join. (I promise that's the last time I'll plug my website! Though you really should check it out—it's packed with tons of book-related goodness.)

I also want to thank my family, who have been supportive of me and my writing in many ways for many years: Hal Peterson; Meg and Jim Ghiglieri; Kristel Peterson and Joe Fahr; Holly Peterson, Skylar Brown, and Travis, Cori, and TJ Fralin; Jean and John Boynton; Nicole, Justice, Joey, and Miri Manha; and my extended family and dear friends near and far. And, last but never *ever* least, Cora, Desmond, and Brett. You give me the courage to continue pressing forward, even when—especially when—it isn't easy.

Finally, to all of my readers, I'm grateful to you for sticking with this series and riding this tumultuous wave alongside me. You are unequivocally, indisputably amazing. Thank you.

ALANNA PETERSON graduated from the University of Washington in Seattle with degrees in molecular biology and nutritional science. *When We Vanished*, her award-winning debut novel, has a growing fanbase of readers all over the world. While researching its sequel, *Where Shadows Grow*, she picked apples in the scorching heat, marched twelve miles in solidarity with farmworkers near the U.S.-Canada border, sipped horchata in Sunnyside, and dipped her toes into the Pacific Ocean at various locations along the West Coast. She is a longtime resident of South Seattle, where she tries to keep up on her overgrown garden and spends a lot of time cooking and baking with her family.

www.ingramcontent.com/pod-product-compliance
Lightning Source LLC
Chambersburg PA
CBHW051628180726
48284CB00006B/1652